Leaving the Tribe

By

Peg Herring

Leaving the Tribe

Editor: Sara Schreiber

Copy Editor: Caroline Krauss

Leaving the Tribe is a work of fiction. Names, characters, and incidents are entirely the work of the author's imagination. Any resemblance to actual persons, living or dead, or events, is entirely coincidental.

ISBN: 978-1-944502-56-0

PART I: MILLA

Chapter One

On the night they hanged the stranger, I should have been home at the dining room table, puzzling out the story problems Teacher Foster had assigned. *If Ethan farms 110 acres, and a bag of fertilizer covers 50 square feet, how many bags should Ethan request?*

But as I helped Mother with supper cleanup in the large kitchen at the back of Grandfather's big farmhouse, two quick raps sounded on the back door. My cousin burst in without waiting for an answer, betraying her eagerness. Her eyes sparkled, her cheeks flushed pink, and her lips parted slightly in anticipation. *Mary Ann is up to something,* I decided.

The house still smelled of dinner, roast pork, potatoes, gravy, freshly picked corn, and poppyseed rolls. Mary Ann brought with her a gust of air scented with the beginnings of fall, cool evenings and a hint of ripe fruit. Seeing that I wasn't alone, she stopped, straightening her posture. By the time Mother turned to look, her hands were folded at her waist and her chin was lowered almost to her chest. "Good evening, Aunt Wendy."

With only a grunt of acknowledgment, Mother continued packaging leftovers from dinner, using sheets of aluminum foil she kept folded in a drawer. I wished she'd at least pretend to be pleased to have a visitor, but Mother's smiles were rare, and her words were saved for giving directions as to what task should be undertaken next.

I was unable to speak. No one knew why, but I was used to it. Despite my disability, I loved words and collected them in my mind like pretty beads. I memorized words I saw in storybooks, phrases taken from the Bible, or terms used by my teachers. I used them in my thoughts, making sentences that pleased me, though I could not express them aloud. *Mary Ann is endeavoring to look demure.* In the real world I communicated mostly through facial expression and simple gestures. That night, to soften Mother's coldness, I smiled at Mary Ann and wriggled my fingers in greeting.

She looked the image of a proper young lady, hair neatly combed, high-necked white blouse tucked in tightly, and a clean blue skirt. The ID tattoo on her arm flashed from under her sleeve as she set her backpack down by the door. Every person in Fairica had one, given a few days after birth to prove citizenship in a tribe. Some people added to their tats to make them prettier, and Mary Ann's parents had let her box her name, tribe, and birth date with a frame of delicate flowers.

She made an effort to look modest, I thought, *like Pastor says we should.* Tonight Mary Ann's skirt hem fell below her knees, but I knew that when there were no adults around, she rolled the waistband to raise it a few inches. "Boys like it," she'd insisted. Once she'd rolled my skirt to show me how it was done. "There. Now boys will notice you, even if you can't tell them how smart and good-looking they are."

At the time, my thought had been *What if Grandmother saw me out in public like this?* The band had felt funny bunched at my waist, and my naked knees peeped up at me in condemnation with every step I took. As soon as Mary Ann left, I'd returned my skirt to its proper length.

"Aunt," Mary Ann asked in her little-girl voice, "could Milla help me deliver the food tonight? Ailing Quarters is full."

She's planning one of her adventures. The realization made my stomach go twisty. While I liked my cousin, who was a few years older than I, Mary Ann thought it was fun to go places we shouldn't, and she didn't mind fibbing about it afterward. I believed that rules were made for a reason, and besides, I hated the thought of anyone being mad at me. While it was tempting to escape the oversight of adults for an hour or two, I always worried about how long we'd get away with doing things nice girls shouldn't.

But if I didn't go, Mary Ann would hunt me down tomorrow and call me a baby.

Mother was frowning, and I sensed she'd say no. Mary Ann saw it too and added further explanation. "The twins on Skyview Farm both got hurt today. One of them, David, I think, climbed into a pen with a bull that didn't want him there. The bull pushed him into the wall and broke his shoulder. Mark jumped in to help David and got his foot stepped on." When Mother said nothing, Mary Ann added, "With those two injured and the cough that's going around, my parents thought Mister Abel could use extra help."

One way the Woods Tribe supported each other was by feeding those who could not feed themselves. A schedule posted weekly in each burg lined up families to donate food, either to Ailing Quarters, where sick and injured people were cared for, or Special Quarters, where the permanently disabled lived. Another schedule lined up unmarried daughters to gather the food and deliver it. Tonight was Mary Ann's turn but not mine. I tried to telegraph a message to Mother. *Say no. Say I have homework.*

Mary Ann added a clincher. "Mother says it's a shame that people grumble about providing food. She says the leader's families should set a good example."

Did I really need to pee, or was I just nervous?

Mother's gaze turned on me, and I focused on wrapping a half-dozen rolls in waxed paper. While I was anxious about Mary Ann's motives, I couldn't help being curious as to what she had in mind. On a September evening when the air was warm, what girl wouldn't look forward to time away from chores and rules? Maybe it wouldn't be wrong to go if Mother said I could.

The decision took a while. Flies stirred on the windowsill, almost dead but not quite. A cricket called from a corner. Finally Mother said, "Milla already had her turn this week, but helping others will make her grateful for what she has."

Comments like that always felt like a slap in the face. What had I done, I asked myself, that made Mother think I was ungrateful?

If Zalea had been there she'd have whispered, "Worrywart Wendy's in a bad mood that never ends." But I reminded myself of the Lord's commandment: *Honor thy father and thy mother.* Our mother had lost two husbands and raised two fatherless girls. We should not judge her for being sad all the time.

My sister Zalea had strong opinions about a lot of things. Even Grandmother, the kindest woman ever, called her "sassy and wrong-headed." While we worked, wiping dust from the windowsills with rags or making neat rows in the vegetable garden with the corner of a hoe, Grandmother would warn me not to "take after Azalea." While I admired my sister's self-confidence and intelligence, I accepted Grandmother's wisdom. There was no way I wanted to be discussed in whispers in the burg, as Zalea often was.

"I'll pack up the rest of this cake," Mother said. "Milla, get a jar of last year's pickles out of the pantry and take it along. We need to use them up, because we've got plenty of cucumbers left to pick, so I'll be making more." I did as she said, adding it to the growing mix of food.

Mary Ann ran a finger along the edge of the plate Mother had emptied to taste the leftover frosting. "Umm. Good." Looking at her from the side, I saw triumph in her expression. My naughty cousin had succeeded in removing us both from the watchful eyes of adults for an hour, maybe more. No household chores. No lectures about propriety. We would entertain ourselves.

"Are you looking forward to music night on Friday, Aunt Wendy?" Mary Ann asked. "Father says you have a beautiful voice. He wishes you'd sing with the others."

Our family was known for musical talent. At any celebration, someone was sure to call out, "A song, Leader Woods. Give us a song!" Grandfather would get out his guitar and strum and adjust until the chords sounded right to him. Grandmother would take her dulcimer from its case and lay it across her lap. She'd once been the lead singer, but her range had narrowed with age. Now Zalea sang melody while Grandmother added alto and Grandfather a resounding bass. I'd felt left out as a kid, but then Grandfather found a flute at a swap meet, its parts nestled into molded depressions in a battered black case lined with purple velvet. There'd been a fingering chart folded into the lid, and soon I was able to stand behind Grandmother's chair, reading the music over her shoulder and adding runs and trills to songs like "Never, My Love" and "Uptown Girl."

Mother had steadfastly refused to join the family band, and she responded to Mary Ann's suggestion with disgust. "I hope my brother doesn't hold his breath waiting for that to happen." Mary Ann turned her eyes to the window, as if she wished she were outside.

"Get your sweater," Mother ordered. As I pulled on my deep green cardigan, she added, "I'm putting three serving spoons in. Make sure you bring them back, and the empty pickle jar too."

Taking a canvas backpack from a rack by the door, Mother put the containers of food into it. When she'd finished, she held the bag so I could put my arms through the straps. "Be home before dark," she ordered as I wiggled a little, adjusting to the added weight. "You never know what can happen after the sun goes down."

I avoided looking at Mary Ann, guessing she'd be rolling her eyes. Mother's constant fears of what "might" or "could" happen were a joke to those who knew her well. *It's not like anything exciting ever happens around here,* I imagined Mary Ann thinking. That was true, but I liked it that way. Home was safe. Home was the best of places.

Grandfather appeared in the kitchen doorway, his expression vague, as if he'd just woken from a nap. He wore a clean shirt, his dress-up pants, and he carried a shoe in each hand. Grandmother appeared behind him, a comb in one hand and scissors in the other. Standing straighter, Mary Ann said, "Good evening, Woodsleader."

His eyeglasses shifted on his nose as he squinted. "Who's this?"

"It's Byron's girl, Mary Ann," Grandmother said. Licking her hand, she smoothed his cowlick flat. "Are you sure you have to go out tonight, Sweetheart?"

"It's important. Where's—the older girl? I want her to come with me."

"Zalea's gone to her room," Mother said, adding, "I made sure she'd finished her chores before she went up."

"It isn't proper for Azalea to go, Ben," Grandmother said. "I'll go with you and wait on the road till you're done. Then we'll walk home together."

“I don’t—” Grandfather stopped midsentence, staring out the window. I turned to look at what he was seeing but there was nothing except what was always there: the big oak tree, the gazebo, and beyond that, the picket fence. Grandfather tended to drift away from conversations lately, but he was very old, probably over sixty.

Apparently forgetting what he’d come for, Grandfather turned and left the room. Grandmother looked from Mary Ann to me, a question in her eyes. The pack had rumpled my blouse, revealing a bit of skin at my waistline, and Mother reached out to tuck it in. “Milla’s going to help Mary Ann tonight at AQ.”

“That’s nice, Sweetheart. Mary Ann, you’re older. You watch out for your cousin.” Grandmother gave me a brief hug and then turned and left, holding the comb ready for when she caught up with Grandfather again.

“Go on,” Mother opened the door and shooed us out. “The sick shouldn’t have to wait on you for their supper.”

Mary Ann led the way, as eager to get away from Mother as she was to help the sick of our community. The pack of food bumped gently on my back as I followed her out the door. I closed it with a soft click, so I wouldn’t get in trouble for making too much noise. At the gate, Mary Ann went through and then held it open for me, and we stepped onto the sidewalk. Though I was still nervous about what our real purpose was, it did feel good to be out from under Mother’s disapproving gaze for a while. The fact that she would probably do the dishes and clean the kitchen while I was gone was a plus too. My chore list would be a little shorter.

“We’ll be done at AQ in no time,” Mary Ann said. When possible, we chose to deliver food to Ailing Quarters rather than Special. “Sick people aren’t scary,” Mary Ann maintained, “but SQ residents make my skin crawl with all their hollering and moaning."

Mother volunteered a lot at Special Quarters, and sometimes she made me go with her. She was different there, talking to the people like they were normal and even smiling sometimes, like when Miss Betsy, who had some bad disease, made a joke. Miss Betsy was okay, but other people in SQ swore a lot, which made me want to cover my ears. A few of the worst ones reached out as we passed, trying to grab our skirts or touch us. While I felt sorry for them, I was half sick the whole time I was there.

Mary Ann had a second reason for choosing to deliver to AQ. Mr. Abel, the night-time caregiver, was a bit of an outcast, so it wasn't likely our parents would chat with him on a street corner or after church. Both families believed that Mary Ann and I stayed at AQ and helped Mr. Abel serve the food we delivered. That "misunderstanding" provided us with an hour to do whatever we chose. Well, whatever Mary Ann chose.

The air had begun to smell different, I noticed. In our land-hold, surrounded on three sides by two massive lakes, the leaves had begun to fade from the deep green of summer to the lighter shades that signaled the first sign of decay. Here and there, a single branch had hurried the process, going as red as an apple or as yellow as a squash. The night was pleasant, cool but not cold, and a slight breeze swept away gnats that otherwise hovered around my nose, mouth, and eyes.

When we were away from the house, Mary Ann stopped under a street light and said in a low tone, "I know where Grandfather's going tonight. There's a trial, and it could end with a Final Punishment."

Taking hold of my cousin's arm with one hand I raised the other, widening my eyes in a silent question.

"Uncle Rolf caught a stranger near his house last night. He's charged the man with trespassing and attempted murder." Mary Ann shook her head, and her long, blond curls twisted on her shoulders. "I want to see it, but I'm scared to go alone." She turned, walking backward a few steps. "I hoped Aunt Wendy would be in the mood to let you go, but you never know with her. She's so grumpy."

Children, obey your parents in the Lord, for this is right. I knew I should turn around and go right back home. However, if I did that, Mother would figure out that Mary Ann had lied. Then they'd both be mad at me.

Unaware of my doubts, my cousin started down the street. "Let's get this stuff delivered." Mary Ann never minded that I couldn't speak, because she always had plenty to say. "Aunt Sally griped at me when I picked up their donation," she told me as we walked along. "She says we coddle the NCMs by giving them free food, and it takes a big chunk out of the tribe's funding. But Grandfather's the leader and he arranged it, so it must be right."

Each tribe in Fairica was paid by the Govt for the goods or services it provided. General grants allowed for projects and programs the leaders saw as beneficial, and individual stipends gave members the means to support their families. Working men got the largest amounts, since they actually provided the goods or services. Smaller stipends went to women with children and the children themselves, to encourage large families and provide future workers.

Non-Contributing Members of a tribe were ineligible for a stipend and therefore dependent on the tribe's generosity. Teacher Foster said Leader Woods' willingness to support so many NCMs was admirable, especially since funds from the Govt had lessened in the last few years. Other tribes expected families or churches or friends to care for their NCMs. If no one was willing to do it, whatever happened was God's will.

When he'd set the rules for his tribe, several years before I was born, Grandfather pledged to take care of members who were unable to work. He'd had quarters built in each burg in our holding, maintained with funds we received for the grains we grew. Both Special and Ailing Quarters were staffed and managed by men, of course, but women were encouraged to volunteer there, since Grandfather maintained that a woman's touch made any place more comfortable. Breakfast and lunch were simple meals, cereal and sandwiches. Evening meals came from donations and were intended to be more appealing. To set a good example, our family sent tasty food in generous quantities when it was our turn.

Like Mary Ann, I'd heard rumblings of discontent about the practice. Zalea said some families either skimped on their donations or sent inferior food. "It's not right," she'd raged at dinner one night. "Stupid people can't imagine ever having to depend on charity, so they tell themselves that those who do are worthless and lazy."

After a nervous silence in which Grandfather kept eating as if she hadn't spoken, Grandmother had reminded Zalea that tribal management was none of her business. Zalea didn't give up. "Those poor people have to either eat what they're given or go hungry," she'd argued. "We should make sure everyone gives their fair share, and the food should be decent."

"Rolf will get to it when he can," Grandmother had replied. "He's overburdened right now, trying to do his own job and Benny's too." Zalea had gone silent. I knew she missed Uncle Benny, who'd meant a lot to her.

While Grandmother had been put out by Zalea's fault-finding, she was a caring person. The next day, while I was on my hands and knees picking bugs off the potato plants, I heard Grandmother ask Rolf to be more vigilant in his duty to AQ and SQ. He'd only grunted in response, but Rolf was like that.

I'd been pleased by Grandmother's action. She'd listened to Zalea's argument and then done something to help the NCMs. Because it wasn't a woman's place to complain, she'd gone to Rolf privately instead of grumping at the dinner table the way Zalea had. Grandfather had a lot of responsibility on his shoulders. The leader shouldn't be bothered with worrying about how much soup each patient in AQ gets for dinner.

Mary Ann and I came to Main Street, and we turned toward Ailing Quarters, which was on the far side of Woodsburg. The largest burg in a holding was named for the tribe. Our other burgs had more fanciful names, like Bent River, Del's Cross, and even Squirrel Hollow. I'd visited some of them, but I was most comfortable in Woodsburg, where everything was familiar and people knew better than to ask me questions I was unable to answer.

The downtown was quiet. All businesses closed by five p.m., so men could go home to their families and the meals their wives prepared for them. We passed familiar buildings set around a grassy square: the grocery store, the bank, the funeral home, the church, the school, and the meeting house. Beyond that were homes, and beyond them, the work yard, where barns, silos, and storage sheds crowded against each other. Parked in rows were pieces of farm equipment, owned by the tribe and used by members to complete their given tasks: tractors, combines, plows, balers, rakes, and more. In the growing dark, the machinery looked like monsters crouched, ready to pounce. My father had died in a farm accident when I was little, and I always felt a little trembly at the sight of the helpful but dangerous machines that farming requires.

If I were leader, I'd have sold the machines and gone back to using horses, like the draft animals we saw on *Wagon Train* and *The Waltons.* I supposed the horses liked it better nowadays, when they were pets and only had to haul around a human or two.

Ailing Quarters sat along the western edge of the burg, past the equipment, the silos, and the barns. Special Quarters was even farther out. Grandmother said that was to give the residents privacy, but Zalea claimed it was so "regular" people didn't have to hear the moans of the dying and the shouts of the insane. If Grandmother overheard, Zalea was sure to get a lecture about curbing her tongue and cultivating an obedient heart. The two were like barn cats forced to share space. They tiptoed around each other, staying as far apart as possible.

Mary Ann interrupted my thoughts, putting a hand on my arm. "Milla, Father's going to look for a husband for me at the Fall Fair." She'd recently turned sixteen, the age when girls could marry. It was hard for me to imagine my cousin as a wife, much less a mother. Mary Ann seemed in many ways younger than I. She always spoke as if she were almost out of breath, and her mind was mostly taken up with pretty dresses she wanted and ways to make her hair feel softer.

Mary Ann's tone turned disapproving. "Zalea will be eighteen soon. I'd be ashamed to be that old without a whisper of a wedding coming up." She was critical of Zalea yet jealous too, since no one could deny that my sister was beautiful. "She's pretty, if a man likes that type," she finished, "but I swear your sister wishes she'd been born a boy."

Zalea doesn't want to be a boy, I replied in my head. *She thinks girls are every bit as smart as boys are.*

Mary Ann returned to her favorite topic, herself. "I had my mind set on Neil, the banker's oldest, but he's decided to go to college."

She shivered. "I'd be old and decrepit by the time he gets done with that. Father will look for a man at the Fair, one who's already got a degree and can take over the tribe's finances right away." She gave a little giggle. "He'll be older, maybe even twenty-five, but at least I'll be well off. Accountants earn a lot more than just a stipend because they take on private clients." After a pause, she added, "I could have you move in with us and help take care of my babies."

The implication was that I'd never have my own, which was possible. My disability was considered unlucky at best, at worst a sign of God's disfavor. "If He can make a baby right," I once heard a man say outside church after services, "why would God let it go wrong?" He'd tapped a wooden post with a knuckle. "Has to be a sign of sin."

In my case, the sinner was Mother, who'd left home for several years and returned with Azalea and no husband. Rumor said she might even have been involved in criminal activity, though no one knew the details. My father, Eric, had married Mother in spite of her past, which meant he must have loved her very much. I had only vague memories of him, a loud voice, big hands, and a scratchy beard. It was seen as a further sign of God's disfavor when Wendy Woods' second child grew up unable to form intelligible words.

"Psst!" Mary Ann pulled at my arm, drawing me into the shadows of a building. Peering out, I saw two men approaching at a lively pace. The taller was a half-step in front of the other, his manner purposeful. Mary Ann's whisper was full of hisses. "Stay out of sight. If he sees us with all this food, Rolf will rant for an hour about the evils of charity."

Rolf's wife, Aunt Sally, had bad headaches, so I was often called in to watch her younger children while she rested. I liked caring for them, even the twins, but their home was different from mine.

Mother made most of our clothes. She would sew dresses for Zalea and then when she outgrew them, they'd become mine. Aunt Sally said sewing made her back hurt, so she ordered clothes for her children by mail. It took forever to get them, which she said was because they came all the way from China. She whispered when she said that, so I knew there was something shady about the process.

Some things I learned from Aunt Sally I guessed Grandmother and Mother wouldn't have liked. Aunt Sally loved to talk about how awful childbirth was, how it felt like you were being split in two and how you bled for weeks afterward. I was a little scared by her tales of excruciating pain. It seemed odd that a woman had to go without food or water from the first pang until her baby was in her arms, even if it was two days later. Still, I told myself that zillions of women had gone through it, including Sally herself eight times. Childbirth was a woman's burden, but it was survivable, most of the time, and if I ever got the chance to be a wife, I'd face it with as much courage as I could.

From being in their home so often, I also knew that Uncle Rolf often disagreed with Grandfather's decisions. "Why should us normal people support cripples and loons who don't contribute their fair share to the tribe?" he'd say. I suspected he included me in that statement, and he didn't even care that I was sitting right there.

We're supposed to love everyone, I thought as my bandy-legged uncle came toward us. Rolf didn't love anyone, so I figured it might be okay to be a little mad at him sometimes.

As the two came closer, I recognized the second man as Gary, Rolf's oldest son. Though generally disliked at school, Gary had a few boys who hung around with him, mostly because he was the leader's grandson. A bully, a cheat, and a loudmouth, Gary was horrible to girls, making public, often nasty judgments on our appearance. He was especially cruel to Zalea and me. He called Zalea a "mud person" and maintained she wasn't really his cousin. He called me "Dummy," often mimicking my attempts to communicate with exaggerated gestures and facial expressions.

The sight of him brought back an incident from the day before. Girls attended classes only in the morning, so we were dismissed at noon. As I'd left the school building, Gary and his little gang had been sprawled on the front steps, eating their lunches and harassing the girls who passed by. When I stepped outside Gary rose and pulled me into a hug. "Hello, Dear Cousin," he said loudly. His hand slid down, and I felt his fingers close on my right breast. Leaning back, he said in pretended surprise, "What have you got under that blouse, little Milla? Are you growing tits?"

While my face burned with shame, Gary's gang of friends elbowed each other and grinned. Leaning close, Gary said in my ear, "If I took you down by the pond and had a look at them, you wouldn't tell anyone, would you?" I swallowed hard, hoping he was teasing, but his eyes scared me. "Oh, that's right," he finished. "You *can't* tell anyone, can you?"

At that moment a voice had called, "Milla? Leader Woods wants you to show me the fence that needs repair."

I'd turned to see Jack, a boy who worked hard and said little, standing outside the schoolyard fence. His calling my name—even knowing my name—surprised me, and I had no idea there was a problem with Grandfather's fence. Seizing the opportunity, I slid out of my cousin's grasp. Gary glared at Jack for ruining his fun, but he didn't try to stop me. I'd noticed he never challenged those who were capable of defending themselves.

As Jack and I walked away together, I went over in my mind what I knew of him. Orphaned at fifteen, he'd gone to the fair and offered himself as a laborer. An old farmer from our tribe, Milton

Woods, had hired him. Only a few months later, Milton had petitioned to adopt the boy. "He tosses bales of hay onto the wagon like they're empty boxes," he told anyone who would listen. "And he does numbers in his head like you've never seen."

Once we were out of sight of the school, Jack stopped, giving me a tight smile. "I think you'll be all right now." I nodded, hoping my expression told him how grateful I was. Though it appeared to take effort, Jack had more to say. "I think you're good the way you are, Milla. You're pretty, and you're nice, and...you don't have to talk to be...good." With that he turned and left. I'd stood where I was for a few moments, stunned by the praise. Not "damaged." Not "imperfect." Not "pitiful." Was it possible I was okay as I was?

Mary Ann touched my arm, interrupting my remembrance. "Rolf and Gruesome Gary are gone. Did you see they were all dressed up? Probably trying to make an impression at the trial."

Resettling our packs, we stepped back onto the street. When we reached AQ, two girls I recognized were coming out the door, their empty packs looped loosely over their arms. Mister Abel stood in the doorway, and his long nose twitched with interest when he saw us. "What have you brought for us tonight, ladies?" Too old to do farm work anymore, Mister Abel tended the sick and injured at night. He lived in a room at the back of the building and ate the same food as his patients. I liked Mister Abel's sweet, gentle nature, but I heard men chuckle about him, saying he'd "never grown a pair."

Abel had two arms, two legs, two eyes, and two ears, just like everybody else. I wasn't sure what pair he was missing.

Mary Ann began unloading her bag. "Mother sent chicken. There's peppers sliced up and a few apple tarts."

"We appreciate it," Mister Abel said before turning to me. I unpacked my bag, revealing my family's offering, fresh-baked rolls, bits of pork cut small, and gravy. Green beans. Half a carrot cake. And pickles.

"Lovely," Mister Abel said as we transferred the food into bowls and warming pans. "Be sure to tell your moms thanks."

While a few older people used informal words like *Mom, Dad,* and *Gramps,* our teachers insisted that respectful words were important: *Mother. Father. Grandfather.*

After Mister Abel rinsed the empty containers in the sink, Mary Ann and I returned them to our totes. I made sure I got our spoons and the jar back. Through the doorway I saw the sickroom, where two rows of beds faced each other. Female patients lay on one side, males on the other. A curtain down the middle allowed for modesty.

Though it was too dark in there to recognize faces, I knew who most of them were. Some were sick enough to need monitoring but had no family to provide it. The nearest hospital was over a hundred miles away, so unless the situation was dire, the sick stayed with the tribe. Others were recovering from injuries, like the twins who'd been hurt by their bull.

In the bed closest to the doorway, Great Aunt Didi dozed. Over ninety, she would never recover from the dozen ills that plagued her. According to the rules, she should have been moved to Special Quarters for her final days. That had become a struggle of wills between Grandmother and Uncle Rolf. "Rules are rules," Rolf said, but Grandmother insisted the oldest living member of the Woods family should be allowed to die in peace where she was. So far Grandmother had won, but whenever Didi's name came up, Rolf's face got red and his hands curled into fists. It looked to me like he wanted to punch his own mother.

Saying goodbye to Mister Abel, we left AQ. As soon as the door closed behind them, Mary Ann jerked my pack off my back. Shrugging her own off too, she stuffed them under a bush. "We have to hurry if we want to see the trial."

My feet stumbled a little as I followed my cousin. I was thinking of the day Grandmother had said, "There are things girls shouldn't see, Milla." She and I had been planting nasturtiums along the fence when Aunt Sally stopped, her whole body bustling with gossip. Stanley Woods had been caught breaking tribal law for a third time, she'd said. If found guilty, he might face the death penalty.

She pursed her thin lips. "Has Leader Woods told you whether he'll support that decision or not?"

"Ben doesn't discuss his business at home," Grandmother had replied stiffly. "It's the men's concern."

Sally's eyes had narrowed at the veiled suggestion she nosed into places she shouldn't, but she didn't seem able to stop herself. "Well, they'll vote tonight, and Rolf says if the punishment is final, they'll hang him right then." She sniffed. "If you ask me, they should do it in the middle of the square at noon. Children need to see the consequences of bad behavior." Grandmother hadn't replied to that, and after a moment Sally went on, no doubt looking for a more sympathetic ear.

My inability to talk had an odd result. Many times, people spoke their thoughts aloud to me as they wrestled with them inside their own heads. Regarding her daughter-in-law's retreating figure, Grandmother had said in a musing tone, "No one should watch a person die who doesn't have to." Pulling a pigweed plant, she'd tossed it over the fence, adding, "Of course the tribe can't let evil people run around loose. In the Old Times they put 'em in prisons, but that ended up making good citizens pay for criminals to eat three meals a day and watch TV." Setting her hands on her hips, she'd stretched her back. "We have to get rid of the bad apples. I just don't think it should become a show for people to gawp at."

Stanley Woods had escaped Final Punishment, I recalled now. Instead of hanging him, the tribe had burned three *X*s on his forehead so everyone could see that he couldn't be trusted. Since then, he'd lived on the outer edge of Woods territory, seldom seen in public and always with a baleful glare that showed how much he resented the punishment he'd received.

"If they actually kill someone, I want to see it." Mary Ann was walking so fast that I had to skip every few steps to keep up. Imagining my cousin's desire coming true made the knot in my stomach get even tighter. I didn't want to see the Punishment, but if I turned back now, Mary Ann would call me "Chicken" and "Sissy-Missy."

Maybe it's just a rumor. Maybe the meeting is about crop rotation or weed control. Maybe by the time we get to the Punishment Place, it will be over.

Mary Ann's thought was similar. "Hurry," she urged. "It will be over before we get there."

It wasn't over. Outside the clearing where punishments were decided and carried out, we stopped in the trees, crouching side by side, and peered through pine-scented branches to where the men of the tribe were performing their civic duty.

Each tribe in the nation of Fairica decided its own rules and the consequences for breaking them. Offenses committed by women and children were handled by husbands, fathers, or other males expected to see that a household abided by the rules. Among males, offenses like petty theft, cheating in business, or misusing farm equipment were punished with extra service to the tribe.

Offenders might pick up trash in the square or wash the fire engine. A second offense meant a harsher penalty, usually shunning for a set period of time. A third offense meant a man could be put to death. More often, if he didn't pose a danger to others, he was branded as a punishment for him and a warning to others.

Any man in the tribe could attend trials and vote on the punishments handed out. Since Grandfather was trusted to mete out justice without prejudice or favoritism, the crowd at a trial was often small, with only witnesses and family members in attendance. That night was different. The accused was not one of us, and the crowd numbered at least a hundred men.

As long as the weather allowed it, trials were held in the open space, where a gibbet reminded those present that the tribe held power over life and death. I'd seen the gibbet lots of times. Often on Sundays, Grandfather put us all in his car and took us for a drive to look for deer and elk. We passed it when we left our holding to go to the fairs. Until that night, I'd only seen a platform with an upright post and a bracket. I hadn't really thought about what it was for. Now a rope that ended in a noose had been added, its color a bright yellow-white due to its newness.

We shouldn't have come. We're snooping into things that are none of our business. I reached out to touch Mary Ann's arm, but I saw from the look on her face that she wouldn't leave now. *And she'll be really, really mad if I do.*

Reluctantly, I turned to the scene before me. Five men stood on the platform. I recognized our local police officer Topper Ned, Gary, Uncle Rolf, and Grandfather. The fifth was a man I'd never seen before. The stranger's dark complexion, hair, and eyes told me he wasn't one of us. His hands were tied behind his back.

Most of the men crowded around the gibbet wore the clothing they'd worked in all day, coated with dust and stained with sweat. Only Rolf, Gary, and Grandfather had changed and groomed themselves. Grandfather wore the stole of authority around his neck, a simple but elegant strip of green cloth with a large, gold *W* on each side. Though I couldn't read it from that distance, I knew the family motto, *Strength and Soil*, was embroidered along the edge. While he wore it, Grandfather represented order, and his word was law.

Uncle Rolf was making his case, and the men on the ground listened closely as his voice rose and fell. Rolf was a good speaker, and he told the story of how he'd come home the night before and heard a suspicious noise. "This man—" He pointed at the stranger, his arm fully extended and his finger aimed accusingly. "—was hiding in the lilac bushes at the back of my yard. The sentries say he didn't enter by the road." Rolf leaned forward. "He *sneaked* onto our land. Why?"

It was a fair question. Honest visitors came by the main road and identified themselves at the crossing. The tribe saw few strangers, being at the far northern edge of the nation, so fences were more a notice than a barrier. While it was possible to avoid the sentries and the occasional patrol, it was suspicious that the stranger had arrived in Woodsburg without making anyone aware of his presence.

Rolf took two items out of a canvas bag and held them up for the crowd to see. "In this man's pack I found this knife and a coil of rope. It's clear he intended to kidnap or kill one of us." Pointing at individuals in the crowd, one after another, he added, "Who did he come here to hurt? Someone in your family, Tim? Or yours, Edmond? Or yours, George?"

"Liar!" I was surprised when the stranger interrupted. So was Rolf, who stopped speaking and turned, his eyes wide. The acknowledged successor to Grandfather as Woods Tribe leader, he was seldom challenged and never insulted.

The stranger turned to face Rolf squarely, his posture defiant, and repeated the word. "Liar."

Rolf spoke to the men on the platform. "Hold him," he ordered. "If he opens his damned yap again—"

"No," a voice called. "He's allowed to defend himself."

"Father!" Mary Ann said in a whisper. "He always feels like he has to stand up for justice, but Rolf won't like it."

Making his way up the stairs to the platform, Uncle Byron took a stand beside Grandfather. He spoke first to Rolfe. "It's the law, Brother." Grandfather appeared to have not been paying attention, and Byron turned to him, leaning close as he repeated, "It's the law, right, Father?" After a moment, Grandfather nodded.

"Untie his hands." When that was done, Byron told the prisoner, "State your case, sir. Tell the truth, as God commands."

The stranger shifted his shoulders to relieve the cramps being tied had caused and pushed a strand of graying hair away from his eyes. "I came here to deliver a message. I didn't announce my presence because the message is private." He made a gesture at Rolf that clearly hinted at contempt. "Everything he said is a lie. I carried no knife, no rope, and I was not hovering in anyone's bushes. This man and two others jumped me and then made up this ridiculous story."

"Yet here before us are the items taken from you," Grandfather said.

The man paused, looking into Grandfather's eyes. After a second he nodded as if some piece of understanding had hit. He then turned to Byron, who remained silent. Apparently he'd done all he was willing to do.

"This man tried to kill me!" Rolf shouted. "Here is the shirt I was wearing. You can see the slit where he tried to gut me." He held up the garment, putting a hand through a long slice near the bottom edge. Feet shifted, and a murmur went through the crowd. "No man should be attacked on his own land." Rolf's voice rang with certainty. "Here we are meant to be safe. We cannot, we must not, abide dangerous interlopers."

Though the crowd wasn't facing my way, I saw heads bob in agreement. Byron looked unhappy, but I guessed he'd seen that the stranger's case was weak. One of the best things about the Woods Tribe was the safety we enjoyed. In the Old Times, people had been attacked in their homes, in their cars, and on their streets. When Mother fretted about letting her girls out of her sight, Grandfather would remind her we were safe on tribal land. Criminals got what they deserved these days, and that was, he often said, good for good people.

Zalea, who had an odd way of looking at the world, claimed women had "traded away" their freedom in some mistaken belief that a system that limited them would also protect them. "But we're not safe," she'd rant. "Look at Gail, married off to an old, creepy man so her father can get access to water for his cattle. And other girls—well, there are lots of them who are either afraid or embarrassed to tell what happens to them."

Though I let her have her say, I thought Zalea was mistaken. The girls we knew didn't have to worry about rapists and sex traffickers, like they had in the Old Times. And Gail's old husband wouldn't live forever. She'd probably get a much better one next time.

Beside me, Mary Ann whispered, "He has to be a renegade. Don't his eyes look mean?"

I'd never seen a renegade before, but Mary Ann was probably right. Tribeless, such men wandered from place to place with no family to protect them and no one to teach them how to behave. "Over time they turn wild," Grandmother said, "like pigs set loose in a forest."

"This man is accused of trespass with criminal intention." Grandfather had stepped to the center of the platform. "The evidence we are given is first, stealth. He stole into our midst without revealing himself. Second, he carried items that show he intended harm." Grandfather's gaze passed over the crowd. "He says he had a message to deliver. Can anyone here explain that or speak for him?"

"You can't do this!" The stranger's tone hinted he knew they could and they would. "I've done nothing wrong."

"One last time," Grandfather said. "Will any man speak for the stranger?"

Silence. The man had been given his chance to speak, to save himself, as the law required.

Straightening his back and setting his feet, Grandfather said formally, "The tribe has spoken. The prisoner is guilty, and under the laws of Fairica may be put to death for his crimes. Sentence is immediate."

After that, things moved quickly. The stranger made no fuss as two cousins took hold of his arms. He let them lead him to the trapdoor without any attempt to resist, though his flinty glare at Rolf hinted what he'd do to him if he were able. He stood where they placed him, shoulders back and head high. Gary put the noose over the prisoner's head and adjusted it so the knot lay under his right ear. He stepped back. The atmosphere grew quiet. Grandfather bowed his head, and all his followers did the same. “Father God, we send this man to you for final judgment. Deal with him as You see fit.”

Rolf pulled the handle. The trapdoor opened, and the man dropped through. At the last moment, I looked away. “He wriggled a little,” Mary Ann said a few seconds later, “but it’s over.” She rose to her feet. “Come on. We’ll have to hurry to beat the men back home.”

Chapter Two

I relived the hanging in my mind, over and over again, as we hurried home: the man's set expression, the squeal of hinges as the trapdoor dropped, and one awful glance backward at the corpse as Mary Ann pulled me away. I couldn't erase the stranger's last moments of life from my memory. Faced with hanging, I would have cried and begged for mercy. He'd been rebellious to the last, unwilling to die but refusing to whine about it.

Still, I asked myself, what might have happened if they hadn't caught the man? Would he have stabbed Grandfather or Aunt Sally? That night my dreams were filled with threatening creatures who were half-human, half-monster. The next morning I woke with a heaviness that made it feel like I was slogging through muck as I went down the hallway to the bathroom. The tribe's men had done the right thing. They'd protected themselves and their people. Why, then, did my stomach feel like it had rocks in it?

It was my turn to get milk, and I trudged down to the dairy barn with a jar in each hand, still plagued by what I'd seen. Returning, I set the jars in the refrigerator and went upstairs to dress for school. Mother and Grandmother moved about the kitchen in a practiced duet, doing their breakfast tasks while staying out of each other's way. Mother had fried bacon, and she poured the grease that remained into a jar to be used again later. Grandmother mixed pancake batter, holding the bowl under one arm as she stirred in the milk I'd brought. I probably looked upset, but neither was paying attention.

But when I went upstairs to dress for school, Zalea noticed. "What's up, Milla?" She was already dressed for the day in a pleated navy skirt, a pale yellow blouse, and flat shoes. Zalea covered a lot of ground in a day, because unlike every other female I knew, my sister had a job.

Just over a year ago, Grandfather's oldest son had died in a hunting accident. Though many had considered him standoffish, no one ever denied Benny's intelligence or work ethic. He'd handled all the tribe's business, keeping track of everything from membership to crop production and submitting the proper paperwork to the Govt. Grandfather had named Benny heir to his tribal leadership, and though any man could apply to succeed a leader upon his death, it was doubtful anyone in our tribe would have challenged Benny for the job.

Benny's death at only forty-one had created a crisis, since the tribe had no one trained to replace him. How would we get grants to buy equipment and plow snow, people wondered. How would families get their stipends? Any disruption in a tribe's reporting to the Govt brought inspectors from the capital, men known for taking months to examine records and assessing large fees in the process. In a surprise to almost everyone, Grandfather had announced that Zalea would serve temporarily as the tribe's financial officer. It seemed Benny had taught her how to do the record-keeping, and she could assure that the Govt stayed out of our paperwork while the tribe and its members got what was due them.

Many said it was a mistake. Zalea was young, and besides, women weren't known for their skill with numbers. Grandfather maintained she would serve only until a qualified male candidate could be found, which had quieted the complaints for a while. But now, almost a year after Benny's death, Zalea still got up every morning and took on a job only she and Grandfather believed she should have. People muttered and shook their heads. Zalea didn't care. Grandmother *tsked* and hinted that it was time she married. Grandfather ignored all the objections, including his wife's.

I understood Grandmother's point of view, but I trusted Grandfather. Yes, it was odd that Zalea did a man's job, but it wasn't my place to have an opinion on it.

Despite our different personalities and the five years separating us, Zalea and I were close. We'd grown up together in a room in the upstairs of Grandfather's century-old farmhouse, where winter mornings left frost on the inside of the windows. Zalea had taught me to write my name by scratching it with a fingernail across the frozen, lacy patterns. While Grandmother and Mother cooked breakfast, we'd bundled up in flannel robes and slippers and hurried downstairs to sit on the grate that let heat from the wood furnace in the basement rise to warm us.

We'd always been oddities in the tribe, since Mother remained unmarried. Some said our lop-sided family structure had allowed Zalea to "go wild." Mothers were notoriously unable to provide the discipline children need, and though Grandfather was a fine father figure, he did have a soft spot for his only daughter's girls. Uncle Rolf often sneered that Ben Woods' "doting" had worked against the teachings that should have turned us into good wife material.

When Zalea asked if I was okay, I shrugged off the question, but she didn't give up. Taking me by the shoulders, she turned me so we faced each other. In my peripheral view, I saw our reflection in the dresser mirror. I had light skin while Zalea's was brown. I was blond with blue eyes, but Zalea's hair was glossy black, her eyes deep brown. I showed all my teeth when I smiled, but Zalea's smile was closed and a little sideways, as if she wasn't sure she wanted to let it out. Zalea was taller than I'd ever be, and while we were both trim, Zalea's full breasts drew attention from men wherever she went.

"What is wrong, Milla?" she demanded. "Use your signs."

While helping Grandfather clear out Benny's house after his death, Zalea had found a book on sign language. A note on the front page said it was a Christmas gift from Benny to Wendy, but he'd apparently never actually given it to Mother.

Young people weren't supposed to keep books of their own, but Zalea didn't care about the rules. She'd brought it home, and together we'd studied it at night, teaching ourselves the signs for letters and phrases. For the first time in my life, I was able to tell another person how I felt and what I was thinking. I'd wanted to share my new skill with the rest of the family, but Zalea said we had to keep it a secret. "They'd have to learn the signs to understand you, which I don't see happening. Grandfather is beyond learning new things. Mother can't be bothered. And Grandmother will say it's the devil's work or some such nonsense. Besides, we'd have to tell that I took the book, and she'll insist I'm a bad influence on you—again."

I could have used my signs to tell Zalea what I'd seen, but she'd have been angry at Mary Ann for taking me to the Punishment Place. She was very protective of me, and she made no secret of the fact that she considered Mary Ann silly. Making an effort to look less gloomy, I signed, *Tired.*

"Want me to ride you to school on my bike?" Though women weren't allowed to drive cars, Zalea had been given an electric bike to use for running Grandfather's errands. "As long as Grandmother doesn't see us, we'll be fine."

Forcing a smile, I shook my head. I didn't like riding the bike on a good day, bumping along as my sister dodged holes and cracks in the roads that grew bigger every year. I planned to walk to school through the woods, soaking up the calming spirit there. Like me, trees didn't speak, yet they conveyed to me a sense that the world was mostly good.

To distract my sister, I held up two different bows and raised my brows in question. "The green one looks good in your golden hair." Sending me a quick air kiss, Zalea left the room and clattered down the stairs. I got out my school shoes and set my work shoes under the bed. When I stood back up, I looked out the window and saw her ride off, pedaling the bike to save battery power.

The woods path was the longer way to school, but I liked the whisper of leaves overhead, the chatter of squirrels, and the feeling of soft earth underfoot. I talked to the trees with my mind, asking if they were as shocked at what happened as I was. I thought the answer was yes, but then, I wasn't sure trees understood the need to rid the world of criminals.

At school, the hanging was the topic of every conversation. Gary was in his glory, telling the story of what happened with emphasis on his role. According to him, the stranger had begged for his life. I looked at the ground as I passed so he couldn't see the denial in my eyes.

I couldn't concentrate on the lessons. The second time I missed him calling my name, Teacher Foster said I must be day-dreaming about some boy. The other students laughed, and I smiled to show I got the joke, but my memory kept replaying the scene from the night before. Over and over, I heard Grandfather's final statement, commending the man's soul to God. Stamped on the inside of my eyelids was the image of the lifeless body, hanging straight down like rotting fruit. No matter how many times I blinked, the image returned.

During civics class, the sound of the door opening caught my attention. I turned to see the tribe's Over-Teacher slip in at the back of the room and take a chair, a pad of paper in one hand and a pen in the other. Teacher Foster's spine straightened a little, and his voice turned crisp. "Oral quiz. Twenty points for each correct answer." After a moment to let the incentive kick in, he asked, "Who can explain the unique advantages of the Fairica System?" Hands shot up. "Marty?"

Marty stood up, turned to face the class, and spoke loudly. "Fairica is a nation run as a business. It's composed of four lateral sections, each overseen by a commander."

"Name them, please. In order."

Looking toward the ceiling, Marty apparently imagined the map that was now behind him. "East of us is the Blue Section. We're Green, then there's Rose, and farthest west is Gold."

"Good. Zach, please explain the organization of the Govt."

Zach stood and turned toward us. "Fairica is headed by Chief Vox." Zach's voice broke on the last word, and a few students giggled. His face turned red, but he went on. "Each section is divided into family groups called tribes, which are overseen by leaders. The members of each tribe work together to either produce goods or provide a service to the nation."

"Very good. Who can explain how the tribal system provides stability?" Scanning raised hands, the teacher said, "Tina."

Tina's shrill voice hurt my ears, but she always knew the answers. "Tribes maintain moral standards. They teach children about their heritage. They deal with crime. And they encourage strong parenting to instill values in our youth."

Teacher Foster glanced at our visitor, a small smile on his lips. He was choosing his best students, showing off their knowledge. "Who can tell us what the Govt gives us in return?" Hands waved, and he called on David.

David stood at attention, as we'd been taught. "The Govt accepts each tribe's product or service and sees that it is put to maximum use. It also provides troops that serve as a defense against foreign invasion and battle internal problems like rebellion and sabotage."

"And why is that necessary?"

"In the Old Times, a corrupt man named Gerald Miller was elected to the highest office in the land."

"How did that happen?"

"There was improper voting, and technology failed us. Miller's administration was so bad that some people rebelled, but the rebels weren't good people either. They were mostly instigators who came here to disrupt law and order. Between the crooks in office and the violence caused by the rebels, the economy collapsed. There was fighting in lots of places, and the nation almost fell apart."

Teacher Foster nodded gravely as he looked around the room. "Who can explain how we found our direction again?"

Once again, hands rose. Billy was called on to answer. "When things got really bad, the people chose a man who knew what we needed to do. Chief Vox drafted the Tribal Reorganization Act, which required every person to join a tribe that suited their background and culture."

A boy raised his hand, and the teacher said, "Yes, Andy?"

"My dad says that was hard for some people, because they didn't really know their families."

"True," Teacher Foster replied, "but Chief Vox had to act boldly. Shifting to the tribal system saved the nation."

Russ, who tended to speak out of turn, offered an opinion. "My dad says whole segments of the country refused to comply with the TRA."

Teacher's tone remained patient. "That's why it's good we elected Chief Vox. He was able to steer our nation through those scary days." Going to a map of Fairica at the side of the room, he touched a gray area between the Gold Section and the Western Ocean. "Chief Vox realized the malcontents on the west coast were of no value to us, so he allowed them to secede. That was a huge mistake for them, and today this area, known as Dorado, is lawless and backward. No one wants to live there."

"The east rebelled too, but they came crawling back once they realized they'd fail without us." That was Steven, known on the playground as "Suck-up Steve." Though it was mean to call him names, he did *really* want to be Teacher's Pet.

Teacher Foster gave an approving smile. "You're correct, Steven. After a bad year on their own, the East Coast region, now part of the Blue Section, begged to rejoin Fairica and share in our success." He surveyed the room. "Now who can tell me how the Woods Tribe came to be?"

Iris raised her hand, rather timidly, and was called on. "Prominent men were allowed to purchase territory for themselves and their tribe. Based on the plans they submitted, the Govt decided how much land they would need. Farm tribes got big tracts of rural land. Factory tribes got manufacturing hubs and the residential areas around them. Service tribes live in or close to the areas where they operate transportation, construction, and other services." More confident with local lore, she went on, "Our leader, Benjamin Wood, applied for and was given the Woods Land-hold. Any man directly related to him was required to move here. Other men could apply to join our tribe and fill positions we needed, like bankers…and teachers." A few kids giggled, and

Teacher Foster smiled, tacitly admitting he was an adopted Woods. "Each man was given work that fit his abilities." Iris' glance turned briefly to the man at the back of the room. "Ours is one of the most successful farm tribes in the country."

Zalea, who knew more than most about tribal business, claimed all wasn't "sweetness and light" between the Govt and the tribes. Her stories of corrupt Govt agents and tribes selling their extra grain "under the table" mean little to me. I didn't care about business. My goal in life was to be a good daughter now and a good wife and mother someday. Grandmother often quoted the Bible's description of such a woman: "...more precious than pearls...and all her paths are peace."

Teacher Foster's summing-up tone brought me back to the classroom. "Very good, students." He spoke as if they'd thought up their answers by themselves, when in fact we all were expected to have portions of our text memorized to be recited on demand.

The Over-Teacher rose and left the room, looking satisfied. Teacher Foster smiled as if he'd passed an important test. "Let's dismiss for lunch a few minutes early, shall we?"

Chapter Three

While I had a little trouble falling asleep the second night after the hanging, I had no more dreams about what I'd seen, and I woke without the sense of dread I'd had the morning before. Everyone said justice had been served. "He shouldn't have been on our land," some said. "He came armed," said others. Aunt Sally summed up the general feeling. "He was not one of us."

Though what was done had been legal, it bothered me that no one had really listened to the man. No one questioned Rolf's story, though anyone who paid attention knew he lied whenever it suited him.

I left for school early and took a short detour to a nearby pasture where a half-dozen horses grazed. Climbing through the split-rail fence, I spent a few minutes petting their necks and letting them sniff my pockets for bits of celery I'd brought along. Standing in the circle of horses, I felt my remaining anxiety ebb. The tribe had been within its rights. The men had acted to make everyone safe. Life would go on as it had for as long as I'd lived.

School was not all that interesting. While I did the work I was assigned to the best of my abilities, much of it was just repeating how great Fairica was. I didn't disagree, but I did wonder how often we needed to read it, say it, and hear it. Yes, the Old Times had been bad. Good people had been in danger from criminals every minute of every day. Women had been turned into the opposite of what we were meant to be. Everyone was addicted to technology. Though it was hard to imagine, there'd been devices people never set down, even to eat a meal or go to the bathroom. It sounded made-up, but older people sometimes talked about having laptops, cell phones, apps, and online news, so at least some of it was real. A few things sounded fun, like choosing movies and shows I wanted to watch instead of the ones

Grandfather picked. Most adults admitted machines had made life easier, but they insisted that too much convenience, too much information, and endless, constant communication had turned us all into lazy, overweight zombies.

"Chief Vox had to act fast to save the country," Teacher Foster was saying as he paced back and forth across the front of the classroom. "He wanted to unite the people, support traditional values, and still respect everyone's rights. Today we have national standards for overall cohesion, and tribal rules to bind members of tribes together. For example, if letting women vote is really, really important to a tribe, they can allow it."

"But why would we?" Chris commented with a sneer.

The teacher acknowledged with a shrug that he couldn't answer that. "Choosing such a practice would reduce a tribe's grant money, but that's only fair. If a tribe chooses to ignore national standards, it must accept the repercussions."

Suck-up Steve said, "We're lucky. Our tribe meets every standard, and we provide lots of grain for the country."

"I wish we kept more of it for ourselves," Russ griped. "My father has this sweet old car called a Mustang stored away in the barn. There's never enough fuel, so it just sits there."

It was true that the cost of operating vehicles, whether cars or combines, was high. Replacement parts were hard to come by as well. Since most of the tribe's income was spent on equipment, seed, fuel, and fertilizer, we generated electricity for our homes with simple solar and wind systems. Most systems were home-built, and to save the energy produced, all but essential power sources were shut down at night in most homes. "God sends the sun every day," Grandfather would say. "He intends for us to work while it gives us light and rest when it hides its face."

Our tribe was recognized every year for hard work and high standards, usually with plaques commending Overall Production and Farm Efficiency. In the privacy of our bedroom, Zalea scoffed at the "so-called prestige" of such awards. "Everyone gets them. They don't cost the Govt much, but people break their necks to get recognized, whether it means anything or not."

An upcoming new prize would go to tribes that recorded more births than deaths in a given year. Rolf had suggested we let men take on second and even third wives to achieve positive growth, but Grandfather hesitated, believing that marriage meant one man to one woman. "God made Adam and Eve," he insisted. "I don't care what some folks did later."

Rolf hate "wishy-washy" way tribe run, I signed to Zalea after Grandfather rejected his proposal.

"How do you know that?"

Sally said.

Zalea had looked surprised. "She told you that?" When I nodded, Zalea's sideways smile appeared. "You are the perfect sounding board, Milla. You listen, but you can't tattle, so people tell you things they should never say out loud."

Of course I could have tattled if I wanted to. My perfectly shaped cursive letters were often tacked to the classroom wall as examples of excellent penmanship. My three-paragraph essays were often returned with a gold star stuck at the top. If I'd written down tidbits I heard here and there, I could have shocked my teachers and the whole tribe. *Woodsleader swore an oath against God,* or *Pastor Thomas says the stipend for churchmen is stingy.* Because I didn't want to make trouble, I listened and smiled and never told what I heard.

On the way home from school that day, I again took the woods path, noting how the light was starting to slant as the sun's path across the sky changed. Around me the colors shifted too, some going bright while others faded into autumn.

"Milla!" I turned to see my sister hurrying toward me, looking upset. When she reached my side, she took hold of my arm as if needing help to stay upright. Her mouth worked a few times as she tried to speak, but nothing came out. Stepping toward her, I signed, *What?*

"Grandfather's dead."

Her words hit like a blow, making it hard for me to pull air into my lungs. I signed, *How?*

"He was stabbed. Rolf says the man they put to death must have had an accomplice."

While grief tore at my heart, anger filled my gut. I'd felt sorry for the stranger, but now I saw that the tribe had been right to deal with him as they had. The tragedy was that no one had suspected a second killer lurking nearby.

"Milla!" Zalea's voice was soft but commanding. "You have to listen to me, okay?"

A hot tear escaped my eye and rolled down my cheek, but I nodded. Zalea took hold of my shoulders and bent so our gazes met. "You and I have to leave here."

This second shock was as great as the first. We'd lost our beloved Grandfather, and now Zalea wanted to run away from home? I pulled away from her grasp, shaking my head.

"Milla. Listen to me." Zalea wrapped her arms around herself, as if she felt cold. "Forty days from now, Rolf will be the leader, and that won't be good for you and me." She turned, looking to the west for a moment. “I wish I knew how to fly the tribe’s plane, but I doubt I could figure it out, so we’ll be on foot.”

Zalea watched my eyes as I took in her words. “Do you understand? With Rolf in control, life will get very bad for us.”

What do? I signed.

“We have to leave. Tonight.”

That seemed ridiculous. *Where go?*

“My father sent for me.” That surprised me, but Zalea explained, “The man who came here, the one they killed? He told me my father is alive.” A truck rattled by on the road, some distance away, and she glanced around anxiously before going on. “He stopped me on the street that afternoon and said he had a letter for me from my father.” Sri Afzal, Zalea’s father, had been some sort of criminal, but we’d been told he died when she was tiny. “I saw that Rolf was watching us,” Zalea said, “so I told the man I’d meet him in the park at midnight.”

That was foolish. What if the stranger had planned to do awful things to her?

“I pretended he’d asked me for directions,” Zalea went on. “I pointed toward Grandfather’s office and then went on, like it wasn’t important.” She shook her head. “I guess Rolf didn’t fall for it, because he hunted the guy down and made up some story about him coming here to kill one of us.” Her voice turned hard. “Rolf got the man killed, when he was only here to give me a letter from my father.”

Your father alive?

Zalea nodded. “The man said that until recently, Sri thought Mother and I were dead.” She glanced around again, fearful we might be seen. “I don’t know exactly where he is or what his tribe is like, but it has to be better than staying here once Rolf is in control." She took hold of my arms. "I'm leaving, Milla. I think you should come too."

The thought of Rolf being leader was scary. It was no secret he thought Zalea and I were a drain on the tribe's resources. Zalea, he reminded anyone who'd listen, should be living with her father's family, not her mother's. As for me, he'd raise both hands and ask, "Who'll marry a girl who can't talk when there were plenty of normal women around?"

But do we really have to run away? I asked myself. *Won't Mother or Grandmother or Uncle Byron stand up for us?* The answer wasn't encouraging. Mother never fought for anything, and besides, Rolf was awful to her, calling her "The Prodigal" and worse. As for Grandmother and Uncle Byron, neither would have the power to stop Rolf once he was leader. They could object, but his word would be what mattered.

The last thought, the one that convinced me, was fear of being separated from Zalea. She was wild and mouthy. She didn't think the way a girl should. But I knew my sister loved me and would protect me. If she said we had to go—

I go.

"Good." She bit her lip. "It would be easier if we left in a car, but women can't drive, and I don't know any men I'd trust." I raised my hands to indicate I didn't have any suggestions, and she went on. "You know that clump of sumac that grows next to the tallest grain silo? Hide in there and wait for me. I'll tell Mother you're babysitting somewhere. Tonight when they're asleep, I'll pack our things and sneak out." Zalea gave me her slanty smile. "It will be late, but don't be scared."

Once she'd hurried away, my mind flooded with worry. How would we get away? How would we deal with the outside world? I'd never in my life been without adult supervision for more than a few hours. Being more adventurous, more used to the world, Zalea might do better on her own. Still, she'd decided to take me with her. Did she know enough to get both of us to a place neither of us knew anything about?

Over the last year or so, I'd learned that my sister did secret things. Once after a bad dream I'd gone to her bed, intending to crawl in with her so I could sleep again. Instead of Zalea, I found two pillows under the blankets. Our bedroom window had been left unlocked and open a little, so it could easily be raised from the outside. Looking out, I'd traced the path Zalea must have taken, down the porch roof, a short jump to the lawn, and out the back gate. I'd gone back to bed wondering how she found the courage to do as she did, and why she couldn't accept that rules are there to protect us.

Grandmother seemed to sense that Zalea wasn't behaving herself. She insisted no man wanted another man's "leavings," so women should remain chaste. "Men are more animalistic than we are," she'd say. "That makes them well-suited for defending their families, but it also makes them less able to control themselves. A woman should never put herself in a situation where a man's urges might cause him to take advantage of her."

Zalea made fun of "Grandmother's Favorite Sermon" behind her back, though she wasn't all that amused. Sprawled on her bed, her face turned toward the window, she'd said once, "The tribe wants to keep its girls in line, so they make purity a goal we're supposed to long for." Her tone had turned hard. "Why don't they lecture the boys about chastity?"

Since she was older and more experienced than Zalea, I figured Grandmother knew right from wrong. What would she say if she learned we planned to run away? As I crouched there in the sumac, I flip-flopped. *Run away. Stay here. Go with Zalea. Stay home with Grandmother. Go where Rolf can't mistreat me. Stay where I know all the rules.*

What if Zalea was just mad because she knew Rolf wouldn't let her continue as the tribe's accountant? Grandmother would support Rolf on that. She had reminded Zalea every day since Benny died that her work was temporary. "As soon as they find a man who can do the job," she'd say, "That will be the end of ledgers and production estimates for you." One night while I was clearing the table I'd heard Grandmother say to Mother, "Zalea needs a man who'll take her in hand."

I'd happened to be facing Mother, and the expression that appeared on her face had been shocking and a little scary. "Any man who hurts Zalea will answer to me," she said, her voice stronger than I'd ever heard before. A dish of mashed potatoes had hit the floor between them. I wasn't sure who'd been holding it, but it broke into pieces, making an awful mess. I hurried to help Grandmother clean it up while Mother turned and went into the kitchen. I saw her start running the water for dishwashing, her back to us, her head sunk low.

Pulling leaves from the sumac branches and shredding them one by one, I waited all that afternoon. Dinner time came, and I wondered if Mother and Grandmother would wonder where I was. Probably not. With Grandfather dead, their minds would be dulled by grief and shock, and they'd accept whatever story Zalea told. Thinking of my beloved Grandfather's death made me sad, and I wiped my tears on the hem of my skirt. There would be a huge funeral for him, and people from all around would attend. Forty days afterward, Rolf would officially take his place as leader of the Woods Tribe. While he wasn't admired, as Grandfather had been, Rolf was clever and persuasive. He could be successful, though not beloved.

My butt grew tired of sitting, the bushes scratched my neck every time I moved, and doubts kept nipping at my mind. I turned up the collar of my blouse. I wriggled to a more comfortable position. But I couldn't deal with the doubts. What if What if we stayed for a week or two to see how things worked out? If Rolf really was a bad leader, we could always run away later. What if there was something that would keep Rolf from being mean to us?

That new thought made me sit up straight. Grandfather had been a very smart man. He knew Rolf didn't approve of Mother and me and especially Zalea. He might have put a note in his will saying how he wanted us treated. If I found the will and read it, I'd know for sure whether we had to run away or not. It would be in Grandfather's office at tribal headquarters. All I had to do was sneak in there, find the will, and take it to Grandmother. She'd know what to do with it.

Leaving the sumac, I went around the back of the silos and made my way to the meeting house. There was a light in Grandfather's office. Creeping under a window ledge, I listened for a while. Hearing nothing, I rose and peeped inside.

Rolf sat at Grandfather's desk, going through a stack of papers. He scanned each one, putting some back where he'd found them and setting others on the desktop. Across the room, her back to me, Aunt Sally stood at a file drawer, doing the same thing. They didn't speak for a while, so the only sound was the soft rustle of paper against paper. About the time I'd decided to leave, Aunt Sally spoke. "Here it is." A few seconds later, "That old bastard." Taking a single sheet of paper to the desk, she handed it to her husband.

Rolf scanned it. "I *told* you he'd been acting funny."

"He was going to name Byron his successor." Sally's tone vibrated with disgust. "Do you think anyone knows?"

Tapping the sheet with his hand, Rolf said, "Look at the misspellings and the overuse of commas. If he'd showed this to my mother, she'd have made corrections."

Sally sniffed. "I'm surprised he had enough of his mind left to make a new will and keep it secret."

"If he hadn't mistaken me for Byron and spilled the beans, I wouldn't have suspected a thing."

Sally made a disgusted face. "So what do we do with this?"

There was a metal waste can beside the desk. Holding the single sheet over it, Rolf took out a lighter and set the flame to it. When the paper turned black and the flame crept toward his hand, he dropped it in. "Gone."

Sally looked around the office. I ducked out of sight. "We'll have to go through every bit of this and make sure there's nothing else that could make trouble for us."

"I doubt there will be." Rolf rose and stretched. "The tribe expects me to become leader, and I will."

"I worry about your mother." Sally brushed her long hair away from her face. "She's not stupid, you know."

"We'll keep her busy planning events. First, the old man's sendoff. Then when the waiting period's over, my installation ceremony. By the time she gets around to sticking her nose in, she won't be able to stop me."

"And your sister?"

"I have plans for her and her kids. They won't like it, but like everybody else, they'll do what the new leader says."

Chapter Four

It was late when Zalea came back to where I waited in the sumac bushes. "I told Mother and Grandmother you're watching the pastor's baby so he and his wife can hold an all-night prayer vigil for Grandfather." She handed me a flashlight and set a knapsack down beside me. "Clothes for you to change into." Opening the zipper, I took out blue jeans, a loose t-shirt, hiking boots, a bandana, and one of Grandfather's caps. Flashing the light inside, I saw more clothes that weren't mine, some toiletries, a notebook and pen, a light jacket, and a heavier, warmer one. At the bottom was my flute, and I felt a rush of warmth for Zalea, who'd guessed I wouldn't want to leave it behind. Taking out a roll of wide elastic bandage, I held it in the flashlight beam, asking a silent question.

"You're going to travel as a boy," she said. "We'll wrap your chest with that and cut your hair short—" The look on my face stopped her, and she sighed. "Milla, boys don't have long hair." She was right, but I felt like crying at the thought of cutting off my "crowning glory." What would Grandmother say?

Grandmother would never know.

Tears rolled down my cheeks as Zalea took out scissors and snipped away my almost waist-length hair. It was strange to feel the weight of it leave me. The scissors went *snick-snick-snick* near my right ear, then the left, then up the back. I felt Zalea's breath on my neck as she leaned in. I saw her in the flashlight's beam, biting her bottom lip as she focused. When she was finished, she wiped away my tears with her thumbs. "I'm sorry, Milla. Sorry we had to do it and sorry I didn't do a very good job. It's kind of crooked, but we'll even it up somewhere along the way."

Hearing the regret in her voice, I signed, *Okay.* I couldn't look at her for fear I'd break into tears again, and Zalea looked miserable as she picked up her pack and stored the scissors in a zippered pocket. "You look as much like a boy as a pretty girl can. When we have to deal with people, look down and don't smile."

Zalea had brought two more packs, one containing her own belongings and one full of food. I was hungry, but when I reached for it my sister cautioned, "Go easy. That's all we have until we find a way to feed ourselves."

As I ate a single peanut butter cookie in tiny bites, we began our exit from the only home we'd ever known. Zalea led the way to the southernmost exit, moving parallel to the road but well off it. It felt weird to be out at night. We didn't dare use the flashlights to guide our steps, but the moon was almost full, and Zalea knew the way. I followed her closely, watching the ground to avoid sticks that might snap and alert others to our presence.

There were obstacles. We had to jump a creek, which got my borrowed shoes damp. I tried not to think about the animals that might be watching us, bears, coyotes, and maybe even a cougar, lying in shadowed places where the moonlight didn't reach. We both gasped once when a partridge flew up in front of us. Then we smiled, aware that we'd given the bird as much of a scare as it had given us. A few dogs barked as we passed outlying farms. They didn't sound worried, only eager to let their humans know there was movement in the woods.

By daybreak we were ten miles from home. I was sleepy, worn out, and grumpy. Sliding her pack to the ground, Zalea said, "We'll rest here for a few hours." Pushing some dead leaves into a pile as a cushion, she took her warm coat from the pack, spread it over her shoulders like a blanket, and settled down to sleep. I tried to do the same, but the earth was damp and hard beneath me. Every nearby sound made me jump. Wafts of cold air up the back of my shirt made me shiver. In that dark, lonely place, I began to understand how different life would be from now on.

Lying there with a rock poking into my thigh, I imagined my bedroom at home, comfortable and welcoming, with shelves Grandfather had put up and quilts Grandmother had made. With that memory, I found myself regretting a particular object I'd left behind, a Barbie doll Zalea had stolen for me.

Once she'd made herself indispensable to Grandfather, Zalea had begun taking advantage of his trust. She went places she shouldn't. She spoke out more than she should. And a few weeks earlier, she'd taken the doll from a storeroom as a gift for me. Coming home with what appeared to be a quilt, she'd revealed the doll when we got up to our room, folded inside the bright covering and still sheltered in its original box. Though it looked new, Zalea said it was at least fifty years old.

Barbie was tall, with long blonde hair and feet molded to fit into high-heeled shoes. Grandmother would not have approved, since the doll wore a bathing suit that left her long legs, shapely arms, far too much of her chest, and all of her stomach exposed. The box also contained a doll-sized towel, a picnic basket, and a colorful ball. My underwear covered more skin than what Barbie had apparently put on to go to the beach.

I was too old for dolls. This one was inappropriate. But my mind whispered, *She's so beautiful!*

"I found her while doing inventory," Zalea told me. "No one will notice she's gone, but you'll need to keep her to yourself." One brow rose. "She's definitely not what Grandmother would call demure."

I'd intended to do as she said, but once Zalea was gone, I laid the doll against my pillow so I could just look at her for a while. *What kind of life did girls have in the Old Times?* I wondered, touching the box gently. *Didn't they get in trouble for walking around almost naked?* Everyone knew that dressing provocatively tempted men to evil thoughts, so I had trouble picturing a time when it would have been safe.

The door opened and Mother said, "Don't forget tomorrow is laundry—" She stopped at the sight of the doll.

I knew I was in trouble. I'd lose the doll for sure, and there might be further punishment for keeping secrets. Mother would want to know where Barbie came from, which meant Zalea would be in trouble too. I waited, keeping my gaze directed at the floor. I deserved whatever happened next.

"Little girls used to play with those all the time." Mother stepped into the room and closed the door. "There were tons of clothes you could buy for them, and houses, even cars." Then the most surprising thing ever happened. "If you plan to keep her, you'll need to find a really good hiding place." After a moment, she added, "Somewhere your Grandmother would never look. I assume Azalea already knows."

After Mother left, I wrapped the doll in the quilt and laid her gently at the back of my closet, under my summer clothes. Since then, I'd taken her out for a few minutes each night before I went to bed. Our bedroom door didn't lock, of course, but I'd set the laundry basket in front of it, so I'd hear it scrape on the floor if someone started to come in.

I hadn't opened the box yet. I'd planned to save that for a special time, maybe my birthday. It had felt funny having the doll. I knew it was wrong, but Mother had kind of given her permission. *How bad can the sin be?*

Lying on the damp ground in the dim woods, I wished I'd asked Zalea to bring the doll. It was a silly thing, but maybe it would have made me feel a little less like I was giving up every single good part of my life.

I awoke hours later. The sun had warmed the air around us, but I felt the need to pee. By the time I found a private spot and took care of that, Zalea was awake and rummaging in the food tote. She took out a piece of beef jerky and an apple for each of us. Setting the food in my lap, I signed, *Go home. Say we lost.*

"I'm not going back," Zalea replied firmly. "We'll reach the Wagner Tribe-hold today. If you've changed your mind, I'm sure someone there will take you home. You can tell them I made you come but you escaped."

I shook my head. *Ask can join their tribe?*

She let out a sharp bark of laughter. "Do you think they'll take on two runaways? No way. They'll take us back to Rolf, and we'll be worse off than we were before."

If we'd been male, we could have said we'd gone camping, and our return home would have met with only a light reprimand for not telling anyone where we were. But when a girl was unchaperoned overnight, any chance she could attract a decent husband was gone. Understanding crashed in my head, loud as a tree felled by the wind. We'd be declared renegades. We were tribeless and alone.

Beside me, Zalea was re-packing her things. "We should get started," she said, glancing at the sun overhead. "The sooner we get off Woods land, the better."

Chapter Five

I was used to walking, but it felt different now. Nothing looked familiar. The trees, though still the birches, maples, oaks, elms, and pines I'd known all my life, grew thicker as we approached the border of Grandfather's land. We heard the growl of traffic on the road, mostly pickup trucks and farm equipment. We stayed out of sight, fighting our way through thickets and cornfields and getting scraped and scratched in the process. We crawled over blow-downs and tiptoed through swampy spots, careful at all times not to stray so far from the road that we lost track of it completely.

When we stopped to pass the canteen between us, I signed, *Where?*

"Stanley Woods can help us," Zalea replied. "I just need to find his place and convince him to do it."

It took a while to find the little house where Mr. Stanley Woods lived, but in the end we emerged from a deeply forested area into a small clearing and stopped, blinking in the light. In the center of the open space sat a house that looked like it was melting into the ground. Slanted walls green with mold. An old pallet for a porch. Window glass so dirty sunlight was unlikely to penetrate. Zalea straightened her back, the way she did when she had a job to do that she didn't look forward to. Then she went to the door and knocked.

"What?" a growly voice demanded.

"It's Zalea Woods, Stan. I need your help."

There was a long silence, but finally we heard footsteps inside. The door opened as if a strong wind had blown it in, and a man peered out at us. The first thing I noticed was the three *X*s above the bridge of his nose. Other than that, Stanley looked like a normal guy, though he was pale, like a weed that grew inside the barn wall and didn't get enough light. He was about Uncle Rolf's age but not his style at all. Mr. Stanley wore a ragged long-sleeved jersey, saggy pants, and dirty tennis shoes. The look in his eyes when he looked at my sister made my stomach turn.

"Well, well," he said in a too-loud voice. "The leader's granddaughter needs my help. Come in." He moved aside, and we stepped into the house, which seemed even smaller inside than it had from the path. Every surface was covered with stuff in various stages of repair: small appliances with innards scattered around them, weather-worn birdhouses, and scraps of fabric now turned into grease rags. Mr. Stanley rubbed his hands together. "What can I do for you, ladies?"

"We need you to alter our tats."

He frowned. "Why, Miss Azalea! That is illegal, as you well know. No one can change the identification given at your birth without a signed order from the tribal leader."

"I know it's illegal." Zalea's chin jutted. "I also know you can do it."

His expression turned sly. "And why would I?"

"Because I will give you what you've been wanting for the last three years."

I saw surprise in his expression, then anticipation. The sick feeling in my stomach turned worse. "Is that a fact."

"It is. Fix my sister's tat first."

Stanley frowned. "You need to understand that any changes I make are only good for visual checks. If you get somewhere they have digital scanners, the changes will show."

Zalea didn't like that, but after a moment she said, "We'll take what we can get."

Within minutes, I was seated at a table that rocked a little if I leaned on it too hard. Zalea put a magazine under the leg to steady it while Stan got out his tools: a device that looked like a pen with an electrical cord that he attached to a battery, bottles of ink, needles, a rag, a bandage, and a jar of cream. It terrified me when he took hold of my arm with his calloused, dry fingers, and I jumped when he made the first prick. After that, I bit my lip and took the pain. I didn't think at first that I wanted to see, but I found myself watching as he remade my tattoo. Under Stan's unexpected artistry, the word *Woods* became *Goodman, Camilla* was changed to *Cameron,* and the day of my birth became the twelfth, not the second. "I made you younger," Stan said, rubbing cream onto my stinging skin. "Never knew a woman didn't like that."

"Milla, you can go outside now," Zalea said. "Sit under that big pine tree while I get mine done." It sounded like an order. When I hesitated, she repeated, "Go. This will take a while, so you'll have time for a nap."

It did take a long time. Stanley's yard was littered with half-done projects, firewood that needed splitting, a feed trough he was apparently repairing, and near the garden, a rusty tiller that looked like it hadn't been moved in years. I sat down on a soft bed of rusty pine needles and listened to the breeze sigh through the branches overhead. I couldn't sleep because my arm burned, so I watched birds fly over, listened to their calls, and said their names in my head. Crows. Sparrows. Mourning doves. A solitary eagle, circling as it looked for food. I was hungry too, and my mind focused, oddly, on Grandmother's snickerdoodles. With that came the memory of the last time we'd made them. Perhaps because of Zalea's constant griping about men being in charge, I'd written a question on a piece of scrap paper. *Why no woman boss?*

Grandmother had been silent for a few seconds, holding the paper as if it were heavy in her hands. Then she'd set it aside and started measuring ingredients into a bowl. "When I was young, Milla, women led two lives. We had to make a home for our husbands and children, of course, but we were also expected to work outside that home. We competed with men for jobs and money, and we tried to show the world how very, very *competent* we were."

The lines between her brows deepened. "That burden on women brought conflict everywhere, in families, between lovers, and among people who should have been friends. Our children grew up without guidance, subject to wild theories and ridiculous assertions. Too many led destructive lives. They took drugs that weren't good for them. They broke laws. They rejected God's commandments. The misinterpretation of male and female roles led to hatred and violence."

It was clear she was upset, and I wished I hadn't asked the question. As she stirred the batter with a vengeance, Grandmother went on. "We finally recognized that women should return to doing what we're meant to do. We're built to bear and nurture children. We're designed to respond to their needs. We're programmed to shape them into decent adults." Setting the bowl down, she finished, "It's better now. We stay in our place, and men handle the world outside the home."

A hinge squeaked, jolting me out of memories and back to Stanley's messy yard. Zalea came out of the house, slamming the door behind her as if she never wanted it opened again. I stood, shouldering my pack, and she showed me her revised tat. She was now Amanda Goodman, and her birth date was September 28 instead of September 18. "Let's go," she said. "Shake the dust of this place off for good."

The sun had begun to sink in the west when we came to the gate between the Woods and Wagner tribes. A small, neatly-kept house sat beside the road. In it lived Gerald Woods, who with his wife and son operated the wooden barrier that allowed entry and exit to Woods land. Gerald was elderly, and the son, Mike, had been hit by a falling tree branch, leaving him with physical and mental disabilities. The work of minding the border wasn't particularly taxing, since our tribe's remote location made security a minor concern. Aside from shipments of grain going out and truckloads of fertilizer coming in, there was little traffic. With no enemies and few visitors, our tribe had erected a fence along the border but posted no armed sentries. Only elderly men watched the gateway, keeping a record of who came and went.

In the past, people had stopped working at a certain age, a practice Teacher Foster said was a terrible waste. In the New Times, everyone contributed. Older women cared for children, tended gardens, and managed social events. Men too old to work in the fields cleaned public buildings or swept the streets to earn their allotments from the Govt. Though a few muttered about arthritis and hip pain as they worked, most were proud to be Contributing Members.

Don Woods, white-haired and bent with age, sat in a shaded area on his front porch, wearing a cap with a green and gold patch that heralded his tribal authority. Hands folded in his lap and chin on his chest, he dozed in a rocking chair made of rough-sawn logs.

Stepping onto the road, Zalea went quietly to the barrier, ducked under the bar, and gestured for me to follow. I hesitated. Crossing the border was an act we could never take back, and all my doubts returned. It didn't help that my left heel burned where a blister had formed and my neck ached from the pull of the loaded backpack. It bothered me that I'd never see Grandmother again, or Mother, or anyone else I cared about. Uncle Byron's twins would grow up without me to watch over them. I would miss the Fall Fair, Mary Ann's wedding, and Christmas services at church.

I might miss all that anyway, I reminded myself. Rolf might marry me to some old man with bad breath or send me to a tribe where I knew no one. It was a hard choice, and I didn't feel capable of making it. Zalea was smart. Zalea said we had to go. Ignoring my sore heel, I hurried to the road and caught up with my sister.

We passed the sleeping sentry without disturbing him. Behind the house I glimpsed Don's wife and son in their garden, digging potatoes. The son used the shovel to turn the plants while the mother pulled the tubers, shook the dirt off them, and tossed them into a bucket. Focused on their task, they never saw us duck under the wooden arm and hurry into the woodlands of the next tribe.

Fifty yards down, the road took a sharp turn, which shielded us from the sentry's view. We walked on the pavement, where the going was easier, until we heard the sound of a big engine behind us. The *chug-chug* of the motor paused and the brakes hissed as the driver stopped to get clearance to leave. In the stillness we heard Mr. Don ask, "What are they saying in the burg about who killed Ben Woods?" We couldn't hear the answer, but the conversation continued.

"That truck is exactly what we need," Zalea said. "Stay here, but watch for me. When I wave my arms, come running." She ran into the woods, leaping nimbly over downed branches and evading low-hanging ones. Soon she was gone from sight, which made me nervous. What if she'd decided to go on alone? I regretted my grumpiness over the last few hours. I should have been more pleasant, so my sister didn't mind having me along.

Then Zalea reappeared, beckoning. I ran to her, my pack bumping against my rear. She was panting with effort, bark clung to her hair and clothes, and one of her arms had a long, narrow scrape. "I need your help. I found what I want, but it's too big for me to move alone."

What she'd located was a large tree branch with several smaller ones protruding from it. "We're going to pull this into the road." I nodded, not sure what she was up to but willing to help. Moving to the side opposite Zalea, I took a firm hold and tugged. Together we hauled the branch from its resting place and slid it, cracking and groaning in protest, onto the pavement.

Zalea led me back into the woods, where she chose a hiding place close to the road. "That truck is headed to a processing plant. It's a long way from here, but it's southwest, and that's the direction we want to go. When the driver stops to move that branch, we're going to climb up into the second grain box and ride with him as far as we can."

Though I recognized the advantage of riding over walking, I was scared. What if the man checked his load before taking off again? What if the truck started moving when one of us was halfway up the ladder? What if I slipped and fell from the top of the box? Seeing determination in the set of Zalea's chin, I managed a nod. I'd thrown my lot in with her, so I had to do as she said.

A few minutes later the truck ground toward us. When the driver saw the branch, he stopped. The cab rocked and the brakes hissed. The man got out, muttering bad words, and examined the problem. Going back to the cab, he got a pair of gloves. Returning to the branch, he gripped it at the fat end and began pulling. Once he got it moving, he turned away from us and faced the direction he was going. Zalea jabbed my arm and we took off, sprinting to the ladder that led to the top of the grain box. I had a close view of Zalea's underpants as we climbed. At the top we hesitated, peering down at the driver, who'd turned back toward us. I saw him remove his cap to wipe the sweat from his bald head. I heard him clap the gloves to clean the bark off them. I saw the cab shift as he climbed back in. Soon the truck shifted into gear and we took off.

Zalea shot me a look of triumph. Our unsuspecting host had never even glanced our way.

The load was wheat. Zalea took a box cutter from her pocket and slit the canvas tarp that protected it from the elements. She gestured for me to dive through. I landed on my stomach, at the same time feeling the truck lurch into the next gear. Grain shifted under me, picky and dusty, but that feeling wasn't new. As kids we'd often used grain bins like sandboxes, digging ourselves into piles of oats or wheat and enjoying the feeling of the shifting kernels beneath and around us.

Once Zalea landed beside me, she reached up and cut the slit she'd made into a V-shape, giving us more light. The truck growled on beneath us, and we watched the sky, beginning a journey to places neither of us had ever imagined.

Chapter Six

We rode for three days. The first two times the truck stopped, we dug ourselves into the grain, hiding in case the driver, whose name was Bill, checked his load. He never did. "Who'd guess we're riding in this itchy stuff?" Zalea asked. We were both pale with grain dust, and she added, "If Bill did look in here, he'd think he'd seen two ghosts."

As we rode, I signed to Zalea what I'd heard Rolf and Sally say as I crouched outside Grandfather's office. "Grandfather didn't trust Rolf," Zalea said. "He wanted to, especially after Benny died, but in his heart he knew Rolf is an evil man."

The second morning, while looking for a hairbrush in Zalea's pack, I spotted a small mesh bag and pulled it out. It contained a roll of paper money called Fairbucks, issued by the Govt and accepted anywhere. There was also jewelry: a ring, a gold chain with a delicate flower pendant, and two bracelets. Holding up the bag, I met Zalea's gaze in a question.

"I took the money from Rolf's house. It's just Sally's petty cash, but it's something. The jewelry isn't stolen." When I waited expectantly, she went on. "I used to go out at night with boys…and with men. Some of them gave me gifts that were very nice, but I couldn't wear them in public. I brought them along so we can trade for stuff we need."

At first I was tempted to ask more about the "gifts," but once I thought about it, I didn't. There was more to my sister than I'd suspected, and something told me I might not want to know everything. I put the bag back in Zalea's pack.

We learned Bill's rhythms and became confident about getting out of the truck. When he stopped at a diner, usually one attached to a gas station, we'd exercise our legs and relieve our bladders. At night he pulled off the road at a convenient spot and crawled into the compartment above the cab, where he had no trouble falling and staying asleep.

Never in my life had I had nothing to do for so long: no housework, no yard work, no schoolwork. We fell into a dreamlike state, with the truck roaring beneath us, the sky above the same yet different, and changes of speed signaling conditions we had no way of knowing about. At times the noise around us increased, which meant we were passing through large burgs. I would have liked to peek at the traffic and the buildings, but Zalea said someone might notice our heads sticking out from where heads shouldn't be.

Once when we got out at a gas station, we saw a white van with MONC written on the side in big letters. That was scary. Mobile Officers for National Compliance, usually known as Monkey Men, were special troops that made sure people behaved. Their power was absolute. No Monkey Man had ever been convicted of a crime. Of course they only killed bad people, but Zalea and I had entered that category. Disobedient. Sneaky. Rebellious.

The wasted hours nagged at me, since I'd been taught that idleness destroyed ambition. Zalea was bored too, until she remembered something she'd brought along. "I took about a dozen books from Uncle Benny's house," she said. "I hid them at the bottom of the feed bin in the chicken coop, but I never had a lot of time to read them with Grandfather's mind failing so bad." She took a small, soft-cover book from her pack. "Most of them were too heavy to bring along, but this one looked interesting, so I stuck it in my pack." Leafing through, she said, "It's a journal that belonged to a woman named Bonnie. I only read the first few pages, but it starts back in the Old Times. She says how much she loved living in a big burg—She calls it a city." Her dust-coated brows rose. "I think Bonnie lived with Uncle Benny, but they never got married. Back then, men and women would do that, live together for a while then split up and find someone new."

I frowned at that. Not only was that sinful, but how did they raise their children right? Every baby deserved a mother and a father who worked together to make him or her safe, healthy, and prepared to be a good citizen.

Zalea skimmed pages as she looked for bits that interested her. "She started writing during the Miller administration." She read aloud, "*Why doesn't someone make these people follow the law? Our whole country is going to be wrecked.*"

Teacher Foster had told us about Miller, a very bad man who'd somehow got control of the nation near the end of the Old Times. He'd let his people raid the treasury for their own benefit and ignore the laws of the nation. It had gotten really bad, because Miller had convinced a lot of people that he was a genius. They simply couldn't believe he'd lied to get into office and continued lying to remain there.

"Bonnie's parents were Miller supporters," Zalea said. "She paper-clipped her mother's letters in here, and they say how Miller could fix all the country's problems if people just let him do what he wanted. I don't think Bonnie ever wrote back to her mother, but she wrote what she wished she had the nerve to say to her in here." Removing a folded sheet of lilac-colored paper from its paper clip, Zalea scanned it and grimaced. "I don't think Bonnie's mother liked Uncle Benny much." Again she read aloud, this time from the mother's note.

> Sweetheart,
>
> I wish you'd come home so we can talk face to face. I want to understand what you're thinking, but it's hard when you're so far away. Maybe I

could come to the city and meet you at a restaurant where we can talk, just the two of us, without that man between us. We need to figure this out.

Mother

Zalea returned to the diary. "Bonnie's answer is short and sweet. *You never understood me and you never will.*"

I thought Bonnie should have done as her mother asked. After all, our parents are our best guides in life.

"Here's another one," Zalea said. This time the stationery was pale yellow.

Sweetheart,

I know you feel differently than we do about Miller's changes to the government, but he's just getting us back to the principles our country was founded on. We simply cannot react to every complaint of inequality and every accusation of injustice. There's right and there's wrong, and we shouldn't pretend the wrong things are okay just because someone's feelings are hurt.

Please come home for a visit, or I can fly down to see you. I promise to listen to what you have to say if you'll promise to listen to me.

Mother

I hid a yawn, wondering why Zalea cared about ancient drama. There'd been a big fight for a while, but Chief Vox had come along and taken the reins of government in his skilled hands. Good and reason won out, and now the rules now were fair for everyone.

Any disagreements between Bonnie and her mother had been resolved long ago.

Sensing my disinterest, Zalea went quiet and read to herself. I took out my flute and played softly, practicing some runs I liked until I was satisfied with them. Taking the flute apart, I wiped each piece carefully before putting it into its case. Grain dust floated in the air like mist, and I didn't want it stored in or on my beloved instrument.

Every once in a while, Zalea got excited about a passage and read it aloud. Often it was a description of what Bonnie's life had been like in the Old Times. While it sounded made up to me, I could tell Zalea believed every word. "Girls went to college as often as boys did," she said. "There were female doctors and lawyers and teachers." She set the journal on her lap. "People wore whatever they wanted. I saw pictures in old magazines at Benny's house showing women in short pants, tops that barely covered their busts, and even see-through dresses. I meant to steal one to show you, but Grandfather tossed them all into the fire."

Zalea had once dared to suggest it would be easier to do her job if she were allowed to wear different clothes. "I have to climb into haylofts and up onto tractors to talk to farmers," she'd argued. "It would be so much easier in pants."

"Skirts are more modest," Grandmother had replied. "Nice girls don't encourage men to think about the cleft."

Bad clothes get girls raped, I signed.

Zalea's brow furrowed. "I don't think it's clothes that get women raped, Milla. I think some people hurt others any time they can get away with it."

Mother says purity gift for husband.

"Where was Mother when I was getting raped at thirteen?" Seeing my shocked expression, Zalea bit her lip. "Forget I said that, Milla. I-I was kidding."

Clearly, she had not been kidding. *What boy did this?*

Setting the journal in her lap, Zalea met my gaze. "Not a boy. A man."

My mind flooded with questions I didn't know how to ask. Sex was mostly a mystery to me. While any farm girl knew where babies came from, I wasn't exactly sure how what I'd seen among cattle applied to people. I'd grown up in a house with three females and Grandfather, who Grandmother said was "too old to get frisky, praise the Lord." I thought maybe a woman could get pregnant if she let a man put his hands under her skirt, but I wasn't sure.

That brought a question. *No baby?*

Zalea's nostrils flared. "Rolf took me to a doctor—at least, a man he said was a doctor."

My jaw dropped. It was our uncle who'd ruined Zalea?

Staring up at the sky above us, she explained. "I remember the guy's house smelled really bad. He took me into this room with a metal table and made me lie on it while he put a…thing inside me to keep…a baby…from happening." I pointed to her abdomen, asking a silent question, and Zalea nodded. "Yes. It's still there."

As my mind reeled with unwelcome thoughts, Zalea went on. "About a month ago, Rolf suddenly stopped bothering me. I was afraid..." She turned to me. "Did he ever—hurt you?"

I shook my head. Though I'd always felt kind of shivery when Uncle Rolf was around, he'd never touched me. I wondered now if the uncomfortable feeling I'd had was because deep down, I'd sensed he wanted to.

Perhaps embarrassed by her confession, Zalea took up the journal again. "Anyway, Bonnie seems very sad about what happened after Miller dropped dead." She read aloud.

> Now that Dupree's taken over, they're bombing big cities, claiming activists have taken them over and ruined them. I stopped watching the news. They parrot Dupree's words and gloss over the wrongs he's committing. I feel like I'm shirking my duty, but I can't read what they say and keep my sanity. Kent is very angry. He says we have to do something. I am afraid, for him, for myself, for all of us.

Who Kent? I signed.

"Her brother maybe. She talks about him a lot." Zalea skimmed a few pages. "Oh-oh. I think Kent must have joined the rebellion. She writes *K is dead*, and then there's a big time gap." She looked ahead. "More than a year. She must have come to live with Benny during that time, but there are just a few more entries." She read aloud.

> Everyone in Woodsburg admires Benjamin Woods, Junior, but no one cares about me. I still look for Kent everywhere, but I know he's gone forever. How could they kill that beautiful man? How could they?

Zalea paged forward again. "Here's the last entry. *I'm not sure I can do this, but I don't have a choice.*" Staring into the truck's dim corner, she said, "I wonder what she had to do."

Since Uncle Benny had lived alone for as long as I knew him, I guessed the final entry meant that Bonnie had decided to leave him. Maybe she'd married someone else, or maybe she'd returned to her own people.

Near the end of the third day, traffic noises increased and we heard engines, horns, and people shouting. The truck made a sharp turn and then proceeded much more slowly. Overhead we saw the upper stories of very tall buildings on either side, taller even than the silos at home. The truck turned again, went up a sharp incline, and stopped. "Be ready to get out," Zalea ordered. Being inside a gravity box when the bottom opened was dangerous, since we might be sucked down into the grain and suffocate. Quickly we gathered our things, stowed them in our packs, and shrugged them onto our backs. The food pack was empty, so Zalea folded it up and put it inside her own.

Staying low, we crawled out of the grain, through the slit, and lay atop the canvas cover. All around us was activity and noise. The sun had been hot, but as it slanted away from us the air cooled a little, so the sweat on my back felt clammy.

Below us men moved into sight and out again, but they were like no men I'd seen before. Their skin was darker than the darkest field hands at home, darker than days in the sun could have made them. Black men. Bill's delivery route had brought us to a tribe of a whole different race.

We had pictures of black people in our schoolbooks, but I'd never seen one in person. The man who greeted Bill was half a head taller, with wide shoulders and muscular arms. He wore an orange-and-black reflective vest and carried a clipboard. "Hey there, Mr. Porter. You made good time."

"Smooth sailing," Bill replied. "Not much traffic and no bad weather."

The man's smile flashed, showing white teeth. "Come on inside, and we'll get the paperwork done."

They went into a shed-like building made of rusty metal. The Black man had to slam the door twice to get it to close. As soon as they were inside, Zalea said, "We need to go."

I would have signed *Where?* but she was already scanning the yard. Pointing to a shed marked *TOOLS,* she said, "When no one's looking, we'll climb down and hide in there until the workers go home for the night."

Now my question would have been, *Then what?* but again, Zalea wasn't paying attention.

Scooting to the back, she paused, waited for her moment, and then swung herself onto the ladder. "Come on!"

I scooted across the canvas, grabbed the ladder, and followed her to the ground. No one hollered, "Look!" or "What you kids doing here?" so we scurried toward the structure and opened the door. Inside was a waist-high platform loaded with tools. On the walls were pegs for hanging belts, chains, and cords. Under the shelf was larger stuff, ten-gallon cans, crates full of odds and ends, a couple of engines, and machines I couldn't identify. Zalea crawled to the back wall and then called, "Can you see me from the doorway?" Standing back, I looked and shook my head. "Good. Get in here with me."

The space was cramped, but it served its purpose. Several times during the afternoon men came through the door, chose some tool they needed, and left again. Each time we held our breath, but no one saw us. While I wasn't sure how Zalea felt, I was terrified.

Being discovered would be bad. Being discovered by a Black man might be worse. I'd heard stories.

"The Blacks have their own tribes," Cousin Kat told Cousin Anna once while I helped them make jam. "It was harder for them, since their bloodlines are so messy, but I guess the Govt helped them sort it out."

"Well, I like knowing they have their place and we have ours." Cousin Anna had responded.

"Yes," Kat agreed. "It's better now that everyone lives with their own kind."

The workers who went in and out of the tool shed were all Black men, but some were light-skinned while others were so dark they blended into the shadows once they stepped out of the light from the doorway. The odd thing was that if I closed my eyes, they sounded just like the men from home. They joked with each other, griped about the foreman's need for order, and discussed the possibility of a win for a team called the Runners. They might have been Woods or Scrantons or Davises. I tried to sign that to Zalea, but she whispered, "Not now."

After a while, my stomach began growling like an angry Doberman. Zalea whispered, "When we get out of here, we'll find something to eat," but my stomach didn't understand future tense. It kept right on letting me know it wasn't happy.

After hours in a crouch that made my legs stiff and my neck ache, I heard a long, shrill whistle. Within ten minutes, the yard around us fell silent. We stayed in hiding a while longer as men came in to put tools away for the night. When Zalea decided it was safe, we crawled out from hiding and stood up. There wasn't much light in the shed, but I could see that Zalea was a mess. I guessed I looked no better. Three days in the dusty grain box followed by an afternoon hiding behind greasy machinery had left us filthy and rumpled. We couldn't go out in public until we cleaned up.

Stripping down to our underwear, we used the last of our water and a fairly clean rag I found to wipe away the dirt, sweat, and cobwebs. I put on my clean set of boy's clothes, jeans and a t-shirt with a flannel to go over it. Zalea beat Grandfather's cap against a shelf to clean it and set it on my head. "You look okay. Now me."

The outfit Zalea took from the bottom of her knapsack was unlike anything I could have imagined. The dress was stretchy, and when she pulled it on, it hugged her body tightly. It was covered in shiny spangles that caught even the tiny amount of light that came through the seams in the shed wall. The neckline scooped low, while the skirt stopped several inches above her knees. I'd seen entertainers at fairs dressed like that, but never a girl like us. Bracing herself against my shoulder, Zalea put on shoes that were definitely not made for life on a farm. She practiced walking in them by going back and forth across the shed floor a few times. Her ankles wobbled at first, but with practice she learned to maintain her balance.

Where? I signed, pointing at the dress.

"I think it belonged to Bonnie. It's pretty, so I took it while Grandfather was using the bathroom." My lips tightened at my sister's audacity, but Zalea said, "Before we leave here, let me have a look at that blister."

Once the sore spot was padded with a piece of rag, I put my boots back on and we gave each other a final inspection. With her hand on the knob, Zalea grimaced, acknowledging that what was out there was scary to her too. Peeping out to be sure the yard was deserted, we slipped out the door, closing it carefully so it didn't make noise.

I'd never seen such an unfriendly place, all metal and hard dirt. The air smelled smoky, like there was a fire nearby. The whole place was silent now except for a metallic sound I identified after a moment as wind lifting a nearby metal vent. Each time a gust died, a louvre fell back into place with a clank.

The yard itself was huge. Massive holding tanks lined one side, some fat and squat, others taller and thinner. They all had pipes and tubes sprouting from everywhere. Across the yard was a pile of grain bigger than any I'd ever seen before. I guessed our tribe's harvest would soon be emptied there, if it hadn't been already.

"What you two doing here?" The voice was raspy and low. We turned to see the man who'd met Bill and taken delivery of his load. Up close he looked even bigger, and his glare of inquiry made me afraid I might wet my borrowed pants.

"We're just cutting through to the next road," Zalea said. Anyone who didn't know her would have thought her tone was casual, but I heard the false note. Zalea was as scared of the stranger as I was.

"Just out for a walk, huh?"

"Yes. My little brother wanted to see what they do with the grain. I didn't think anybody would mind if we took a look."

The man's lips twitched with humor, and I couldn't tell if that was good or bad. The image of the stranger who'd been hanged for entering our land uninvited flitted through my head. At the very least we were trespassers. Worse crimes might be laid at our door.

"Where'd you come from?"

"We live over there." Zalea pointed in what had to be a random direction, since neither of us knew what was where.

"Over there." That lip twitch thing happened again. "So you're Tribe Mihn?"

Zalea sensed that was wrong. "Um, no. Farther over."

"You walked fifty miles to show your little brother an ethanol plant."

She was floundering. "It was a nice day, and…"

"Don't bullshit an old bullshitter, girl. Where you from really?"

Aware she was trapped, Zalea tried a different approach. "When you come to work tomorrow morning, sir, we'll be gone."

That made him shake his head. "Girl, you ain't going to make it to tomorrow morning. The people around here gonna eat you two up and spit your bones into the river."

Licking her lips, Zalea tried again. "That's nothing to you. Let us leave, and—"

"I bet your little brother there is hungry." The man must have seen my involuntary response to the mention of food, because he grinned, showing those white teeth. For some reason, I started to feel like we were going to be okay. "Come with me to my house," he proposed. "My wife will feed you supper and you can sleep in our spare bedroom." His voice took on a persuasive tone. "In the morning you might feel like going back home." Raising a hand, he vowed, "Nobody will hurt you, I promise."

Zalea opened her mouth, no doubt to argue that we were fine, but I nudged her with an elbow. While I was a little scared of the Black man, I was more afraid of the others he'd mentioned, the ones who'd eat us and spit out our bones.

After a glance at me, Zalea said, "We can pay." Taking off her backpack, she dug out the bag of jewelry and showed him one of the bracelets. "Tomorrow morning before we leave, I'll give this to your wife."

She seemed willing to ignore the fact that the man was big enough to knock us both in the head and take the whole bag. With a straight face but a twinkle in his eyes, he said, "Keep it. Someday, you'll get a chance to help another person, and I expect you to pass the favor on." Making a sweeping motion with his hand, he said, "Let me escort you to my chariot."

Within minutes, we were leaving the plant in the man's pickup truck. We stopped at a gate that slid open when he passed a card over a metal box. "My name's Floyd, and I'm Jefferson Tribe. Who are you?"

"I'm Amanda," Zalea said. "My brother is Cameron. We're Goodman Tribe, from out east."

"Pleased to meet you." Mr. Floyd checked the traffic before pulling onto the road. I'd never seen so many cars and trucks before, and they all appeared to be in a hurry. For a while, the only drivers we saw were Black men, but when we reached the center of the burg, I saw people with different complexions, different eye shapes, and different statures. Most pedestrians carried bags, briefcases, or boxes. In cars and trucks, drivers focused on the road, their expressions serious.

The buildings were huge, not just one- or two-story structures like at home, but rows and rows stacked on top of each other, with window after window exactly the same.

"Scrunch down," Mr. Floyd ordered. "I can't have anybody wondering why you two are with me."

We did as he said, but Zalea asked, "You're not supposed to give people rides?"

"Did you see any men that looked like me traveling with kids that look like you?"

"Um, no."

"That's because it's against the law. Your tribe's law. My tribe's law. The Govt's law. Races don't mix except to do business. I can sell you fuel or buy your grain or maybe help if you get a flat tire, but we aren't allowed to socialize."

Because everyone is more comfortable with their own, I thought. As Grandmother always said, "That's just how it is."

We drove through an area where tall buildings stood side by side like blocks. I caught a glimpse of a huge, shiny arch rising hundreds of feet into the air. I poked Zalea and pointed, and she asked Mr. Floyd, "What is that?"

"It's kind of a miracle," he replied. "The Arch shouldn't have survived the war, but somehow it did." He grimaced. "You used to be able to ride to the top of it, but these days it's just for lookin' at."

He turned into a driveway and then, to my horror, drove down a ramp that took us underground. I didn't even like Grandfather's basement much, and now I was in a huge space made of dank, dark concrete. In dim, grayish light provided by sconces embedded in the walls, Mr. Floyd parked in a space outlined by painted lines. Turning to us, he said, "We need to ride up in the elevator, but I'd just as soon not have to explain you to anybody. I'll go ahead and make sure it's clear. When I signal, get over there fast as you can, okay?"

We nodded. When he was gone Zalea spoke, but I didn't know if she was talking to me or to herself. "We could run. He'd never catch us."

Thinking about the people who'd eat us, I touched her arm and shook my head.

“Okay,” Zalea said. “Take this and slide it up your sleeve.” She held out a paring knife. “If he tries anything, stab him in the eye.”

I did as she said. The blade lay against my skin, cold, like a warning. Was I willing to stab Mr. Floyd? I had to be. No way would I let him hurt me or Zalea.

Mr. Floyd approached the elevator, a device I’d heard about but never seen or used. When he reached the doors they opened, and a woman with two small children came out. All three wore nice clothes. The mother spoke to Mr. Floyd, who smiled as he answered. That helped me relax a little. His neighbors weren’t scared of Mr. Floyd, and they didn’t look like cannibals either.

Once the woman and her kids were gone, Mr. Floyd gestured at us. Zalea opened the truck door and exited, closing it softly after I got out. The sound was loud in the echo-y area, but we hurried toward Mr. Floyd, who ushered us into the car and pushed a button. A door slid across the open space, making the garage disappear.

I got a funny sensation in my stomach when the elevator began its climb. It was scary but interesting. I was being carried upward to—I checked the button Mr. Floyd had pressed—the tenth floor. Beside me, Zalea reached out and took my hand. From the clammy feel of it, I guessed she was as nervous as I was. Not that she’d ever admit it.

When we stopped moving with a gentle jolt, the doors slid open again, revealing a blank wall across a wide hallway. Mr. Mr. Floyd leaned out, looked both ways, and then said, “Come on.” We followed him, turning right and passing door after door. Did people really live this close to each other day after day? I wondered. Where did the kids go to play kickball? Where did they keep their horses and cows? Where did a person go for a few minutes of quiet?

Hums, voices, bumps, and the occasional bark of a dog told me that there were lots of people in this place. We came to a door marked *1014*, and Mr. Floyd took out a key, unlocked it, and gestured for us to enter ahead of him. Once we were inside, he closed the door and called, "Lila, I'm home."

Home for Mr. Floyd was an apartment with a wide living room, a kitchen behind a half wall on one side, and a hallway down the other side that contained four doors. From one of those came a woman who stopped dead when she saw us. She took in an astonished breath. "Floyd? What—?" She couldn't even complete the question.

"I found them on the grounds at work," Mr. Floyd said. I sensed the scene he'd imagined had been less difficult than the reality he now faced. "They've been hiding in one of our sheds all day. I figure we'll feed 'em and—"

"You should have called the toppers. They'd have come and taken them off your hands."

Mr. Floyd's brow furrowed. "I couldn't do that, Li. They're just kids."

Going into the kitchen, Mrs. Floyd opened the oven door. The smell of roast beef that emanated made my stomach do a little dance. Closing the oven, she moved to the counter and dumped a bowl of dough onto a cutting board. Her expression indicated a struggle to reach a decision, and she beat the dough with her fists with more force than seemed necessary. "Trespassing is a crime," she said. "Tribal Officers of Protection handle such things."

He gestured at us. "Look at them, Li. They ain't going to blow up the machinery."

"Well, they ain't going to fit in here." Taking a rolling pin, she squashed the dough flat. "We have guests coming tonight."

Mr. Floyd slapped his own forehead. “Damn. I forgot.” Turning to us he said, “Look, you two. If we feed you supper, can you stay in our guest room and be quiet?” Zalea nodded, so I did too.

“What you gonna tell the kids?” Mrs. Floyd cut the dough into squares and began rolling the squares into balls.

“It might be good for them to meet people of…people who are different. You know how much stupid stuff they hear about…them. Maybe they need to learn a little truth.” To us he said, “My kids went on an outing with a church group after school today. They’ll be home in about an hour, and I’m gonna tell them your dad is a truck driver. He brought you along on his run, but his rig broke down. He’s getting it fixed, and I invited you here so you wouldn’t have to sleep on the ground at the plant. Does that sound okay?”

We both nodded again, but Mrs. Floyd was not convinced. “The boys will know they aren’t supposed to be here, and look at that girl, Floyd. What you gonna tell our boys she is?”

“I’ll explain that the rules allow for emergencies.” He raised his hands in a plea. “They’re hungry, Li, and you know if they wander around out there, bad things are gonna happen to them.”

She huffed out a breath, still not pleased. “I suppose if the boys tell their teacher that their dad brought a white boy and a light brown girl home for dinner, he’ll assume they’re making up stories.”

Mrs. Floyd took two more potatoes from a bin under the sink. Hurrying over, Zalea took them from her. “I can do that.” Taking up a peeler that lay on the counter, she went to work, obviously eager to convince the woman we weren’t going to be a problem.

“Thank you,” Mrs. Floyd said in a formal tone. Opening the freezer, she took out a small, square package. “It’s too late to add more meat, so I'll cut it up small and add another side dish. I hope y'all like corn." At that point I was so hungry I wouldn't even have turned down beets, my least favorite food in the world.

When Zalea finished peeling the potatoes, she added them to a pot already on the stove. Mrs. Floyd inspected her work, seemed satisfied with it, and turned on the burner below. I saw her nose twitch when she got close to Zalea. "Maybe you two would like to wash up before dinner." After a pause, she added, "Have you got something less…flashy to wear?"

Zalea looked at Mrs. Floyd's modest dress and then down at the spangled one she wore. "Um, yes."

"Great. Once you're clean, put your other clothes on and hide that." Looking embarrassed and a little resentful, Zalea grabbed her bag and disappeared into the bathroom.

Mr. Floyd sat down at a small desk near the door to deal with the day's mail. Mrs. Floyd was busy in the kitchen. Left on my own, I wandered the living area, making comparisons. The Jeffersons' apartment was in many ways nicer than Grandfather's house. The appliances in the kitchen were shiny and square. I noticed the refrigerator didn't make bumpy, burpy noises like the one we'd had. While the furnishings weren't the heavy, classic pieces we had at home, they looked newer and more comfortable. There were tall, graceful lamps on the end tables and soft rugs underfoot. There was a telephone on the desk where Mr. Floyd perused the daily newspaper. Framed photos hung on the walls, some of the family, others of what I assumed were relatives. It was odd to see Black people posed, smiling, or caught at candid moments, playing a game or laughing over a birthday cake.

I knew modern Black people didn't live in huts or wear loincloths like in the Tarzan movies, but from what I'd heard growing up, I'd assumed they were backward. Now I saw that wasn't true. In fact,

Mr. Floyd and his wife seemed a lot like Uncle Byron and Aunt Ariel. They discussed news items from the paper. They joked about his boss, who apparently loved her cinnamon buns. And even though she was disgusted with her husband for bringing uninvited, illegal guests into their home, Mrs. Floyd brought him a cold beer and pinched his shoulder as she set it before him.

Instead of windows in the living room, the apartment had a sliding glass door that led to a small balcony. I would have liked to go out there, but it was evening, and I was afraid I'd let in a draft. Standing before the glass, I looked out at buildings that went on and on. In the dark they were only silhouettes spotted with light. Some were tall, some squatting low but spread wide. The view impressed me, not so much for its beauty but for the extent of it. There were people in all those buildings, but not a speck of farmland in sight. How did they live?

Along the edge of the balcony sat wooden boxes with plants growing in them. I identified mint, basil, and sage. There were also tomatoes, but not the ones I was used to. These were only the size of grapes. Seeing my gaze, Mrs. Floyd said from the kitchen, "Prices are high. It pays to grow what we can."

After about twenty minutes Zalea returned, wearing a gray skirt and plaid blouse. "Your turn, Cameron."

Floyd showed me to a bathroom where he'd set out clean towels and washcloths. When he left, closing the door behind him, I spent a moment appreciating the towel, which was softer than the ones at home and smelled faintly of lavender. It took me a minute to figure out how the shower worked, but I got it. I was surprised by the power of the water, which pounded on me in a pleasant, relaxing beat. Its warmth was constant as well, not the too-hot-and-then-too-cold way the shower at home tended to run. I washed my skin and hair vigorously, watching bits of grain circle the drain as I rinsed.

When I was finished, I put on my clean set of boy clothes and went back to the Jefferson's living room. Zalea and I sat on the couch while Mr. Floyd sat opposite us and his wife continued to fuss in the kitchen. When their twin boys, aged six, arrived home, their reaction to our presence was almost funny. They came in tussling over a baseball cap they'd found on the sidewalk. Seeing us sitting on their couch made them glance at each other, eyes and mouths wide open, and then erupt in nervous laughter.

"These are our guests for the night." Mr. Floyd gave the prepared story as the boys' eyes flickered between him and us. I tried to appear masculine. How did strange boys approach each other? With a smile? With a glare? I settled for a direct look, keeping the corners of my mouth from turning either up or down.

"And listen here." Their mother's tone was serious. "You are not to talk about them outside this house. Got it?" When they both nodded, Lila turned to us. "This is Jonah, and that's Jacob. You won't be here long enough to be able to tell them apart." That was true, since they were identical. "Jacob, show them where they'll be sleeping. Jonah, go set the table."

Dinner began badly. Mr. Floyd did his best to make conversation, but he didn't get much response. He talked about his day at work. He described the new building going up downtown. His family responded with single words. "Nice," or "Really." Finally, maybe out of desperation, he asked, "Would you like to tell us what it's like where you come from?"

After a brief pause, Zalea said, "We're a farm tribe. We don't live in buildings like this. Each family has its own house, some close together but others far apart. We grow grains, like wheat, corn, oats, and sunflowers."

One of the boys overcame his shyness and asked, "Are those the big ones?"

"Yes." Zalea replied. "Like this." She made a circle with her hands, bigger than her own head.

"And you cut stuff down when it's ready and bring it to my dad so he can turn it into gas." That was the other twin.

"Yes."

"That's how the tribes work together," their mother told them, "but everyone lives in their own spot, so we feel safe." With a glance at us, she finished, "It's best if we stay among our own kind."

When the meal was finished, Zalea helped Mrs. Floyd in the kitchen while Mr. Floyd, the boys, and I moved the living room furniture against the walls to open the center space. With the help of Jacob—or maybe Jonah—I set a half-dozen folding chairs around the room for their guests. Mrs. Floyd arranged crackers, meat, cheese, and nuts on pretty plates and set them around the room. The last one she gave to Zalea to take to the guest room, a hint that she'd warmed to us a little.

By then it was almost eight. "Time for you to disappear." Mrs. Floyd followed us down the hall and stood in the doorway, checking to see that we had everything we might need. The room was nice, with pale yellow walls and deep green carpeting. The bed was large and covered with a green, silky cover, lighter than the quilts we used at home. Satisfied that all was in order our hostess said, "Lock the door behind me, so no one wanders in here looking for the bathroom. Stay quiet. Get some sleep. Tomorrow morning early, if you still want to go on, Floyd will drop you off in Sidell territory, where you'll blend in better." She hesitated, her hand on the doorknob. "Was home so bad that you had to run away?"

Zalea gave her a direct look. "Yes, ma'am. It was."

Mrs. Floyd frowned. "I don't think you know how hard it's going to be out there on your own."

"We're grateful to you for helping us out."

"Don't be grateful to me," she said with a wry grin. "I do what my husband says, though sometimes I think he's got rocks in his head." I followed her to the door and locked it, as ordered. Soon we heard the doorbell ring, and voices rose in welcome and response. That happened over and over, until I guessed there were at least twenty people out there. All of them would be Black. While the idea might have scared me before, it no longer did.

I had other concerns though. Tapping Zalea's arm, I signed, *Where we go?* Her lips clamped shut, and I guessed she didn't want to admit she had no idea. *How you know where?*

Zalea scowled. "The man who would have taken me to my father told me he lives in Dorado." She looked down at her hands. "I wished I'd known they arrested him. I'd have gone to the Punishment Place and spoken for him."

I doubted a girl would have been allowed to stand up and speak at a meeting of men. Even if Zalea had tried, Uncle Rolf's account would have been believed over anything she said. Had the man been innocent, as Zalea insisted? Looking back I recalled his courage, his defiant stance in the last moments of life.

"It probably wouldn't have helped," Zalea admitted, "but I'd have spoken up anyway." Tears formed in her eyes, but she blinked them away. "Dorado is a whole different country from Fairica now, but if we can get there, I'm pretty sure I can find my father." "Pretty sure" didn't sound promising to me, but Zalea said, "We should rest, like Mrs. Lila suggested."

We lay on the bed, Zalea reading Bonnie's journal while I took out the notebook she'd brought along. *Left Sept. 10,* I wrote. I'd meant to start a record of our travels, but I couldn't recall how many nights we'd been gone. Was it four or five?

Light from the living room shone under the door, and we listened to the sounds of the Jeffersons' party. It was somebody's birthday. The hum of conversation formed a background as bottles clinked and dishes were set down with soft thuds. After a half hour, I heard a strum of introductory guitar chords. Someone began to sing. A few voices joined in, then more. I'd heard the song before. It was about choosing to be happy, and while I didn't know all the words, there was something about a room with no roof. The guests joined in, and there was hand-clapping and harmonizing. It sounded like gatherings we'd had at home, and I felt a stab of loneliness.

"Seems like they're having fun," Zalea murmured. When the first song ended, another began, softer and unknown to us. For a moment I imagined getting my flute from my backpack and going out to join the musicians. I imagined their surprised, pleased faces when I added breathy arpeggios to the melodies they sang. Zalea might have taught them a few songs they didn't know, like "Time in a Bottle" or "Seven Bridges Road."

Then I remembered what a shock seeing us would be for the Floyds' guests. These people weren't our tribe or even our race. We had nothing in common, even if the music made it seem like we might. I drifted off to sleep to the sound of "Hallelujah" from the living room and Zalea's light snore close by.

In the morning Mrs. Floyd knocked sharply on the door, and I staggered over to unlock it. "Not many patrols this early," she told us, "so hop to it. I don't want Floyd getting stopped with you two in his truck."

Zalea yawned, stretched, and slid out of bed, wearing her slip as a nightgown. Lila held out a navy blue cotton dress with a white belt and three-quarter sleeves. "This is a little tight for me, but I think it will fit you. It won't call attention to you like that one you came here in."

"Thank you."

Mrs. Floyd rolled her eyes. "You can thank me by forgetting who we are and where we live. I'm pretty sure you won't get through today without being arrested."

After she left, Zalea regarded the spangled dress hung over the back of a chair. "When I saw the pictures in Benny's magazines, I thought that's what women wore in bigger burgs, but I guess I was wrong. That dress must have been from a long time ago."

For years after she left him, Benny had kept Bonnie's stuff. He must have loved her very much.

Zalea stuffed the dress into her bag. "I'm going to keep it. Maybe other places are different from here."

Mr. Floyd checked the elevator to be sure it was empty before taking us down to the garage. There he checked again, found it clear, and gestured for us to hurry to his truck. Soon we were on the road, Zalea and I ducked down so that all we could see was skyline. Mr. Floyd was nervous, and I guessed his wife's disapproval had made him aware of the dangers of the situation. "If anyone catches Floyd with you two, he'll be in serious trouble," she'd told us as we prepared to leave. "Our tribe would punish him with a fine at best, maybe worse. A white tribe would hang him from the nearest lamppost."

And what would happen to us? That, I guessed, would depend on the tribe. Some might make allowances for our youth. Others would treat us the same way they treated Mr. Floyd. After all, it might be argued, if we were good girls, we'd be safe at home, not wandering the streets tempting men to evil deeds. As the tops of lampposts passed, I imagined my sister's body suspended from one and shivered.

It was a relief for all of us when Mr. Floyd pulled over and shifted the truck into park. "Across this road is Tribe Sidell territory," he said. "If you keep up a good pace, you can be out of the metro area by dark." His brow furrowed. "You'd be a lot better off if you had travel passes, but I'm not sure how you'd get them."

"We'll figure it out," Zalea said. "Thank you for everything."

His mouth drooped. "I wish I could do more."

"You've already risked enough for us. We'll be fine." Taking a look around to be sure no one was watching, Zalea opened the truck door and got out. "Come on, Cameron." I followed, waving goodbye to Mr. Floyd, whose pressure on the gas pedal suggested relief at being done with us.

Hurrying across the street, Zalea turned down the first alley we came to. Day had arrived, but between the buildings it was still fairly dark. Opening a brown paper sack Mrs. Floyd had given her, she made a little squeal of pleasure. "Breakfast!"

Sliding our backs down the bumpy brick wall, we sat on the cold cement and ate biscuits sliced open and stuffed with slabs of ham and chunks of cheese. We'd refilled the canteen from the Jeffersons' sink, and we passed it back and forth, taking sips to wash down the food. When we finished, Zalea wadded up the sack and the napkins and took them to a smelly trash bin farther down the alley. After she'd dumped the bag she turned back, opened the bin lid, and peered inside.

I got up and joined her, asking a question with my eyes. "I thought maybe we could find an old pass in here." Zalea pulled herself onto the edge of the metal bin. "Shine your flashlight in there, will you?"

Putting a foot on a metal strut, I lifted myself up and lit the bin while Zalea scanned the mess of discarded food, paper, and clothing. It smelled bad, but finding even one travel pass would be worth the effort. We saw nothing worthwhile.

"Can I help, ladies?" We turned to see a man with a broad, pleasant face and a high, shiny forehead. His easy smile suggested friendliness.

Zalea climbed down from the trash bin. "We threw our travel passes away by accident. I put them in a bag last night for safekeeping. This morning my brother thought it was trash and tossed it."

"So you're just passing through the area?"

"We're on our way south." Zalea glanced at me. "To meet our parents."

"I see." The man kneaded his hands together for a few seconds. "What you have to do is go to the Dept of Travel, tell them what happened, and apply for replacement passes."

Zalea licked her lips. "What would they need from us to issue those?"

He rubbed at his chin. "They'll run a check on your ID tats to see when and where your passes were issued."

"Oh."

The man looked from Zalea to me and back again. "Maybe I should go with you. I used to work there, and the people there remember me." His left brow quirked as he added, "I could probably get them to skip all the rigamarole and give you what you need."

"Why would you do that for us?"

His smile revealed crooked bottom teeth. "I've been in the situation you're in. You need to get somewhere, but you don't have the paperwork. It's hard, worrying that every topper you see is an enemy. I don't think it's right for everyday citizens to have to account to the authorities for every move they make." He paused, tilting his head. "You want my help or not?"

Zalea shot me a raised-eyebrow look, asking a silent question. I gave a little shrug to indicate I'd do whatever she decided. We'd been scared of Floyd Jefferson, and he'd turned out to be really nice. This man seemed nice too, and he was white, so we didn't have to worry about being seen with him.

Apparently Zalea's thoughts went the same way. "Thank you, Mr. …"

"Ripley. Gus to my friends." He swept a hand toward the street. "My car is that way."

"Your car?"

"The office is about a mile from here. Much faster to ride."

Zalea gave me a second look. When I shrugged again, she sighed, like she was tired of the weight of decision-making. To Mr. Ripley she said, "That would be great. Thank you."

When we got to Mr. Ripley's Honda, a woman sat behind the wheel. That was odd, not only because I'd seen very few women back home who could drive, but also because she was so tiny she could barely see over the steering wheel. Still, she smiled sweetly at us, and her white hair and blue eyes reminded me of Grandmother. "This is my wife, Marilyn," Mr. Ripley said. "These ladies need to visit the Travel Office, dear. Can we help?"

"Of course," she replied. "It's not that far out of our way."

He got in up front. Zalea and I got into the back seat. As soon as the doors closed, I heard a click that made my spine tingle. I tried the handle, but it didn't open. Mrs. Ripley started the car and pulled away from the curb.

"Why did you lock us in?" Zalea asked.

"For your safety," Mr. Ripley replied, but his smile had turned smug.

"We've changed our minds," Zalea said. "We'll walk to the Travel Office."

"I don't think so." The wife's tone was hard now, and her eyes, when they met mine in the rear view mirror, were even harder. "There's a Supply Squad not far from here that will be thrilled to get their hands on the two of you."

It was a threat I'd heard irritated mothers use to calm disobedient children: "If you don't behave, I'll sell you to the goons from the Supply Squad." Gangs of violent men made their living by capturing those who had no tribe to protect them. It was said they prowled in vans, scooping up their victims and tossing them into the back like sacks of mail. Though they weren't part of the Govt, Supply Squads were generally left to operate because they served a purpose. Businesses needed workers for dangerous jobs. Drug and medical testing labs needed test subjects. And the sex trade constantly demanded new, young women. I'd assumed—hoped—Supply Squads weren't real. I sensed we were about to find out differently.

"Our parents will be looking for us," Zalea said, but the fear in her voice undercut the believability of her words.

"I doubt that," Mrs. Ripley scoffed. "Kids skulking on the street at five a.m. got nobody to care where you are."

"This isn't legal."

The woman turned briefly to look at her. "So sue us."

"Where are you taking us?" As she spoke, Zalea touched my leg. Without betraying her movements to the couple, she'd taken off her belt and looped it into a noose. With her free hand, she mimicked grabbing something and turning it sharply.

My eyes went wide as I grasped her intention. Zalea planned to attack the man. She wanted me to take control of the steering wheel. What then? Stop the car somehow, I guessed. It was a desperate plan, but I nodded understanding.

Unaware, Mrs. Ripley chatted as if we were old friends and she was helping us out. "We aren't that far from a Supply Team's base, so you'll be in good hands very soon."

"You're scum." Zalea was spreading her noose wide enough to slip over Mr. Ripley's head. "But you know that."

The woman's tone turned resentful. "We can't live on Gus' stipend alone. The Govt is so damned *stingy* with old people."

"You'd probably starve on the streets any—" Mr. Ripley made a strangled sound. Zalea had dropped the belt over his head, and she braced her feet against his seat, pulling him backward.

"Gus!" Mrs. Ripley reached to the side to help her husband, which gave me my chance. Lurching forward, I grabbed the wheel and wrenched it to the right. The car bumped over a curb and onto the sidewalk. Seeing a driveway ahead, I steered into a parking lot. Mrs. Ripley flailed at me with one hand while she fought me for control of the wheel with the other. It did her no good, because the car hit a lamp post and stopped abruptly. Her face hit the steering wheel, and blood spurted onto the dashboard. "My nose!" she hollered. "You broke my nose, you little bitch!"

I turned to see how Zalea was faring. Mr. Ripley clawed at the belt around his neck, but without air, he was quickly losing strength. Zalea held on, pulling backward with all her might. Finally he slumped in his seat, his face purple. His wife, pressing the base of her nose with a knuckle, called us terrible names and promised all kinds of retribution. She turned in her seat to swat at me, but Zalea reached into her backpack, took out our metal canteen and, holding it like a rock, whacked her on the head. With a moan, she too went limp.

When I could think again, I looked around, fearing passers-by had seen what happened. Apparently no one had. Cars zipped by on the street, unaware that we'd smashed into the light post. The lot itself was empty, since it was still early. As we sat there, panting from exertion and crying a little, I signed, *Dead?*

Reaching tentatively over the seat, Zalea touched Mr. Ripley's neck. He moaned and turned his head a little. I touched the wife's arm. A pulse pounded steadily in her wrist. *Alive,* I signed.

"I wish we'd killed them." Zalea shouldered her pack. "Let's go."

I signaled *Wait!* and pointed to the woman's neck, where a pass said *Visitor to Tribe Sidell.* The dates spanned three days.

"Of course they're outsiders," Zalea said. "Creeps like them wouldn't hunt in their own backyard." I took Mrs. Ripley's pass, wiping the blood splattered across it onto her dress. Zalea took the one from around Mr. Ripley's neck, and we traded. "The photos don't match," she said, "but from a distance, we'll look legitimate."

That proved to be good enough. All that day and the next, no one stopped us to ask our business. I worried that the Ripley's would report us, but Zalea insisted they wouldn't. "Those two are like rats. They'll crawl into hiding and lick their wounds."

Chapter Seven

"The worst part of this," Zalea said a few days later when we came to a fence with signs announcing yet another tribe's territory, "is not knowing who's fussy about checking on visitors and who isn't."

For me it was all horrible. We never had enough to eat. We slept in barns and utility sheds. The warm, soapy showers at Mr. Floyd's house were long behind us, and we were stinky again. We tried to keep the parts that showed clean, but it felt like dirt was burrowing between my toes and making itself a permanent home.

There were other bothersome things. To earn money for food, Zalea made me play my flute in the public spaces of small burgs. We'd set out a tin can, I'd play "Country Roads" or "Wichita Lineman," and kind people passing by would drop in a coin or two. Tribes came and went, some large, some smaller and more compact. The O'Haras loved my music. The Zelinskis asked if I knew a polka. (I did not.) The Muramoto tribe, a group that seemed more prosperous than most, listened politely and donated generously, which made Zalea dance with joy when she counted the day's profits.

The tribes blurred as we traveled and Zalea admitted she sometimes forgot whose land we were crossing. Some were unwelcoming, and we hurried through. Others were used to strangers and tolerant, even kind. Sometimes a local topper would order us to move on, using the harsh voice Zalea claimed was common to all petty men of power. We never argued. We'd pack up and go, shaking off the embarrassment and trying again in the next burg. No one saw the thin, blond boy I appeared to be as any threat to public peace. Toppers in small burgs didn't carry scanners, which were expensive to buy and operate, so there was little chance we'd have our tats zapped and found to be fakes.

Zalea said we were safe, but still, I didn't like being treated like a neighborhood nuisance.

What bothered me most was the fact that while I played for people, Zalea stole from them. When a woman set down her bag of groceries to listen for a few minutes, my sister helped herself to whatever was on top. If a store owner wandered out to see where the music was coming from, Zalea slipped inside and took stuff we needed: a cake of soap, a bottle of insect repellant, or fresh batteries for our flashlights.

Real meals were hard to come by. In one of the minor burgs belonging to a tribe called Rizzo, we passed a shop that smelled so tantalizing that even Zalea was tempted. Going inside, she parted with one Fairbuck in exchange for two warm, triangle-shaped bits of baked bread with vegetables, meat, and tomato sauce on top. It was delicious. When I begged her to go back for more, she refused. "We have to save our money, Milla. We'll need to bribe the people at the border to let us cross." We went on, but that night, sleeping on two hay bales in some farmer's barn, the generous meals around Grandmother's table filled my dreams. I woke up with tears on my cheeks and stared out at the stars until Zalea woke. There was nothing for breakfast that day, so we moved on once again.

Growing up on a farm had made us strong, which was good. We walked long distances every day, at times making our way through fields, swamps, and thick woods in order to avoid being seen. My arms turned brown below the sleeves of my t-shirt, like the "farmer's tan" Grandfather had always had. Cold October rains drenched us. Autumn winds fought against our progress, pushing us backward. My ill-fitting boot was torture until Zalea used her box cutter to make a slit in the spot that rubbed. That gave my foot more room, but it also let water leak in. I dried it carefully each night, and Zalea checked to make sure it didn't show signs of infection. Eventually the blister healed. Our backs adjusted to the weight of the packs, which varied depending on what we were able to beg or steal to put into them. Fields, orchards, and gardens offered the chance to help ourselves to fruits and vegetables. I missed the taste of meat, and I recalled Lila Jefferson's pot roast with hauntingly vivid clarity.

Each time we reached a border between tribes, we scouted the new place to see how much we'd stand out. On the lands of the Yoder Tribe, where the men all wore suspenders and the women white gauze caps and cotton aprons, we rested during the day and traveled at night. In places where people looked generally like us, we crossed in daylight, making better time. Always we avoided sentry posts by wading through swamps, climbing fences, or making wide circles around them. No way did we want to be asked to show our travel passes or have our ID tats zapped.

Zalea claimed we were headed southwest, though I wasn't sure she knew where that was. We had no compass, so we followed the sun and bore right when a choice presented itself. I wished there was an adult we could ask, because I worried that our path to Zalea's father was based more on hope than reality.

A few times we came upon big celebrations, and Zalea said it was safe to join in. "People don't expect to know everyone at a party that size," she'd say. "We'll get a free meal and a sense of where we are." When we saw a car in front of a church decorated with a *Just Married* sign, we cleaned ourselves up and followed the crowd into a tent where the reception was being held. Zalea dragged me inside, greeting this person or that as if she expected them to know who she was. We filled plates from the long row of tables at one side and sat down in a corner to eat. At the head table was the happy couple, and on either side of them were two other women. Zalea asked a woman sitting near us who they were.

"Wives," she said. "Millie is wife number five. Jim's got the money, and we don't have enough men to go around."

We joined other celebrations, some commemorating local events, one a funeral. Zalea coached me to pretend to talk to her sometimes, so my muteness wasn't obvious. "If someone speaks to you directly I'll tell them you're shy," she said. "I don't know if anyone is looking for us, but if they are, they'll have mentioned that you don't speak." It made me feel bad to know that my disability made things harder for her. I promised myself I'd be more cheerful. I'd play my flute and not worry about Zalea's thieving. I'd eat what we had and keep a smile on my face. I'd—

Zalea swatted my arm. "Look!" She pointed to where men were setting up tents in an open area. "It's a fair."

Her excitement was contagious. Fairs attracted people from all over, so our being strangers would not be a problem. Zalea would be able to ask questions and determine where we were. We might learn of a faster method of travel, like a truck heading in the direction we wanted. Last but not least, there was food everywhere at a fair. We'd be able to fill our bellies.

The day had warmed nicely, and we waited for dark in a pleasant grove of trees where a river ran through. After assuring ourselves that we were alone, we took off our outer clothing and bathed in the water, sharing the sliver of soap Zalea had in her pack. Once we were clean, we washed the clothes we'd been wearing and hung them on a tree branch to dry.

As I put on my only other outfit, Zalea shook out the dress Lila had disapproved of. "Tonight, I'll be the distraction and you'll be the snatcher," she told me. "We look for a man carrying a tray of food, maybe for his family or a group of friends. I saunter by and give him a little smile. When he turns to look at me, grab one thing from the tray and walk on, slow and casual. Most won't even realize they're missing something. If they do, they won't know who took it."

Though stealing was a necessity, I'd never actually done it myself. I was already feeling guilty, but Zalea's plan made sense. My pretty flute tunes couldn't compete with the noise of the fair, but in a crowd of strangers, mostly men, Zalea's looks were the perfect distraction.

When evening came, we slipped onto the fairgrounds and mingled with the crowd. Though we were far from home, this fair was much like those we'd attended. There were games to play, entertainments to enjoy, and rides that mostly went around really fast. People were enjoying themselves, pointing, talking, and laughing, distracted by the lights and the commotion. Zalea pinched my arm gently. "Time to get something to eat."

Taking off her jacket and tossing it to me, she stepped ahead, swinging her hips. She walked as if it was perfectly natural for a beautiful young woman in a stunning dress and spiked heels to parade through the crowd. I followed, watching as she caught the eye of almost every male. The dress was noticeable enough, but Zalea herself was beautiful. She'd brushed her hair behind one ear and added a flower picked from a ditch. When a man carrying a cardboard tray of elephant ears turned to stare after her, I took one as he passed. I was sure he'd turn back and catch me, but once it was in my hand, my fears lessened. I wanted that warm, doughy treat. Opening my knapsack, I dropped it in. Then I circled around to catch up with Zalea.

In less than fifteen minutes, I picked up a candied apple, a hot dog wrapped in waxed paper, and a roasted turkey leg, all from men who paused to watch Zalea go by. Despite my earlier reluctance, I felt a little sense of pride in being the provider of food for once. I learned to identify what I wanted quickly and scan the crowd to make sure the man was alone. Then I'd slew toward my target, snag the food without slowing, and walk on. Only someone watching closely would notice, and no one was. A few times I heard exclamations of surprise behind me when a loss was discovered, but by then I'd already dumped the prize into my pack.

Once we'd covered the grounds, Zalea disappeared into a spot between two tents where it was dark and quiet. Glancing back to make sure no one was watching, I joined her. We spread our jackets on the ground, sat on them, and began eating. We took turns gnawing bites off the turkey leg. Zalea tore the elephant ear in two and gave me half. She halved the apple with her box cutter and took a bite. "Sticky," she said around a mouthful, "but good."

Voices at the side of the tent interrupted our meal. "I've missed you so much," a man said. "It seemed like it took years for the carnival to circle back here again."

"Me too," another voice said. "I could hardly stand being away from you all this time."

The second voice was also male. I looked to my sister in confusion, and she mouthed a single word, "Gays."

I'd heard kids at school claim there were men who loved other men, but I'd never believed that could be true.

Sounds told me the men were embracing, maybe kissing. I looked at Zalea, who shrugged as if to say, *I was right.*

A third male voice, from farther away, demanded, "What's going on back here?"

"N-n-nothing."

"Looks like something to me." The third man raised his voice. "Hey! We got two twinks back here!"

From a distance, voices answered, “What? Where?” Coming closer, someone demanded, “You two need lessons in how a man should behave?”

With a “stay here” gesture to me, Zalea pushed herself to her feet, straightened her spangled dress, and stepped around the corner of the tent. In a flirty tone she asked, “Could we have a little privacy, gentlemen?”

“Who are you?” It was the man who’d discovered the other two.

“The three of us have an agreement,” Zalea said coolly. “You’re getting in the way.”

There was a brief silence. I imagined the men who’d been ready to teach the gays a “lesson” adjusting their thinking. “You’re going to screw ’em both?”

“Well, I haven’t seen their money yet.” Zalea’s tone turned teasing. “But we’ll work it out once you go on your way.”

Another silence followed. Then the man said, “I wouldn’t mind having a piece when you’re finished with them.”

“Sounds nice.” I could not believe my sister had said that. “But you’ll have to wait your turn.”

There was a general shuffling as the group that had interrupted retreated, muttering among themselves. After a moment one of the original two voices asked, “Why did you do that?”

“I was pretty sure they planned to beat you bloody.”

“No doubt. Why did you stop them?”

“I guess I don’t think people should be knocked around just because they’re different.”

The result of Zalea's action was that she and I got to sleep in a real bed that night. One of the queer men, Dale, worked for the carnival as a roustabout. When Zalea confessed that she and her little "brother" were runaways, he insisted we should sleep in his quarters. "Ernie and I have a place we go to that's private, so you're welcome to use my bunk all night."

It confused me to know that Dale, who seemed like a really nice man, was in fact a pervert, while the men threatening him, who'd sounded really mean, were the right sort of males. Men loving other men wasn't natural.

One of the carnival's trucks contained quarters for the workers. Each person got a space about six by six feet, with storage overhead. Dale led us down the row of doors and stopped at a compartment marked "D. M." in chalk. While it was just wide enough for a sleeping mat, I liked the fact that there was a metal hook-and-eye fastener on the door. "Toilets are a few doors down," Dale told us. "No one will bother you here, and I'll be back early in the morning."

"Do the other carnival workers know about you and Ernie?" Zalea asked.

He shrugged. "Carnival people tend to live and let live."

"I've heard being queer isn't a crime everywhere," Zalea said. "Why don't you and Ernie move so you can be together?"

"Ernie's got his mother and sister to care for. Until he finds husbands for one or both of them, he has to stay with his tribe." He took a corduroy jacket from a nail near the door. "Thanks again for helping us. It took guts."

"If you ask me, it's common sense," Zalea said. "You can't beat someone into not being gay."

Wishing us a good night's sleep, Dale left. I locked the door behind him, which made me feel a little bit safe for the first time in a while. Turning to Zalea, I signed, *Different okay?*

"I knew I'd hear from you about that." She patted the mat, and I sat down beside her. "How well do you really remember Benny?" I shrugged. Kind but distant, Uncle Benny hadn't come to family gatherings. He hadn't joked with me like Uncle Byron did. Everyone said he'd been good at his job, but overall he'd seemed uninterested in interacting with people.

"Benny was the family's Golden Child as a kid," Zalea told me. "He was good-looking, well-liked, and talented in lots of areas. At college he played baseball and did pretty well. He got a degree in finance and then a really good job in a big city, one of those places where everybody lived all mixed together. When the Old Times ended, Benny had to move to where his tribe was, like everyone else. I think that created a big problem for him."

I sensed the story my sister was weaving related somehow to what we were currently experiencing, and her next words proved me right. "I think Benny was gay."

I turned to her, widening my eyes to show how surprised I was. Zalea nodded. "The Govt had outlawed homosexuality. Benny might have been imprisoned or even killed if people in the tribe knew. I think he offered his friend Bonnie a place to live if she'd pretend to be his wife, or at least his girlfriend."

My mouth had dropped open, and I made an effort to close it as Zalea went on. "In Bonnie's journal, she wrote that the man she loved, Kent, had died. She was really sad about that, and she obviously didn't get along with her parents, so she wouldn't have wanted to go back to her own tribe. I think she agreed to pretend to be Mrs. Benny Woods. They must have lived together for years, but then at some point, Bonnie left. I think she was sad to leave

Benny behind. Remember the last line of her journal? *I don't know if I can do this…*"

Bad for Benny, I signed.

"Yes. I think Grandmother and Grandfather knew the truth, but they still pressured Benny to get married." Zalea sniffed. "I used to hear Grandfather go at him." Zalea imitated Grandfather's gruff voice. "'The next leader of the Woods Tribe has to set a good example for his people.' Benny would get this weird expression on his face, and I didn't know what it meant." Zalea frowned. "When Grandfather's mind started to fail, Grandmother pushed Benny even harder. 'We can find you a nice girl, Sweetheart,' I heard her tell him once. 'You'll become the man I know you can be.'" Shaking her head, Zalea finished, "I think Benny ended the problem the only way he could."

I was unwilling to believe suicide had been the only solution available to my uncle. *Tribe help him.*

Zalea chuckled. "Yes, they tell us a good, strong family will straighten out all your kinks. From what I've seen, 'helping' involves lots of prayer and tons of pressure." She shook her head. "I don't think prayer works when your heart isn't in it, and I'm pretty sure pressure just makes everything harder."

Had my uncle really killed himself rather than live what to him felt like a lie? I signed, *He try harder, be normal*?

"What is normal? Dale and Ernie fell in love, even though they've only ever seen men matching up with women. Where did that attraction come from?"

I had no answer, but Zalea saw that my brow was still furrowed. "You were born mute. I was apparently born with a questioning nature and a smart mouth. Neither of us is 'normal' according to people like Grandmother." In a burst of anger, she finished, "I'd like to know who put them in charge of saying what's normal."

God did. I only thought it, and I tried not to let my face show it. I was at that moment realizing that Grandmother had been right about Zalea. If we followed her way of thinking, there wouldn't be any rules at all. Families would lose influence. Ties within the tribe would weaken. The whole country would fall apart.

My sister was all mixed up. That was why Mother used to chew at her lip when Zalea spoke her mind at dinner. It was why Grandmother had often felt it necessary to take her aside and give her a good talking-to. Why Teacher Foster had said upon meeting me, "So you don't speak. That will be a welcome change after having your sister in my classroom."

I felt sick. Believing she knew better than her elders, Zalea had thrown away her chance for a good life with the tribe. Worse, she'd dragged me along, ruining my chances too.

Faking a yawn, I turned away and settled, as if ready to sleep. Zalea spooned in beside me. Lying still and breathing slowly, I let my mind buzz with arguments I'd have made if I were able. People living in groups needed rules to follow. Babies were taught not to touch fire. Toddlers learned not to play in the road. Teenagers were made to understand that we didn't have sex before marriage. Such teachings kept young people from facing unpleasant consequences.

Of course instruction didn't always prevent disobedience. I recalled Will, a boy of seven, who'd burnt his father's barn to the ground while playing with matches. He had to stand up in church, tell everyone what he'd done, and apologize to the tribe and to God. A girl in Zalea's class named Ursula got pregnant at fifteen. That was kept a secret, though not as much as her parents thought, and she was shipped off to another tribe to marry a man who'd accept her child as his in exchange for money. The disobedient few served as lessons for the rest of us: *This is what happens when you don't follow the rules.*

When a member chose a course that was harmful to their tribe, family, or self, it was up to the family to fix it. While the Bible made that clear, that wasn't the only source of proof. Study after study showed that a person in crisis had a stronger chance for survival when family support was available. Benny could have been helped if he'd submitted to the rules.

Zalea spoke in the darkness. "Members of our tribe break the rules all the time." I didn't turn toward her, but she seemed to know I was listening. "Rolf's the worst. He goes on 'business trips' where he gambles and sleeps with women. Grandfather knows it—knew it and reined him in when he could, but mostly he covered for Rolf to 'protect our reputation.'" I felt her breath in my hair as she let out a sigh. "We punish guys like Dale, who aren't hurting anyone, and we let men like Rolf strut around pretending they're good when they're actually—" Her voice broke. "He's pure evil."

We slept then. Zalea woke me as the morning sun made the metal wall beside us click as it warmed. "We should go."

I'd just zipped my pack closed when the latch rattled. Seconds later, a pounding fist made the walls shake. "Where's the girl, Carnie?" a loud voice called. "I want my turn with her."

It was the man from the night before, and from the way his words slurred and the nonstop pounding, I guessed he'd spent the night drinking. Zalea's gaze flickered around the space like a trapped bird, but there was no other way out. I made a desperate plan. I'd open the door, kick the man hard in the shin with my heavy boot, and we'd run.

Than another voice sounded. "What are you doing here?" It was Dale.

"The girl. Are you done with her?"

There was a pause as Dale decided how to answer. "I promised her breakfast if she stayed all night."

"I told you I wanted her next, but then I couldn't find either of you."

"We were having a good time," Dale said. "It seemed a shame to end it."

"Listen, Carnie. My money's good as yours. Get the slut out here now."

Another pause. "Tell you what," Dale said. "I'll fight you for her. If I win, you leave. If you win, I give her up."

Dale was slightly built and of average height. The single glimpse I'd had the night before of the other man had left an image in my mind of the Philistine from the Bible, Goliath. I heard a note of glee as he replied, "Deal."

"All right then." Dale's voice rose a little. "Let's go outside, where there's room to move."

"Sure, Little Man. It won't take long." He raised his voice. "I'll come back for you, woman."

A glance between us affirmed understanding that Dale was giving us a chance to get away. As the men's footsteps receded, Zalea stood staring at the door. "I can't let Dale do this, Milla. Stay here. I'll…fix this and be back later." Before I could react, I heard the click of her receding steps on the wooden floor of the trailer.

Zalea intended to save Dale a second time by doing what the big man wanted her to do.

I couldn't stay put. Opening the door, I peeped out into the corridor. All was quiet. Turning back, I took up our packs and started after Zalea. As I hurried down the ramp, a languid voice behind me called, "Dale must be fond of your friend. That's one big galoot he's going to fight."

The person who spoke might have been male or female. Short, fluffy hair surrounded a square face. Greenish eyes regarded me with lazy humor. Blue jeans and a flannel shirt that had seen better days covered a shapeless, straight-up-and-down body. Coming down the ramp, the person joined me on the dusty ground. Putting my hands on my cheeks, I pantomimed fear. "Don't worry about Dale," was the response. "In fact, you and I might follow along and cheer him on." With a little salute the person said, "I'm Pat. I run the Ferris Wheel."

Pat led the way. I followed, my mind in a mess. In spite of Pat's assurances, Dale was going to lose. First, he wasn't very big. Second, he was gay, which meant he was a sissy. I wondered if Dale's friends might help, but then I recalled that carnival folk, always suspect in the eyes of the law because of their lifestyle, tended to mind their own business when trouble came along. When Dale lost the fight, the big man would claim Zalea as his prize. We should be putting as much distance between ourselves and these grounds as possible, but I didn't know how I'd convince her of that.

Dale had led his opponent to the midway. "Is this okay?"

Goliath nodded. He'd sobered up slightly, which was probably worse for Dale. He took a firm stand and raised his arms, causing the muscles to bulge. "Are you ready, Little Man?"

By some form of carnival telegraph, a small crowd was gathering. I recognized several people I'd seen the night before, men who ran the games and rides, a woman who'd danced with a snake in a filmy skirt, a couple of boys with manure-coated boots who'd apparently left animal care duties to see the fight. Zalea stood near the back, apparently trying to decide what to do. I took hold of Pat's sleeve and dragged my new friend to her side. Understanding what was needed, Pat said, "Dale knows what he's doing, Dearie. There's no need for you to panic."

Though Zalea looked doubtful, she nodded. We turned toward the fighters, who stood a few feet apart. Goliath rocked back and forth on his feet, stepping left and then right as he gauged his opponent. Dale stood easily, waiting for him to make the first move. When Goliath let out a primitive bellow designed to unnerve his opponent, Dale only smiled. One of the carnies near us said, "This should be good."

It was, if a person enjoyed seeing a very large man hurt and humiliated. Though he did his best, Goliath never laid a hand on Dale. Each swing of his fist was deftly avoided, either with a duck to one side or a quick lean backward. When Goliath's misses unbalanced him, Dale struck without delay, landing blows on the big man's face, gut, and kidneys. Soon his teeth were outlined in blood, his left cheek was swelling toward his eye, and he tried desperately to shield his right side from further damage. When he found it impossible to land punches, Goliath tried to kick at his opponent. That was a mistake, because Dale caught his foot and gave it a sharp jerk upward. Goliath landed on his back, gasping as he tried to get wind back into his lungs.

"Are you done?" Dale asked calmly. Unable to speak, Goliath nodded. "All right then." Dale gestured at the crowd around them. "We don't want any trouble with your tribe, so no one here is going to say a word about what just happened. If you decide to run your mouth, every person here will swear you came to this fight of your own free will and got beat fair and square. I suggest you tell your friends you fell and hurt yourself last night when you were drunk. They'll believe that, since the drunk part is true." After a pause Dale said, "If you prefer, we can keep fighting."

Goliath wasn't bright, but he knew he was beaten. He gasped out a single word. "No."

I wanted to clap for Dale, but the crowd remained silent, probably aware that it was best not to antagonize the local man further. Two men came and helped Goliath to his feet. Zalea and I stayed out of sight as they escorted him off the grounds.

"Will he make trouble for your people?" Zalea asked.

"If he does, his friends will find out he got his ass handed to him by a man half his size." Pat gestured toward an awning where food was being set out. "Have breakfast with us. We've got plenty."

There was indeed a lot to eat, though the company was unlike any I'd seen before. Carnival workers were an odd lot, a tribe made up by choice, not blood. Pat explained that he'd been designated a female at birth but "had a problem with the doctor's opinion." Down a few chairs were conjoined twins who said that for them, carnival life was preferable to the Special Quarters their tribe maintained. A man with warts all over his face and body said his family had encouraged him to become a carnie, since it was unlikely any woman would want to marry him. I found him hard to look at, but Zalea gave him one of her best smiles as she asked him to please pass the salt. Others in the group seemed nice, though most had what I thought was a wild look about them. Carnies were people who didn't fit the rules, yet as I sat with them, listening to their chatter, I got the same feeling I'd had listening to the Black men as we hid in their tool shed. These people were different from me in some ways, yet in the most important ways, we were the same.

Dale joined us, setting down a tray loaded with scrambled eggs and ham. "You were amazing," Zalea told him. "Where did you learn to fight like that?"

"In the Old Times, my father was a mixed martial arts champion." His grin was tinged with sadness. "He taught me how to fight, but he couldn't make me into the man he wanted me to be."

"So you left your tribe."

"I was sent to live with these people when I was sixteen."

"I'm sorry your tribe didn't want you," Zalea said. "It's their loss, not yours."

He shrugged. "I didn't mind this life until I met Ernie. Now all I want is a place where we can settle down together."

"What does Ernie's mother think about him being gay?"

Dale stopped with a forkful of ham halfway to his mouth. "What does she think? She thinks the man I love is looking forward to choosing a wife and starting a family, like every other red-blooded man in Fairica."

Though we'd tried to keep up the pretense that I was a boy, the carnival people knew better. "You don't walk like a boy," Pat told me, and the snake lady said, "She don't smell like one either." They also shrugged off my muteness. "I got a sister that can't hear," one man said. "They put her in SQ even though she's the smartest one in the whole damned family."

"Is that why you two ran?" Dale asked.

"Our Grandfather died, and our uncle is horrible," Zalea replied. "We figured we'd be better off on our own."

"And where will you go?"

"My father lives in Dorado. We're headed there."

Dale whistled. "That's a long way."

Zalea grimaced, acknowledging that. "Is it possible we could travel with you for a while? We'd work for our keep."

Dale shook his head. "We're only licensed for the Green Section, so this is as far west as we get."

Pat had an idea. "Our manager is going into the Rose Section today to pick up some rice. It's only forty miles or so, but it would be forty miles you won't have to walk."

"Will you ask him if we can ride along?"

"I will," Pat said, "but you could stay with us. It's not a bad life, and the Govt mostly leaves us alone."

Zalea shook her head. "I have to find my dad." To me she said, "I know you're tired. If you want to stay with them—"

I was tired of walking. I hated being hungry all the time. I thought Zalea was wrong about a lot of things. But I felt safer with her than with strangers. Besides, I'd formed a plan. Once we found Zalea's father, I'd ask him to talk to Uncle Rolf. They'd discuss it man to man, work things out, and I'd return home. I signed, *I go with you.*

Chapter Eight

Harold, the carnival manager, wasn't thrilled with Pat's request that he take two runaways with him on his visit to Chiltonburg. "What do I do if somebody asks who they are?" he demanded. "Lie through my teeth?"

"Drop them off before you go into the burg," Dale said patiently. "That way no one will connect them to you." Harold voiced a few more complaints, which Dale and Pat ignored, and then ordered us into his pickup. As the carnival people gathered to wave goodbye, I noticed again how weird they were: odd clothing, odd tattoos, odd lifestyles. Still, I'd felt safe with them. Not only safe, but welcome.

Harold was a talker who kept turning his head to look at us as he spoke, which made me nervous. Forgetting his earlier objections to our presence, he waxed eloquent on the lifestyle of carnival folk. "People like us used to make movies or sing or dance or act. 'All the world's a stage,' you know, and we were the players, the Beautiful People. Then all of a sudden, things changed. They said we were debauched—" He said it again, liking the sound of the word though not, apparently, its meaning. "Debauched! You coulda knocked me over with a feather first time I heard one of 'em say that."

I noticed Zalea staring ahead, as if trying to encourage Harold to do the same. He did, but only for a second or two. "In two shakes of a lamb's tail, Miller's people outlawed most of what was called show business." He raised a hand, index finger pointed upward. "But Vox knew people need to be entertained or they get grumpy, like old billy goats. His Govt concocted theater tribes, people like us who travel the countryside and give the population a break from their monotonous lives." His voice rose as he repeated one of his barker lines. "So here we are, folks! We're in your neighborhood, ready to provide a few laughs, a few thrills, and a little ra-a-a-azzle dazzle!"

"Vox wanted working people to stay where he'd put them," Zalea said.

"Exactly right. We come into a rural area, set up our tents, and show 'em things they haven't seen before. Take Maggie, our elephant. Poor old girl's on her last legs, but she's still as popular as ice cream at a picnic." Harold waved at the land outside the windshield, which was low and flat. "Maggie loves rice, and that's what they grow around here. Whenever we get close, I drive over and get a truckload for her."

"That's nice of you."

"Good business," he corrected. "Guy's gotta take care of his assets." Again Harold turned in the seat to look at us, and I fought the urge to point at the road ahead. "We start with music, to set the mood." He *de-dah-deed* through a few bars of a lively tune. "We show 'em the animals, Maggie, a ring-tailed lemur named Samu, some clever dogs, and a couple of African parrots. We offer games of skill, because men are natural competitors and the girls love to see them show off." Using both hands, he mimed aiming a gun, and I saw Zalea's hand twitch, ready to grab the steering wheel if necessary.

As the truck veered toward the ditch, Harold took hold of the steering wheel again and straightened our course. "In the tents, we've got different entertainments. The men like watching Tammy the Snake Lady, half-dressed, wriggle all over the stage with Casper wrapped around her neck." He sang a bit of the snake lady's song, pounding the steering wheel as if it were a hand drum. "You probably met Roger at breakfast. Little guy, but come night-time he's our Wild Man of Borneo. He's got this hairy costume and fake fangs. We put him in a cage, and he growls like he's nuts and rattles at the bars. The girls scream like steam whistles, and the men squeeze 'em tight, so they feel safe." He batted his eyes. "Very romantic."

"And fake," Zalea said.

"As a three-dollar bill." Harold turned to us yet again, and I watched the road for him. "When I was a kid, they had whole TV shows with people pretending to compete for their lives in some dangerous place, ignoring cameras and film crews while they ran around in some jungle. The viewers had to know it was fake, but they slurped it up like soup." He shook his head. "The Romans called it 'bread and circuses.' For most people, having work, enough money to survive on, and a little entertainment once in a while is enough to keep them going."

Harold's disregard for the road was making me crazy. It wasn't very wide to start with, and it had cracks everywhere, so we bumped back and forth like three balls in a box.

Zalea was thinking along the same lines. "This road could be in better shape."

"The Chilton Tribe don't like company much," Harold said. "They're an odd bunch."

"Odd how?"

Harold made the classic body squirm of a gossip about to dish dirt. "Their leader, Lincoln Chilton, is batshit crazy—excuse my French—but he's also very, very rich. Made a fortune back in the Old Times selling mattresses. He supported Gerald Miller like nobody else, but when Miller died he went quiet, apparently unwilling to support Dupree's excesses. When Vox got elected, Chilton bought a tribe-hold where the people grow rice and long for the days when Miller was in charge." Hesitating before making his big point, he finished, "Chilton claims that Miller still talks to him in his dreams."

Zalea shook her head in disbelief. "Ri-i-ight."

"You don't believe that. I don't believe it. But people who missed old Miller flocked to join Chilton's tribe like chickadees to a feeder. I guess they aren't hurting anything, clinging to the idea that Miller would have saved them if he'd lived. But from what we know about the man now, it's just—" he hesitated but in the end decided to say it, "—nuts."

"You're taking us into a tribe full of nuts." Now Zalea's disgust was tinged with dread.

"If rice wasn't hard to come by these days, I'd steer clear," Harold said. He pulled off to the side of the road at a sign that said, *Unauthorized Visitors Unwelcome*. "Here's where you two get out." He pointed. "See that foot trail? It cuts directly across the Chilton land hold. If I was you, I'd go right on to the next tribe."

Zalea opened the truck door and slid out. "Thank you, Mr.—um, Harold." I followed, waving a thank you.

"Good luck to you." Putting the truck into drive again, he sped off. The resulting silence was both peaceful and unnerving. Harold's jazz riffs beaten on the steering wheel and accompanying "Bop-bop-de-bop" lyrics had been irritating, but the silence now and the prospect of trekking across the land of a tribe hostile to strangers was daunting.

Zalea's sigh told me she was thinking along the same lines, but she managed a smile as she shouldered her pack. "Let's push it and get through this tribe-hold as fast as possible." She started down a trail bordered on both sides by tall, sweeping plants, pushing aside branches that leaned into the way as she went.

Chapter Nine

As we walked, I tried to estimate our current location on a map of Fairica I pictured in my head. Since we'd just crossed into the Rose Section, we were near the center of the country east to west. We'd come quite far south, which Zalea said was good. While the nights here were cool, the days warmed nicely. I could no longer name the trees and plants we saw nor identify the birds from their calls. Even if I caught glimpses of them, I still didn't know their names. If I hadn't understood how far we were from home before, I knew it now.

The trail Harold had pointed out soon turned to a raised platform, dissecting large sections of what I guessed were the rice fields the Chilton Tribe was known for. Where the harvest had been done, damp ground and stubble remained. Other sections were still crowded with three-to four-foot plants that looked nothing like I'd expected rice to look. Tripping along the wooden boardwalk, we twice came to hinged segments that opened like a drawbridge. "They must pull these up to move equipment from one field to another," Zalea said.

After what felt like hours, we stopped to rest. The day was hot, and sweat ran down my spine, dampening the band I wore to flatten my breasts. Zalea took out a sack Pat had handed to her as we left. Inside it were leftovers from breakfast, hash brown potatoes, chunks of ham, and scrambled eggs. It had all jumbled together, but we squatted on the wooden platform and ate every bit of it gratefully, scooping the food with our fingers and licking the grease off after each bite.

Once we'd eaten, we took to the trail again. The boardwalk ended, and we followed a slightly squishy path with tree roots interrupting its smoothness. I couldn't help imagining the poisonous snakes I'd heard inhabited the south. Were they slithering around us right now? Scanning the ground constantly, I listened, trying to interpret every noise. Who knew what kinds of beasts made their home among the odd, droopy trees and the low shrubs with leaves like knives?

Late in the afternoon, we came to a place where a river had been dammed to form a pool that practically begged us to jump in and cool off. Zalea went ahead a bit to make sure the spot was isolated. While she was gone, I examined the edge of the pool carefully. I found nothing that resembled alligator foot-prints, which was a relief. "There's a burg up ahead," Zalea said when she returned. "We'll wait until dark and then go around it." I pointed at the pool, and she nodded. "Yes. In the meantime, we can go swimming and wash our clothes at the same time."

Wading into the cool water we did exactly that, diving under to wet our hair. Toward the end we splashed each other, as we'd done when we were kids. Clean and refreshed, we stretched out on a grassy spot, napping as our clothes dried.

When dark descended we went on, approaching the burg cautiously and stopping in some trees at the edge. An area lit by perhaps six alternating street lamps revealed a road that cut between two rows of house trailers. We began a long semi-circle, going around the perimeter to avoid patrols. Most of the homes we passed were in poor shape, with broken blinds at the windows and junk piled outside the entry door. Many had green mold climbing up the side walls. There were several with gardens, most not much bigger than a gravesite. A couple of times we passed dogs, but both were chained to posts. One was asleep and didn't hear us. The other barked until a voice from inside called, "Shut up, Boozer!"

It was a relief when we came to the far side of the burg, but Zalea stayed off the road a while longer in case someone came down it. That's how we found the park.

Zalea actually bumped into the gateway. I heard her mutter a bad word as she rubbed her shoulder. "What is that?" she asked, and we stood back to see the rest of the metal structure. Across an overgrown side road, an arch stretched. There were letters, but it was too dark to read them. Getting out her flashlight, Zalea aimed it upward. "Gerald K. Miller Memorial Park," she read aloud. The man who'd almost ruined our nation? "Come on. I have to see this."

We entered an area about a half-acre in size. A flagstone path led to the right, where we saw the statue of a man, a little bigger than life size. Miller wasn't pictured in our textbooks, but I'd always imagined him with horns and a tail. The statue made him appear kind-faced and noble. There were two jarring notes. First, the statue was coated with something like gold, so he looked like he'd been touched by King Midas. Second, the gold surface was nearly obscured by bird poop.

"Guess the locals have given up on maintenance," Zalea said softly.

We followed the path, which curved into the woods. As Zalea pointed her flashlight ahead, we came to a series of thick metal posts, each with a huge portrait mounted on it. They all pictured Miller as some hero of legend, King Arthur, Julius Caesar, Hercules, and Davy Crockett. Again, the impression the display had been intended to create was ruined by neglect. The portraits were spattered with dirt, their vinyl casings were black with mold, and in places, there were bullet holes where someone had used them for target practice.

The path curved again, and we came to a second statue, this one showing Miller older and heavier, but still strong. A smile lit his face, which was again gold, and he held his arms up in blessing. Here the woods had taken over, and the piece was overgrown with some vine-like plant that almost hid it completely.

We turned again, following the path back to the gateway. Along that span was a huge mosaic, set before a three-sided wooden frame. Here Miller was depicted walking arm and arm with Jesus in a lovely garden. After years of listening to Zalea's complaints about "Sunday School Jesus," I was aware that a Semitic man's coloring would have been more like hers than mine, but this Jesus had light-brown hair, white skin, and sky-blue eyes.

Again, the display was in need of care. The wooden frame had weathered, so the paint was gone in several places. In others, the wood had separated and curled. The mosaic itself was missing pieces, most shockingly at Miller's right eye, so that he looked both crazy and spooky.

Then we were back to the gate. As we walked away, Zalea turned once to look back. "I suppose he deserves to be an afterthought to history," she said, "but it's wild that even Miller's most devoted followers have forgotten all about him."

Chapter Ten

The last day we spent crossing Chilton territory was difficult. The heat ramped up, the land turned swampy, and insects came out in force. Our arms were in constant motion, trying to shoo them away. That evening, we came to a split-rail fence with posts scored with a *W.* "Tribe Wiggins," Zalea said. "Hallelujah." Climbing through, we walked on until we crested a hill and looked down. "Look!" Zalea said, pointing. "A train."

I'd seen trains in movies. I'd balanced precariously on abandoned, overgrown metal tracks back home. But I'd never seen a real, operating train. This one, a shiny silver engine with dozens of cars behind it, sat motionless at a tidy station with a wide platform. We hurried down the hillside, where Zalea asked a uniformed man where the train was headed.

"Lots of places, little lady, but the line ends at Greensburg."

"Is that either south or west of here, by chance?"

"South and then west." He frowned. "Didn't they ever show you a map at school?"

Zalea assumed a meek look. "Our teacher says we can be good wives without knowing about maps and things."

"Your teacher is right," the man said, pushing his bottom lip out. "Pretty as you are, I guess you don't need to be clever." He shook a finger in her face. "Make sure you can cook though. Even a pretty woman should be useful in the kitchen."

"I will, sir." When we'd turned a corner and were out of the man's sight, Zalea stuck her tongue out in a useless gesture of rebellion. "Jackass!" Then she turned to business. "Milla, we need to get on that train."

I raised my hands: *How?*

"Walk through the station. Pretend you're looking for someone, and find out what time the train leaves."

I did as she said, though the idea of getting on the train made me nervous. We couldn't buy a ticket because we had no valid travel passes. We'd have to stow away, which was probably a really big crime. If we were caught would we be shot? Hanged? To calm myself, I did something Grandmother had taught me. "Deal with your fears by imagining they're bread," she'd say. "Take a big bite, chew it to squash it down, and then swallow it deep inside." I tried, but hopping a train was still a very big chunk of dread-bread to handle.

Departures were posted on a sign board. Beside it was a clock that said the time was 3:23. The train would leave at 6:05. I went back outside and relayed that information to Zalea. "That's perfect. I've been watching them load the cars. A man goes through and opens up five or six at a time. Trucks pull up alongside, and workers move the goods from the truck to the train. When they're done, the first man comes back and locks the cars up. If we slip in after the loaders are done but before the lock-up man returns, we'll have a ride all the way to the border."

It wasn't difficult. We watched as workers filled one open car and then a second. When the crew reached the third car, Zalea approached the first car in a crouch, grasped the metal frame, and hauled herself up onto the wooden floor. Quickly, she turned around and extended a hand to me. Being shorter I had a harder time, but I managed to get the top half of my body into the car. Zalea grabbed the waistband of my jeans and pulled me in the rest of the way.

Appliance-sized boxes were piled almost to the roof, with a narrow aisle left in the center. Shifting every other one slightly, we formed steps we could climb. I went first and Zalea followed, flopping onto the top box with a grunt of achievement. "The lock-up man will give the car a once-over," she said, "but unless he climbs up here, he won't see us."

In the foot of space left between the top box and the roof, we spread ourselves out, taking off our packs and laying them close by. "I think we have about forty-five minutes." Zalea opened her pack and took out two doughnuts she'd stolen from a vendor outside the station. She also had a three-quarters-full bottle of Coca-Cola. "A man set it down, so I took it," she said when I raised my brows. "I always wanted to taste it, but Grandmother says it isn't fit for human consumption."

After we'd eaten the doughnuts, we tried the Coca-Cola. Zalea let me go first, and she laughed when the drink made my eyes water. It fizzed in my throat and all the way down, so sweet that I grabbed the canteen and took a swig of water to wash the taste away. Zalea took a drink, licked her lips, and took another, frowning. "It is really sweet," she said, "but I like it." I held up the canteen, indicating I'd stick to water.

Noticing her pack was half-unzipped, Zalea made a choked sound. "My purse is gone." Turning it upside down, she emptied the contents, shaking every item of clothing and fingering every object in hopes she was wrong. When she didn't find the purse that contained our money and jewelry, she looked stricken. "I set my pack down for just a minute when I went in to get the doughnuts." Her voice shook. "Now we can't pay to get across the border."

Though I was unsure about leaving Fairica, I knew Zalea had her heart set on it. For the first time, she seemed to lose hope. That was bad, because if Zalea lost her nerve, we were both in trouble.

A rattle sounded below, and the car went dark. The click of the locking mechanism told us we were stuck inside the car for—how long? We had no way of knowing.

Outside, men shouted commands and passed along information. The engine rumbled. A long, shrill whistle sounded, hurting my ears. After making sure our stuff wouldn't fall between the boxes if they shifted, we waited, both eager and anxious, for the first jolt of movement. A loud *Clunk!* made me jump, but Zalea said it was only the couplings shifting into place. Slowly at first, the train rolled forward. The initial noise was huffy, like an exhausted runner, but then it sped up, and there was less air, more engine. A gentle rhythm began, a combination of swaying and chugging. From time to time the car groaned as it strained on a curve, but on the straightaways, there was only the clickety-click of metal wheels on metal track.

"There must be other ways to cross the border," Zalea said after a while. "I might even be able to telephone my father and ask him to help." Her voice got stronger as she finished, "We'll figure it out when we get there." *Typical Zalea.* I'd been thinking we could go back home. We'd say we climbed into the truck for fun but then fell asleep, and when we woke up we were lost. I'd even let my sister be the hero of the story, saying she'd found the way back despite many setbacks.

Zalea spoke again, killing that dream. "At least we're going in the right direction. We'll get there, Milla."

The train's rocking motion was relaxing, and Zalea's breathing soon slowed, but sleep didn't come to me for some time. Every clack reminded me of the speed at which we were moving away from home. And there was more danger ahead, because everyone knew there were tons of Monkey Men along the border.

I missed the farm, the dew-wet grass in the morning and the quiet, snowy nights. I missed the bawl of calves when they lost track of their mothers and the hoot of owls near the back porch at night. I missed lightning bugs in June and Christmas in December. I even missed school, where the teacher had checked our hands every morning to be sure they were clean and the boys had to hang their caps on hooks along the wall before they could take their seats. It would be different now without Grandfather but still, it was hard to accept that I'd never see home again. What if Zalea and I had to spend the rest of our lives wandering, friendless and homeless?

With a sigh, I rolled onto my back. Though I didn't like this new life, I didn't know how to change it. I had to trust my sister and hope that somehow, someday, we'd find a place where we could both be safe.

Chapter Eleven

When I woke the next morning, Zalea was lying on her stomach, using a slit of light that came through a translucent panel in the roof to read Bonnie's journal. I stretched, wondering what we had to eat, but she had something else on her mind. "Bonnie says Miller was a terrible person. He and his bunch of corrupt clowns wrecked everything, so the people had no choice but to revolt."

Whatever Miller did back then, the Govt had fixed it, so I didn't care. I did care that our food pack contained two raw potatoes and nothing else. I rubbed my belly. *Hungry.*

Zalea set the book aside, marking her place with a scrap of paper. "I don't think my father was really a criminal. I think he opposed Miller's corruption by organizing a rebellion, and he died because of it."

I handed her the larger potato and signed, *Bathroom?*

"I think we can get out when the train stops." Zalea pointed at the roof. "There's a hatch."

We crawled to the foot-square trapdoor on all fours. Rising to her knees, Zalea felt around the edges to find the latch. After several grunts of exertion and one bad word, she managed to undo it and push the trapdoor open. A square of sky appeared above us. Clouds came and went like dandelion fluff as the train rattled along. I was a little scared that someone would know we'd opened the trapdoor, but no horn sounded. The train didn't slow. No face appeared in the opening.

"Let's leave it open," Zalea said. "When the train stops, we'll climb out and look around."

I hoped that would be soon, because my bladder wanted badly to be emptied. I was relieved a half hour later when the train whistle sounded, metal ground on metal, and the car jolted to a stop. Climbing out the hatch, we surveyed the ground below. One side of the train was all activity, people getting on or off, workers hurrying to do their assigned tasks. On the other side, the train faced a five-foot pile of railroad ties and not much else. We climbed down, went behind the stack and did our business, and climbed back to our little nest in minutes. As the train whistle sounded, warning of imminent departure, we resumed our place in the boxcar with that issue resolved.

Over the course of the day, we learned that the train made different sounds depending on its reason for stopping. On short stops to pick up passengers, the engine idled down but didn't stop. We stayed where we were then, unless nature's call demanded a quick climb to the ground and a dash between buildings or into bushes. Longer stops, when cars were added or subtracted, took more time, so we were able to work on other goals. I returned to being an entertainer, sitting on the platform and playing my flute. When people stopped to listen, Zalea watched for chances to steal their food. Sometimes she took snacks stuffed into the side pockets of passengers' bags. Other times she filched items from vendors: drinks, sandwiches, or candy bars. "I only take one from each," she said in a slightly defensive tone as we split a Hershey bar. "I don't want to hurt anyone's profits, but we need to eat." I nodded, thinking that Grandmother would have strongly disapproved of both our stealing and our diet of candy, chips, and crackers.

From signs at stops and bits of conversation, we tried to figure out where we were. I heard two men talking about a lake visible in the distance. One of them called it Parker Lake, but the other chuckled. "I know the leaders got to rename everything to suit themselves, but around here we still call it by its old name, Thunderbird Lake. Lots more interesting."

One afternoon as I played "Piano Man" on the platform, a well-dressed couple left their car and strolled its length, apparently stretching their legs. They were flanked by four tough-looking men who seemed to see everyone around them as a possible threat, even me. The train crew put on their best behavior, with lots of "Good afternoon, sir" and "Wonderful to see you, ma'am" comments as the couple considered whether they wanted something to eat. The man, fortyish with fair hair, fair skin, and a smile that never went past halfway, kept his eyes focused somewhere in the distance, as if heavy matters occupied his mind. The woman, a few years younger, smiled at the people around her in a general sort of way. She was the height of glamour, I thought, clothing, makeup, shoes, and hair all perfectly chosen and arranged to heighten her attractiveness.

The man passed me without notice, but the woman stopped, watching my fingers move on the keys of the flute. "You're very good," she said when I finished my song. She nudged her husband, who pulled out a Faircoin and dropped it into the can I'd set out for donations. I smiled to acknowledge both the compliment and the gift.

Behind the couple came two men pushing a cart piled with food and drinks. I saw Zalea sail by and snitch two cans of soda while the men ogled the couple, possibly memorizing the details of their appearance so they could describe it to friends and family later. Dropping the sodas into her backpack, Zalea moved on.

The woman lingered near me. "Peter," she said, "does this boy remind you of anyone?"

"No." He gave her arm a little tug, and she turned away. They got back on the train, two attendants going ahead while the other two scanned the platform for possible danger. The eyes of everyone there followed the couple, and while they looked away, I saw Zalea slip into the depot, where, I learned later, she found an unattended food booth and scooped up a ham sandwich for each of us. “Everyone was gawking at those people,” she said as we ate our prizes. “They must have been VIPs.” I didn’t care. The lady had been nice, the man generous, and the distraction they’d created meant Zalea and I had reasonably full bellies.

That night, disaster struck. A few hours after we nodded off to the train’s gentle rocking, I was awakened by the screech of metal. Before I had time to understand what was happening, a violent collision sent me hurtling against the front wall of the car. I reached out both hands to stop from hitting my head and felt a sharp pain in my left forearm. The car tilted to one side, and I rolled until I hit the wall with a force that took my breath away. The screeching and grinding seemed to go on and on. There were more jolts as car after car smashed into the one ahead of it. I heard Zalea cry out, a short, sharp sound.

Finally there was silence, and I tried to sort out what had happened. The train must have hit something and derailed. It took several seconds before I could turn my mind away from thinking about what had happened and focus on what I should do about it.

My left arm hurt like nothing I’d ever felt before. Touching it gingerly with my other hand, I realized both bones were broken, though they hadn’t pierced the skin. I sat up, leaning on my right arm, and as gently as I could, slid my left hand between the buttons of my flannel shirt. Then I removed my belt and made it into a sling to support the spot where the break had occurred. It still hurt to move, but the pain was bearable. I had to find Zalea.

Slithering over the boxes, pulling myself along with my good hand, I searched until I found my sister. She lay against the wall of the car, limp and still. I couldn’t see well in the darkness, but when I touched her face, my hand came back bloody.

This could not be. Zalea, my strong, capable sister, could not be lying crumpled against the slanted metal wall of the train car. Zalea was always there. Zalea always knew what to do. Zalea should be telling me this was just another bump in the road. That things would be okay.

Reaching out again, I shook her shoulder gently. There was no response. I touched her face again. Did her skin feel cold, or was fear creating false reports?

Then I became aware of voices outside. People screamed. People shouted. Their words hardly penetrated my consciousness, frantic as I was, but the fact that help was available did. Again I patted Zalea's face, desperate for her to awaken and tell me what to do. She remained inert. My hand found a small miracle, a flashlight, and I turned the light on Zalea. She looked terrible. In addition to a wound on her forehead, I saw that the wreck had shifted the boxes, pinning her legs. I tried to pull them off her, using first my undamaged arm and then my feet, but they were too heavy.

I had to get help. My gaze went to the open hatch, which barely showed in the dark of night. Cradling the elbow of my broken arm with my good hand, I made my way to it and crawled out onto the roof, which now slanted almost to the ground. Ahead of me, the train engine lay completely on its side. Several cars directly behind it were also turned, but their connections to each other had broken, so they lay on either side of the tracks, some flat, some crumpled. Behind the car we'd been in were more cars, some tilted, but no more tipped over. I made my way to the ground, biting my lip at the pain each movement caused. Once there, I moved toward the passenger cars, where the people were.

The first few workers I approached were too upset to pay attention. I slapped at their arms and tugged on their sleeves, but one look told them I wasn't badly injured. A man in uniform pointed to a bank of earth along the train track and ordered, "Go sit over there. EMTs will be along soon to look you over."

How could I tell them it wasn't myself I was worried about? I pointed at the car, signing *Help sister!* No one understood. Crewmen were helping passengers exit the train. Some were bleeding, all were upset. I looked okay. I couldn't explain my need. I wasn't even a paying passenger. My concerns would come last.

I didn't give up. I couldn't, not with Zalea in that train car, bleeding and possibly dying. One by one I approached the crewmen, frantically trying to get their attention. Over and over, I was ordered to sit down and wait for assistance.

There were questions about what had happened. I heard the word *sabotage* and an opinion that renegades were responsible. I didn't care about the why at that point. Though I tried to hold them back, tears flowed down my cheeks. *Sister*, I signed over and over with my good hand. *Help*.

Then a hand touched my arm. "Slow down, dear." I turned to find the beautiful woman I'd seen that afternoon at the station. Her clothes were dirty and her hair was disheveled, but she said softly, "I know a little ASL, but you'll have to start over and slow down."

Trying to do as she said, I signed the two words again. "Your sister is hurt." She got it. "Where is she?" I pointed, and the woman said, "You were riding in a freight car?" I nodded, unable to care if we were caught and punished. Zalea might be dying, might already be dead.

"You're mute?" the woman said. I nodded. A little smile played at her lips. "And you're a girl." I nodded again, and her expression revealed satisfaction at her own cleverness. "My daughter is about your age."

Worry for Zalea consumed me. *Sister,* I signed again, and the woman nodded. "I'll send someone to find her. Which car was she in?" Recalling that the car had *D & N* on the side, I signed that. "All right. Come with me."

Ambulances had arrived, and the woman led me to one. "This child has a broken arm," she said in a regal tone. "See to it that she's transported to a hospital and treated. I'll be along as soon as I can."

The medic was deferential. "Yes, ma'am."

I hesitated, looking back at the train, but the woman said, "I'll make sure they bring your sister along as soon as possible." She squeezed my arm. "My husband is commander of the Rose Section. These people will do as I say."

The ride to the hospital was scary. Not only did my arm have an extra bend between elbow and wrist, but I'd never been in an ambulance before. I'd never traveled so fast. Never been under the care of medical people. The medic had to cut my shirt off. When he saw the wrappings that bound my breasts, his expression revealed no surprise, no censure, nothing. I should have been relieved, but all I could think about was what would happen next.

What happened was medical care. I was taken to a hospital and given the first injection I'd ever had. It put me to sleep, and when I woke, my arm was straight again, held in place by wrapping that looked like fishnet. I was in a hospital bed, in a room with ten or twelve others, all female. In a chair near the bed was the woman who'd helped me. When I opened my eyes, she rose and came to my side. "How are you feeling?"

I shrugged, unable to say how I felt until I learned how Zalea was. I raised my brows in question, but the woman had her own agenda. "My name is Giselle Vail." Glancing at my wrist, she said, "I'm told there's an issue with your tattoo. No one in the Goodman Tribe claims you." Her voice was kind as she asked, "Are you perhaps a runaway?"

There was no sense denying it, so I nodded.

"I see. Can you write your real name down for me?" She handed me a bit of paper and a pen, and I wrote *Milla*, using my best penmanship so the lady would know I'd had a good education.

Mrs. Vail read the name aloud. "Milla. Very pretty. Now Milla, don't worry about your legal status. We can delay investigation of that until we see if things work out between us." She gave me a few seconds to process that, and I felt the muscles in my neck relax a little. "As I told you, I have a daughter about your age. You and Isabel look very much alike."

I tried to smile. While it was hardly pertinent to train wrecks and my missing sister, I was grateful for her kindness.

"I've been looking for a companion for her." Mrs. Vail's beautiful face turned sad. "Isa is very lonely, and I think she'd be happier with someone like you around." She let me process that for a moment before finishing, "Please consider coming to live with us. If you agree to be a friend to our little girl, you'll have a life like you never imagined."

Shaking my head, I signed *Sister*.

My visitor's face turned even sadder. "I'm sorry, dear. I'm afraid your sister died in that awful accident."

Chapter Twelve

The next day, Commander Vail and his wife came to the hospital to learn my decision about going home with them. "I sent for my car to take us the rest of the way," the commander said after his wife introduced him. His smooth baritone dropped lower as he added, "Neither of us is excited about getting back on a train for a while."

"Stay with us at least until your arm is healed," Mrs. Vail said. "We hope you'll decide to stay longer, but of course that will be up to you." The commander left the room, and she added in a confidential tone, "Don't worry about the legalities of your situation. Peter is taking care of it." Did that mean they'd adopt me into their tribe? Was that something I wanted? It was kind of them to consider it, since they knew nothing about me.

Sensing my indecision, Mrs. Vail gave my undamaged arm a squeeze. "I know you'll love our home. Once upon a time it was a park, so there's lots of space. We call it Eden, like a little piece of heaven."

Making the decision on my own, without Zalea to hash out the pros and cons with me, was hard. I'd found sleep difficult the night before as pangs of grief, stabs of fear, and blows of doubt hit me over and over. Should I ask the commander to contact my tribe? Surely he could do that, but it meant dealing with Uncle Rolf. It was customary for a tribe to pay the expenses involved with returning runaways, and I doubted he'd be willing to do that. Grandmother would want me back, but would she even know I'd been located? Uncle Rolf might tell the commander to do with me as he saw fit.

The Vails seemed eager to have me come to live with them. While it was possible they meant to sell me to a Supply Squad or turn me over to the Monkey Men, I didn't get that sense from them. Mr. Vail was an important man, one of the nation's six commanders. His wife was beautiful and gracious. I doubted that people like them bothered to personally gather up runaways and dispose of them.

I really didn't have a choice. The Vails wanted me, and while I wasn't sure why, I thought they would keep me safe. And after weeks on the road, it would be nice to no longer have to sleep in the woods and steal to eat.

Yes, I signed to Mrs. Vail. *Thank you.* I was surprised by her reaction. I couldn't remember a time when someone had clapped their hands at the prospect of spending time with me.

In less than half an hour we left the hospital. It was still early, and the morning was cool. I shivered when the nurse wheeled me outside. Everything I'd had was lost in the accident, including my jacket. Seeing my discomfort, Mrs. Vail ordered, "Get the poor child out of the cold. She's had a bad enough time already without getting sick as well."

The car that waited was unlike any I'd seen before. Long, black, and shiny, it came with a brown-skinned driver of about Zalea's age who was extra tall, very muscular, and strikingly handsome. When he saw us coming he got out and opened the door. I smiled to thank him as I got in, but he appeared not to notice.

The car was roomy and smelled like pine trees. We settled inside, the Vails facing forward and me on a cushy seat that faced them. Closing the door, the driver went around to the front and wedged his big frame into his seat. Once his door closed with a muted *clunk!,* it seemed like nothing outside mattered. "We're ready, Grae," the commander said. Starting the engine, the driver pulled smoothly out of the parking spot and onto the busy street. He navigated heavy traffic for about twenty minutes, making smooth turns and stopping for red lights. When we went up a ramp onto a busy, well-maintained highway, he accelerated to cruising speed.

The lady said the trip would take several hours. "We have a house in the capital because my husband's work is there, but I can't stand the place when the weather turns cold. Our real home is southwest of here, where the temperature suits me better." Southwest. I was continuing the journey Zalea had laid out for us. Tears stung my eyes, but Mrs. Vail went on, "We'd never taken the train before, and I doubt we'll be doing it again."

No one had explained to me why the train had derailed, but I recalled someone mentioning sabotage. Could it have been because the Vails were passengers? Some people hated the Govt, but what kind of monsters hurt and killed innocent people to make a political point? I considered signing that question to Mrs. Vail, but the commander's blank, bored face scared me a little, so I didn't.

About two hours later, Grae turned off the wide highway onto a smaller but well-maintained road. The land was grassy and rather desolate. "Eden is remote," the lady said. "We enjoy the privacy it offers."

After another hour we turned again, and the countryside changed from open to forested. The road got narrower, snaking between trees and shadowed by branches. When we came to a high metal fence, two men stood outside a sentry shack. One opened the gateway while the other waved us through, his manner stiff and respectful. After more maneuvering, we came to a second gate, this one allowing entrance into a walled area. I had the sense we were close, and suddenly the view to my left opened, revealing a small, sparkling lake. Between the road and the near shore was an array of outbuildings, all decorated alike with rustic shutters and matching paint. Around the last curve, we came to a large open space. On my right was a house like nothing I'd seen before. *Eden isn't a home,* I thought. *It's a palace.*

Built on a bluff overlooking the lake, the wide mixture of one and two-story levels shone in the noonday sun, all adobe brick and gray glass. The red tiled roof seemed to go on and on, now low, now high, then low again. A terrace lined the second story, its roof shading a row of perhaps ten double doors from the harsh sun. The house stood against a second, higher bluff thick with trees, so that it framed the elegant architecture. The ground below was terraced, with a variety of fruit trees, flowering bushes, and shrubs trimmed into fanciful shapes.

The car pulled up to the front door and stopped. Grae got out and opened the door, standing as if at attention as we exited. His thick frame, all muscle, strained against the seams of his uniform. His gaze flickered over me as I exited the car, but I couldn't read his thought. He might have been trying to figure out who I was, but he might simply have been considering whether I needed help getting out due to my casted arm.

I followed my hosts up several steps to the house, where a woman wearing a plain black dress stood waiting. A ring of keys hung from a lanyard attached to her belt. While her lips turned upward in a smile, her eyes were watchful, their deep brown depths unrevealing.

"Mar," Commander Vail said. "I hope everything is ready."

"It is, sir. Madame. It's good to have you home again." I'd never heard a woman called "Madame" except in movies, but I'd never seen real servants outside of movies. While Grandmother hired a man or two to come in when they had extra work to do in the yard, no one in the Woods Tribe served another family full-time. I noted that while Mar and the driver, Grae, were brown-skinned with dark eyes and black hair, the Vails were fair-skinned and blond.

"Where is Isa?" Madame Vail asked.

"At the stable, Madame." The woman's face and voice were blank, but I detected a tinge of disapproval in her voice.

"This is Milla," Madame Vail said. "She'll be…helping out with Isa. Put her in the room next to hers."

"Yes, Madame." She turned to Milla and bowed slightly. "Welcome, Miss."

"She can't speak." Commander Vail made it sound like a choice I'd made.

Another flick of those brown eyes made me feel judged, but not in a bad way. "I see."

I followed Mar through the house. Though I tried not to "gawp," as Grandmother would have put it, I'd never seen anyplace like it. Everything the Vails had was…extra. The curtains were extra full. A couch we passed was extra-long, the chairs beside it extra-padded. The lighting fixture overhead was extra-large, and while its dozens of bulbs weren't lit at midday, I imagined the extra brilliance they'd provide at night.

All through the house, in alcoves and on tables, were works of art like nothing I'd ever seen. At one that was particularly impressive, a squarish head made of green stone, I stopped. Noticing, Mar explained, "The commander collects Olmec artifacts. Pieces like this were made by my ancestors, long ago." After a moment she added, "Now they belong to others."

The room I was given could have come from a fairy tale. The walls were painted soft blue, and snowy white curtains framed floor to ceiling windows. The double doors I'd seen from the car stood open onto the terrace, which overlooked the lake. Though I was dying to go out and take in the view, I listened politely while Mar explained the routines of the house. “Isa has already had her lunch, but I will bring you a tray. Do you prefer a chicken or tuna sandwich?” I put up one finger, choosing chicken, since I was unfamiliar with tuna. “Milk or juice?” Milk sounded safe, so I put up one finger again, adding the sign for *thank you.* With the first evidence of warmth I’d seen from her, Mar said, “Cook made cupcakes this morning. I’ll bring you one of those too.” I signed *Thank you* again. “You have no things?” When I confirmed that, Mar said. “Isa has plenty of clothes that will fit you.”

I thanked her a third time, and Mar left. Hurrying outside, I turned slowly from left to right, admiring the view. It was quite different from home. Many of the trees were unfamiliar. The soil had a sandy look. The lake had a reddish tint. At a boathouse near the shore, wide doors stood open revealing several kinds of watercraft. A dock a few yards down from it practically begged me to sit at its end and dip my toes in the water.

Zalea would like this place. It made me sad that she would never experience what I was seeing now: a different climate, odd trees, and exotic plants. Nor had we ever lived in luxury, with servants to find a person clothes to wear and bring her food to eat. Would Zalea approve of the commander and his wife? I didn’t know, but then, I didn’t know myself how I felt about them. They seemed nice, especially Mrs.—*Madame*, I corrected myself. Madame Vail.

Mar returned, knocking softly and then entering with a tray she set on a small table. While I ate my sandwich and a delicious chocolate cupcake, she went through a connecting door to a larger, fancier room with frilly lace everywhere and an abundance of pink. She returned with three dresses, some separates, and a nightgown. Under one arm she carried two pairs of shoes, one a lace-up canvas, the other a pretty flat with a strap that buckled. Laying the clothing on the bed, she said, “One more trip,” and disappeared again. On her return, she had an armful of underwear, socks, panties, and a bra. "That might be too big for you," Mar said, pointing at the bra. "Isa has a large bust."

Taking up the bra, I fingered the cups. Given a needle and thread, I could adjust them to fit, but I wasn't sure how to get that across. To my surprise, Mar signed, *We change this?*

Eagerly I answered, *You sign.*

"They thought for a long time that Isa would never speak, so Madam and I learned ASL," Mar explained. "Isa never showed a minute's interest in it. Then one day, I think she was six, she suddenly started talking. She…Isa takes her own time doing things." Mar sighed, and I guessed that was a burden for her and maybe for others. "Anyway, I remember a little of it, so if you go slow, I can probably figure out what you say."

I fix bra needle thread, I signed.

"All right. I'll get that for you."

Meet Isa?

Mar's lips tightened. "She's gone horseback riding. You have time for a shower and a nap too, if you like." She opened a door to reveal a bathroom. "When Isa returns, wait for me to come up and take you to meet her."

Mar left, and I investigated the bathroom that appeared to be all mine. I'd never seen so many soaps, one for hair, one for body, one for face alone. The towels were thick and soft and smelled spicy. I stood under the shower for a long time, holding my casted arm outside the stall so it didn't get wet. The warm water running over the rest of me eased my bruises, which showed purple and green along my shoulder and hip.

When I finished bathing, I put on the nightgown Mar had provided, turned back the silky-soft coverlet, and lay down on the bed. I was tired, but it took a while to get to sleep. My new environment, as fancy as it was, felt stressful. I didn't know how to behave, didn't understand what was expected of me. Grief at losing Zalea clawed at me, as did the fear of going on without her. I wondered about Isa, who was apparently important to my future. Madame Vail had said I'd be her companion, which sounded like she hoped we'd become close. I didn't know if people could simply decide to be friends, but I was willing to try. Perhaps Isa would ease my loneliness and help me get past the loss of my home, my family, and most recently, my strong, loving sister.

Unexpected tears burned my eyes, and I cried for a while. So much of my pain was my own fault. I'd broken many rules. I'd run away from my tribe. Zalea had initiated it, and Uncle Rolf was indeed mean, but I'd gone along, and my punishment was fitting. I'd lost Zalea forever. I had no home except with strangers.

Wiping my eyes, I called to mind Grandmother's advice, "Enjoy the good times but be ready for the bad ones," and my religious training. There was a time for every purpose under heaven. I mourned now, but someday, I might laugh again.

I should be grateful for the chance I'd been given. I was in a lovely place, with adults to guide me and the chance to prove I could be obedient. I could mold myself into a better person by helping Madame Vail, the commander, and their daughter however I could. I drifted off to sleep determined to make the best of my new life.

When I woke, the clock on the bedside table said three-thirty. I got up and dressed in the clothes Mar had provided. The bra was indeed too big, but I put a sock in each cup and vowed to fix it later. I chose the plainest dress, which was a little long but otherwise fit well. The shoes felt tight but not painfully so. In the bathroom mirror, I experienced a moment's regret for the loss of my waist-length hair. Taking up a brush, I smoothed what was left, straightening the tangles that had resulted from letting it dry while I slept

After that, I sat in a chair, looking at the lake, until Mar's soft knock came again. She opened the door without waiting for an answer. The look she gave me said she approved, either of my looks or my state of readiness.

"I've told Isa about you, and she wants to meet you right away." Mar stepped to the connecting doorway, indicating I should follow.

The room I'd glimpsed earlier was even more elaborate than I'd thought. The bed had a canopy, the first one I'd even seen in real life. One whole wall was shelves with dolls, perhaps fifty of them, in costumes of different eras and cultures. I noted a Cinderella, a Chinese princess, a native American, and a Thai dancer. I would have liked to examine them, but Mar led me to the bed, where a girl lay sprawled, eyeing me with distaste.

Madame Vail hadn't been exaggerating when she said her daughter and I looked alike. Except for Isa's larger bust, we were very similar, from our builds to our coloring and even our facial features. The biggest difference was Isa's expression. Her jaw jutted forward. Her eyes were narrowed to slits. She was angry, but it wasn't a reasonable sort of anger. Something in her eyes told me that Isabel Vail could not understand the world around her and didn't know why. Her response was to be mad about it.

Isa lay on her stomach, wearing a culotte skirt and a long-sleeved blouse. Cowboy boots with reddish dirt on them lay next to her on the bedspread. A battered Stetson hat lay on the floor, where she'd apparently tossed it. Her posture telegraphed the same unhappiness I saw on her face.

"Isa," Mar said, "This is Milla. She'll be staying in the room next door."

She spoke directly to me. "Who said you come here?"

Mar responded, and I guessed she'd already answered that question. "Your parents invited her. If you need me to have your father explain why, I can ask him to do that." Isa's eyelids drooped for a second, and I sensed she didn't want her father explaining anything. That led to a glimmer of understanding. It was no doubt demanding for anyone to be a powerful man's only child. It would be more so if that child had difficulty comprehending life's complexities.

Mar spoke again. "I think you will like Milla once you get to know her." Isa nodded woodenly, accepting necessity without an ounce of grace. "I'll leave you two to get acquainted. You're both invited to dinner, so be downstairs by six." With that, she left.

The room was silent, but tension crackled between us. I stood perfectly still for perhaps a minute, unsure how to break the ice. Isa ignored me, fiddling with a device I'd never seen before. From where I stood, I could see dancing figures and hear music. After a while I realized Isa was watching a cartoon. I'd never seen a screen that small, and I took a step closer. The second I moved, a boot came flying at my head. I ducked and it sailed past, hitting the wall with a thud. "I no want you here," Isa shouted. "I want be only one!"

I wasn't sure what to do. I could retreat to my room, but would it remain mine if Isa didn't want me there?

Just then the door opened and Madame Vail bustled in. She had changed from her travel clothes to more casual ones, but she looked every bit as elegant as before in a full-skirted dress and matching, low-heeled shoes. "I see you two have met."

I nodded. Isa ignored her. Madame turned to me, her face flushed pink. "Isa has…difficulty establishing relationships with others. I—" With a glance at Isa, she began again. "Isa's father and I hope you can help her become better at dealing with people." Her tone lightened. "When I saw you that first time at the train station, I noticed how much you and she look alike. I thought, 'How sweet it would be if Isa had a twin!' Of course I thought you were a boy at that time, so I just went on." She clasped her hands. "But God heard my thought and brought us together a second time." She licked her lips. "It's tragic that you lost your sister, but now you have the chance to help me and Isa and the commander." She gestured at the room. "Do you like our home, Milla?"

I nodded, which made Madame clap her hands again. How easy it was to make her happy! Turning to her daughter, she said, "Isa, Milla is going to show you how a young lady should behave. If you're good, your father will be very proud." A frown appeared on her brow as she finished, "And you won't feel so angry all the time, because people will like you."

"Her stupid," Isa interrupted. "No talk." She pointed at her own chest. "I talk good!"

"Yes, you do," Madame said enthusiastically. "But Milla doesn't stomp her feet and rush around like there's a fire. She doesn't glare at people." Taking hold of my shoulders, she turned me toward her daughter. "She doesn't go around with her bottom lip stuck out so far we could hang a lantern on it. While it's true you can speak and she can't, it's often best for a girl to be quiet and let the men talk. If you learn to be more like Milla, your father will find you an excellent husband."

With that Madame left the room, clearly convinced she'd provided the best kind of encouragement. I looked at my feet, horrified to have been presented as an ideal to be copied. Giving me a look of pure hatred, Isa spun on her heel and stomped onto the terrace, her back rigid with outrage.

Going back to my room, I closed the door. Mar was standing beside the bed, arms folded. She'd obviously heard the whole exchange, and she seemed to disapprove of the approach Madame Vail had taken. "This won't be easy for you, but I don't suppose you have a choice." I gave her a rueful smile. Mar moved around the room, straightening pillows that were already in place and adjusting decorative items a quarter inch here and there. "I told you Isa didn't speak until she was six. She didn't walk until she was three, didn't feed herself until she was almost seven. She's nearing the age when she should marry, but she's completely unready. Her mother needs a miracle, and I'm afraid she wants you to provide it."

I shrugged and then signed, *I try.*

That made her smile. "I will help when I can."

A young woman named Lucia came to get us ready for dinner. After she'd helped me choose a slightly more formal dress than the one I had on, she went to deal with Isa. The door was open, so I saw that the whole time Lucia was buttoning the girl's dress, fixing her hair, and buckling her shoes, Isa slapped at her hands and face, making honking sounds of laughter. She tried to bite too, but Lucia was apparently aware of that possibility. Twice I heard a clack as Isa's teeth came together without making contact with her target.

The struggle continued, and I turned away, sickened by the delight Isa took in harassing someone who was trying to help her. I would soon be in a similar position, I realized. I was supposed to change a girl who'd apparently been allowed to act like a wild creature for thirteen years.

When Mar came to take us downstairs, Isa quieted. As we descended, her expression was sulky but fearful as well. Dinner with her parents wasn't usual for Isa, I realized.

The dining room was like everything else in the house—extra. Extra big, extra fancy, extra expensive. I'd already figured out that the house was air-conditioned throughout. That was something Grandmother would have enjoyed, I thought, since she was always too warm. The four of us sat at a long table that could have held a dozen more guests. We occupied one end, the commander at the head, his wife on his right, and on the left Isa and then me. Three different women served the meal, setting bowls and plates before each of us and then backing away. When I finished a dish, one of the women would step forward, take it away, and replace it with another. If the commander or his wife expressed a wish for an item, they hurried to provide it. The servers resembled Mar, with the same dark hair and eyes. I decided they were hired workers, not members of the Vail tribe. That was odd, because while tribes often sought out experts in other tribes and engaged them for specific jobs, there was nothing special about serving food. Apparently no Vails wanted the jobs these women held.

Madame Vail disliked silence. She talked through the meal like a bright parrot, her green and gold fingernails clicking on her wine glass. The commander's responses were mostly grunts, and Isa ignored her. I tried to respond with appropriate smiles and nods.

We were served foods I'd never had before and foods I was familiar with that were served in new ways. I liked the spicy rice, the beans they said were "refried," and the meat and cheese wrapped in thin round bread called a tortilla.

"We're so happy that you're here to be with our girl," my hostess said in her breathy tone as we ate. "We've…um, we've let Isa have her way a bit too much." The commander coughed lightly and took a sip of water, but his wife went on, "We believe she'll learn quickly now that you're here."

Isa hadn't appeared to be listening. She had, in fact, been shoving food into her mouth like she hadn't eaten for days. At her mother's comment, however, she picked up her plate as if it were a disc and tossed it across the room. It hit a large stone fireplace at the far end and broke into pieces. Red sauce dripped from the mantel edge and spattered the hearth.

"Out!" The commander hit the table with the flat of his hand. "Take her out!"

Two of the women came forward, their faces grim, and took Isa by the arms. She fought them, making angry grunts and flailing, but they were obviously practiced. Gripping her wrists with one hand, they pulled her, chair and all, away from the table. Each woman took hold of the waistband of her dress with her free hand and, half-dragging, half-carrying, took her from the room. Isa fought and swore and raged, but she couldn't escape. The sound of her struggles faded as the unhappy trio mounted the stairs.

Vail turned to his wife, his face flushed with anger. "I don't know why you do this, Giselle. She never makes it through a meal without going off."

Tears filled Madame's eyes. "I thought she'd do better with her new friend beside her."

The commander gave an irritated sigh. "You can't expect the girl to magically change Isa in one afternoon." He looked at me, and I didn't know whether to meet his gaze or look down at my plate. I chose the latter, and he spoke as if I weren't there. "I doubt she can do what the finest teachers and doctors haven't been able to." Shifting in his chair, he added, "I'm willing to let you have your little experiment, but don't expect me to tolerate Isa's presence until you have real results." The remaining servant had begun to clean up the mess Isa made, and he barked at her, "Take the girl back up to her room. She may have her dessert up there. Isa will go without."

On the morning of my second day I was up at six. I was to take lessons with Isa at nine, so I had time to explore the area outside the house. I met several people on my way. Everyone seemed to know who I was and why I was there. Most greeted me and went on. A boy of about eight asked where I wanted to go, and I shrugged, unsure. "There's figs in the orchard that are ready to eat," he said. "Want me to show you?"

I nodded, and he led the way to a tree bent with fruit. "The ripe ones come off easy," he said. "You want the ones that feel soft but not mushy." Selecting one, he handed it to me, and soon I was enjoying a taste that was new and delicious. I'd been too shy to go to the kitchen and ask for breakfast, so it was filling as well.

Saying he had chores to do, the boy went on. Still munching, I walked all the way around the commander's house. A few times I circled briefly into the orchards, where apple, peach, pear, and orange trees stood in various stages of production. Hoping it was okay, I picked an orange and ate it as I went. No one I passed seemed to mind my presence or the theft of the fruit. I returned to my room with sticky hands and a satisfied appetite.

When it was time for lessons, Mar escorted me to the classroom. Isa was already there, sitting sulkily at a table. Before her was a map of Fairica and a selection of crayons corresponding to the sections: Blue, Green, Rose, and Gold. She'd apparently been told to color it correctly, but so far there were only random scribbles across the sheet.

There were items in the room I'd have liked to examine: a world globe, the device I'd seen Isa using earlier, and more books than I'd ever seen in one place before. The walls were hung with pictures and graphs I might have perused, but a narrowing of Isa's eyes dared me to touch anything she considered hers. I sat down at the table, as far away from her as I could get.

Tutor Frank, apparently the latest in a long line, had planned a math lesson, but mostly he said the same things over and over. "Please sit down, Isa. We have work to do," or "Isa, let's show your new friend how good you are at addition." Inevitably, his encouragements turned to threats. "If you don't behave, I'll have to tell your father." Isa apparently knew he wouldn't, because her behavior didn't improve. As the session went on, he gave up trying to control her and spoke only to me. Isa invented excuses to pass behind my chair, pinching my neck and laughing as if it were the funniest trick ever.

Lunch was better, because Mar sat with us while we ate. While Isa wasn't exactly sweet to her, Mar had a dignity about her that prevented Isa from harassing her the way she did other servants. Mar didn't cajole or threaten. She expected Isa to behave, and it worked.

As Mar cleared away the dishes, Madame Vail bustled in with a ledger clutched to her ample chest. "Isa, Milla, I'm going to show you how I manage the household." Isa made a honk of derision, which her mother ignored. "Good wives spend their husband's money wisely," she began, sitting down between us. She opened the book, which contained neat columns of numbers headed with terms like *Groceries* or *Furnishings*. "Most wives are given an allowance so they can plan efficiently." Widening her eyes, she cautioned, "We need to be vigilant, because tradesmen know how bad women are with numbers. If we don't pay attention, they inflate the prices of goods or overcharge for services." Leaning toward us, she finished in a lower tone, "It pays to watch the servants too. I trust Mar, of course, but the rest of them?" She waved a hand. "Those people simply don't have the same moral code we do."

I'd seen Madame's handwriting, which was flowery and big. The numbers in the book were square and neat. My guess was that Mar actually kept the household accounts and Madame pretended to oversee her work.

Isa could not have cared less about her mother's instruction. She'd already turned on the device called a tablet. Touching the screen, she began watching a cartoon cat chase a cartoon mouse. Seemingly unaware, Madame prattled on the clever ways she saved her husband's money. "It was my idea for the staff to share quarters," she boasted. "We were able to close three cabins completely." Her lips worked, apparently at an unpleasant memory. "Multiple families living in one house required some adjustment, but it's not like the staff is home that often. They're working."

When her mother finally said we could go, Isa took off like a hound released from its tether. The lady turned to me. "You can see that Isa is smarter than she first appears, yes?" If by "smarter" she meant clever at getting away with bad behavior, I had to agree, so I nodded. Madame's smile was worth the fib. "My girl isn't…slow, like the doctors say. She just needs a friend who understands her, like you, Milla." After a moment she said, "Do you like your name, Milla?" When I smiled to indicate I did, Madame said, "All right, then. Off you go."

I spent the next few days with Isa, encouraging her when she behaved and avoiding her feet, fingers, and teeth when her anger overflowed. The servants kept small chocolate candies wrapped in foil in their pockets to use as bribes. Isa found sweets irresistible and often forgot what she was upset about when offered a treat.

She'd toss the wrapper onto the floor, stick the candy in her mouth, and turn to me, certain I'd be jealous. Mostly what I felt was relief. One less tantrum to suffer through. One less bruise for myself or one of the servants.

Life at Eden was colored by the shadow of Commander Vail, who spoke little and expected much. He was often gone on business, and it seemed to me the house was more peaceful then. When he was in residence, the atmosphere was tense, even fearful. As the man in charge, the commander was nothing like Grandfather. He consulted no one in his decision-making, and I overheard him telling Donnie, his estate manager, "My job is to lead. Your job is to see that everyone follows." Everything we did was based on the commander's beliefs, experiences, and whims. Unsure of my place in his estimation, I avoided him whenever possible.

Madame Vail was different from other women I'd known. Though she seemed to believe she led a busy life, she did almost nothing for herself. Obsessed with her looks, she often shared beauty secrets with Isa and me as if they were vitally important. Isa paid no attention whatsoever. I was shocked at how far Madame believed a wife should go to remain attractive to her husband. Men should never see what their wives did to maintain beauty, she told us. Those things were taken care of in secret. When the commander wasn't around, Madame used eye-masks, facial oils, and body creams, particularly one that claimed it would keep the breasts from "falling." She waxed places I didn't even want to hear about. She made Mar set bees on her skin, claiming their sting plumped and firmed it. I kept imagining Grandmother's amusement at her frivolous pursuit of youth, and I suspected Zalea would have had a lot to say about intestinal cleanses and therapeutic mud baths.

The estate ran smoothly due to a well-trained and surprisingly large staff, and I liked most of them. Only Donnie, the manager, seemed to disapprove of me, lifting his nose when I was nearby. Again I imagined what Zalea would have said about Donnie's obvious conceit. Everything about him, his slicked-back hair, his carefully-kept fingernails, even the hint of makeup to darken his eyelashes, suggested he was obsessed with his looks. Though Donnie and the commander worked out regularly together, I noticed that neither of them seemed interested in doing actual work.

On my fourth day at the Vail estate, Mar asked if my arm was healed enough that I might start riding with Isa in the afternoons. "Madame would like you to go, but if you don't want to, I can tell her—"

I ride, I signed. Not only did I love horses, I also looked forward to any chance to be outside. As beautiful and as comfortable as the Vails' home was, I liked fresh air and sun on my skin.

Mar sent one of the boys to see to the preparations while she fetched one of Isa's riding outfits for me to wear. After we adjusted the fit with a belt and a little sleeve-rolling, we walked to a paddock attached to the long side of the stable. Divided doors stood open, allowing the horses inside to look out. Isa was already there, wearing her cowboy hat and boots. Taking one look at me, she shouted, "No!" and stomped her foot. "No her!"

"Your father wants the two of you to do things together," Mar said firmly, opening the gate and gesturing me inside. "If Milla goes back to the house, I'll have to tell him why she didn't go riding with you today."

Isa paused, her jaw tight. Despite her intellectual challenges, she understood what her father's anger meant. Turning away abruptly, she folded her arms on her chest.

Grae, the commander's driver, appeared from the stable leading a dappled-gray mare for me to ride. I was struck again by his size, I guessed six feet six. He was no lumbering giant, but moved with natural grace as he turned the horse toward the gate. "You've ridden before?" he asked. I nodded yes. The cast would make things more difficult, but I was sure I could do it. I petted the horse's nose and neck, letting her get used to my touch and smell.

Grae seemed pleased by that. "This is Dolly," he said. "She was Miss Isa's horse until the commander bought Princess for her a month ago. Dolly is easy-going, and she knows the trails, so all you have to do is stay on." I stepped forward, ready to mount, and then hesitated, stopped by my casted arm. "If you don't mind, Miss." Putting his hands on my waist, Grae lifted me as if I weighed nothing and set me on the horse's back. Grasping the horn with my good hand, I settled into the saddle and set my feet in the stirrups.

"Me." Isa led her horse to where Grae stood and indicated he should help her mount. Obligingly, he lifted her onto Princess, a spritely black with dainty feet and a sleek shape. As she took up the reins, Isa gave Grae an uncharacteristically sweet smile. I noticed, but he apparently didn't.

Going back into the stable, Grae got on his own horse, a big-boned buckskin he introduced as Royal. Mar, who'd been watching, opened the paddock gate to let us out. Grae asked, "Which direction would you like to go today, Miss Vail?" Isa pointed toward the hills on the northwest side of the estate. Nodding, he led the way.

A few minutes later, we exited the north gate and followed a trail that skirted the lake for a time. It was manicured in a way I'd never seen before. Neat wooden signs pointed out spots of interest and the distance to them. Benches set along the way offered spectacular views of the lake. I would have liked to stop and look, but Isa rode on, apparently with a goal in mind. "Rocks there," she said, pointing to where a turnoff wound up a steep hillside. When we reached the spot she'd chosen, Isa stopped, dismounted, and pulled on heavy gloves. Leaving Princess' reins on the ground, she started up the rocky incline, sending pebbles rolling toward us in her haste.

"You might as well dismount," Grae told me. "She'll be up there a while." He helped me down, explaining, "Isa likes rocks." He pointed at a leather satchel hung on the horn of his saddle. "She'll spend about twenty minutes up there, making a pile of what she finds today. When she's done, I go up and put them in that bag." His tone turned amused. "I carry them back to the house and take them inside. Mar hauls them up to Isa's room and sets them on the balcony. Isa looks at them at night, before she goes to sleep. Tomorrow morning, she'll no longer want those rocks. Mar will bring them back down to me, I'll toss them, and Isa will go looking for new ones."

I looked up to where Isa knelt, digging one rock after another out of the ground and either tossing it aside or setting it onto the pile she was making. She focused on the task in a way she never did in the classroom.

As we waited, I pointed to a plant and widened my eyes in question. Grae said, "That's yucca." When I pointed to another, he got the idea that I was interested in learning about the area. He seemed pleased to share what he knew, and he talked for some time about the local terrain and plants. I was fascinated by the live oaks, which spread out along the ground rather than up, the way trees I was used to did. Grae pointed out a spicebush heavy with red berries, a bald cypress, and a patch of whitish-yellow flowers he said were wild indigo.

As he talked Grae grew more animated, telling me about some coyote pups he'd seen. By chance I happened to glance up. Isa had paused her rock-collecting and stood looking down at us, fists clenched and planted on her hips. I rolled my eyes at Grae, who turned and saw trouble brewing. In a casual voice, he called, "Ready to stop for today, Miss?"

Isa's hand flashed in response. A rock flew past my shoulder. I hadn't seen it coming, but luckily, her aim was off. Taking large steps, Grae climbed to where Isa stood and put a hand on her arm, speaking softly. "I have been telling your friend about the plants that grow here. She comes from far away, so she doesn't know the things you know." Isa's expression didn't change. Turning toward the rock pile, Grae said, "I'll load these up for you, and then we can start back."

Isa didn't toss any more rocks, which I took as a good sign. Grae began loading the bag while she made her way down the steep slope, her face still frozen in anger. Without a glance at me she took up her horse's reins, set her foot in the stirrup, and mounted in one swift motion. Once there, she gave the animal a sharp kick in its sides with her booted feet.

If her plan had been to ride off without us, that wasn't what happened. The kick startled the horse, and she bucked violently, arching her back and twisting to one side. Isa tried to grab the saddle horn but missed. Sliding backward, she landed hard on the trail. Sprinting downhill, Princess disappeared from sight.

Racing to Isa's side, Grae examined her for injuries. "No hurt!" she insisted. "Get horse!"

"Stay with her," Grae told me once he was satisfied Isa was okay. He glanced back in the direction of the house, as if afraid someone there might have seen the incident. "I'm willing to bet that little horse will be up for sale tomorrow."

When he was gone, I helped Isa to her feet and walked with her a few steps to make sure everything worked. I was surprised when she took hold of my arm, pulled me close, and ordered, "No tell Father." I tried to pull away, cowed by her demanding tone, but she squeezed tighter. "Father sell Princess. Maybe mad at Grae." In a harsh tone, she finished, "You tell, I hurt you."

I got it. While Isa didn't care about much, she loved Princess and had a crush on Grae. Seeing an opportunity to gain her trust, I put a finger to my lips and shook my head. My smile made a pact between us. After a moment, Isa smiled too.

Cracking in the nearby brush signaled Grae's return, and he appeared on the trail, leading the horse, who was now calm and obedient. As Isa took the reins from him, she gave a haughty command. "We not tell Father this."

He frowned. "What if he finds out? What if you have a concussion or a cracked bone?"

Isa pointed at me, then herself, then Grae. "She no tell. I no tell. You no tell. He no find out."

Approaching Grae, I swept a hand from Isa's head to her feet and back again, highlighting her lack of injury. I made a praying gesture. *Please?*

Grae sighed. "If you'll watch her tonight to make sure she's okay, I guess we can keep it to ourselves."

When he turned to the horses, Isa gave me a grin that indicated we were co-conspirators now. It was, I hoped, a step toward what the Vails wanted me to accomplish.

Chapter Thirteen

"Our house up north isn't like this one," Madame Vail said as she checked her brows one more time in the hallway mirror. Her dress, which showed off her tiny waist, was blue with large black buttons for trim. "It's smaller and much less elegant. Peter says we must maintain what he calls 'optics' in the capital, where everything we do is public." Other than the modesty of their "political" home, she claimed, Capital Center itself was lively and entertaining. In a tone warm with approval, she added, "Because Isa has been making such good progress, the commander agreed that the two of you can come along and join the festivities celebrating our nation's re-birth."

Isa had been less nasty of late, though she still tended to see those around her either as obstacles or means for getting what she wanted. I'd found I could often derail an impending tantrum by taking hold of Isa's hands or wrapping my arms around her. If I got to her before she erupted, Isa's chin would relax, and her eyes would lose the wild look that signaled loss of control. I wasn't sure if she wanted the personal contact or if it simply helped her to know that someone was there.

The problem for me was that my calming influence required Isa and I to be together every waking hour. Even at her best, Isa was still Isa, demanding and incorrigible. When Tutor Frank assigned us a task, Isa would announce, "Milla do it." She insisted we be served the same foods, whether I felt like having macaroni and cheese every day for lunch or not. And Isa expected me to accompany her everywhere, even to the bathroom.

With me as guarantor of Isa's good behavior, the commander had decided to take her to the celebration at the capital. Grae would drive us, though I now knew that was a job he hated. While Isa scoured for rocks each afternoon, Grae shared his thoughts, maybe in friendship, maybe in unconscious acknowledgment that I couldn't tell what I heard. We were careful to stand a good distance apart and pretend he was providing lessons on native plants and animals. Grae pointed as he spoke. I pretended interest in whatever he pointed at. Once Isa was convinced we were simply passing the time, she would focus on her digging and sorting. Only I knew that Grae spoke not to instruct but to share his heart.

"I'd just as soon stay here and take care of the horses," he told me one day, "but the commander decided I should drive for him. He flies there and back most of the time, but sometimes he wants his car in Capital City, so I take him up there and deliver him where he needs to go."

When I frowned to ask why, he blushed. "I think he likes…I mean, I'm kinda noticeable." I nodded, acknowledging that Grae was impressive, both in size and appearance. "Donnie used to be his guy, but one day the commander ordered him to teach me the job." Grae rubbed at his jaw, and I had a feeling it was an unconscious memory of pain. "Donnie wasn't happy about it and neither was I, but you don't argue with the commander."

Had Donnie hit Grae for getting a job he hadn't asked for and didn't even want? Having seen that the workers on the estate avoided him whenever possible, I guessed Donnie turned any unhappiness he experienced into an excuse for physical punishment.

Though not one of them was as impressive as Grae, the guards on the estate were tough-looking men with hard eyes and belts that bristled with weapons. They were obsequious toward the Vails and dismissive of everyone else. Donnie, their boss, walked around with a cold stare on his face and his fists curled to keep his large arm muscles flexed. He seemed to have decided I was beneath his notice, and I took that as a good thing.

"The first time I drove the commander to the capital," Grae told me, "I was sure I was gonna throw up all over the car." A scrape of Isa's trowel had reminded him of her watchful presence, so he pointed to a tree as if telling me about it. I went over and peered at its leaves. While my back was to him Grae said, "Yesterday he told me I'll be moving to the capital full time when I turn eighteen next month. I told him I'd rather stay here, but he acted like he didn't hear."

From Grae's shared thoughts and snatches I heard from the others at Eden, I'd surmised that the workers on the estate had little say in what happened to them. While the Tribal Reorganization Act had promised land and autonomy to every group, the brown-skinned people on the commander's estate had no leader of their own and decided nothing for themselves. Any agreements between tribes were supposed to result in mutual benefit, but I saw no advantage for Grae's people in working at Eden. Commander and Madame Vail ordered Mar, Grae, and the others to do everything for them, from heavy labor to personal care, but they took no interest in them as people.

Lucia, the woman who cleaned my room each morning, gave her explanation of the relationship one day as she wiped dust from the baseboards in my room. "The commander is an important man. He advises Chief Vox. He oversees hundreds of tribes. He takes care of the big things for us, and we take care of the little things for him."

When it was time for us to leave for the capital, Grae loaded a half-dozen suitcases into the car. "One for each of you," Madame had said at breakfast. "We're a nation of equals, so we mustn't show off."

A nation of equals? I thought as we passed through the gates and left the commander's luxurious home behind. That was an illusion the Vails worked to maintain in public while in private they used their people like slaves. The Tribal System wasn't supposed to work like that.

Grandfather had been proud to share equally in the work and the rewards the Woods Tribe earned. He'd often spoken of the first few years and the struggle to unite our tribe and make it successful. Once that was accomplished and we began to prosper, he'd insisted that all men benefit equally. He'd refused special treatment like a bigger house, a fancy car, or more money. Commander Vail could have taken lessons from Ben Woods.

The house in the capital was certainly less grand than Eden. There was only one servant, Cara, who seemed to resent having five people to feed and clean up after. "Usually she has only the commander to please," Madame Vail told me when Cara fussed about "elbow room" and schedules. "She's known him since he was a boy, so he's a little scared of her."

The house had only three bedrooms, which meant I had to bunk with Isa. Madame Vail and the commander slept in the same room, which they never did at home. Since Cara occupied the third bedroom, Grae rolled up in blankets on the living room couch. When I woke the next morning he was already up, and I helped him fold his blankets and stack them in a corner.

"I don't care where I sleep, but I hate the city." Tossing the pillow he'd used atop the pile of blankets, he added, "Donnie's home and mad that I'm here, and I'm here and sad that I'm not back there."

Isa came in at that moment, rubbing the sleep from her eyes. Grae and I went silent, waiting to see if she was in the mood to be jealous. I knew Grae was aware of Isa's crush on him and embarrassed by it. He lived in fear the commander would find out and choose to be angry with him, though he'd done nothing to encourage it. The only blessing, he'd told me, was that Isa knew her father would disapprove, so when the commander was around, she did her best to hide her infatuation.

"I'd better get the car swept out," Grae said in a casual tone. "The commander will be heading to the Capitol soon."

Isa watched him go and then turned to me, her gaze faintly accusing. Sniffing the air, I pointed to the kitchen, where Cara was making French toast. After a second, Isa said, "We eat!" and led the way.

That week was an eye-opening experience. The nation's capital, which had been moved to the center of the nation during the rebellion, showed me that the marvels older members of my tribe had sometimes mentioned were all true. The capital had a bus and a subway system. There was a library five stories high. Our second night there, the Vails took us to a concert hall. Though Isa grew bored and sulky, I fell under the spell of the music, leaning on the balcony rail and listening to every nuance of sound. My fingers twitched as the flutists played, an unconscious longing to recreate their part on the flute I'd lost when the train crashed.

The downside to the trip was realizing how backward I—in fact, everyone in our tribe—was in comparison to residents of the larger burgs, often referred to by the old term, cities. At home, talking on the phone had been a rare experience. Movies were shown on special nights and limited to what Grandfather considered worthwhile. Financial transactions were accomplished by barter or check. In Capital Center there were phones in every home, sometimes two or three. Everyone had a TV. The commander had a small card that he handed over to pay for things. It was all very impressive, though I noticed that people didn't interact the way they did at home. It was all, "Yes, please," and "No, thanks," but there wasn't a lot of warmth involved.

After seeing so much I'd never seen before, I could almost believe Zalea's contention that women had once started companies and held elected office. I wished I could talk about it with her, because it confused me. Though Fairica wasn't what I'd thought it was, I still believed the way we'd grown up had been good for us. Hard work had made us strong. Firm rules had guided us to honor and integrity. While parts of Fairica had turned away from Chief Vox's vision, they could be brought back. We shouldn't throw away a whole system of government because of a few weak spots.

Looking at the calendar on the commander's desk, I realized I'd been gone from home almost forty days. Rolf would be installed as the new leader soon. Would our tribe continue strong under my uncle's guidance? Rolf was selfish and, I knew now, evil as well. That didn't bode well for the Woods Tribe's future.

The reason for our visit to Capital City was to celebrate the eighteenth anniversary of the TRA. All commanders and their families were expected to attend. Evening events were planned for the adults, and daytime activities allowed parents to include their children. There was concern about Isa's first visit to the Vox Mansion, since it was a luncheon for immediate family only. Madame Vail spent a great deal of time instructing Isa on how to behave when she met Chief Vox. As usual, her approach was "We hope you'll—" and "Please try to—" weak statements with no backbone to them.

The morning of the visit, I was headed to breakfast when I heard the commander's iron-edged voice and stopped outside the dining room doorway. "—do anything to embarrass me. Do you understand?" In the silence that followed, I tried to guess Isa's reaction. Was she making an effort to appear obedient, or did she have that stubborn expression that presaged a violent outburst? Should I go in and try to calm her, or would that make matters worse?

Isa's father was clear about his intentions. "If you don't behave, Isabel, understand this. When we leave here, I will personally drive you to the nearest Special Quarters and leave you there. You won't have your precious tablet. You won't get to choose what you eat. No chocolates. No Mar to wait on you. No horses. No pretty clothes." His tone got even harder. "If you don't do exactly as I say, I will put you where I should have put you ten years ago, no matter how hard your mother cries."

I felt a stab of sorrow for Isa. While she was unpleasant to be around, she lacked the ability to analyze her own behavior and correct it. With the right kind of encouragement she might have learned to behave better, but she had a mother who pretended she was fine and a father who couldn't stand the sight of her. No wonder she always seemed ready to explode.

"Cara has laid out clothes for you," Commander Vail went on. "You will add nothing. There will be no rocks in your pockets or in your socks. When you meet Chief Vox, you will smile at him. If he asks a direct question, you'll say 'Yes, sir' or 'No, sir.' No more, do you understand?" After a moment he added, "If I thought I'd get away with it, I'd take the other girl and pass her off as my daughter. At least then I wouldn't have to worry about you shooting off your big mouth."

I ducked behind the couch just in time to avoid Isa, who hurried to our room with her head thrust forward and her hands balled into fists. No wonder she was so mean. And no wonder she resented me.

Grae dropped the Vails at the Mansion and returned. Cara, it turned out, was his aunt, and with the Vails gone, he caught her up on what was happening with their relatives at Eden. Once that was covered, Cara glanced at me. "What does she know about us?"

"Milla has seen how we live," Grae replied.

"Then you know that we are enslaved." Cara's tone was harsh. Grae flashed me a look, the kind of apology young people offer their friends when older relatives start in on their favorite rant.

Cara either didn't notice or didn't care. "In the Old Times, we worked for a wage. When Vox came to power and said he'd be fair to everyone, he didn't mean us."

I frowned to show confusion, and Grae explained. "We aren't citizens of Fairica. Vox called us "guest workers," and our 'hosts,' men like Commander Vail, guarantee our good behavior in return for our service."

"Their requirements are simple," Cara said. "We do whatever they say. If we try to leave, they hunt us down and kill us. They're allowed to use 'constructive punishment' to assure our compliance." Cara's voice turned cold. "They have the nerve to insist that it's good for us, because we have places to live and food to eat and schools for our kids." She sniffed. "We get as much of that as they want to give us for as long as we do exactly what they say."

Grae shifted his shoulders abruptly. "I'd better go. It's almost time to pick them up."

When he was gone, Cara asked, "Has he told you about the fighting?" I shook my head. "The commander's newest idea is having Grae become a cage fighter. The commanders all love the sport—if that's what you call it—and it's become fashionable among them to have their own fighters." Her nostrils flared. "Kind of like a gamecock or a dog you train to provide entertainment for your friends."

I gestured at the door Grae had exited, my expression unbelieving. Grae didn't seem like a guy who'd want to fight.

“He doesn’t,” Cara said, reading my thought, “but the commander doesn’t care what Grae wants.”

As the week went on, I thought about what she’d said. Did Madame Vail know Grae and Cara and Mar were slaves? Did she approve? Why couldn’t they have their own tribe? How would Grae convince the commander he didn’t want to fight for the entertainment of his friends?

Our time at the capital ended with a gathering at the Mansion for the commanders, their families, and other dignitaries. I attended, feeling very out of place as photographers snapped stills and videographers followed our movements. Madame Vail was thrilled at the comments about her daughter and her lookalike companion. Friends and acquaintances oohed and aahed over our similarities and congratulated Madame on her goodness. “I knew you had a big heart,” one woman told her. “It’s so kind of you, taking in an unfortunate child and changing her life.”

The next day we returned to Eden. That afternoon when she came to clean, I noticed that Lucia’s right eye was swollen shut and bruised black. Pointing to it, I raised my palms, indicating I wanted an explanation.

“I had an accident.” Her words didn’t ring true, and I set a hand on her arm, signaling I wanted more. After a second of hesitation Lucia said, “I spilled the commander’s coffee and stained his sleeve.”

I was horrified. The commander had hit Lucia?

Seeing my expression, Lucia shook her head. “When a person doesn’t pay attention, bad things happen to her.” She returned to cleaning the windows in the terrace door, chattering about new kittens that had been born while I was away.

What gave the commander the right to hit Lucia? It wasn't fair, no matter how important he was.

What I'd heard from Grae and Cara and Lucia made me wonder exactly what my status was. Was I part of the Vail Tribe or was I, like my new friends, just another person they could order around?

PART II: AZALEA

Chapter Fourteen

You start out thinking life is okay, right? Then one day, and I guess that day comes at different times for everyone, you realize it isn't. You realize that the people around you, every single one of them, plead or push or poke to get you to do what they want, be what they want. Behind the happy family picnics and singalongs at the meeting hall, everyone, from upright citizens to loving relatives to complete assholes, are out to control you.

I was thirteen when I realized that. Even before, I knew some people, including my Grandmother, wished I were someone else—or wished I were some*where* else. Mother never explained why that was, because that would have meant crawling out of the shell she'd built around herself. But I saw people's eyes slide toward me when the pastor talked about the wages of sin. I felt their disapproval when I asked questions not considered proper for a female. And I heard snarky comments about spending resources on a girl who didn't belong. *Children live with their father's tribe, not their mother's. If she weren't Leader Woods' granddaughter…*

I couldn't be like other girls, and at some point I stopped trying. I resented being told what to do by men who were clearly not very smart. I hated having to say "Yes, sir," when they told me to stack the firewood the way they liked it rather than a way that made more sense. Grandmother harangued me with lectures on deportment. "We women choose to let our men lead us," she'd say. "The tribe recognizes that it's best for our children."

But the tribe wasn't great for me or for Milla. She was "imperfect," and too many assumed she was stupid just because she couldn't speak. And me? I was an outsider from Day One. I didn't look like them. I stuck out everywhere I went. Those who tried to be nice said dumb stuff like how lucky I was to not have to worry about getting sunburned. The ones who weren't nice said things that were downright mean. I learned to meet their eyes and stare until they got embarrassed and looked away. Few were brave enough to risk Grandfather's wrath by actually saying out loud that I should be kicked out of the tribe.

Rolf was. Uncle Rolf. Rolf the Heir. Rolf the Pedophile Bastard.

It was Rolf who informed me at the age of thirteen that my father had been a rebel who blew up innocent people because he held fanatical beliefs and came from a foreign background. My weak-minded mother had married him in a drug-induced haze, Rolf claimed. My "daddy" had gone to prison shortly after I was born. Mother had been headed that way too, but Grandfather's intervention had saved her. Back home, with the strong support of her family, Wendy Woods had learned to live like a normal person again, but she was stuck with a reminder of her wicked past. Me.

In return for those truths, Rolf raped me twice a week for almost three years. If I closed my eyes, I could still hear his voice in my head. *Come here to me, brown girl. Come be nice to your Uncle Rolf.*

I could have gone to Grandfather and told him what was happening, but I didn't. For one thing, tribal teaching said that women, though we were "weaker vessels," had great seductive powers over men. Sinful sex started when a woman tempted a man. Why else, it was argued, did God visit the punishment, a child with no legal father, on the female?

The other reason I kept quiet was Rolf's threat. If I didn't do as he wanted, he told me, he'd take my little sister. To make him leave Milla alone, I shut my eyes every time he touched me and counted it a victory. In fact, as Milla turned from a child to a young woman, my fears for her led me to actually work to keep Rolf's interest. I began our "relationship" as a reluctant amateur, but I learned to be, if not a polished seductress, at least a competent one. In time I used my skills on men other than my uncle, getting satisfaction from their infatuation with me and the kick I got from fooling Grandmother and Mother. I was not the good girl they'd raised me to be, but that was nobody's business but mine.

In those years, I felt utterly alone. Every sermon on lust seemed aimed directly at me. Every time Grandmother pursed her lips and commented on my improper demeanor, I wanted to shout, *Do you know what your son does to me on Mondays and Thursdays, when I'm supposedly cleaning his house?* There was no one I could talk to, no one I felt comfortable telling. Then one day I began helping Uncle Benny with record-keeping.

I came into Grandfather's office with a message from Grandmother and found him and Benny sorting through a mess of wet, sticky papers, shaking their heads as they tried to read blurred words and numbers. A careless cleaner had spilled bleach on the desktop, ruining the paperwork Benny had been doing for the tribe's end-of-year accounting. "All the information is written down somewhere else," he was telling Grandfather, "but it's taken me weeks to enter it on the correct forms, and now they're ruined."

"You'll have to redo them," Grandfather said.

"I will, but it will take at least a week, and the deadline is Friday."

"Three days." Grandfather's lips pulled in, covering his teeth. "Can one of the clerks help?"

Benny looked doubtful. "It will take someone who's really good with numbers."

"I can do it," I said before I could stop myself.

They both turned to me as if I'd said I could spin straw into gold. Benny's expression hinted I'd be told to go away and mind my little-girl business. But Grandfather said, "Azalea's always reading over my shoulder and asking me to explain this or that about our business. She's really smart." I waited for him to add, "for a girl," but he left it at that.

Benny frowned at me. "You like finance?"

I shrugged. "Numbers make sense to me. Way more than people do."

"In what way?"

Though I'd known him all my life, Benny was a stranger to me. A loner, he lived in a small house outside of town. He went to church, as the law required, but usually left without speaking to anyone. He didn't attend parties or barbeques or music nights. Since I didn't know what he wanted to hear, I told him how I felt. "People change," I said. "Laws are subject to interpretation. Words have different meanings to different people. But numbers are what they are. They either add up or they don't."

In the silence that followed, I felt myself blushing. After a moment Benny said, "All right, Azalea. Let's see if you and I can get this done."

"Grandfather," I said, "will you send word to Uncle Rolf? Tell him I'm needed here so I can't clean his house today."

Benny and I got the work done and submitted on time. He said I had a gift for business, and as we worked, he taught me about spreadsheets, percentiles, projections, and operational systems. He was smarter than anyone I'd met before and always willing to answer my questions. When I frowned he'd explain again, using different words, until I got it.

Once when Grandfather was out, Benny and I were checking each other's figures with a couple of calculators. "Before the Govt took over," he said, "All of this would have been done by computers. They saved us a lot of dog work."

I was surprised to hear him speak approvingly of the long-banned devices. "It's too bad they got to be dangerous."

Benny gave me an odd look, and for a moment I felt very, very young. But all he said was, "Yes, I suppose it is."

When we finished the end of year reports, Benny found more work for me to do. Soon I became a fixture at the office. There were raised eyebrows, but Grandfather allowed it, claiming I showed real talent for the work. For once I was grateful the leader could do whatever he liked.

After a month or so, Benny and I could almost read each other's minds, at least as far as numbers were concerned. He started making jokes only I would get. (*Why do plants hate math? It gives them square roots.*) When I made mistakes, he caught them and showed me how to avoid them in the future. In time, the uncle I'd thought of as distant and odd became the closest thing I had to a friend. Though I tortured myself with fears that one day he'd touch my cheek or "accidentally" bump my breast and ruin everything, he never did.

"You have the perfect mind for numbers," he told me once. "You could easily be an accountant."

I was comfortable enough by then to give him a sarcastic eyeroll. "Have you noticed that I'm female?"

He shook his head. "What a waste we've made of talent in this new time."

"You think girls should be allowed to be accountants?"

"I do, and you're more than halfway there already."

I sighed. "What good is it? I'll never really be one."

"You'll know that you're capable," he replied, "and I've made sure Father knows. Who can say what might happen?"

In the year we worked together, as trust developed between us, Benny told me how corrupt and self-serving our Govt was. He showed me how he protected our tribe, first by backing up every record and second by providing a little "extra" for the officials who came to inspect our books. He called them *satraps*, a word I had to look up. "They're supposed to be loyal to Vox, but self-interest tends to win when there's little risk of getting caught."

In my ignorance, I thought Benny would be happier if he socialized with others. When I suggested he should come and hear the family band, he only smiled. "I don't think I will, Azalea, but it's kind of you to think of me."

Then one day he went out into the woods and didn't return. While most men of the tribe hunted and fished, some with more passion than they showed to their families, I'd never known Benny to be interested in such pursuits. When he was missed, they went looking and found his body. A tragic accident, they said. While climbing between the strands of a barbed wire fence, he'd accidentally discharged his rifle. The bullet had gone through his head, killing him instantly.

With my beloved uncle dead, my despised uncle stepped in as heir to tribal leadership. Rolf made it clear he thought I should be sent back to women's work, but even though (maybe because) his mind was failing, Grandfather insisted I continue as bookkeeper. Using what Benny had taught me, I made myself indispensable to the tribe.

Grandmother must have seen her husband's struggles—the long pauses, the wrong word choices, the general vagueness in speech—but she never let on. Mother probably noticed too, at least when she came out of her funk long enough to pay attention. He told the same stories over and over. He forgot what he'd said three minutes ago. On days when his mind worked as it should, he pushed himself to get lots done. I knew he sensed there were worse days coming.

I continued balancing columns and drafting reports, but I also began writing out what Grandfather needed to say at meetings. I used the words he'd have used if he were well, and with the notes, written in large print so he could read them easily, he usually did okay. Grandmother took to standing beside him when he performed his duties, and I'd see her mouth move as she reminded him what came next.

When the news came that Grandfather was dead, I knew I couldn't stay. My understanding of the tribe's business meant Rolf would need to get rid of me, probably by arranging a marriage to some man outside the tribe. I wasn't sure what he'd do with Milla, but knowing it wouldn't be good, I convinced her to run away with me.

Though I made mistakes along the way, we did all right until the night the train crashed.

I woke with a splitting headache and a bandage on my forehead. The view out the window told me I was at least three stories off the ground. A row of beds containing female patients stretched on either side of me, many sleeping, one talking with a visitor, a couple gazing into space. Men in scrubs moved around the room, checking readings, changing dressings, and writing on charts hung at the foot of each bed.

“Good, you’re awake.” The man wore a white smock. The bell of the stethoscope he wore around his neck was tucked into the top pocket. His brown hair, overlong and kind of droopy, hung over his face, making it look like an animal was trapped up there. When he got close I read his badge: *Derek Kazinski, Medical Resident.* Though he was older than I was by at least five years, the impression I got was one of innocence. His examination of me was so carefully non-threatening that I almost chuckled. Up close I saw places where he’d missed spots while shaving, and there was a button missing from the cuff of the plaid shirt he wore under the smock. I guessed that Derek lived alone, and I realized that he was impressed with me to the point of being tongue-tied.

His step back from my bed was almost military in its execution. “You, um, look much improved this morning. Do you remember what happened?”

It came back in a rush: Milla and I trying to find my father, the train, and the crash that had sent me sliding into the metal sidewall. “Train crashed,” I replied. “When was that?”

“A week ago. You had a concussion, so you’ve been doing a lot of sleeping. Any pain? Headache? Neck stiffness?”

“No.”

“Good. We found no signs of permanent damage, so now it’s just a matter of letting yourself heal for a while.”

“I was traveling with my si…” I caught myself. “…sibling. Do you know anything about that?”

He glanced vaguely around the room. “I can ask if anyone came in with you.” He returned in only minutes, his expression grave. “I’m sorry. The girl who was with you died in the accident. From what I understand—” He went on, but all that registered was that

Milla was dead. My little sister, the only person left on earth who'd truly cared about me.

I felt my chin quiver, and tears flowed down my cheeks. The doctor put a hand on my shoulder, a clumsy attempt at comfort. Recovering control took a while. He offered cheap, scratchy tissues from a nearby box, and I used four of them to mop my nose and eyes. Clearing his throat, he said, "I'm sorry to distress you further, but there's a problem with your identity tattoo. We were required to report it to the Govt, so now that you're awake, an agent will be coming in to interview you."

Another blow. If—when—my tat was found to be fake, bad things would happen. Being on the train illegally suggested I was a renegade and a criminal. There was real possibility I'd be executed, my body tossed into a waste pit and forgotten. After all, who cared what happened to a disobedient, disconnected female?

The doctor didn't press me about my identity, but he did hang around for a while. I performed all the tests he set for me, pressing against his hand with mine and letting him test the reflexes in my legs. I'd returned to normal function, he told me, and aside from ten stitches at my hairline, I was probably fine. While I thanked him for his encouragement, there was no way Doctor Derek could know how not fine my life was. I was in all kinds of trouble, and I was responsible for the death of my sister. I would never forgive myself for that.

As the doctor had predicted, a man with a clipboard entered the ward later that day and stopped, running his gaze over each woman there with a purposeful air. He wore a black t-shirt with a padded vest over it that said *MONC AGENT* across the chest in large yellow letters. He was festooned with weapons and devices I had no explanation for. His hair was covered with a knitted hat, so I couldn't see its color. Sunglasses hid his eyes, despite the fact that he was inside.

As the Monkey Man homed in on me, the other women nearby found ways to avoid making eye contact. One I'd talked to an hour earlier sent me a single pitying glance and then closed her eyes, pretending to be asleep. Though I'd never seen one before, the Govt enforcers struck fear into the hearts of everyday people. This one had come to ask me questions I didn't know how to answer.

"Warman 2nd Rank Moline," he said by way of introduction. "Your tat won't scan, so I'm here to determine your placement." Taking out a pen, he asked, "Tribe?"

I had decided to stick to my original story, which went with the fake tat Stanley had provided. "Goodman. We sell and service farm equipment all over the Green Section. I'm not sure what's wrong with my ID."

He looked me over, his glance lingering briefly on my breasts. "There's no record of you in that tribe."

"It must be a mistake." If I could delay discovery of the truth for a day, or even a few hours, I'd be gone. Pretending to be struck with a possible reason, I said, "We got a new clerk last month. Maybe he didn't know how to find the record."

Moline wrote that down. "What are you doing so far from your area?"

My best bet was to play Silly Female. "My sister and I thought it would be fun to ride a train, but we didn't realize we wouldn't be able to get out once we got in." I let my voice turn breathless. "We called and called, but no one heard. Then we crashed." I didn't have to fake grief as I added, "My sister died."

"So I heard." His gaze kept dropping away from my eyes and down to my chest.

In an attempt to distract his attention from me, I asked, “How did the accident happen?”

“Saboteurs.” Moline raised his shoulders in an angry shrug. “We do our best to catch them, but we can’t predict where they’ll strike next.”

“Why would they wreck a train and hurt innocent people?”

He huffed dramatically. “There was a VIP aboard.” Shifting his feet, Moline said, “I’ll contact the Goodman Tribe directly. If you’re theirs, and if they’ll pay transport, you’ll be returned home. What happens after that is up to them.” He didn’t say what would happen if the tribe refused to acknowledge me, but I was relieved to know I wouldn’t be hauled outside immediately and shot.

When Moline left, I took stock of the situation. He’d learn, probably within hours, that the Goodman Tribe had no idea who I was. Then my fate would be up to the Monkey Men. Before that happened, I had to get as far away as possible.

Climbing out of bed, I closed the curtain around it. In a cabinet I found the clothes I’d been wearing and put them on, despite a large bloodstain on one shoulder of the dress. I left my hair loose, so that it hid most of the stain.

By the time I was dressed I felt light-headed, but I was desperate to get out of there. I sat down on the bed to put on my shoes. After few minutes of rest, I’d walk out of the hospital as if I were a departing visitor. My heart sank when I looked up and saw Doctor Derek peeping through the curtains.

“What are you doing?” His tone was low, which boded well for secrecy.

“I’m—I lied to a Monkey Man,” I told him. “I need to get out of here before he comes back.”

He thought about that. “You’re a runaway?”

“I’m, uh, switching tribes.”

“Without permission from your current one.”

“Well, yes.” Meeting his gaze, I ran a hand over my breasts. “Help me, Derek, and I’ll do whatever you want.”

His expression revealed anticipation, and I guessed I’d soon have a safe place to stay until I was steady on my feet. The bargain I proposed to Derek brought Milla to mind. My little sister’s death was tragic, but at least now she’d never know the awful things I’d done to get my way.

Despite my hatred for Rolf, I had two reasons to be grateful to him. First, I didn’t have to worry about getting pregnant, no matter who I gave myself to. Second, he’d helped me see my body as a way to get what I wanted from men. I’d been very careful with my choices. I’d never had sex with the men of my tribe, at least not until I needed Stanley’s help with our tattoos. With men I met outside our tribe, sometimes at fairs and other times on business for Grandfather, I’d managed the same way I tolerated Rolf’s pawing. In my mind, I traveled to a place where I was alone. It was warm there, and the landscape was completely different from Woodsburg. Strange birds croaked odd songs, a breeze brushed my skin, and the sky was a different blue. That way I ignored the sweating face hovering above me, whether Rolf’s or some other man’s.

It took Derek less than five seconds to make a plan. “Put the hospital gown back on,” he ordered. “I’ll bring a wheelchair and take you out like you’re going for tests.” He looked around. “Do you have belongings?”

“I had a knapsack. Dark red with black arrows stitched onto the front.”

"I'll see if I can find it. Wait here."

While he was gone, I had a brief argument with myself. Could I trust him? The lust I'd seen in his eyes argued that I could. Derek knew how to get me out of the hospital. That was good. He'd take me to his home, which would give me time to figure out what to do next. Putting the hospital gown over my bloody dress, I laid a blanket over my lap and sat on the bed, waiting.

Soon Derek was back with a loud, way-too-cheerful comment about taking me to X-ray. While he wasn't good at subterfuge, it didn't seem like anyone paid much attention. When he helped me stand and pivot to the chair, his hand briefly cupped my breast. Seeing he'd found my knapsack and hung it on the chair handles, I looked up at him and smiled.

Derek pushed me along the ward, down a hallway, and onto a long ramp. "There's an elevator," he said, "but it hardly ever works." On the second floor we went down another hallway to a ramp that took us to the ground floor. Pushing a door open with one hip, Derek turned the chair and pulled me outside. Bright natural light caused me to wince, but he pointed at a cream-colored car parked next to three large trash bins. "We're going over there."

Pushing the chair to the car, Derek opened the back door and helped me inside. "Stay down. Maybe take a nap. I've got to finish my shift."

The seat was hot from the sun, but I did as he said. Derek set my pack on the floor beside me. "About three hours," he said before he closed the car door.

When he was gone, I again weighed my options. I could walk away and leave my rescuer behind, but I was still wobbly on my feet and besides, I had no idea where I was. I shouldn't try to navigate an unknown burg alone and dizzy.

Alone. Tears came again then, tears for my situation and tears for Milla, for the life she'd never have and the loss her death meant for me.

I was sleeping when Derek returned, and I let out a yelp of surprise when the door opened. "Shh!" he cautioned, looking around anxiously. "I brought food." He got in up front.

Accepting the bag he handed over the seat, I took out a chicken salad sandwich, potato chips, and a cold soda called Dr. Pepper. I was so hungry that I ate the sandwich without stopping to remove the pickles.

As he drove, I asked Derek where we were. "This is Dunhamsburg," he told me, "but you'll see people from everywhere. The Dunhams manufacture industrial equipment. Other tribes have contracts to come into their burg and provide services. At first those people lived around the edges of the city, but it became more convenient for the Dunhams to let them live inside their boundaries."

"I've been through a few big burgs, and it seemed like the tribes were starting to mingle there too."

I saw his shoulders rise and fall. "The Govt wants us to remain separate, but it's hard to enforce. Take me, for example. I'm here to study medicine, and I have to live somewhere. Even though it's on the Dunham land-hold, my apartment building rents mostly to students like me." Derek gave me an over-his-shoulder grin. "You'll be safe there. Medical students are so exhausted from the wicked long hours we work that we don't even notice who comes and goes."

The apartment, a fourth-floor walkup in an ugly metal and concrete building, wasn't nearly as attractive as the Jefferson's had been. I said it was really nice.

“Student stipends are skimpy,” he told me, “but once I get my medical license, I’ll make good money. Twenty hours a week working for the tribe combined with a private practice will make me very comfortable.”

“Good for you,” I said, putting on a smile. “Now tell me what kind of girl you like.”

My time with Derek wasn’t bad. He was clean, he didn’t demand anything weird, and he had a TV. I was dizzy the first few days, so sitting still was about all I wanted to do. Though I’d seen TVs, I’d never actually controlled one before. Derek showed me how to turn it on and off and find different channels. Though I spent a lot of time in his big reclining chair, I did leg lifts and arm exercises, determined to get in shape for when I could hit the road again.

Television was fascinating at first. I could watch dramas, comedies, and informative programs any time of the day or night. The thrill faded when I realized that other than the daily news, the shows were decades old and chosen to represent what the Govt considered good family values, like *Bonanza, Gunsmoke, Little House on the Prairie,* and *The Waltons*. In old police dramas like *Dragnet* and *Highway Patrol*, the stories were sometimes choppy. Derek said that was because they’d been censored to remove references to divorce or infidelity, which were considered unacceptable for children.

News shows focused on Vox’s latest successes in crime-fighting, cost-cutting, and business growth. Prominent tribal leaders were praised for building unity. I watched a beauty pageant where ten attractive women of about my age told the interviewer they couldn’t wait to marry and become the mothers of strong sons and virtuous daughters. A science documentary presented the accepted truth that Man was caregiver for the earth, expected by God to make choices about how to use its resources. "Some must die so Man can live" was the conclusion reached.

Probably due to Uncle Benny's influence, I saw that it was all designed to convince the public that things were great and couldn't possibly be any better. Bland-faced men spoke often of how happy the citizens of Fairica were. Though our progress was the envy of the world, they claimed, Vox had chosen to close our borders to outsiders. Foreigners were innately untrustworthy, and they told vicious lies about Fairica.

In the end I turned off the TV and set about cleaning Derek's apartment. He kept it fairly neat, but when I looked into the corners and under the bed, I saw a need for a good scrubbing. That I could address, thanks to Grandmother's training.

By the fifth day at Derek's place, I was feeling healthy again. I also sensed that he wanted me gone. While he certainly enjoyed the sex, I noticed he kept the curtains closed throughout the apartment, all the time. When he left for work, he'd peep out the door first to be sure no one got a look inside. Clearly he was nervous about harboring a runaway. Because he was a nice guy, he didn't suggest outright that it was time for me to go. I questioned him at length about the area, aware that once I left, I'd be completely on my own.

There'd been a minor outcry when I disappeared from the hospital, Derek said. Their closed-circuit cameras hadn't worked for months, so our exit hadn't been recorded. The Monkey Man had been furious to find me gone, but he'd seemed to think no one on staff would have been brave enough to help a fugitive escape. "They'll soon lose interest in you," Derek predicted. "There are lots of runaways in the cities these days, and the Govt's record for catching them gets worse every year."

"Why is that?"

He grimaced. "Mostly because the test for getting a Govt job is loyalty to Vox, which doesn't attract the most competent men. Add to that the need for Monkey Men to ignore cruelty and injustice, and the choices are limited."

"It sounds like you don't think things are going well in Fairica."

"I guess it depends." He set one hand out, palm up. "Tribes that produce a good product or provide a necessary service do okay as long as they keep their expenses low. But the poorer tribes and even a lot of the ones in the middle are floundering. My church does outreach twice a month, so I've visited tribes where food is in short supply and disease runs rampant. They have no programs to help their members, because they just don't have the money."

Derek's observations made me angry at our Govt, but I also felt lucky to have been raised in the Woods Tribe. Everyone mattered back home, at least they had under Grandfather's leadership. Whatever his failings, Ben Woods had seen to the sick and the disabled. He'd encouraged education, at least his version of it. The character of the leader colors the lives of every individual, whether in a tribe or in a nation.

We just didn't have enough great leaders.

When he set off to work on the fifth morning, his shirt button back in place and his hair trimmed to a more attractive style, I didn't tell Derek I was leaving. Though we'd done all right together, we hadn't formed a real bond. When he returned and found me gone, all he'd miss was the convenient, nightly sex.

I'd chosen a Saturday, hoping the toppers would be too busy on a weekend to watch for one renegade girl. Putting on my modest dress, which I'd managed to wash clean of bloodstains, I did my best to make myself look like an upstanding citizen, pinning my hair up and slapping the dust off my backpack. A search of Derek's desk netted me an outdated travel pass in a plastic sleeve, which I hung on my belt so from a distance I'd appear legitimate. In the corner of a desk drawer I found a little ball compass. Just after eleven a.m., I left the apartment, consulting the compass every once in a while to make sure I was heading southward.

As I left my place of sanctuary, it felt like I'd lost track of my plan and my path. Partly that was because I was for the first time all alone in my journey. I tried not to dwell on Milla and how much I missed her. I'd dragged her away from the home she loved, forced her to live like a wild bird, eating what we could forage and flitting from place to place, and then gotten her killed. What kind of sister does that?

The temperature was warm, not like at home, where October meant jacket weather most mornings. Trying to look like I belonged, I walked briskly along the sidewalk as the city buzzed and bumped around me. I got used to the traffic again, following the lead of the pedestrians around me, walking when they walked and pausing when they paused.

Store after store offered clothing, furniture, food, appliances, and more as I passed. City people had a much wider choice of goods than we'd had in Woodsburg, but they also had to contend with noise, traffic, and a much faster pace. Surrounded by concrete and bricks, I found myself missing things like weeds. How often had I walked past a tuft of Queen Anne's Lace and ignored its delicate perfection? How many milkweed pods had I split open as a kid, brushing the soft scales with a finger and watching them fly away on the breeze? How many times had I been ordered to pull grapevine from Grandmother's maple trees for fear it would strangle them? As I walked the hard sidewalks of the city, I couldn't even see a tree, much less rescue one.

"Are you lost?" The voice made me jump, and I turned to find a woman looking at me questioningly. I'd stopped on the sidewalk, gazing into space and muttering to myself. "I thought there was a bus station around here," I replied. "I must have turned the wrong way."

"It's two blocks that way." She pointed. "Turn left at the next corner and keep going until you see it on your right."

I smelled the buses before I actually saw them. Three long, gray hulks idled at the front of the property while several others sat parked at the back. A large bulletin board on the station wall held a map and gave departure times. One of them made me whisper, "Yes!" A bus would head southwest to a place called Wellsburg in less than two hours.

The news reignited my determination to be on my way, but I still had problems to solve. Derek had said long-haul bus drivers were required to check for travel passes for everyone who boarded, and they had to be specific to the bus route. In addition to that, tickets weren't free. I no longer had money or the jewelry I'd planned to trade with. I couldn't even offer sex in exchange for a ride, since the drivers were on duty and on a schedule.

Maybe if I hung around, I'd get a chance to steal a pass for Wellsburg. I went inside the station, which was comfortable in a commercial kind of way. People waited, some pacing, some napping, some watching a large TV mounted overhead on the wall. It was tuned to the national news, and the seat I took faced it, so my eye was drawn to what was being shown. Wherever the story was coming from was colder than here. People wore coats as they exited limousines at some event, and I saw them button or zip up as the wind hit them. I watched idly for a few seconds but then, frowning, I leaned forward to get a better look. Either my quick movement or an involuntary sound I made caused a woman beside me to look up from her knitting and ask, "What?"

I pointed at the TV screen. "Do you know where that's happening?"

She looked up and shrugged, revealing disinterest. "They're at Capital Center, celebrating the anniversary of the TRA. The final event is a luncheon at the Vox Mansion for the commanders and their families."

More cars pulled up before the elaborate home, each dropping off a man, woman, and a number of children. Each man shepherded his family to the portico and then turned to face the cameras. When all four groups were in place, Vox emerged, wearing a double-breasted overcoat and gloves and leaning on a gold-topped cane. He gave a short speech of welcome. While I'd seen pictures of him, I'd never seen him live. He was shorter than I'd envisioned. Older too.

"We're here to celebrate seventeen years of success," he told the crowd. "Eighteen years ago, I accepted the task of repairing a nation torn in two by conflict, ruined by economic collapse, and decimated by rebellion. With the help of the commanders present with us today, I worked tirelessly to bring us back from the brink. My greatest achievement, I believe, was the Tribal Reorganization Act. With it came a return to unity, a return to prosperity, and a return to peace."

"As long as you don't rock the boat," a man near me muttered. Realizing he'd spoken aloud, he took on an apologetic tone. "I don't mean what Vox did was bad. We needed a strong man back then, but now they could let us have more say."

"We have a say," a woman objected. "We tell our leaders what we need. They tell the commanders."

"Who only listen when they want to," the man argued. "Our leader wants to stop making people get vaccinations, but the Govt said if he does, our stipends will get cut."

"That's only fair," a man farther down the row said. "If your tribe isn't willing to act for the good of everyone, you shouldn't share in the nation's bounty."

The first man lapsed into angry silence. I returned my attention to the TV screen.

"Building the nation of Fairica has not been easy," Vox was saying. "Our place in the world is still threatened by those who tell lies about us, and those who willfully misunderstand our policies. Here is my pledge to you. I will not weaken my resolve in order to receive the approval of strangers. We have the right to govern ourselves as we see fit."

He went on, but none of it interested me much. I was waiting for the camera to pan so I could confirm or deny what I thought I'd seen earlier. Finally Vox finished speaking, and the people standing on the steps of the Mansion began filing inside. There, with a stern-looking man, a beautiful woman, and a girl of about her age, was my sister Milla. She had one arm in a cast, and she looked uncomfortable at being the center of attention, but she was undeniably alive.

"You okay?" The woman was regarding me with concern, and I guessed I'd spoken aloud. I hoped I hadn't let loose with one of Grandfather's curse words.

"I—I thought I saw a person I knew on the TV."

She smiled at the ridiculousness of that statement. How would I, with my scuffed shoes and worn dress, know any of the luminaries present at a national event? Rising, I left the station. No question now of taking a bus to Wellsburg. I would delay my search for my father to take on a different one: finding Milla and learning why I'd been told she was dead.

Chapter Fifteen

To get out of the flow of foot traffic on the sidewalk, I turned into the first alley I found. Halfway down, I dropped my bag on the ground and sank down atop it so I could think about how to proceed. It appeared that Milla was living with one of Fairica's commanders, but aside from the one who ran our section, Commander Dunn, I didn't know one from another. I did know they were required to live in their sections. That meant the family I'd seen on the TV would leave the capital when the festivities ended. Where would my sister be going?

"What are you doing down there, Missy?"

I looked up to see a stout, dark-haired man blocking the alley entrance. He was dressed in gray, with a gold badge pinned to his shirt. His pants were a slightly darker shade, and his gray hat matched them exactly. A patch on the hat had gold lettering: *TOP.* For a second I berated myself for not choosing a spot out of sight from the street. Taking a few steps into the alley, the topper stopped and tapped his toe, impatient for an answer.

"A man was following me," I improvised. "I ducked in here to get away from him."

"Haven't seen you before." The topper's narrow eyes got even narrower. "Come here and show me your tat."

I froze, unsure what to do, but a hoarse voice called from the street, "Hey, Top! How are your hemorrhoids today?"

Looking past the officer, I saw a guy of about my age standing at the alley entry. He bounced lightly on his feet, as if unwilling, or maybe unable, to remain still. His appearance suggested he'd put on whatever came out of a charity bag, loose pants, a shirt with the sleeves cut off, leaving ragged edges, and a necktie in pinks and purples. His red hair floated around his head like a cloud of fire, and his shoes were blotched with paint of every color imaginable. The expression on his plain, freckled face revealed pure joy at the confrontation he'd initiated and clearly intended to continue.

"Dak!" the topper made it a swearword. "I've warned you…"

"Oh, right," the boy interrupted. "Dak, don't bother the nice topper while he's doing his job. Dak, don't call the toppers Bargain Basement Monkey Men. Dak, don't make Topper Belham run. It makes his ass hurt."

The topper's face went purple with rage. Turning away from the guy, he slid one hand behind his back, and I saw him draw his stunner from its holster. His index finger found the trigger, and his fist closed firmly around the grip. Taking two apparently casual steps toward the young man, he said, "You're a smart-mouthed little bastard."

Apparently Dak knew exactly how this would go. Despite the danger he faced, his expression revealed enjoyment. Dancing on his toes and throwing air punches like a boxer preparing for a fight, he egged the officer on. "And smarter than you and all your buddies put together, Top."

The topper took another step toward him, still trying to make his approach seem casual. I felt a touch on my arm and turned to see a girl every bit as raggedy as Dak leaning down next to me. She jerked a thumb over her shoulder, indicating I should go with her.

Pushing myself to my feet, I grabbed my bag and trailed her down the alley. Sensing my movement, the topper turned and saw that he had to decide which of us to chase. His anger toward Dak must have won, because as the girl and I rounded a corner and started down a narrow street, no footsteps pounded behind us. We turned onto a larger street and ran for a few blocks before my rescuer ducked into a second alley. I stopped, stymied, when we came to a fence, but she climbed it like a cat and then turned to offer her hand to help me scale it. As soon as I landed on the other side she took off again, tossing a reassuring grin over her shoulder.

We ran on, both puffing after a while, until we came to a ramshackle neighborhood full of old, empty buildings. At a doorway that appeared to be boarded up, the girl slid her hand behind a board and lifted a hidden latch. Another grin hinted at her enjoyment of the surprise she was providing. Both the door and the boards nailed across it swung outward, allowing access. Urging me inside with a gesture, she followed and latched the door behind us.

We stood in the dark for a moment, letting our eyes adjust and our breathing slow to normal. Resting my hands on my thighs, I raised my head to look around. At least fifty sewing machines, much larger versions of Grandmother's Singer, sat in a block at the center of the large room. Huge windows on the second and third floors must once have provided light for the workers, but years of neglect had left them almost opaque. Along the walls were rows and rows of empty shelves. This had once been a factory, I realized, one of many that had closed during the Old Times and never re-opened. I tried to imagine the place as it had once been, humming with the sound of shuffling feet and industrial motors. Vox had promised a return to prosperity for everyone, but that obviously hadn't extended to this place. Every surface was coated with grime. Looters had taken anything useful, leaving behind the heavy machines, scattered papers, and bits of metal and string. I smelled old rubber, dust, and urine.

With a gesture, my rescuer indicated our destination, a spiral staircase at the back of the building. She led the way up it, her feet almost silent on the metal treads. I followed, noting she had more energy than her slim body and pale complexion would have led me to expect. We entered what had once been an office, with a desk, filing cabinets that were spotted with corrosion, and an office chair that tilted badly. Openings overlooking the floor below on three sides called to mind a manager monitoring his workforce by watching from above. A second glance made me choose a different pronoun. On a coatrack in a corner, matted now with dust and insect carcasses, was an umbrella, pink with a black ruffle along its edge. On the door, a battered but still-readable sign said, *Angela Voorhies, General Manager, EasyWear Shoes. She* had looked down on *her* workforce.

Sweaty from fear and exertion, I followed the girl's lead and slid to the floor. We examined each other silently for a few seconds. My savior had pale blue eyes, thin lips, and sandy eyebrows. She wore a sack-like dress with a hole near the hem that had probably resulted from a brush with a protruding nail. Her hair was tied up in a kerchief, but strands of deep auburn showed at the neck. With the red hair came freckles, lots of them. Like Dak, she wore athletic shoes painted with wild designs and bright colors. I guessed they'd found a supply of EasyWear shoes that had escaped earlier looters and personalized them to their own satisfaction.

After a few seconds I whispered, "What about Dak?"

She waved away my concern. "He'll be along."

Almost as she said it there he was, grinning and hardly out of breath. "Once you get to know Dak the Magnificent, you'll never doubt me again." Stepping forward, he held out a hand. "And you are?"

I remembered the name on my tattoo. "Amanda."

Dak's grin got wider. "You don't look like an Amanda to me, but it's as good an alias as any." He didn't bother to ask my tribe and make me lie a second time. "I'm Dak of the O'Donnell Tribe, which is and isn't a tribe. We're kind of magical." He gestured at the girl. "This is Frieda, of the same tribe."

"I can introduce myself, Dak." Her tone was petulant. "Don't be playing the host and shit."

Dak rolled his eyes at me. "Our Frieda is a bit of a Libber." At my look of confusion he explained, "One who believes that females are every bit as useful to the world as males are." Tossing her an impish glance, he added, "She might be right, but don't tell her I said so."

Frieda examined me, frowning. "I suppose you were taught that women are nothing but baby machines."

I found myself wanting to impress this odd, ragged girl. "I was told that, but I have ears, eyes, and a brain, so it didn't work."

A nod said Frieda approved of my answer. Though she interested me, Dak was a talker. "We saw you were in trouble with Topper Belham, so we did our thing."

"Thanks for that. It was brave."

"Fun," he corrected, raising a finger. "And we're always looking for fun."

"You harass toppers on purpose?"

Dak batted his eyes. "Only every time we get the chance."

"Why?"

He spread his hands as if the answer were obvious. "Because they're assholes."

“Oh.” That was true at home too. Men generally applied to be toppers because they enjoyed ordering others around.

“We don’t have any land of our own,” Frieda explained, “so our tribe gets shit from every topper in the area.”

“You’re a tribe but you have no land?”

“We had land once,” Dak said. “Then our leader disagreed with stuff the Govt was doing. He stood up to them, said we had the right to be heard. The Govt said, ‘No, you don’t.’ They had him shot, and then they took away our tribal status as a warning to everybody else.”

“I didn’t think they could do that.”

“They kinda make up the rules as they go.” Frowning at the wall behind me, Dak said, “We were meant to be builders, but these days the only work an O’Donnell can get is collecting garbage, killing rats, or clearing clogged sewers.”

“That’s not fair.”

“Like I said: They’re assholes.” He sang the last part and danced across the room. Dak seemed different from any male I’d met before, with no sense of the “manliness” I’d been told came with facial hair and outdoor plumbing.

When a scrape sounded downstairs, he crouched quickly beside me, putting a finger to his lips. We waited in silence as footsteps scraped on the tile floor below: a half dozen and a pause, another half dozen and another pause. Belham or one of his fellow toppers was down there, listening for a clue to our presence. I worried he’d hear my heart beating like a drum in my chest. Dak and Frieda seemed calm, though they squatted on their haunches, ready to run if necessary.

After a while, the steps retreated and the door slammed shut. Dak rose, peered out the glassless window to the factory floor, and then did a little dance of joy that ended with a flourish, one hand up high, the other low. "Belham hates stairs," he said by way of explanation. "Give it a few minutes so we know he's gone, and then you can be on your way."

His casual suggestion filled me with dread. While I had no claim on these odd people, I felt safe in their company. It was hard to think I'd soon be on my own again.

"Don't be an ass, Dak," Frieda said. "Can't you see she hasn't got anywhere to go?"

He leaned close, his brows questioning. I smelled peanuts on his breath. He saw something in my eyes. "Okay," he said, flopping onto the floor beside me. "Tell us your story. How'd you get here? How'd you hurt your head? Where are you going?" Then he sang, softly in case the topper was still around, "What Are You Doing the Rest of Your Life?"

"My sister and I were on a train that derailed. We got separated, and the people at the hospital where I was taken told me she was killed. Less than an hour ago, I saw her on TV." My last words came out in a tearful waver. "I have to find her."

Dak pointed at the travel pass on my belt. "I take it that's not yours."

"No. I, um, borrowed it from a guy I met."

"Let me see." Taking the pass out of its sleeve, I handed it over. Dak squinted as he sounded out. "De-rek Ku-zin-ski, med-i-cal res-i-dent." With another of his giggles, he said, "Good gravy, Amanda! It's a wonder you got this far."

I tried to smile. "A girl does what she has to."

Frieda frowned. "How old are you?"

If my calculations were right, I'd had a birthday since we left home. "Eighteen."

"Then you're a woman, not a girl. Don't belittle yourself."

"I wasn't—"

"No sense arguing with Frieda," Dak warned. "She's convinced we need to go back to the Old Times."

"I know things were different for women then," I said. "We had jobs and bank accounts."

"Yes." Frieda nodded enthusiastically. "We were pilots, doctors, fashion designers—anything we wanted to be."

"My grandmother was a school superintendent, but when I asked her about it once, she said it was a mistake."

Frieda nodded. "Women have learned to believe—or pretend to believe—they never wanted to be anything but wives and mothers." She pointed a finger at me. "If you ask me, they gave in way too easily." After a second she added, "Not my mother though. She never stopped fighting the patriarchy."

"Where's your mother now?"

"Dead." Her tone suggested she didn't want to talk about it.

Dak turned to practicalities. "What are we going to do with Amanda, Frieda?"

"I bet Walter could find her sister."

He frowned. "Do you think he would?"

"He will if you ask him to."

"You're probably right." Dak raised a finger dramatically. "Then as soon as it's safe, we're off to see the Wizard."

We stayed in the old factory until it was dark outside. Dak led the way, I followed, and Frieda brought up the rear. We slipped through alleys and down deserted streets until we came to the downtown area, where people who were much better dressed than my new friends arrived in cars and went into softly-lit restaurants for dinner. Though a few of them glanced at us slant-ways, no one acknowledged our presence. "That's how it is for the O'Donnells," Dak said softly. "They tolerate us 'cuz we're useful, but nobody gets too close."

I had noticed their strong, unpleasant odor, which I guessed was due to the work they did and a lack of bathing opportunities. Dak greeted others of his tribe as we passed along. Most were tattered and silent, moving in the slumped posture of the chronically exhausted. I wondered how long Dak and Frieda would maintain their exuberance in the face of poverty and hopelessness.

"Why didn't the other tribes step up and defend you?" We'd stopped behind a dumpster to avoid a topper patrol car.

Dak scratched at his head. "If the Powers-That-Be can convince *most* of the people that *some* of the people deserve what happens to them, they've got themselves a scapegoat. Since our troubles, we get blamed for all the local crime. The toppers and the Monkey Men are violent with us, because, don't you know, that's all creeps like us understand." Dak peered around the trash bin and then jerked his head back. "I bet there are shit tribes in other places too. Authority needs someone to blame for everything. Ba-a-a-ad men." With a grin for Frieda, he added, "Bad women too, of course."

The patrol car finally drove off, and we moved on, Dak in the lead and Frieda and I following behind like baby ducks. Our destination was only a few blocks farther, an old cinder-block building in the center of a well-lit area. Though it was large, the structure had once been larger. One whole wing had been reduced to rubble, probably by a bomb. Though the damage wasn't recent, that part had been left a ruin. Walled off with plywood and left to decay, its roof and upper stories had caved in on themselves.

The remaining two-thirds of the building was intact, and I saw lights on inside. Reading the sign over the doorway, *Fairica Institute of Citizenry and Govt, Rose Section,* I stopped short. Had Dak and Frieda rescued me from the toppers only to turn me over to the Monkey Men? "What's this?"

Dak gave one of his giggles and swatted me on the arm. "*This* is where Walter lives."

"In a Govt building?"

"Can you think of a better spot for a wanted man to hide than in the bad guys' basement?"

"Where's the stuff?" Frieda asked.

"In the ceiling in the park restroom." To me he said, "We're going in as repairmen, but I only have two outfits."

"I'll wait out here." Frieda frowned at the gray structure. "That place gives me the creeps anyway."

Through an open gate was a pleasant little park with a pond, some benches, and a slightly incongruous piece of heavy artillery from some long-ago war. Frieda sat down on a bench while Dak disappeared into a pit toilet. When he returned, he had a canvas bag full of items we'd need for our mission. We pulled on the coveralls that would identify us as repair workers. Mine smelled pungently of sewage, but I tried to ignore that. Once I'd zipped it all the way up, I piled my hair on top of my head and hid it with the cap Dak provided. Again I had to ignore its condition, the greasy headband and the brown thumbprints along the bill. "Pull it down low," Dak ordered. "No offense, but you don't look like a guy."

He provided a large pair of cotton gloves to give the impression I had "man hands," and last, he handed me a bag of plumbing tools with a long holding strap. "Hang the bag in front so it covers your chest." When I did that, Dak stood back and nodded, indicating approval. "The institute's got plumbing problems that never really get fixed," he said as he zipped up his own coverall. "Our people go in and out all the time, and the guards are pretty lax these days. Rumor says their paychecks don't always arrive on time, so why should they care what happens?"

Had Vox become corrupt, the way Miller had? Shoving the question away, I focused on the immediate future. Dak was taking me into a building that belonged to, was dedicated to, and served the Govt. That was dangerous. It was scary.

I looked around at the park. The vine-covered fence hid the city from view. It felt safe here, and for a moment I wished I could just stay, out of the traffic, away from the toppers, and live among the ducks and the squirrels.

But if I didn't go with Dak, I stood no chance of finding Milla. Sighing, I touched a tree trunk for luck and followed him out of the park, across the street, and through a side door into the Institute.

He was right about the lax security. When Dak said we'd come to clean up a mess in a third-floor washroom, the man at the desk didn't even look up from his crossword puzzle. "Elevator's broken. You gotta take the stairs."

"Right. Thanks."

We did take the stairs, but we went down, not up. As soon as we were out of the guard's sight, Dak did a little dance of joy, his face lit with deviltry. While he was clearly enjoying our incursion into enemy territory, I was terrified we'd be found and punished in some horrible way.

None of the men I'd known before would let themselves act as silly as Dak did, which made me realize something. Women weren't the only ones who were hidebound by the conventions of our time. Men in my tribe were expected to be industrious, serious, and conventional. Dak was none of those things, but having seen him in action, I thought he had more courage than most. His outcast status seemed to give him the freedom to act inappropriately for a male. What did his silliness matter when the so-called "good" people judged him worthless before they knew anything about him?

At the underground level, a folding gate extended across a corridor on our right. It was padlocked, and a large sign said, *DANGER-NO ENTRY*. Ignoring the latch, which was secured with a padlock, Dak went to the other side and used the blade of a jackknife to pop the pins out of the hinges. The gate contracted, letting us through, and he replaced the pins partway, so the gate appeared to be in place. That done, he set off down a dark corridor.

The place was a mess, with walls caved completely in places and debris strewn everywhere. Dak produced a flashlight, which became necessary as we got farther from the staircase. "What happened here?" I asked as we stepped over rubble.

"At the end of the Old Times, a bunch of cities got bombed. The news blamed the rebels, but my dad said that was bullshit, because rebel forces didn't have access to planes. It was more likely the old government's last stab at destroying the opposition." He helped me over a large girder that blocked the way. "When Vox took over, there wasn't money to rebuild, so lots of times they just blocked the wrecked part off and ignored it." He gestured ahead. "Walter's lived down here for years."

"Nobody sees him coming and going?"

Dak frowned. "To be honest, I don't think he ever leaves. We bring him stuff, food and whatever. First my dad did it. He passed the job to me once it got so he couldn't get around good." He wriggled his sandy brows. "The guy's weird, but I kinda like him."

We'd reached a door, and Dak gave two quick knocks, paused, and knocked once more. After a few seconds, the door opened and a deep voice said, "Dak! How goes it, young man?"

"I brought a friend who needs your help." Dak shoved a hand at each of us. "Amanda, this is Walter. Walter, Amanda."

The man's pale face registered distrust. "I am not acquainted with this person, Dak. You must be aware that I—"

"One of the commanders has got her little sister," Dak interrupted. "They claim she's dead, but Amanda saw her on TV."

Shaking his head, Walter muttered, "Those scoundrels like them young." Stepping back, he invited, "Come in, then."

Probably fifty or more, Walter wore a t-shirt that said *Y2K Not?* and short pants that had more pockets than I'd ever seen on one garment before. His pale face was unlined, but his bushy beard was streaked with white. At his invitation, we entered his domain, a room about twenty feet wide by forty feet deep. A half-dozen big TVs lined one wall, each screen with a different view: a weather map, a news show, what looked like a military mission happening in the dark of night, and a Bugs Bunny cartoon. On a table below each screen was a keyboard. Some were large, like Grandfather's typewriter; some had just enough space for two hands. Around them were various metal rectangles, some cube-shaped, some tall.

Benny had described rooms filled with computers, but there were more here than I'd ever imagined in one place.

Past the equipment was Walter's living area, a hot plate and a small refrigerator in one corner and a couch he apparently used as a bed in the other. In between was a big trunk that I guessed held his personal belongings, since bits of t-shirt and underwear hung over the edge. The air smelled strongly of fried meat and seldom washed male. While he might have been embarrassed, there was nothing but pride in Walter's voice when he said, "Welcome to my domicile."

"I have to go upstairs and pound on something, so they think we're working," Dak said. With an exaggerated military salute, he added, "Toilet Patrol, reporting for duty!" took the bag of tools, and went out the door.

Left on our own, Walter and I exchanged slightly embarrassed looks. He had no reason to trust me, and I had no way to convince him he should. Gesturing at the array of screens, I asked, "Where did all this come from?"

"I pilfer the Govt's trappings and employ said trappings against them." Walter scratched under his beard. "Poetic justice, one might argue." His doubts seemed to rise again. "Now, introduce yourself properly, so that I may differentiate you from, say, a basket of apples."

Since I guessed Walter was a former rebel, I tried to make a connection that way. "My father fought against Miller and Dupree in the Old Times," I told him, proud for the first time in my life to share that information. "His name is Sri Afzal."

Walter rolled his eyes upward for a second. "I believe I might have heard of him, but of course it's been some time."

"I think he'd have fought against Vox too, but by the time Vox came along, Sri was in prison."

"Then your father and I would have occupied opposite positions," Walter said. "For almost one year, I was Allen Vox's top expert in the field of computer technology."

I didn't know whether that made us friends or foes, but Walter had apparently come to a decision. "Might I offer you an orange soda while we get acquainted?"

Minutes later we were seated on battered computer chairs, turned away from the monitors and toward each other. I had a bottle of overly sweet bubbly stuff I'd been ordered not to set down anywhere near the equipment. "I don't mean to be fussy," Walter told me in a decidedly fussy tone, "but it's difficult these days to replace equipment that is damaged."

"Right." Setting the bottle on my knee, I held onto it firmly with one hand. "So you worked for Chief Vox as a computer…" I didn't know what they were called. "…worker?"

"Information technician," he supplied. "I served as such in the army and excelled at it, so when Vox won the referendum, he requested that I work directly for him, monitoring the nation's internet capabilities." Seeing my look of confusion Walter asked, "Have you ever used a computer?"

"No. I saw one once in our storeroom at home." I waved a hand. "It was a lot bigger than any of these."

His eyes rolled upward. "A desktop PC." It sounded like I'd mentioned one of his oldest and dearest friends. "To put it simply, the internet once connected each individual computer to other computers. The system was immense and mostly unregulated. It grew up higgledy-piggledy, and by the time Miller came into office, it was in chaos. Miller used computers against the citizenry, collecting information he had no right to have. That wasn't new, of course, but Miller believed he was unstoppable. He made no secret of his crimes and in fact used information to threaten his enemies. Rebels—I'm assuming your father was among them—tried to find ways to stop him." He frowned. "Their methods were extreme, but I suppose they believed that once Miller was gone, what they destroyed would be fixed."

"So this…internet was wrecked when Chief Vox came into office."

"Not completely wrecked, but it certainly wasn't in good shape. When Vox called me in, I expected the job would be repairing the damage, but he wanted the internet shut down completely."

I recalled Grandmother saying how out of hand computers had gotten. "You couldn't even order a hamburger without dealing with some machine that made it ten times harder than speaking to a human," she'd say. "Buying anything, getting into a museum, even parking your car required dealing with technology. It changed all the time, so you had to keep up or look like a moron."

We'd been told in school that the internet had become inherently unsafe. Besides Miller's people stealing everyone's information, something called Artificial Intelligence had begun taking over people's lives. Computers would have ended up our overlords, our teachers said, with humankind under their control instead of vice versa. "I guess technology got really bad," I told Walter. "It made people too lazy to think for themselves."

Walter's smile reminded me of the one Benny used to give when I'd said something dumb but he didn't want to embarrass me. "It would be hard to argue that is completely erroneous," he admitted. "It's true that fewer and fewer people wrote, read, or even *thought* without using a computer to make it easier. We spent far too much time staring at screens and failing to analyze what we saw there."

He rested his chin in one hand. "My little nieces, at maybe eight and ten years old, spent hours each day surfing the net and farming their auras."

I didn't ask for an explanation of that but motioned for him to go on.

"The computer, a tool that should have been freeing and uplifting, turned out to be constricting and polarizing. What might have helped us find out about other people, other cultures, and other ideas turned us angry, xenophobic, and mean. We discovered we could hurt others from a distance, and far too many of us enjoyed it." Walter frowned. "About once a week, some deranged individual went over the edge and moved from vomiting hate from behind his keyboard to procuring a gun and killing complete strangers."

"That sounds bad."

Taking a slurp from his coffee cup, he nodded. "The amount of misinformation and disinformation that circulated was disgusting. People believed conspiracy theories they could easily have debunked with a modicum of effort. Many people tired of trying to learn the truth and focused instead on tiny parts of the internet that made them happy." Another sip of coffee. "Cat videos were big. And something called Wordle."

"My grandfather believed we're better off without all that. He said we have less mental illness and anxiety now."

"I won't say he's wrong, but we gave up a lot too. As is true of any advancement, technology is not good or evil on its own. Computers allowed advancements that were stunningly helpful."

"Then why did Chief Vox cut off access to them?"

"He claimed the shutdown would be temporary. We'd rebuild it, he told us, but with better safeguards. When the system was secure and safe, we'd restore access to everyone." Walter sighed deeply. "He was not honest about his agenda."

"Vox had plans you didn't know about?"

"He wanted the internet to be available only to certain people. His people."

"How?" I pointed at the computers. "Can't anyone catch information out of the air if they have one of those?"

Walter shook his head. "Internet access requires protocols called IPs. Without them, there are no connections."

"You stopped letting regular people have IPs?"

"I didn't, no. As soon as I realized what Vox had in mind, I went to him. I explained that we would literally be responsible for death and chaos if we did as he proposed. Medical devices would fail. Traffic systems would go dark. People would freeze in winter cold and bake in summer heat. Businesses would fail. Delivery systems would choke, with no one knowing where anything was, how much there was of it, or where it was supposed to go."

"What did he say?"

Walter pressed his lips under his teeth for a few seconds before answering. "Vox called it an acceptable loss. That's a military concept that allows a certain number of casualties or damages in the context of a larger operation." His voice turned bitter. "He said that as a soldier, I should understand that we were acting for the greater good we'd achieve. People would go back to being active, he said. They'd perform physical labor and feel the satisfaction that accomplishing such work brings. They'd think for themselves. They'd become better people. They'd be productive and therefore content."

"I'm guessing you thought he had deeper motives."

"Yes. I'd been flattered by his trust in me, and I must say, the man spoke well and seemed honorable. But I realized that he'd be letting chaos reign mostly so he could gather and hold onto power." Walter's words came faster. "I went to the other technicians. I tried to make them see how wrong what Vox was proposing was."

"What did they say?"

"They said they trusted Chief Vox. They said the people of this country did too." His expression turned disgusted. "I would guess that the generous paychecks we'd begun receiving figured in for most of them as well."

"What did you do then?"

"I contacted a dozen or so people in the government who I believed had integrity and told them Vox was not what he appeared to be. I said he would turn into a dictator if people didn't step up soon and stop him." His smile was a grimace. "One of them, perhaps more than one, went to Vox and told him what I'd said."

"Vox fired you."

"No." It was softer this time. "He tried to kill me."

Allen Vox, Chief of Fairica, was a man every teacher I'd ever had praised to the skies. While he hadn't done things the way I'd have done them, it was hard to believe he'd murder someone for speaking out.

It was clear Walter believed it, so I asked, "How did it happen?"

"A few nights after I began airing my concerns, I was at home when I heard a cat crying in the alley. I have always had great affection for felines, so I took a little meat from my fridge and went downstairs to feed the poor creature. About a minute after I stepped outside, a huge explosion rocked my apartment, which was directly overhead."

"Could it have been an accident, like a gas leak?"

"That was the official story the next day, but no. The side entrance opened onto an alley. I was kneeling under a portico, watching the cat eat, and I noticed a car parked on the street. The engine was running—It was cold that night—and a passing car's headlights lit the interior for a few seconds. I recognized the passenger as a member of Vox's security team. I recall thinking, 'What's he doing in my neighborhood?' just before boards, bricks, and glass started raining down on me."

"What did you do?"

"When I recovered my senses, I sprinted down the alley to where my car was parked and drove away, sans coat, sans hat, sans gloves. I located a series of ATMs—That's a computer of a certain type that dispensed cash from a person's bank account. I hit three and collected all the money I could. Then I started driving. The next day I sold the car to a second-hand dealer. I bought a bus ticket, then another and another, mostly at random but going south, out of the cold weather."

"And you ended up here."

"Yes. I wasn't in pristine condition. I had cuts and bruises. I was terrified of everyone. I wandered into an alley, hoping to sleep for a few hours. Dak's father was there, looking for metal to sell for cash. When he saw the gash on my shoulder and the fear in my eyes, he insisted I go with him to his home. He fed me. He gave me a bed to sleep in. He took care of me."

As Dak had done for me. Ironic, I thought, that those who had the least were often the most generous, both with their goods and their courage.

"Once I became myself again, I pondered for some time what I wanted to do. I could escape the country. I could change my name and my looks and start a new life. Neither of those ideas pleased me. Instead, I decided I would use my skills to monitor and oppose the Govt."

"So you moved in here."

"Dak and his father had stumbled across this room while tracing the building's plumbing pipes, and it was exactly what I needed. I moved in and began foraging at night, when daily operations ceased. I'd go upstairs and subtract a single piece of furniture or bit of equipment from here and there." Pointing at the couch, he chuckled. "You'd have been highly entertained to see me dragging that monstrosity down three flights of stairs and pulling it over piles of debris. Spreading my choices out over months, I managed to acquire servers, processors, monitors."

I opened my mouth to express doubt, but he added, "There's so much mismanagement here that they hardly notice when something goes missing. Now I turn the Govt's resources against them."

Looking again at the row of monitors, I said, "We don't have any of this where I come from."

"And you will not, because the way things are, the people of Fairica hear what the Govt wants them to hear and read what they want them to read." He gave me a look. "I would venture to guess your tribe has two, maybe three telephones."

I nodded. "It's expensive to run lines and—"

"It doesn't have to be." Walter moved to a chair draped with an old quilt. Its wheels squeaked in protest as he rolled up to one of the keyboards and typed in a command. A picture appeared on the monitor above it. "This photograph is from the Old Times, when anyone could access the internet. At a library or even a restaurant, a girl like you could look up any piece of information known to Humankind." I watched as he scrolled through images of tall metal towers hung with odd-looking attachments. Next came rooms full of people focused on small screens, and then huge, vault-like areas filled with rows of stacked devices with bright-colored wires connecting them to each other. "Vox returned the country to the 1950s. I think that's because he has idyllic memories of his own childhood." Walter raised a finger. "Not authentic. Idyllic."

"I can't believe people gave up so much knowledge, so many possibilities."

"The fact that it happened reveals what fear and mental exhaustion can do to an entire nation." With that, Walter's manner turned businesslike. "Now if you'll answer a few questions for me, I'll see if I can find this sister you're looking for."

When I explained about seeing Milla on TV, Walter typed in what he called a command, his face close to the screen as he worked. When the news footage from the Capitol appeared, I said, "There! That's her." I almost touched the screen in my excitement, but the look of horror on my host's face stopped me.

"Okay," he said when I'd pulled my hand back. "That's Commander Vail." Walter typed again and then read for a moment. "Vail has only one child, a daughter named Isabel. She doesn't appear in public often, and—" He hit a few letters, the screen changed, and he scanned the information there. "I think there's an issue with her."

"Like what?"

"Look here. I hacked into the commander's household accounts." He indicated a long list on the screen. "Those are the names of private tutors who've come and gone from their home in the last few years. I would guess Isabel is Special Quarters material, but they don't want to admit it."

A knock on the door told us Dak had returned. Walter let him in and then went back to the footage of the family emerging from the car and taking their place on the porch. Commander Vail stood stiffly, his arms at his sides and his face stern. His wife looked beautiful but stressed. Though she smiled and waved to onlookers, she kept glancing at her daughter. A few times her hand went out as if to pat the girl's shoulder, but each time she apparently thought better of it and did not.

The daughter, Isabel, radiated tension in her expression, her posture, every part of her. Her hands twitched. Her feet moved from side to side stiffly, like a robot. On her face was a grimace apparently meant to resemble a smile. As I watched, my sister reached out and took the girl's hand in hers. At Milla's touch, a change came over Isabel. Though she still didn't look happy, she calmed somewhat. When the time came to shake Vox's hand, her smile seemed almost genuine.

It was clear to me why the Vails wanted my sister in their home. Milla's sweet disposition, calm manner, and innate kindness made her the ideal companion for a girl who didn't fit the pattern females were expected to follow. It didn't hurt that the two were so similar in appearance. Standing side by side they looked darling, like a matched set.

"Where do these people live?" Dak flopped into a chair, watching as Walter typed to find the answer to my question.

He found me a map. "The Vail's estate, Eden, is about two hundred miles from here."

That was far, but I'd come a long way already. "How can I get there?"

Walter frowned, but Dak pointed at a highway that ran along the eastern edge of the estate. "Truckers use that road. If you could find one going that direction, you might offer him a deal."

"What kind of deal?"

Dak frowned. "It would have to be cash. Taking on illegal passengers is a big risk."

"If you don't need anything more…" Walter's fingers wriggled, an unconscious sign that he was eager to get back to whatever he'd been doing when we arrived.

Rising, Dak said, "C'mon, Amanda. Walter has lots to do."

"Do I owe you…?" I stopped, embarrassed.

"No, no," Walter said. "I do what I do as a 'Screw-You' to the Govt."

Thanking him, I followed Dak out to the corridor. As he let us through the accordion gate again, I said, "Dak, I don't mind paying with sex if a driver would accept that in return for a ride."

He laughed aloud, slapping a hand over his mouth to muffle the sound. "If Frieda found out we even considered that, she'd murder you and me both."

I gave a little huff of frustration. "Maybe Frieda doesn't understand what it's like to have nothing but yourself to offer."

"She understands." The words came out gruffly. "Sex would still be the last bargaining chip Frieda would consider." After a second he said, "Maybe you can earn some money. Can you sew or fix a broken refrigerator or repair a roof?"

"No." After a beat, I said, "I can sing." When he merely shrugged, I said, "I used to do my tribe's financial records."

"Really?" We'd left the building, and he stopped on the sidewalk. "The guy who kept our records had a heart attack, maybe a month ago now, and we're due to submit paperwork to the Govt." He pushed his hair back with a hand. "I heard the new guy is having problems figuring out the dead guy's system, so if you could help with that, I bet he'd pay enough to get you where you want to go."

"That sounds perfect, Dak."

The O'Donnell's new bookkeeper, Tom, was stymied by his predecessor's methods. I sensed some hesitancy about letting a female show him up, but I said if I couldn't help, he didn't have to pay me anything. With nothing to lose, Tom opened the books and let me peruse them.

The recently departed bookkeeper's work turned out to be excellent, but he'd used a personal shorthand that made it seem indecipherable. Once I figured out what each abbreviation stood for, I shared it with Tom. Then I helped him set up his own system going forward. After three long days bent over a desk, bumping elbows with the geeky Tom, I received the cash I'd been promised. In the meantime, Dak had rooted out the names of a few truckers who might be amenable to a bribe. I was practically on my way to Eden.

The first trucker I talked to was willing, but he wasn't scheduled to go that way for at least a week. I went on to the second name, Cal. Dak knew where he ate his breakfast each morning, so I approached him there, presenting my case as he shoveled eggs over easy into his wide mouth and washed them down with coffee.

I told him where I wanted to go and what I could afford to pay. Without looking up, he said, "Give me half right now. Meet me on the corner of 31st and Winter at six this afternoon. If you don't climb into the cab before the light changes, I go on without you."

Since I had most of the day to kill, Frieda, who'd been sharing her space in the attic of a friend's home with me, suggested we visit her friend Heather. "She's like a living book," Frieda claimed. "You can ask her anything about history, and she'll tell you the truth, not Govt lies."

Frieda led the way, dodging the toppers with an almost magical sense of where they'd be and how to avoid them. As we walked, I asked about her family. "Ain't got one," she said in what she tried to make seem a casual admission. "I guess Dak is my family these days, but who knows how long I'll put up with his shit?"

"What happened to your real family?"

Frieda shrugged. "My father was killed in a bombing when my mom was pregnant for me. When I was six, she got sick. We couldn't afford a doctor, so she died. That left me and my sister Ginny. She's gone now too."

"I'm really sorry. I felt awful when I thought my sister was dead."

"She didn't die." Frieda turned to me and I saw tragedy in her eyes. "Ginny was sixteen and pretty. They took her."

I got a sick feeling in my stomach. "A Supply Squad."

"Dak saw it happen. He tried to help, but there were three goons, big ones. They threw him into a brick wall and broke one of his arms. He was lucky they didn't take him too, but I guess they were just after women that day." She sniffed. "At least Dak tried. Everyone else on the street just stood there and let her get grabbed."

Unable to stop myself, I took a look behind us. What if those rough men were watching right now?

"Like me, Dak's got nobody since his dad died last year. We hang onto each other."

"Are you two…" I didn't know how to phrase it politely. "…engaged?"

She laughed. "It's not like that. Dak's crazy for this girl in the Conway Tribe, Elaine, but there's no way her family would let her hook up with an O'Donnell." She gave a disgusted snort. "He moans a lot and walks around all sad, so when I can, I arrange for the two of them to meet up. I pretend to be Elaine's friend from school, and I invite her to go somewhere, like on a picnic or whatever. Once she's out of her parents' view, I leave her and Dak alone together."

"It's nice that Dak gets to spend time with the girl he loves."

Frieda grimaced. "Things never get very far. Elaine's mother told her she can get pregnant from deep kissing, so all poor Dak ever gets is a peck on the cheek." Now she chuckled. "It's kind of sad, but if you ask me, most of what we call love is pretty pathetic." After a moment she added, "All I want from life is a few laughs. I like frustrating the toppers and learning things I didn't know before." She waved at the dirty street. "The rest is pretty miserable."

"You helped me. That thought should make your life less miserable."

She sighed. "Yeah, score one for Dak and me on that, but I'll be honest. I'd rather it was my sister I'd saved."

Frieda went quiet, and I gave her the gift of silence. Nothing I could say would lessen the grief of knowing a beloved sister was now a slave, used by men who had no honor and no conscience. Or she might be dead, which was both a tragedy and a possible blessing.

When we arrived at a ramshackle building, Frieda warned, "Heather's old and she's been through a lot, so move slowly and keep your voice down."

"Got it."

She led me into the building and down a set of stairs to basement apartments along a hallway that smelled of mold. We passed at least a dozen doors. Behind them I heard the hum of conversation, an occasional burst of laughter or anger, and several different types of music. When she knocked on a door marked U-8, a voice called, "Who is it?"

"It's Frieda."

I heard slippers shuffle across the floor, one stepping, one dragging. The door opened with a slight creak, and a woman peered out. Though she was old, her eyes were alive with interest. Her expression became concerned when she saw me behind Frieda. "Who's this?"

"Amanda," Frieda said. "Dak and I rescued her from the toppers."

Heather's brow furrowed. "How do you know the Monkey Men didn't send her?"

"If you'd seen how scared she was, you'd know. She ran away from some farm up north."

"What tribe?" When I hesitated, she said, "Don't lie to me. It's not necessary, and it will just make me angry."

"Woods."

"Who's the leader?"

"Benjamin, at least he was. He died. Now Rolf Woods is in charge."

"Is he any good?"

I shook my head. "Not even a little bit."

"That's what I heard." I must have looked surprised, because she added, "Yes, I'm old, but I still hear things." Heather stepped aside. "Come in." We entered an apartment stuffed with books, some with bright covers, others dull brown or navy. Some were as thick as planks; others I could have read in an hour. A title that caught my eye, *The Handmaid's Tale*, brought to mind Hagar, Sarah's servant in the Bible. I remembered saying once in Sunday School that I thought she got a raw deal. With a smirk, our teacher had said it was no surprise I'd side with Hagar. "You're descended from her son, Ishmael, but it was Isaac, *our* ancestor, who fathered the tribes of God's people." The kids had snickered, and I'd felt my face warm with embarrassment and anger.

We'd never been encouraged to read much except the Bible and our textbooks, but after Benny died, I read a couple of his books at night, after Milla was asleep. I'd enjoyed *The Outsiders* for its view of what teenagers had once been like, and *Slaughterhouse 5* for its ability to make me think about the world in new ways. Most of all, I'd liked slipping into a story and seeing life from someone else's perspective. I'd wondered what it would be like to curl up with a book in some cozy corner and read for a whole afternoon. But Grandfather had needed me, and Grandmother would not have approved.

Heather offered me a chair, a glass of water, and a cookie. I accepted all three, which seemed to please her. Did spies not accept cookies? Maybe they feared being poisoned or dosed with truth serum. I watched her limp around her tiny kitchen, pouring glasses of water and putting a half-dozen applesauce cookies on a plate. She set it between us, and as I munched, Frieda asked, "Heather, will you tell Amanda what happened at the end of the Old Times?"

Heather smiled fondly at my new friend. "I keep telling Frieda we have to live in the world we have, but she'd like to return to a time that's long gone."

Frieda rapped her knuckles on the table. "I only want everyone to be treated the same." With a mock glare at Heather, she added, "You're the one who taught me that throughout history, whenever women get close to equal rights, a bunch of men band together and say, 'No more of that!'"

Heather chuckled. "If I'd known you were going to go all feminist about it, I wouldn't have gotten you started."

"Heather fought against all of the chauvinists," Frieda told me. "Miller, then Dupree, and then Vox."

"And look where it got me." Heather glanced around the stuffy little apartment, but I noticed that she also laid a hand on her damaged leg and rubbed it gently.

"I read a diary someone left behind," I told them, "so I know a little about how things used to be. What I don't understand is why, if women used to have so many choices, they let them be taken away."

Heather smiled sadly. "Most women back then believed they'd be fine when it all shook out. After all, it wasn't *their* rights that were under threat. It was only the people who didn't *deserve* those rights." She made a *tsk* sound. "It was like they believed that justice can be withheld from some while the rest go merrily along, unaffected."

"How was it done? If women could vote back then, and run for election, and express their opinions—"

Putting up a hand, Heather stopped me. "We could go back a long way with that discussion, but let's focus on Gerald Miller. He got elected to the highest office in the land by telling so many lies that it was hard to sort through them all. He maneuvered his yes-men in the legislature into declaring a recess and sending everyone home. Then he issued what he called a 'National Rebalancing Order,' claiming that women in positions of responsibility were impeding the nation's progress. He ordered them replaced in all leadership roles, and he directed that women's finances would henceforth be accessible only to their nearest male relative. CEOs and university presidents were not only out of a job overnight, but they were also required to ask their husbands, brothers, and fathers for money to buy anything from tampons to lunch at Applebee's."

"The men let that happen?"

Heather smiled. "They were handed large amounts of someone else's money. How hard do you think most of them objected?" Her hands made a flicker of movement. "Of course we sued in the courts. We won judgment after judgment, but Miller simply refused to abide by those decisions. Any financial institution that questioned his blatantly illegal move was harassed so badly that most backed off and did as they were told."

Frieda had a comment. "You know at least half of those men agreed with Miller. No more women in their boardrooms. No need to refrain from sexist jokes. No more having to listen to some woman who thinks she's as smart as you when you know your male brain is superior."

I set the remains of my cookie on the napkin. "Surely some people spoke against it."

"Of course," Heather said, "but those of us who did had no idea the price we'd pay. I was part of a group of lawyers who fought Miller's excesses wherever we could. We won more than we lost, but every time, he'd just go in some new, even crazier direction. Chaos is a very destructive force in government, because it's hard to know where to fight, who to fight, and how to fight. Often our efforts were seen as negative by the public. Some said we were hurting Miller's attempts to make our nation great. I for one spent over a year in jail on a contempt of court charge that was completely fabricated."

So Heather had been imprisoned for her part in opposing Miller, as my father had.

"Was Miller that smart? It sounds like he was really clever about getting his way."

Heather's lips twisted. "He was actually quite stupid. The people he surrounded himself with weren't all that smart either, but they were determined. The nation simply wasn't prepared for an administration that ignored the law and refused to recognize anyone else's right to apply it. Miller sent armed forces to any place people organized against him. He messed with the finances of those that opposed him. He harassed businessmen who spoke up. He cut off funding to organizations that objected." Her eye color seemed to turn from green to gray. "I never would have believed it could happen in our nation, but I watched as it did."

"But then Miller died."

Heather gave a tiny smile. "That felt like a relief, but it actually made things worse. Miller's successor, Tim Dupree, didn't have the charisma his boss had, but he did have a strong desire for power. Dupree took a step even Miller hadn't dared: he sent the military to bomb what he called, 'nests of vermin' in our city centers."

"He bombed his own people?"

"The fact that his orders were obeyed is a testimony to the uncertainty of the times. Newspeople said nothing. Generals went along. Pilots dropped bombs on thousands of their own countrymen." Heather rubbed the spot between her pale eyebrows. "History teaches us that when people can't decide between right and wrong, they tend to obey authority and absolve themselves of responsibility."

I shook my head at the picture of chaos her words evoked. How had a nation admired for decades as a beacon of freedom turned into such a nightmare?

Folding her hands, Heather set them on the table. "One day, Allen Vox stepped into the spotlight. He didn't represent either side. He claimed no agenda except a desire to heal the nation. He said he could bring us out of the crisis within six months. He seemed authentic, and his promise sounded good."

"People liked his idea of a middle-of-the-road solution," Freida put in.

"Even when Vox told us about his idea for a tribal system, it sounded idyllic. What we didn't see was that he intended to make himself into a feudal king."

"Why did people fall for that after the mess with the other two?"

"Ordinary people were depressed, exhausted, and broke. Men with the means to become land-holders were thrilled with the idea of having their own little fiefdoms." Heather's smile was thin. "Even rebels like me told ourselves small units would be more representative. We thought any problems that arose would work themselves out over time." Heather tilted her head at me. "Tribes are okay for a lot of people. You have work to do and an identity that suits you. You grow up with people who look like you, worship like you, and think like you."

I huffed a laugh. "That's not how it went for me. That's why I'm on my own now, with no tribe at all."

Chapter Sixteen

As the semi bumped along the road that night, I rode in the cab behind the driver's seat, looking over Cal's shoulder periodically at the patch of road his headlights illuminated, the flash of reflectors along the verge, and the occasional squashed armadillo. Darkness hid the countryside. The road was mostly deserted. Cal was not a talker. To amuse myself, I imagined a debate between Heather, the historian I'd met that afternoon, and Grandmother, whose explanations and exhortations had shaped so much of my childhood. Grandmother gave Vox credit for two decades of peace in Fairica. Heather claimed he'd completed the destruction Miller began.

Grandmother had always claimed the tribal system was a big success. "Everyone here feels like they belong," she used to tell us, "even people who aren't direct relatives." That was at least partly because the Woods Tribe was made up mostly of Anglo-Saxon types, medium height with a slightly square build, fair skin, light hair, and blue or green eyes.

Heather had claimed many of the nation's greatest minds and talents had moved to other countries rather than comply with the TRA. "The Govt's official stand was that they were glad to see the 'malcontents' go," she'd said, "but those malcontents were our artists, thinkers, musicians, inventors, and creators." Her smile rueful, she'd finished, "Once the Govt took control, Fairica became pretty dull."

Lulled by the hum of the engine, I dozed for a while. When the truck slowed sharply, I woke and saw we were approaching the junction where I'd continue on foot. I'd be about ten miles from the Vail estate, Cal had said. The truck's brakes hissed as he slowed and pulled over to the side. His eyes met mine in the rearview mirror, and I took out the second half of the payment we'd agreed on. It left me with almost nothing, but Cal had been good in his way, bringing leftovers from his meals and letting me have the bed while he napped in the driver's seat with his jacket laid across his chest.

As the truck roared away, I stood in the gray of early morning, looking down the road I was supposed to take. Neither Dak nor Walter had been familiar with the area around Eden, but Walter had forged a travel pass that would allow me to move freely as long as I behaved myself. Dak had found a contact near the Vail estate who was friendly to what he called "people like us."

"There's a restaurant called Dick's near the turnoff. "Ask for Renee. Say that she and your mother used to swim in the Boudica River as kids."

"Boudica?" It sounded like Boo-da-kuh, a word I'd never heard before.

"She was a rebel way back, did great for a while but failed in the end." He shrugged. "Like your dad, I guess."

I paused for a few moments, looking at the landscape. I was much farther south than I'd intended to go. Dorado, the truck driver had told me, was seven hundred miles to the west, which had made me cry a little in the privacy of my borrowed bed in his truck cab. Still, I had to find Milla before I could think about going on.

The two-lane road I'd arrived on continued southward, while a dirt road went southeast and a narrow paved road went northwest. About twenty yards along the dirt road was a clapboard building, slightly rundown. That was my initial destination. Shouldering my pack, I started through the gray dawn toward it.

Vail's estate sat to the west, where the flat, relatively treeless terrain I now walked turned forested. There the land rose sharply and peaks of rock stuck out above the tree line. I pictured the map

Heather had found in one of her books. It showed that the Vail estate, Eden, had once been a national park. A long, narrow lake formed its eastern border, and mountains protected its western side. That had been all we could find, but Dak said Renee would be able to tell me more about both the estate and its residents.

I shivered, missing the jacket I'd lost somewhere along the way. The air was damp, and it felt like I was wrapped in a wet blanket. A second blanket, one made of loneliness, weighed on me as well. I missed Dak's cheerful rebellion and Frieda's serious defiance. Even Silent Cal had been a human presence. Now I was completely on my own. It seemed like I inhabited a black hole somewhere in the universe, far from friends, far from family.

Had it been a mistake to leave Woodsburg? I hated and mistrusted Rolf, but I liked other members of my family. Even Grandmother, who nagged at me constantly, had been trying in her way to help me become an obedient and therefore desirable woman. I even knew that somewhere behind Mother's tight expression and unwelcoming arms, she loved Milla and me. I'd seen it sometimes, a flash of affection in her eyes for one or the other of us before she remembered herself and turned away.

Would it have been so bad to let them find me a decent man, to settle down to a life everyone claimed would make me happy in the end? I'd have friends. I'd have Milla. I sighed. Too late to think about that now.

The restaurant was a square, two-story building. The map had showed a small burg farther down. While locating the diner out of town seemed odd, I realized its regular patrons would know it was there. Additional patrons would come from travelers passing by on the highway, seeing the place, and stopping for a meal.

The place had clearly once been a house, and it had a wide yard all the way around it. A sign over the door, white with plain black lettering, said, *Dick's Place—Good Food.* Behind the building were a couple of storage sheds and a long woodpile. In front was a large parking lot, unpaved and pitted with spots where rain had carried away the softer soil. Boxes overflowing with pink flowers sat on either side of the door. Alongside the building was an ancient Oldsmobile with its trunk yawning open.

A man and woman who looked to be in their early sixties were unlocking the doors as I approached. The man wore a wide back support belt and walked with a limp. The woman was homely and prune-faced. "Good morning," I said. "I'm looking for Renee. She and my mother used to play in the Boudica River together." I stumbled on the name. The woman glanced at the man, who raised his brows.

"Lucky you." Pushing the door open, the woman gestured for me to precede them inside. "You found me." She pointed. "That's my husband, Dick."

The place held about ten tables, most square with seating for four. A large round one in a corner had eight chairs, and I imagined men there, sipping at mugs and discussing the impossibility of understanding their wives.

Closing the door behind us, Renee began loading a large, discolored machine with ground coffee. Dick went into the kitchen, turned on the griddle, and began cleaning it with a spatula, long scrapes interspersed with clangs as he shook the gunk into a metal pan on the side.

"What can we do for you?" Renee asked once the coffee machine started burbling.

"I need to visit Commander Vail's estate." That got me a look, so I added, "My sister's there, and I need to talk to her. Do you think I can get permission to do that?"

"From Peter Vail? I doubt it." Renee's face twisted with disgust. "Unless you have something he wants…" She waited expectantly, but I shook my head. "I heard they have a girl living with them," she said, "but I'm pretty sure pedophilia is the one crime Vail isn't guilty of. So what is your sister doing there?"

"I don't know, but I need to ask if she's there by choice."

Renee and Dick communicated silently, a questioning look from her, an affirmative response from him. Taking a bowl from a cupboard, Renee began breaking eggs into it. "Come back around noon."

I glanced at a display case on the counter that contained a few of yesterday's baked goods. "Maybe you have chores that need doing," I said. "I'd be happy to work for one of those fritters."

She looked me over, taking in my snarled hair and rumpled clothing. "How about three meals and a place to sleep tonight? There's room upstairs if you don't mind bunking on an old couch."

I spent the morning cleaning while Renee and Dick conducted business, cooking breakfasts for crews of men heading out to work on some project, pouring and refilling cups of coffee as they joked with regular customers. The smell of fried eggs and ham wafted up the narrow wooden stairs as I swept insect carcasses out of windowsills and wiped years of smoke and grime from the windows. Furniture that had been used downstairs when the place was their home now took up most of the upstairs space. Dick, who talked more than his wife did, told me they now lived in a cabin along a nearby river. "It's kinda shabby," he admitted, "but we like getting away from the smell of fry grease at night."

The plate Renee brought up for my breakfast was generous and delicious. Sitting on a bench under a wide window, I ate every bit, took my plate and silverware down and washed them, and went back to work, already looking forward to lunch.

Once I'd cleaned the windows inside, I went to work on the outside. As I squirted and scrubbed with vinegar water, something brushed my leg. I started, but looking down, saw that it was only a black-and-gray tiger cat. "Hey, buddy," I said, bending down to scratch its ears. The cat allowed it for a moment and then moved off.

When I mentioned the animal Renee said, "That was Roscoe, who is always, always, looking to get inside. Waits by the back door and tries to get past me any time I go out. Dick feeds him, claims cats keep worse critters away."

At noon a woman arrived, stepping out of a pickup truck driven by a serious-looking man in a green uniform shirt. After a few minutes, Renee called me to the kitchen to meet her. "Madame Vail often sends Lucia to get pastries for the commander's breakfast. Lucia, will you tell Amanda about your duties for the Vails? She starts work next week at a place in Towerburg, and she's never served rich people before."

Lucia readily agreed, and Renee suggested we go out to the back porch to talk. Taking my elbow, she held me back for a moment, saying, "Get what you can from her, but don't tell her more than you have to. The girl has no more brains than your average anole lizard."

Outside, I asked Lucia to tell me about the estate and what her role was there. She chattered on for some time before mentioning Milla's name. "I had a friend named Milla once," I said. "Does this girl like living on your estate?"

"I think so. She came to us with a broken arm, but it's healing."

"How did that happen?"

Lucia's eyes widened. "They were all in a train wreck, the commander and Madame Vail and Milla. She was with her sister, but she died."

So they'd lied to both of us. The Vails wanted Milla to live with them, apparently to help them deal with their unruly daughter. I recalled Walter's guess that she was probably SQ material.

"I'm sure they'd say they did your sister a favor," Renee said later when I told her what I'd learned from Lucia. "The Vails assume that what they want should happen, whether others like it or not. The servants out there are no better than slaves."

"Why would the Vails treat their own people like that?"

"Maybe you didn't notice, but the Vails are blond with light skin. Lucia and her people look more like you, with brown skin and dark hair." Renee gave me a look. "Is your sister—?"

"She's very different from me. In fact, she and the Vails' daughter look almost like twins."

"Huh." Renee shook her head. "Giselle Vail gets an idea in her head that she thinks is cute, and she'll be fascinated with it for a while. A few years back she had the workers release hundreds of rabbits on the estate, because they looked so picturesque hopping around the grounds. Problem was they reproduced like—well, like rabbits. They ate the grass, chewed the bark off the commander's expensive fruit trees, and drove out the other small animals. The staff spent months hunting them down and repairing the damage."

"Lucia says their daughter behaves better with Milla there."

She chuckled. "From what I hear, that would make everyone on the estate happier."

"I need to talk to Milla and find out if *she's* happy."

Renee's left brow rose. "If they told her you're dead, I doubt they'll let you walk in there and tell her otherwise."

"Then I'll have to sneak in. I'll catch Milla alone and ask if she wants to stay with the Vails." When Renee looked doubtful, I repeated, "I can't just leave her there without knowing how she's being treated."

She thought about that. "I know she and Isa go riding most days. You might be able to get her alone then." Her brow knit. "Still, from what I hear, there are guards everywhere."

"How can I get an idea of the layout?"

"Ask Dick." She gave me a wicked grin. "There are deer in the woods, and when he was younger, he and his friends used to sneak onto the property to get themselves some fresh meat every once in a while."

"So it can be done."

"It could back then. When his father died and he took over, the commander put cameras everywhere, so it will be harder now." Noting my dismay, Renee finished, "Ask Dick if he thinks it's possible. If he does, get him to draw you a map."

"It's possible," Dick said as he opened hamburger buns and spread them on the grill to toast. "There are lots of guards, yes, but the estate is huge, so it's hard to cover. The cameras are in obvious places, along the fence, along the inner wall, and mounted over the doors on every building. But surveillance depends on the attention span of the people watching the cameras, and that is a really boring job. Say you've got fifty cameras and two guys watching. They might see you slip by, but they might not." He turned to me. "You have to be willing to take that chance."

Telling myself I'd be just a blip of movement, easily dismissed as a deer or a coyote, I said, "I am."

Dick was able to sketch out a surprisingly complete diagram of the estate on the back of a placemat, with *X*s marking where the guard shacks were. By the time he was done though, he'd changed his mind about my chances and decided I'd never make it. "Don't worry about me," I told him in the breeziest tone I could manage. "I've always been a stealthy type." Grandmother would probably have used the word *sneaky.* Either way, I had skulking skills, from slipping out of the house at night, from reading tribal records I wasn't meant to see, and from spying on Rolf in hopes that I could somehow, someday, pay him back for what he'd done to me.

It was cloudy the next morning, and I cursed (under my breath) with frustration, guessing there'd be no horseback riding if it rained. I continued my service to Renee and Dick by extending a trench behind the restaurant where they buried their waste. I'd heard him mention to her that it needed doing, but Dick was in no shape for hard labor and Renee was busy cooking, baking, waiting tables, and cleaning up. When I said I could do it, I read approval in her eyes. She found me a pair of gloves to protect my hands from blistering, showed me what the job entailed, and left me to it. As I worked, the clouds rolled away and the sun began beating on my neck. The threat of rain had passed.

Soon I was headed for the Vail estate, guided by my compass. "Go due west," Dick had advised. "When you come to a cyclone fence with barbed wire along the top, follow it south. Watch carefully as you go, and I'm pretty sure you'll find a break." He grinned. "They keep fixing them, but the local poachers just make new ones. That will get you inside the outer perimeter. It's patrolled with ATVs, so you'll hear them coming and have plenty of time to hide. The difficult part will be getting past the inner perimeter. It's a brick wall with cameras all along its top."

Looking at the map he'd drawn, I'd asked, "Can I get around it by going into the lake?"

"There's a barrier there too. I haven't seen it, but I hear its some sort of grate that arcs from one end of the perimeter wall to the other, so people can't get to the lakeshore from outside."

"Wow. It sounds like they really don't want visitors."

"They don't want outsiders knowing how they live," he said. "'All animals are equal, but some animals are more equal than others.'" I guessed he was quoting something, but the sentence meant nothing to me. I was focused on finding Milla.

The way was easy until I came to the high wire fence Dick had described. It looked sturdy and forbidding, but I followed it, watching carefully, until I spotted a place where the metal had been cut and repaired with wire. I only saw it because of Dick's prediction and the way the cut edges caught the light a little differently.

Twisting the wires apart with pliers Dick had loaned me, I let myself through the fence and continued silently through a deep woods, listening for patrols. Renee had dug out Dick's camouflage coat, which helped me blend into the leaves. When I heard an engine some distance away, I dropped to the ground, put my face to the dirt, and waited. The ATV went by, its pace unhurried. Raising my head, I saw a uniformed man looking left and right as he passed. He paused for a moment, letting the machine idle as he looked carefully around. I barely breathed, but soon he went on, unaware he had company in the woods.

Once the ATV bumped off, I rose and continued. Soon something sparkled on my right, and I realized I was seeing glimpses of the lake between the trees. I knew the estate lay along its shore, so I simply kept the water on my right as I continued forward. After about three hours, I came to the inner wall Dick had described, which was formidable. Twice my height, it was stuccoed smooth and topped with nasty-looking spirals of barbed wire. I looked around for a tree with an overhanging branch, thinking I might climb up, crawl out over the wall, and drop down on the opposite side. They'd apparently thought of that. All overhanging branches had been cut back, leaving the trees close to the wall with round scars, all at about the same height.

I stood there for some time, frustrated to be so close to my goal and stymied by mute bricks and twisted metal. The estate house was inside that wall, perhaps a half mile from where I stood. I could hear sounds of human activity, an engine, a hammer pounding, the scrape of some other tool. Sunlight blinked on the water, and I turned toward it. Maybe I could get in via the lake.

Making my way to the shore, I stood in the cover of the trees and looked out. The lake was about ten feet away. Above me, a camera mounted atop the wall panned back and forth, monitoring the lake surface. A metal grid fastened to the wall with bolts extended across the shoreline and into the water. Slanting until it extended only a few inches above the lake surface, the mesh enclosed a section of the lake about the size of a baseball field.

If I went out twenty feet or so, I could easily crawl over the mesh, but if I did that, the camera atop the post would reveal my presence to guards somewhere who'd respond quickly and perhaps violently.

Thoughts of giving up came and went quickly. I would defeat Commander Vail's security. It had become a contest between us in my mind. All I wanted was a few words with my sister. He should not be able to keep me from that.

Anger at Vail was swept from my mind when I noticed a plant at my feet that I'd never seen before. A thick mat of green leaves with tiny white flowers, it covered perhaps six square feet of water, bobbing lightly as ripples tipped it up and down. Tightly clustered, the plants looked a little like a rug. Or a cover. A floating clump of weeds.

Taking out my trusty box-cutter, I hid my backpack in the trees and waded into the water, being sure to stay back from the cameras' range. Slicing the tightly-woven plants from their roots, I cut an irregular shape just big enough to cover me. Though I winced a little at the thought of the bugs that might be nesting among its strands, I arranged it over my head, shoved the box-cutter into my bra, and slid into the water. Forcing myself to move slowly, as I imagined drifting vegetation would do, I swam out to the point where the barrier protruded only a few inches from the surface of the lake. Since a clump of weeds shouldn't be making a sharp right turn, I curved slowly toward the grid. When my hands grasped it, I pushed myself over, hoping my butt didn't make too much of a bump as it cleared the barrier.

Once I was inside the boundary, I turned again and floated my way to shore, raising my head every few seconds to make sure there was no one nearby to notice me. Two people passed, but they were carrying a ladder between them and on their way somewhere. When they were gone, I waited for the camera to turn away and then crawled onto the shore. I laid my cloak of greenery near the wall for use on my return trip and moved into the trees, eager to explore my options for moving around the estate unseen.

The commander's boathouse was wide and squatty with big, open doors on either end and a hoist to carry boats out to the water and back in for storage. It was painted red with black trim and had lots of wrought iron decoration. Standing back from it, I spotted cameras over both doors. Anyone going in or out would be seen by those charged with watching for interlopers, so I decided it was best to avoid buildings in general. The land leading away from the lake was terraced, and each slant upward was planted with fruit trees. I made my way through lemon and grapefruit trees to the middle level, where I came to the stable. It had the same red walls, black trim, and wrought iron curlicues I'd seen on the boathouse. A camera at the peak of the roof pointed down at two doors, a small one for people to use and large double doors for horses and machinery. I climbed through another orchard and saw the house clearly for the first time. Nothing Dick or Lucia had said prepared me for Commander Vail's home.

It sat about thirty feet above the lake. I counted ten different sections, each roofed with red tile. Some were open to the air, others enclosed. Along the front, a sunken swimming pool had its own small waterfall with a slide along one end. I didn't count the number of windows on the second floor, but there were a lot. Greenery planted around the stuccoed walls made a beautiful contrast to the adobe, the red tile roof, and the turquoise water of the pool. My sister was living in a mansion. The people who'd told her I was dead spoke of equality and justice while living like princes and forcing others to wait on them. Hypocrites.

Reminding myself of my mission, I climbed the sturdiest tree I could find to get an overall look at the grounds. About two hundred yards to my left a guard shack sat beside what looked like the main gateway. In the opposite direction was a break in the wall that was probably the second gate.

Between the main gate and the house was a large garage. Next to it was a roofed portico where a half-dozen ATVs sat idle. Along the wall was a row of small, cabin-like units that I guessed were living quarters for the help. Behind the house, a high ridge formed a backdrop and suggested the going in that section would be rough.

Having gained a better sense of where I was, I went back to the stable. If Milla had gone riding today, she'd be returning soon.

Taking cover in the trees, I settled down to wait, my still-wet clothes slowly drying around me.

After a while I dozed, but the nicker of a horse woke me. Opening my eyes, I saw a strongly-built young man ride toward me on a large, tan horse. Behind him came Isabel Vail on a beautiful black, and then my sister Milla, riding a slightly overweight gray. I almost exclaimed aloud at the sight of her. She wore deep blue culottes and a blouse with a fitted bodice and puffed sleeves. A hat with a wide brim shaded her face and neck from the sun. Trim boots peeped out from the hem of the skirt. In spite of Grandfather's position, Milla had never had clothes so fine to wear at home.

The little party came into the paddock, fairly close to me. I turned my gaze on Isabel, trying to decide what she was like. As she chattered to her companions, I recognized that her sentences were odd. Connecting words were often left out and pronouns were misused. And she talked about rocks with far more enthusiasm than I'd ever heard before.

Milla smiled at Isabel, showing interest in the same way I'd seen her do when Aunt Sally rambled on about her sick headaches. The big guy helped her dismount, and she and he exchanged looks that acknowledged they were being patient with poor Isabel. They didn't seem irritated, just aware.

Milla seemed happy. She had always loved horses. She was dressed well. And who wouldn't like the lifestyle she'd been offered? If she was expected to be nice to a girl with intellectual disabilities in order to live here at Eden, Milla, who was as kind as anyone I knew, would be able to do that.

The guy took the horses and headed for the barn. The two girls went toward the house, Isabel holding Milla's arm and telling her some long story. I stayed where I was, my intentions turned to dust. After weeks of semi-starvation, hiding out, and sleeping rough with me, my sister had found good fortune. Lucia said the Vails were thrilled at how much Milla's company had helped their daughter, and it was rumored they were making plans to adopt her. That would mean she'd be sought-after as a wife, which I suspected was what Milla most wanted to be.

Was it fair of me to interrupt that new life to ask my sister to go back to traveling with me? We were renegades, heading to an unknown destination, looking for a man who was nothing to her. Did I even matter now? Milla thought I was dead, and she appeared to be better off without me.

"There might be someone on the grounds." The voice came from somewhere to my right. "Clay saw movement on the boathouse cam, and he says it looked human."

"Did you alert the others?"

"We've got two crews on the north side right now, out of range. I'll go that way until I can raise them on the radio."

"Okay, I'll keep an eye out around here."

"Donnie wants you up at the house to help make sure the family's okay."

"Will do."

Footsteps receded, going in opposite directions. Any chance that I might talk to Milla had disappeared. She was now being guarded by men with guns.

Remembering how pretty she'd looked, how relaxed, I told myself Milla was okay. I was the one in danger, since the whole estate would soon be crawling with men looking for me. I headed for the lake, dragged my cloak of vegetation around me, and left the Vail Estate the same way I'd come.

Back at the diner, I asked Renee if I might stay one more night. She agreed but didn't ask what my plans were. It was best for both of us if I went on my way without sharing my destination with her. I didn't have to worry about her tattling, and she wouldn't have to lie if someone asked where I'd gone.

The diner closed at six. About a half hour later, Renee and Dick were getting ready to head home when we heard knocking at the door. "Officers of MONC," a man called. "Open up now!"

Renee glanced at Dick, who nodded understanding of her silent command. "Come with me," he ordered in a low voice.

I followed him up the stairs, two at a time, while Renee called, "I'm coming!"

Darting into the room I'd slept in, I grabbed my pack. Dick gave the room a quick once-over and then led me to the window seat where I'd sat to eat my breakfast the day before. He pressed a spot at one end of the bench, and the front panel opened with a click. He caught it, lowering it silently to the floor. "In there," he whispered. Crouching, I rolled into the space. Dick closed the panel, and I heard his steps on the stairs as he left me in darkness.

It was maddening to lie there, unable to tell what was happening. I was terrified that at any moment the panel would reopen to reveal a masked Monkey Man glaring at me. Footsteps sounded below and above, and bits and pieces of what Renee told them reached my ears. Yes, there'd been a woman with long dark hair. She'd traded a day's work for meals. Her voice faded as she followed them back downstairs, but I thought she claimed I'd left hours ago. I only heard rumbles after that, but I assumed Dick backed up his wife's story. It didn't sound like the intruders were convinced, and a yelp from Renee made me shiver with fear.

For as long as they could, Renee and Dick would claim I'd come and gone, just another renegade in need of a meal. But violence often accompanied the Monkey Men's interrogations. How much would my hosts suffer before they either convinced the men of their honesty or broke down and gave me up?

I wondered too who'd called to report me. The truck driver? A patron at the diner? Lucia? The answer didn't matter. I had to protect myself and my hosts by staying quiet until the officers left. Then I had to get away as fast as possible.

After they'd searched everywhere they could think of, I heard the rumble of boots as the men congregated downstairs. A voice gave orders, but I only heard bits. "—stay here tonight." … "—morning, we'll bring in dogs." … "—your eyes open, got it?" The answer was incomprehensible, but the tone was affirmative. The front door opened, and the last words I heard came from outside. "—put some ice on that eye." The tone was amused, and I guessed the man who'd given Renee the injury was now prescribing treatment for the swelling.

A large vehicle pulled up, stopped for a few seconds, and then drove off. I heard Dick ask Renee a question. "I'm fine," she replied. "Let's go home." Then it was quiet.

Though I wanted out of the confining space, caution whispered that the fact that neither Renee or Dick had come to release me meant they could not. It wasn't easy to lie there with my legs cramping, breathing air that was stale and dusty, but I lay still, listening. After a long silence, the scrape of a chair downstairs confirmed my fears. Men, two of them, it turned out, had been left on guard in hopes of catching me. The tenor of their conversation turned from cautious observation to gradual relaxation and finally to casual storytelling. They'd convinced themselves I was gone, so there was no one to watch for. That meant they had nothing to do all night but entertain themselves. One did most of the talking; the other listened and laughed a lot.

From time to time one of them would get up, making the chair legs grate against the floor. I'd hear the opening and closing of a cupboard or cooler door and the thump of plates as they served themselves from Dick and Renee's stores. After each break, talk resumed. I waited for hours, hoping I didn't go crazy in my tiny prison and betray my presence. Finally the talking stopped. I made myself count to three hundred. No sound came from downstairs. It was time to go.

Slowly, slowly, I searched the wood around me for the catch that would release the front panel. Once I found it, I turned it carefully, holding both parts so there was only a soft click as they separated. With great care, I lowered the panel to the floor and rolled out, pulling my pack with me. I took a minute to stretch my legs, release my shoulders, and ease the crick in my neck. Then, clicking the panel back into place as quietly as possible, I rose to my feet and tried to figure out how I'd get past the guards and out of the diner unseen.

I knew from my cleaning efforts the day before that the upstairs windows were all painted shut. The staircase ended next to the kitchen door, which had full-swing hinges. The front door locked with a key, but the one in the kitchen had a panic bar. If I could get down the stairs and into the kitchen without being seen, I could go out that way.

Tiptoeing down the stairs, I listened for a while and then peeped out to get a look. Dressed in their usual black t-shirts and pants, the men sat facing each other at a table near the front door. Between them were a half-dozen empty plates and two almost empty glasses. One man rested his head in the corner where the booth met the wall. He faced me, and his mouth hung open. The other man supported his face with one hand, his elbow on the table. Both sets of eyes were closed.

As I was about to step out from the staircase, the second man's hand relaxed to the point that his chin fell out of it. With a "Huh?" he sat up, opened his eyes, and looked around. Shrinking into the shadows and quieting my breathing, I waited for several long minutes.

He tried to stay awake; he really did. He drummed his fingers on the table. He finished whatever was in the glass. He rubbed his neck and stared out the window at the dark. But gradually, weariness overtook him again. This time he didn't lean on his hand. He set his forearms on the table and laid his head atop them, creating the most comfortable position he could manage in the circumstances.

When his soft breathing again indicated sleep, I stepped from the stairway into the kitchen. Pausing in the unlit room, I oriented myself to the layout I recalled: an island in front of me, cabinets and appliances on both sides, the exit door on the far wall. As part of my duties I'd oiled the door's hinges and hardware, so there shouldn't be any squeaks.

Though being so close to two Monkey Men made my teeth grind together, I couldn't leave the diner empty handed. Opening a cupboard, I took a loaf of bread and put it into my pack. In the cooler I found a small ham and stuffed it in too. I put half of the money I had left in a bowl in the cupboard as payment. With the satisfying weight of food on my back, I felt my way to the exit door, grasped the panic bar, and ever so slowly, pushed it down.

The result was a terrible clatter. The Monkey Men had wedged a broomstick under the panic, and it dropped onto the floor, bounced a few times, and then rolled until it hit a corner. Shouts sounded from the dining room as my pursuers scrambled up from their naps and tried to figure out where the noise had come from.

It was too late to retreat. Stepping out the door, I let it close behind me but paused on the back step, unsure where to go. The area around the diner was open, with no friendly woods to hide in. My only options were the sheds and the woodpile, none of them great hiding places. The men would have flashlights, so the darkness wouldn't hide me for long.

I ducked behind the woodpile just as the door opened. "Was it the girl?" one man asked. "Did you see her?"

"I didn't see anything. Just heard the commotion."

Two bright beams appeared to my left. "You look out here," the first man ordered. "I'll take a walk around the building." One of the lights wheeled over my head and then disappeared.

While the Monkey Man searched the sheds, one by one, I thought of a way to find better cover. The trench I'd dug the day before was about twenty feet away and long enough that I could lie down in it. If the men didn't approach it and shine their lights in, they wouldn't see me, and from a distance, I didn't think they'd see there was a trench there at all.

Sprinting away from the woodpile, I launched myself into the trench just as the shed door slammed. I felt my head meet dirt, tasted it in my mouth. I tried not to move, not even to breathe, as the flashlight beam moved back and forth above me. Was any part of me visible? I didn't think so. Had he caught my movement out of the corner of his eye? I hoped not. Rising, falling, left then right, the beam of light moved over the area.

The kitchen door opened and the other man called, "I think I found the culprit, Jerry. This fellow was in the kitchen, sniffing around the counter."

The flashlight beam swung away from me. "A cat made all that noise?"

I let out the tiniest sigh of relief. Roscoe must have sneaked in as I went out.

The man chuckled. "I figure he put a foot on that panic bar and shifted it just enough to knock the stick loose." He spoke to the cat. "Nosy critter, ain't ya?"

I raised my head in time to see the man dump Roscoe on the ground, none too gently. The cat scampered away as if he'd been swatted. The men went back inside, unaware that my freedom, maybe even my life, had been saved by a stray cat.

The next few days were cold, lonely, and miserable. Because someone had reported my presence at Dick's diner, I stayed completely away from people. I traveled on foot and followed my compass, going directly west whenever possible. I would get to the border. I would cross into Dorado somehow. After that, I'd figure out how to locate my father.

When I judged I was far enough from Eden, I started hitchhiking. Cal had told me it was fairly common in the Southwest, and as long as I kept my paring knife handy, I'd be safe. I got rides from a pastor who tried to convince me to return home, an elderly man who regaled me with stories of his youth, and a couple of truck drivers who just wanted someone to talk to. All except the pastor made passes at me, but none of them pushed it very hard. I was pleased with my progress, and I even gave the last trucker a kiss before climbing out of his rig at a crossroads.

In a burg called Glazier, I was walking past a gas station when a panel van pulled into the parking lot. Lettering on the vehicle said *Farley Home Furnishings, Farleyburg*. The back doors were half-open, due to rolls of carpeting that extended beyond the vehicle's length. The doors were tied together with twine, and a red fabric flag at the end of the carpet rolls warned other drivers to be watchful. Farleyburg, I recalled from the map, was only fifty miles or so from the border.

"Hey, Mister," I said to the driver. "I'm heading for Farleyburg. Any chance you'd give me a ride?"

He didn't even look my way. "Get lost, bitch."

Well, that wasn't very nice.

When the driver had gone inside, I regarded the van's open doors. Might I go along as a secret passenger? I took a look through the gap. Rolls of carpeting of different types and colors filled the cargo area. Atop them was underlayment, soft, foamy rolls about four feet wide. If I crawled on top of the carpet rolls and covered myself with the padding I could ride unseen, hopefully all the way back to the van's home base in Farleyburg. It was a risk, but I decided it was worth it.

Tossing my pack ahead of me, I squeezed between the doors and rearranged the cargo space to make myself a nest which, while not exactly comfortable, would do. Eating a chunk of Renee's bread, I sipped at my canteen and then settled in. When the driver returned with something that smelled of cinnamon and a soda pop, the two of us set out for Farleyburg.

I tried to sleep along the way, but thoughts of Milla interfered. Had I done right to leave her with the commander's family? Did she miss me like I missed her? Of course she'd have been glad to learn I was alive, but then she'd have been faced with a difficult choice. I couldn't promise her security or comfort or a happy resolution to our quest. Milla's loyalty to me would have collided with the new life she'd found, one that appeared to be secure, comfortable, and resolved.

Each time the van stopped, I took stock of the opportunities that presented themselves. If my driver parked near a store or another vehicle, I had to stay put. But if the back of the van faced a blank wall or a line of bushes, I slipped out, took care of my personal business, and got back in before he returned. On the road he sang a lot, and it wasn't good. The guy knew all the words and some of the tunes to his favorite songs.

The hardest part for me was judging where we were and how far we had to go. I knew I had to leave the van before it reached its destination, but I had no way of knowing when that would be. Farleyburg had looked like a fairly big city on the map, so I hoped I'd be able to tell by the increase in traffic. No way did I want to reach Farley Home Furnishings and come face to face with men who opened those doors expecting to find only carpeting.

A hint to our position came from one of my unwitting host's songs. "Three days on the road, and I'm gonna make it home tonight," he bellowed, and I got the sense he meant it. When the van slowed and began turning down one street after another, I guessed it was time for me to get out. As quietly as possible, I rolled aside the underlayment and scooted to the back of the van. The traffic around us helped, keeping the driver focused ahead and covering small noises I made.

Looking out, I saw lots of lights and plenty of cars. I bit my lip as I practiced in my head what I had to do. The next time the van stopped, I'd get out. Other drivers would see me, but I didn't think anyone would leave their vehicle to chase me down. My driver might realize what was happening, but again, would he leave the van at a stoplight to pursue me?

My chance came when an alarm clanged ahead of us. Looking over my shoulder at the front window, I saw wooden barriers lowering to block traffic due to an oncoming train. Cursing softly, my driver braked to a stop.

Behind us, the driver of a car leaned forward, fiddling with either the radio or the heater. Behind him sets of headlights glowed in a line, perhaps six or eight of them. Seizing my chance, I slid out the rear doors and onto the street. My action caused the man in the car to look up, surprised. Behind me I heard my driver say, "What the—?"

Giving the man in the car a cheerful wave, I ran toward the nearest dark spot. Voices rose behind me, questions from nearby cars and shouted threats from my driver, but I'd been right. Not one of them was willing to abandon their vehicle in the street. The van driver might report the incident to the local toppers, but I'd be long gone by the time they arrived.

I ran parallel to the train tracks, just far enough away from them to be out of the light. At first I raced, then I trotted, and finally I walked as fast as I could manage. After about a half mile, I turned back. No one behind me. My neck relaxed a little, so it no longer felt like a hand hovered behind me, about to squeeze it. When I reached a well-lit area, I slowed to a walk and tried to look like I knew where I was going.

The city of Farleyburg curled around a hill like a decorative scarf. On my left, the train that had stopped the carpet seller's van rattled around the rise and disappeared from sight. To the right lay the population center, with headlights, neon signs, and street lights everywhere. Drawn toward darkness, I climbed the hill, feeling the ground slant sharply under my feet. I passed buildings as I went, but no light showed inside. From time to time I met a person or two, but not one of them even glanced at me. They lit their way with flashlights, so I figured it was okay to get mine out and take a better look at my surroundings. Light revealed that the buildings I passed were not just empty, they were damaged. Farleyburg had been bombed at some point. The section now below me, the flats, had either escaped damage or been rebuilt. Here on the hillside, ruined hulks had been left to rot. I plodded on, unsure what I was looking for.

I needed a place to rest in safety and figure out my next move, and an empty building seemed perfect. It came down to a random choice, a two-story building marked *Condemned-No Entry.* Its front entrance gaped open, the double doors completely gone. Over it was part of a sign: *—ry's Live Theater.* Under that in smaller letters was *—rls, Girls, Girls*! Stepping cautiously through, I listened for a moment. Nothing. My light revealed a water-damaged wall lined with poster-sized frames. The pictures inside them were ruined, their bright colors washed away. Behind the partial wall were rows and rows of seats, also ruined by rain and wind. Beyond them was a stage, or what was left of it. There was no sign the place was inhabited. While I did hear movement in the corners, I was pretty sure it was rats, not people.

Alongside the ruined stage, a broken staircase led to a loft. From it a catwalk crossed to the far side of the stage, no doubt useful for whatever productions had been held there. Though the stairs had been blown into splintered, broken sticks, a banister still ran up the wall they'd once been attached to. Looking up at the area above, I decided that would be a good place to get a few hours of sleep. I had plenty of climbing experience from childhood: trees, barn lofts, even ruined bridges we'd scaled to use as diving boards over the river.

Grasping the banister with both hands, I set a foot on it, testing to see if the bar would hold my weight. When it did, I pulled the other foot up and, hand-foot-hand-foot, began the perilous climb to the loft. I looked up, not down at the splintered boards and protruding nails below me. I didn't let myself wonder how long the banister would hold after years open to the weather. And I didn't let myself imagine what, or who, I might encounter on the loft above.

The answer was no one at the moment, but there were signs that people slept there: grubby blankets, battered dishes, and piles of clothing. I tested the catwalk, crawling onto it on hands and knees, ready to dodge back to safety if it gave out. It shivered a little but remained in place. On the other side was an alcove, out of sight and big enough for me to lie down in.

Conditions in the alcove weren't ideal. There was only a bit of roof overhead, so if it rained in the night, I'd have to decide which half of me I wanted to keep dry. There was also nowhere to pee. From the smell of the place, I guessed other residents had solved that problem in the most convenient way possible. Despite those drawbacks I was off the streets, out of sight of toppers and Monkey Men. I had half of the ham and some of the bread I'd taken from Renee and Dick's diner. Using my box cutter, I sliced off a chunk of ham and ate it. Then, with my pack as a pillow, I lay down to sleep.

I woke to voices. Peering around the partition, I saw two men and a woman in the loft. A battery-operated lantern gave a dim view of them shaking out the blankets I'd seen earlier. They weren't just passing through, I realized. This was their home. Should I wait until they were asleep and try to sneak past them, or reveal my presence and hope for the best?

Coughing lightly, I stood and stepped onto the catwalk. "I'm sorry to intrude. I needed a place to sleep tonight."

"How'd she get up here, Moe?" That was the younger of the two men. "Nobody knows about the ladder but us."

"Must be part squirrel." The other man's face was shadowed, but he sounded old, maybe forty. I saw the scrawny arm that held the lantern, jeans with ragged hems, and a pair of battered boots.

"Well, she can't stay here." That was the first man, whose face showed as he leaned into the light, trying to get a look at me. His eyes were set too close together, and while I know it isn't fair to judge a person on looks, that and his nasty tone made me decide I didn't like him much.

The woman, who had a cloud of red-brown hair and waist impossibly small compared to her bust and hips, spoke more kindly, though they all seemed to think I couldn't hear them. "She's probably just passing through."

"I am," I said. "I'll be gone tomorrow."

The younger man appealed to Moe. "We barely take care of us. How we gonna—"

"Jeez, Mart," the woman said reproachfully, "Nobody's talkin' about adopting her. She just wants to sleep here."

"What if the toppers are after her? What if they come with dogs and stunners and clubs? You think they'll let us be?"

"You're right," Moe said, "but Steph's right too." To me, he said, "Come morning, you'll have to move on."

"Fine."

Mart still wasn't happy. "What if she tells people about our spot? Pretty soon we'll be crowded right out."

"Where are these people gonna come from, Mart?" That was Steph. "Looks to me like she's all alone."

“It’s stupid!” Mart turned away abruptly, and I heard him muttering grievances as he arranged his bed.

“Give us a look at you,” Moe ordered, and I shone my flashlight toward my face. “You’re young.”

“A runaway, I guess,” Steph said. I nodded then turned off the light.

“Mart’s right,” Moe told me in a warning tone. “We can’t let you stay.”

“I understand. I’m sorry to bother you. I’m—” A rush of emotions: losing Milla, being tired and broke, and now facing the animosity of strangers, made tears sting my eyes. “I’m going somewhere, but I’m—It’s been hard.”

“You’ll be okay,” the woman said. “Everything will turn out good for you. I just know it.”

They turned away then, and I heard them settle in along the outer wall, where there was enough roof left to shelter them from the elements. I slept again, this time a little better. In this ruined place, at least I wasn’t completely alone.

I woke when the sun rose high enough to peep through missing sections of the roof. Sitting up, I watched it turn the ruined building gold. I needed to pee, but I stayed where I was, not wanting to disturb my fellow residents. To take my mind off my bladder, I took out the journal, which I’d neglected since losing Milla. Removing one of the letters written on pastel stationery from its paper clip, I read another note that Bonnie’s mother had written.

> Sweetheart,
>
> I’ve been calling and calling, and I know you’re choosing not to answer. I’m sorry your friend

> Kent died. You know I don't condone violence, no matter how much I disagree with a person's lifestyle. If only you and I could talk, face to face. You need family right now. You need your mother, who loves you in spite of everything. Please call me.

In the journal Bonnie had written the response she apparently couldn't convey to her mother.

> We were supposed to be this big experiment, the nation where everyone had a voice. Well, the experiment failed. We can't be too different. We can't be "unnatural." I am what I am, Mom, but your response has always been, "We can fix you." No thanks.

Like my Uncle Benny, Bonnie had been queer. That meant that like him, she'd have had to hide her "unnatural" feelings from the tribe or risk having a *Q* tattooed on her forehead. I guessed they'd agreed to present themselves as a couple before coming to live in Tribe Woods. That was clever, though it was sad that they had to pretend.

When sounds across the room told me the people I'd met the night before were waking up, I followed the catwalk to their space. Steph had already rolled her blankets and set them along the wall, where they became her backrest. In better light, I saw streaks of gray in her hair and wrinkles at the corners of her eyes. Beside her, Moe was tearing strips of cardboard from a box and inserting them into his left shoe, apparently to seal a hole.

Opening my pack, I took out the remaining bread and ham. "Would you share a meal with me?"

“We’d be thrilled.” Moe had a leprechaun face, knobs everywhere, and lively eyes. His enthusiasm was immediately endearing.

I handed the meat to Steph, who set it on a piece of cloth and cut four slices with a knife she carried on her belt. I handed out slices of bread, and we each made ourselves a sandwich. Steph made a fourth and set it aside for Mart, whose sleeping form resembled a pile of rags. Re-wrapping the remaining ham, Steph gave it back to me. Moe gazed at it longingly until it was out of sight in my bag.

When Mart groaned and stretched on his blankets, Moe called, “Our visitor brought food, Mart. Come have a sandwich.”

Rising, he joined us. Though pleased by my gift, Mart still wasn’t pleased with me. “Did you tell her she can’t stay here?”

“You might thank her for sharing her food, Mart.” Moe’s tone was a warning.

“Thanks,” Mart muttered in the least thankful tone ever. “I still think she’s going to bring us trouble.”

“The best thing we can do is to help her on her way,” Moe said. Turning to me, he asked, “Do you have a trade? We might be able to help you find work so you can make enough money to travel on.”

“I’m good with finances.”

Moe chuckled. “Nobody we know has any money. Anything else?”

I thought for a while. “I can sing.”

That made Steph smile. “What kind of songs do you know?”

"Lots. 'When Will I Be Loved?' 'Heartache Tonight,' 'Walk Like an Egyptian.' Stuff like that."

Moe turned to Steph. "I wonder if Larry might know of a group that's looking for a pretty face up front."

She liked that idea. "I'll find him today and ask." To me, she explained. "A long time ago I was an entertainer, right here in this spot. It was Larry's Live Theater back then. Farleyburg got bombed in the fighting, and they shut the theater down. Said what we did was indecent." She flipped a hand, mimicking the outrage of people she clearly didn't like. "My old boss Larry sets up tours for bands nowadays. I'll ask if he knows of a group that needs a girl singer."

Though the idea scared me a little, I needed money. "That would be great. Thank you."

Mart had finished his sandwich in about three bites, and he glanced at my bag as if wondering what else I had in there. When I didn't offer more, he returned to his bed, lying down and turning his back to us.

"Don't pay my grumpy son any mind," Steph said. "I'll be back before you know it."

Moe got out the ladder I'd heard them mention the night before. He'd made it from scrap lumber, he said as he set the rickety frame in place. "When we're here, we haul it up. When we go out, we hide it behind the rubble downstairs."

"Very clever," I said. When he grinned at the compliment, I saw that most of his back teeth were missing.

"Keeps us safe. There's plenty of folks around here who'd steal what little we got if we weren't hard to get to."

When Steph was gone, Mart tossed back his blanket and announced that he too was going out. "I'll see you at work tonight," he told Moe. Setting his hands and feet on the ladder frame, he slid down it like a fireman. He was out the door a second later.

"How do you have jobs but no place to live?" I asked Moe. "In my tribe, every working family gets a house."

"That ain't how it is here," Moe said. "Our factory runs three shifts, six days a week. Mart and I work third, since the pay's a little higher, but the cost of living keeps going up." He waved a hand at the rubble around us. "A lot of houses and apartment buildings got destroyed in the war, and nobody's building new ones."

"Your tribe doesn't provide housing?"

He frowned. "Steph and I had an apartment until about a year ago, but it came to the point where we had to choose between having a roof over our heads or eating every day." He gestured at the loft. "You can see which one we chose. Mart couldn't get a place either, so we kinda had to let him come in with us." Moe's tone signaled regret.

"Why doesn't your leader do something to help?"

"Cuz he's a crook, that's why." Moe's face narrowed. "Back in my father's day, laborers joined together to get a fair deal, but that's illegal now. You won't recall it, but once upon a time, the government helped the people." He shook his head. "Now it's every man for himself."

"I'm sorry things are so hard for you."

He accepted my sympathy with a nod. "Mart's real bitter. Says nobody's good to us, so we shouldn't be good to nobody."

An hour or so later, Steph returned. Moe rose to take her hand as she stepped from the ladder to the loft, her expression revealing satisfaction. "Larry knows of a band that's supposed to start a tour tomorrow. Their girl singer got appendicitis yesterday and had to have surgery, so they told him this morning they'd have to cancel the first few weeks of their tour. Larry had me go and tell them about you, and the head guy said you should come in and audition for him tonight." The best part for me was when she added, "They're heading west."

Grandfather had always said my voice was amazing, but he was my biggest fan. Could I stand on a stage and sing without him behind me strumming his guitar, without Milla's flute adding harmony and color, without Grandmother filling in the chords on her dulcimer? Could I perform for a crowd of strangers? If that was what it took to move on, I decided I could.

We spent the afternoon in Moe and Steph's little nest, telling stories about our lives. They were interested in experiences I thought of as mundane, like picking apples. "Apples right off the tree," Moe said, shaking his head. "Not much fresh fruit around these days." His brow furrowed. "They got them fruit pies at NationMart, though. I s'pose they're the same thing."

When evening came, we shared more of my ham and some canned green beans Steph warmed on a tiny hotplate. Once we'd eaten, Moe left for his job at the factory, which was an hour's walk. When he was gone, Steph gave me directions to the place where I'd find the band manager, putting on her coat as she talked. "I told him you'll need a place to sleep, and he said you can stay on the band's bus tonight if he takes you on. If he doesn't" she warned, "you should know there's a curfew at ten. Once you hear a long, shrill whistle, the toppers can arrest anybody that isn't authorized to be out."

She was ready to leave, and I asked, "What do you do while Moe and Mart are at the factory?"

Steph looked around before answering, as if afraid she'd be overheard. "It's what they call dead-work."

"What's that?"

She gestured widely at their surroundings. "People die in these ruined buildings almost every day. The Govt pays me to find them and haul them to a burial pit a few miles from here. Moe found me a wheelbarrow, and me and a friend wrangle the bodies into it and take 'em out there." Folding her hands, she finished, "We split the bounty sixty-forty, on account of the wheelbarrow being mine."

I frowned. "Why—?" I stopped, unsure how much I wanted to know.

"They're afraid of disease, and of course there's the smell." One side of her mouth lifted in an approximation of a smile. "They want it done in the dark, so nobody sees how many dead there are." Looking away, she added, "Wish I didn't."

When Steph was gone, I waited a few minutes and then put on my backpack and descended the ladder. I set it in its hiding place behind a pile of rubble on the ground floor and, seeing no one on the street, left the building. Only a few steps down, I heard a voice behind me. "Ain't you a pretty thing, out all alone at night."

Turning, I made out the shadow of a man in the doorway of a derelict building. The light was dim, but I could see that his gut hung over his belt like it was trying to slide down his leg and get away. Ahead of me was an alley, and parked in its entry was a brown panel van with its motor running. Out at night, alone, I'd been spotted by a Supply Squad.

"I don't suppose anyone's gonna miss you." The man's tone vibrated with threat. As he stepped onto the cracked sidewalk behind me, his smug smile and relaxed posture hinted he'd been expecting me. Behind him someone moved, slinking into the shadows. When the second man looked over his shoulder once, I recognized Mart's beady eyes and slimy grin. I spent a half-second regretting the fact that I'd shared my ham with him.

When the goon stepped onto the moonlit sidewalk, I saw that he was middle-aged and overweight. Lack of physical exercise showed in the tension on the buttonholes of his shirt. His cheeks hung over his jawbone. His ankles puffed over his shoe tops. In a footrace between us, I was the favorite. He held a stunner in one hand, but since we were about thirty feet apart, I was out of range at the moment.

The van presented a problem, because while I might outrun the fat man, I couldn't outrun that. I turned and squinted, trying to see the driver, but all I could make out was a messy mop of blond hair and two pale hands clutching the steering wheel. If I ran, the driver was ready to chase me down.

But he was parked in the alley, facing the street. What if I chose an escape route they didn't expect?

Turning away from the man on foot, I ran directly toward the driver's side of the van. The fat man shouted, "Hey!" The driver looked surprised, but I saw realization dawn in his eyes. I could run right past him and down the alley. He would have to pull the van out into the street and turn it around in order to follow, which would give me a good head start. He did what I'd hoped he'd do. He opened the door, intending to get out and stop me as I ran by.

He was a shade too late. I'd reached the van, and I slammed into his door as hard as I could, catching him with one leg halfway out. As he screamed and swore, I headed down the alley, praying that the darkness I was heading into led to openness on the opposite end. I tripped over unseen objects. I skirted a pile of rotting crates. I ran toward a dim rectangle of light that told me I might get through this if I could keep my feet and fend off my fears.

Behind me the two men spoke excitedly to each other, making a plan. I hoped the driver was hurt badly enough to be out of service, but if not, I guessed he would drive around the block and try to locate me on the next street. The older man would follow me through the alley. I focused on speed, pumping my legs like pistons, so I'd have a few seconds to decide what to do when I emerged on the next street.

My pursuers probably knew the neighborhood better than I did, and they had the advantage of the vehicle I couldn't outrun. I needed to find a place to hide until they gave up looking for me.

An idea hit that was possibly genius, possibly stupid. At the first opportunity, I turned right. At the next block, I turned right again. A third right turn brought me back to Moe and Steph's place, a short distance from where the fat goon had stopped me. First I peeped carefully around the corner. The street was quiet. I couldn't even hear the van's engine. Ducking into the ruined building, I hurried toward the wrecked stairs. I didn't have time to get the ladder out, so I squirrel-climbed the handrail a second time, pulling myself onto the floor above and rolling out of sight. I lay there, lungs burning, listening for sounds of pursuit. I pulled air in through my nostrils and let it out through my mouth. I forced myself not to gasp or sob or cry. The goons wouldn't expect me to come back here, would they?

No one came into the building. No one spoke in hushed tones below me. No footsteps sounded on the sidewalk outside the ruined doorway. While I couldn't say how long the goons would hunt for me, it seemed that I was safe for the moment. I thought of Freida's sister and all the others who hadn't been lucky enough to escape the Supply Squad goons. What sort of society lets children be used and disposed of like old rags?

I waited an hour, listening to the silence below me, before leaving. Since the ladder was on the ground floor, I grasped the edge of the catwalk, let myself down as far as I could, and dropped to the stage, landing the way I'd heard paratroopers did: balls of the feet first, then calf, thigh, hip, and back. My version wasn't pretty, but I sustained no serious damage.

The place Steph had directed me to was a small club called Leon's. As instructed, I went to the stage door at the back and knocked. A long, bony face with heavy-lidded eyes peered out at me suspiciously. "You're late."

"I made a wrong turn and had to backtrack."

The man stepped back to let me in, then turned and led the way down a narrow passage to a small wooden stage. "I'm Pel," he tossed over his shoulder. About thirty, with shoulder-length hair, Pel might have stepped straight off the Van Halen CD cover Grandmother kept hidden in her bedroom at home. I'd sometimes snooped through them when she was out, interested in the days when people dressed like that, posed like that, lived like that.

"I'm Amanda."

"I guess you know our problem." He ran a spread hand through his blond hair, pushing it back, but it immediately fell back to where it had been. "This tour we're starting could make our name here in the Southwest. We don't want to cancel and disappoint our fans, but Lulu had emergency surgery. Doc says she can't join us for at least two weeks."

"That's too bad."

"Thing is, we're good, maybe great. There are big things in store, and we've worked hard to get where we are. I don't know if I want to take a chance on some unknown singer with no following."

Looking around, I formed a different opinion. While I knew nothing about the music business, I guessed from the condition of the building and the stuff on the stage that this was a small-time operation. I did know a little about men, and I recognized that Pel was full of hot air. "I'm here," I said casually. "Your singer isn't."

Jumping lightly from the stage to the floor, Pel took a seat at the first table. "Sing something for me."

No accompaniment. No warm-up. No encouragement. I moved slowly to center stage, my eyes on its scuffed surface as I gathered courage around me like a shawl. For once Grandmother was on my side, at least in my head. She whispered a suggestion, and I began with Jim Croce's "Time in a Bottle."

"Nice ballad style," Pel interrupted after I'd sung a few lines. "Now give me upbeat."

Raising the volume and the intensity, I struck a pose and gave him a chorus of "Hit Me with Your Best Shot."

"Not bad," Pel said. "You'll have to learn to project better, but we can work on that."

"Does that mean I'm going with you?"

"Don't get all excited," he said in a patronizing tone. "You carry a tune and you're good to look at, so until Lulu's well, you're our girl."

Chapter Seventeen

I rode with The Papas and Mama for ten days, singing at towns all along the way. Professional concerts were largely frowned-upon by the Govt, but in the Gold Section, as long as entertainers began with a prayer and ended with "God Be With You Till We Meet Again," they were mostly left alone. "Our shows make people happy," Pel opined as he lit yet another cigarette, "and there's less to be happy about in this country every year."

I wore Lulu's costumes, but since she'd soon be back, I couldn't alter them. She was bigger than I, so I made the dresses fit with safety pins up the back, which resulted in uncomfortable lumps of fabric. I made her shoes stay on my feet by stuffing the toes with old rags. From the front I looked okay, and as long as I shuffled my feet a little, the shoes stayed on.

Familiar with most of the songs in their repertoire, I quickly picked up the rest. In addition to Pel, who sang lead and played guitar, the band members were Arch, the rhythm guy, who was usually stoned, and Ian, a truly talented musician who sang harmony and played a dozen different instruments. I added tambourine or maracas if a song lent itself to that.

Though Pel grumbled that I didn't "shake it" like Lulu did, audiences responded well to us. Pel and Arch had corny routines they did as comic relief, and for one of them I had to cross the stage in a come-hither manner. I hated it. Every time I strutted past them, I heard a voice in my head. *Come here to me, brown girl. Come be nice to your Uncle Rolf.*

We traveled on an old school bus Pel had converted by taking out every other seat in the front half and hanging curtains to make each of us, four band members and the two roadies who took turns driving, a square of personal space about the size of a closet. The back of the bus was loaded to the roof with equipment. I didn't mind the cramped quarters, didn't mind the smell of marijuana, didn't mind the roadies coming on to me (They didn't really expect to get anywhere). I didn't even mind Pel's resentment of the fact that I wasn't Lulu. We ate three meals a day. I was safe. We sailed through checkpoints with minimal scrutiny. Best of all, each mile brought me closer to my father.

Ian, who loomed over everyone at six feet six, took me under his wing, treating me like his little sister. He explained the routines and gave me hints on how to deal with Pel, who was conceited, irritable, and irritating. Ian and I were usually the first ones up in the morning, so we'd find a place to get coffee, sit on benches damp with dew, and talk. I told him my reasons for coming on the trip, leaving out any specifics. He was sympathetic. "Nobody should have to live with family that don't treat them right."

"You had to leave your family too?"

"Had to?" He frowned. "Not really. My parents are good people. My tribe's contribution is operating heavy equipment. We dig, dredge, bull-doze, that sort of stuff. When I told my dad I didn't want to do any of that, he asked what I did want to do. When I said, 'Make music,' it was like I'd stabbed him."

"But music is good."

"It is," Ian allowed. "But neither of my parents get it. I visit sometimes, and I can tell they're waiting for me to grow out of this phase I'm going through." He grinned. "I'm thirty-two. I know how I want to spend my days, but Mother and Father are sure I'm kidding myself."

Our travels had brought us to a land of wide open spaces that were stark but beautiful. As the bus ground along, we passed rock formations that looked like giant children had piled them there to entertain themselves and then gone home to dinner. "We're close to the border with Dorado now," Ian told me in his ultra-bass voice. "There's lots of smuggling going on around here, stuff the Govt doesn't want us to have. Most of the locals like it, so they look the other way."

On the twelfth day Lulu joined us, pale but on her way to recovery. She made it clear from the minute she stepped off the bus that I was no longer welcome, and the way she snuggled in under Pel's arm told me a lot. There was no longer a place for me with the band, which was okay except that I was again in a depressingly familiar situation: no papers, no friends, no idea what the lay of the land was, and no idea how I'd move on.

That night I watched the show from the audience. Pel was right, Lulu was a better entertainer than I, though she'd have been in trouble back in our tribe, where shows had conformed to Grandfather's strict standards of decency. Here I saw only enjoyment on the faces in the crowd when Lulu shrugged out of her jacket and did a sexy shimmy as a finale.

When the show was over, I helped the band pack up. We toted drums and amps and guitar cases back onto the bus. Pulling me to one side, Ian gave me an envelope of cash that signaled the end of my employment. "I talked to a local who said there's a smugglers' camp a few miles out of town," he told me as I tucked the money into my pack. "It's a cliff with caves in it, like little apartments." I frowned, and Ian shrugged. "Maybe if you offer to pay them they'll take you to Dorado."

"They're more likely to slit my throat and toss my body to the cougars."

He rubbed at his beard. "They're businessmen, not killers." He ticked off points on his fingers. "They know how to get across the border, which you don't. The desert is hot in the daytime and cold at night. There are checkpoints to avoid and patrols coming through at odd times." He sniffed. "Lots of people want to leave Fairica these days, so stopping them at the border has become a priority for the Govt."

While Ian was right about most of it, I had no clue how to contact a bunch of smugglers or even find out exactly where they were. In the end it came down to chance. As we finished loading the equipment into the bus, I noticed a man watching from across the street. When I looked his way he tilted his head in greeting. I turned to Ian, who held out his arms for a hug. "It's been great having you with us, Girlie. Good luck with…everything."

"Thanks." I was reluctant to let go of him, since when I did, I'd be on my own again. The rest of the band, except for Lulu and Pel, wished me well, and I managed to hold back my tears as they climbed aboard. When the bus doors closed and I turned away, the guy was in the same spot, looking at me with what was clearly an invitation.

A local might know where the caves Ian had mentioned were located. Crossing the street to where he stood, I said, "Hi there. What's your name?"

His name was Ren, and he was clearly married but trying not to show it. "I came to the show last night, and when I saw you up on that stage, singing so good and looking so beautiful, I couldn't look away. I came back tonight, but that other girl took your place."

"You're sweet." I put a purr into my voice. "I noticed you in the crowd too. You were the cutest guy out there."

Ren was eager to take me somewhere we could be alone. His house wasn't an option, he said, because he had relatives visiting.

Ignoring the lie, I made a suggestion. "I heard there are caves in a cliff near here. I'd love to see them."

He frowned. "Bad people hang out in those caves."

I laid a hand on his chest. "Couldn't we sneak in really quietly and just take a peek at them?" When he hesitated, I added, "It'll be scary, but I'll be okay if you're with me."

He still hesitated. "It's dark now. You won't be able to see nothing."

I fluttered my lashes. "But I'll be able to see in the morning, when the sun comes up."

Milla would have been shocked. Frieda would have been mad at me. I didn't care, and it turned out okay, in an almost funny way. Ren asked me to wait a few minutes and returned looking pleased with himself. He took me to his car, and we drove a few miles out of town. Turning onto a small sideroad, he parked the car in the trees. We walked the rest of the way, crossing a sandy spot and stopping when a hilly section rose before us. "The caves are over that hill," Ren told me. "At sunrise we'll climb up there so you can get a look at the bad guys."

That was when Ren revealed the reason for his smug expression. He'd brought along a cloth bag, and from it he took a blanket and a bottle of tequila. In whispers, lest we attract attention from the smugglers' camp only a hundred yards away, we drank to our new friendship, to the stars, to chance encounters.

Actually, only one of us drank. I kept passing Ren the bottle, but when it was my turn, I only pretended to drink. I teased him a little about being able to hold his liquor, so he naturally had to prove that he could. He drank deeply, and soon he was slurring his words. Not long after that he was nodding, and with a few more slugs, he drifted off mid-sentence. While I'd been prepared to give him what he wanted if I had to, it seemed like a victory to get my way without slaking some creep's lust one more time.

The next morning I told him he'd been amazing, which seemed to make him happy. The morning was cold, and we shivered in our light clothing as Ren helped me climb to a spot where we could lie on our bellies and look across at the caves. Dim light from within revealed figures moving around, and he pulled me back from the edge. "We should go. We do not want to get caught spying on these people."

We returned to the town together, but Ren's mind had already moved on. I guessed he was inventing the story he'd tell his wife about why he hadn't come home all night. As soon as we parted, I retrieved my pack from where I'd stashed it and started back to the caves.

The sun was overhead when I reached the spot where Ren and I had awoken that morning, and the temperature warmed until my armpits and spine were damp and uncomfortable. As I approached, I studied the lay of the land. Two curved rock formations edged a river, like hands cupped around it. One rock wall was pitted with the caves I'd seen from above that morning. The other was blank, with only the occasional hardy shrub clinging to it and somehow finding sustenance. That was where Ren had led me to look down on the encampment. Puffing a little in the heat, I again climbed to the top and watched, trying to form a plan.

Beyond the caves, the river widened and curved out of sight. Seeing a glint of metal reflecting sunlight on my right, I moved down the ledge a bit until I could see that it was the grille of a truck parked around the bend. Scooting farther down the ledge, I saw two more trucks parked half in, half out of the river. They must have driven through the river itself to get there, but the hiding place was ingenious. The trucks were invisible from most viewpoints, and the water covered their tracks.

Going back to my original spot, I watched the little community that occupied the caves. Ladders had been lowered, and people went about various tasks. I noticed one man of maybe sixty, because he moved with some difficulty and had suffered a disturbing facial injury. One cheek was sunken, apparently from its supporting bone being shattered beyond repair. Despite that he greeted anyone he met cheerfully. As I watched, he climbed each ladder with a sack slung over one shoulder, went inside the cave briefly, and then climbed back down. The sack got fuller as he went. After he'd visited all the caves, the man walked downriver a good way and then dumped the bag's contents on the bank. It was clothing. Taking a cake of soap from his pocket, he knelt on the bank and began washing the items, scrubbing out the stains and rinsing with clear water. He hummed a song as he worked.

If I returned to ground level and stayed close to the canyon wall, I'd be able to approach the man without being seen by anyone else in the camp. I'd assure him I wasn't a threat and ask if they'd take me back to Dorado with them. The answer might be no, but if that was the case, I could simply run away. He was old and lame, and while he might raise the alarm, I'd have time to run and hide before the others figured out what was happening and where. While some of the men carried guns, the old man did not, so he couldn't shoot me. Besides, what gang would have one of their toughest men doing laundry?

Backing down the opposing cliff, I found the stream and followed it until I came to the spot where the man was working. He didn't hear me coming because of the plops and squishes he made as he worked.

"Sir?" He jumped a mile. "I'm not here to hurt you."

That didn't help. In fact, his expression told me he didn't understand what I'd said. Since I had no language but English, I acted out words, as I'd once done with Milla. "I" (pointing to my chest) "no" (shaking my head) "hurt" (mimicking a blow) "you" (pointing at the man).

His face relaxed a little, and I went on. "I need your help." Looking at me blankly, he shook his head.

I pointed to my mouth. "English?"

He thought about it. Finally he set aside the shirt he'd been washing, stood, pointed to the ground, and said what I interpreted as *Wait here*.

That was scary, since he might well return with people who might beat or even kill me. I looked longingly back the way I'd come. Did I have time to escape? If I did, I'd never know if the smugglers could help me get into Dorado. I had no other prospects. I would beg whoever returned with the old man to listen. I'd promise to do whatever they wanted if they helped me get out of Fairica. I'd...probably end up floating in the river, face down. I was close to bolting when the old man returned with another man, this one maybe thirty. The old one stopped on the far bank, but the newcomer waded the river, undeterred by the water that swirled around his boots. When he stood toe to toe with me, he asked brusquely, "You want something?"

Both men regarded me with blank faces and hostile eyes. How could I convince them I was worthy of their help? There had to be a reward in it for them, but all I had to offer was a little bit of cash now and the promise of more later.

"My father lives in Dorado. I was told you could take me there."

The man smiled, but it didn't make him seem any friendlier. "We're not in the business of skip-tracing deadbeat dads."

I didn't know what the last part meant, but I got that I was being refused. "My father sent a man to bring me to Dorado, where he lives. The man…died, but if you can help me find Sri Afzal, I think he'll—"

His whole demeanor changed. "Sri is your father?"

"Yes."

He said something to the older man, who hurried off. "Come with me," he ordered. "Hector will want to meet you."

I crossed the river, doing my best to keep my shoes dry by stepping on outcropping stones. The man headed toward the cave wall at a steady pace. By the time we reached it, a man, Hector, I assumed, was descending the ladder at one end. He was solidly built, about thirty-five. His feet seemed light on the rungs, and when he reached the bottom, his dark eyes assayed me as if I were a rock he'd been told might be a diamond. After a moment he said, "You have his eyes."

"You know my father?"

Hector swept a hand, indicating the camp. "Sri is in charge of all this." He pointed to a cave a few feet down. "Come with me. Diana will want to hear what you have to tell."

I followed Hector up the ladder into a cave where he introduced me to Diana, a deeply-tan woman with straight blond hair pulled into a knot at the back and tied with twine. "This girl claims she knows what happened to your husband."

Diana's face was stony as I told the story. When I finished, she was silent for some time. Afraid she'd blame me, I said, "I'm sorry. If I'd known what they were planning—"

"You could have done nothing." Her voice was raspy. "In this country, a woman doesn't control her own destiny, let alone that of another."

After a moment, I said, "I intend to control my own life from now on."

Diana's lips twitched in what seemed like approval. Turning to Hector, she said, "She can stay with me until we leave."

It would be two days, Hector told me, before they returned to Dorado. They could not communicate with my father in that time, since the Monkey Men were able to pick up transmissions by phone or radio. I'd have to wait until their work was done, but then they'd take me to my father.

In my time in the caves, I learned how convenient they were as a temporary camp. Besides being easily defensible, Hector's people had found and enlarged passages behind the "apartments" in several directions. The smugglers knew them well and could elude anyone who came looking for them simply by retreating into the cave's dark recesses and coming out somewhere else.

As Sri's daughter, I was treated with deference, though I detected suspicion from one or two. I understood their doubts, because I had no way of proving who I was until my father confirmed my identity.

The first man I'd met, Andy, did the cooking and cleaning for the group. He was kind to me, seeing that I got special bits at mealtime, the softest slice of bread, the most tender chunk of meat. Because he found English difficult, we couldn't communicate much, but Diana obligingly translated. Noticing he had trouble following, even in Spanish, I waited until he was outside and then asked, "What's wrong with Andy?"

"Nothing," she said bluntly. "At least there was nothing wrong with him before the Monkey Men got hold of him."

"What did they do?"

She licked her lips. "You don't want to know." It seemed for a few seconds that she wasn't going to say any more, but then she changed her mind. "Most times when they catch us, they kill us and leave our bodies to rot. But they knew that Andy was part of Sri's inner circle. They wanted him to tell them where Sri was, so they…didn't kill him." Her eyes were bleak. "As soon as we heard he'd been captured, we did everything we could to find him. Eventually we did, but we took too long. Now Andy's brain doesn't work like it should." She managed a smile. "But he won't give up. He insists on doing what he can for the effort, even if it's only cooking and cleaning for the rest of us."

"And what exactly is the effort?" I asked. "I know smuggling is profitable, but it seems like you have other motives."

Diana nodded. "We bring in items people can't get in Fairica, books the Govt considers unsuitable and that sort of thing. Mostly we supply electronics, so your people can rebuild their communications systems and start getting real information again. They need to hear the truth about your Govt. In some tribes people are starving while leaders take advantage of their positions to build massive wealth for themselves. Govt workers are mostly incompetent, corrupt, or both. The people we deal with share what they learn with others, which we hope will eventually bring your so-called Govt to a complete and ignominious end."

I'd sensed for a long time that the Govt's insistence on controlling the lives of its citizens was wrong. In my recent travels, I'd seen evidence of the damage it caused. How, I wondered, had the Govt convinced people to give up their rights, their choices, their humanity? Why did people fool themselves into thinking that one man knew what was best for everyone?

When I asked Diana those questions, she shook her head. "The only explanation I can see is fear. They made people afraid of anyone who didn't look like them or act like them." She met my gaze. "Most of the time, hate is fear in disguise."

The three trucks I'd seen had been "liberated" from an army transport fleet. "They're tough," Hector told me, "and they can go almost anywhere." Each night, he and his crews went out to make deliveries to various burgs. When all the goods had been dispersed, we prepared to return to Dorado. I rode with Diana and Ernesto, a driver Hector claimed could make the trip blindfolded. We started late in the day, and as we traveled, the sun grew fatter and then sank below the horizon, leaving a brief period of yellow glow and then darkness.

We traveled at night and on highways, but occasionally the radio on the dashboard would squawk three times, stop, and then squawk twice. That was a warning, and we'd turn off into what appeared to me unnavigable territory. Ernesto was unbothered by the bad terrain, and he always found a place where we could stop and wait for the all-clear, six short squawks. Once I saw what it was we were avoiding. A van with the MONC logo went by on a bridge above us, unaware of our presence below. When they were gone, Ernesto drove back up from the ditch, and we continued on our way.

Shivering, I asked, "If they catch us, will they kill us?"

"Yes," Diana replied calmly. "Your Govt decided that trials and prisons for people like us aren't worth the time and expense." I must have looked surprised, because she explained, "I don't think anybody ever said, 'This is the new rule,' but the Monkey Men started killing anyone they caught who didn't have an ID tat. They also kill those who are with them. You must be a criminal, or you wouldn't be hanging out with criminals. No one ever questioned it. They have immunity as long as they're acting for the Govt." She turned to look at me. "When we didn't hear from Chad, I knew I'd never see him again. I cried, because I loved the man. Then I promised myself I'm make the assholes who run this country pay."

The trip was long, and though I was nervous, I soon fell under the spell of road noise and vibration. My head drooped a few times, until finally I leaned it against the back window and dozed. It was still dark when I was jolted awake by Ernesto's, "Shit!" Opening my eyes, I saw lights had come on ahead, revealing two vans, a sawhorse-like barricade, and men with really big guns. Hector slammed on the brakes, no doubt intending to turn around, but something he saw in the rearview mirror stopped him. "We've got Monkey Men ahead and behind."

My heart began to race, and my knees bounced like twin rabbits. I wanted to scream. I wanted to be so quiet they wouldn't know I was there. Most of all, I wanted to be somewhere else.

"Trade me places," Diana ordered. It took me a second to comprehend, but I did as she said, rolling under her to the right while she slid over me to the middle of the seat. Once we'd done that, she slid to the floor and curled up, out of sight.

Ernesto had stopped the truck, though he left the engine running. A masked man stepped forward from the barricade, aiming a gun at his head. "Get out."

From the floor, Diana said, "Do what he says. Close the door as quick as you can."

I looked at her in disbelief. Did she think they wouldn't find her in there after they killed the rest of us? "Make a scene," she whispered. "Cry. Faint. Scream."

Opening the door, I slid to the ground and closed it behind me. I was at the edge of a paved road. Behind me were the other two trucks in our convoy. Behind them, two white vans blocked our escape.

Six of the eight men who'd been waiting at the barricade stepped forward until there was one of them on either side of each truck. They held their guns ready as the smugglers opened their doors and climbed out. On the faces of our people was understanding that they'd soon be killed. We were ordered forward, into the headlights of the first truck. I saw Hector's expression shift subtly when he realized Diana was missing. It wasn't exactly a hopeful look, just acknowledgment of a chance that hadn't been there before.

Everything about the Monkey Men was scary and designed to be that way. Their faces were covered, so only their hard, cold eyes showed. They shoved their gun muzzles close to our faces, and I couldn't help but imagine a bullet tearing through my brain. They moved almost in rhythm, their heavy boots crunching on the pavement. When Andy didn't move into line fast enough, one man kicked him hard, sending him stumbling forward. The others laughed, and one called out, "That's why you people will always be inferior. You never shift out of first gear."

A man with no mask sauntered toward us, into the spill of the headlights. He wore a smile, pleased that he'd netted a dozen of Sri's people and three of his trucks. No doubt he'd be a hero back at headquarters when he told how he shot us all down as if we were mad dogs.

I turned to look at the faces of my friends. There were signs of fear, traces of regret, but mostly, there was anger. Hector caught my eye as if asking a question, and I remembered what Diana had told me to do. *Make a scene.*

It didn't take much for me to appear hysterical, since I was already close. As the Monkey Men herded the last of us forward, I began begging, "Let me go. I haven't done anything wrong. Please let me—"

A slap from the unmasked man knocked me to the pavement. "Shut up, bitch!" I heard the others laughing as I struggled to rise to my feet. My ears rang. Bursts of light exploded inside my head, blurring my vision. When one of Hector's men stepped forward to steady me, the one who'd hit me calmly drew a pistol from his belt and shot him in the head.

I was sure I was next, but shots sounded from behind me. The man who'd hit me clutched at his eye and fell, hitting the ground hard. A second man clutched his thigh, screaming with pain. Wresting the wounded man's gun from his hands, Hector started firing. One of the others picked up the dead man's firearm and did the same. Soon there was shooting all around me. I crouched down, using the body of the Monkey Man as a partial shield. Our former captors, not so brave now that the tables had turned, dived for cover.

"The vans!" Hector shouted. I looked up to see the two vehicles that had been behind us coming our way. They came fairly slowly, since they had to pass close to our trucks to avoid sinking into the soft sand at the sides of the road. Gunfire blazed from the passenger sides, and another of our men went down. I stood frozen, unsure what to do, but Hector ordered, "Stay behind me." I followed him as the vans bore down on the spot where we'd been standing. A few feet off the road was a slight dip, hardly worthy of being called cover, but Hector shoved me toward it. "Get down on your belly and stay there," he said, and then he was gone.

I did as I was told, actually burying my head in the sand. Then the truck I'd been riding in made a growl of acceleration. Looking up, I saw it jolt into gear and start moving. It lurched to one side, ramming the van that was passing on its right. Slewing from the impact, the van went off the road, where it tipped crazily, its right-side tires sunk to the hubs in sand. Two of Hector's people hurried up behind it, wrenched the doors open, and pulled the Monkey Men out onto the ground. I couldn't see what happened next, but Hector's men were the only ones who returned to the fight.

The truck continued forward, crashing into the blocks set up across the road. The two men there scrambled to get out of the way, but one moved too slowly. The truck's impact sent him spinning through the air along with pieces of the barrier. The other man fled into the dark, but a few seconds later he stumbled back into the light, blood dripping from his neck. He fell onto the road and lay there, unmoving.

After it plowed through the barrier the truck stopped, backed up a few feet, and turned around. It had to go off-road to do that, but its heavy tires had no problem navigating the soft ground. After its bumping turn, the truck pulled back onto the road, sending another Monkey Man flying, and sped away. The second van stayed on the pavement as it turned around and followed. The passenger fired wildly as the retreating truck slewed back and forth, making it a harder target to hit.

That left the Monkey Men's force badly depleted, but by my count, there were at least four men somewhere in the darkness with guns. I lay there, shaking, unable to interpret what was happening. Once the sounds of retreating vehicles faded, a tense silence fell over the area. Then a voice called, "One down."

Perhaps a minute later I heard a strangled cry. A different voice said, "Two to go, by my count."

After a brief silence, a voice called, "We surrender."

"Come into the light," Hector ordered. "Leave your weapons on the ground."

Two Monkey Men stepped into the headlights of our truck with their hands raised. One of Hector's men now held an automatic weapon taken from them. Soon others of our party emerged from the darkness.

One of the Monkey Men spoke to Hector. "Don't kill us. We just did what we were told."

A radio attached to the dead leader's belt squawked to life. "We caught up with the truck, sir," a voice reported. "Dumped the body. Back in ten."

His face hard as stone, Hector raised the muzzle of his borrowed gun and shot both of the Monkey Men. "Let's go."

Two men picked up the body of their dead comrade while Andy and one of the women helped a man who was bleeding climb into the back of the truck. Once we were loaded, Hector knocked on the back window and Ernesto, who'd climbed in up front, took off, bypassing the wrecked barrier and knocking aside the white vans that sat behind it.

"They killed Diana."

Hector's lips were tight. "She knew what would happen."

Slouched against the wall of the truck, I cried for a while, though I managed to make no sound. Diana had sacrificed herself so that we could get away.

As adrenaline ebbed from my system, I fell into a sort of coma-sleep, unable to rest, unwilling to think. We roared on through the night, mostly silent as we thanked our lucky stars and our brave friends for a few more hours of life.

I woke to find that we were in the mountains. The road was rough and unmarked. The view outside my window made my stomach churn. Nobody seemed bothered by the narrow road and the steep cliffs beside us. After some time, the truck veered off the road to an even worse one. We bumped up a narrow trail and came to a halt when there was nowhere else to go. Around us were high rock walls. Before us was a bunch of loose stone and a timber blockade with a sign: *Danger! Do Not Enter!*

"Time for you to get out," Ernesto said.

Obeying, I climbed down and joined the crew who'd been riding in the back of the truck. "Hector's gotta turn the truck around so we can load up," one of the men told me.

Though it seemed impossible, he did it. The second truck had stopped back a way and sat waiting while Hector jockeyed his vehicle 180 degrees, moving a few feet with each turn. As he did that, two men approached the wooden blockade with wrenches and did something at its four corners. Within minutes, they lifted the whole thing and moved it to one side.

I was looking into a hole, about six feet wide and six feet high. It was black inside, but near the front I saw ancient rails that had once allowed a cart to be moved in and out.

"A mine."

"Once upon a time." Hector had come up beside me, and he regarded the hole as if seeing it through my eyes. "There are old mines all over up here, and caves too. Over the last couple of decades, we managed to hook them together to make ourselves an unobserved pathway into Dorado."

Noise from the depths of the tunnel alerted us to the approach of someone. I looked to Hector, frightened, but he said, "That's the replacement crew." Soon several ATVs loaded with boxes of goods exited the tunnel. The two crews greeted each other and then began loading the goods onto the trucks. "When they're done, we get the quads and they get the trucks." He sighed. "I have to go let them know why we only have two."

Approaching a woman of about his age, Hector took her aside. I saw a look of sadness form as she listened. Gesturing at the road behind us and then at the tunnel, I guessed Hector suggested she might want to return with us, but the woman shook her head. He nodded, put a hand on her arm as if in benediction, and returned to me.

"You'll ride with me," he said, gesturing at an ATV. "As soon as we reach the other side, I'll text Sri and tell him you're here. I'm sure he'll want to come and meet you."

Once the machine was emptied of its cargo, Hector turned it around. "Hop on." Soon we were zooming along, too fast in my opinion, toward Dorado. The passage felt narrow and eerie. In some places it smelled dank, in others, slightly dusty. Sometimes there were lamps along the way. Other times I could only see the few feet our headlights illuminated. The walls loomed close, making me claustrophobic. I tried not to think about the massive weight of rock pressing down on the structure.

Hector had nothing to say, so for a while there was only the sound of our vehicle. In time I heard others and realized that Hector's crew had come up behind us. Finally we stopped in a spot that at first seemed like any other. We were in a natural cave now, not the man-made hole we'd started from. A string of lights showed me that there was a doorway ahead.

"Hop off."

I did as he said, and Hector followed suit, approaching the metal door. He said something into an intercom and waited. In a few seconds the door rose upward, revealing what appeared to be an automotive repair shop. With a formal bow, Hector indicated I should precede him. "Welcome to Dorado, Zalea."

I stepped into the shop, blinking a little at the bright light. People working in several areas looked at us, registered our presence, and then went back to what they'd been doing. Hector stepped aside and composed a text. When the rest of the crew was out of the tunnel, the door lowered back in place. A pocket door in the auto shop wall closed, and I heard the latch click into place. There was no sign there was an opening behind it.

Ernesto went into an office at one side of the building and spoke to a woman there. She approached us just as I heard a sound that told me Hector had sent his text. "I hear it was bad last night."

"Yeah." His tone said more than the single word.

"Our people will find the body and bring her back if we can."

"Tell them to be careful."

She gave him a look. "Like they don't know that?"

Another sound from Hector's phone indicated he'd received a reply to his text. After reading it, he hit a single key. "I'll take Zalea to meet Sri." Going to a board studded with nails, he took a set of keys hanging on one marked, *H*. "Then I'll go see Diana's family."

I was silent as Hector drove me to the meeting place. Sadness for Diana's death was hard to set aside. The fact that I would soon come face-to-face with my father was both exciting and nerve-wracking. What if he took one look at me and decided I wasn't who I said I was? What if he was a bad man? Though Hector and the others had been good to me, leaders of smuggling gangs were seldom known for kindness and caring. What if my father had changed his mind about wanting to see me? After all, my tribe had killed Chad, his friend. Diana's death, while not really my fault, might be another barrier between us.

When he pulled in at a restaurant/gas station, Hector didn't get out. "He's waiting inside," he said. "Look for a guy wearing a turquoise ball cap." I got out and Hector drove off, no doubt focused on the sad news he had to convey. I stood in the parking lot, clutching my backpack, my mind aboil with a strange combination of hope and fear. How would I convince my father that I really was his daughter?

Shouldering my bag, I went into the restaurant. I paused in the doorway, surveying patrons who were eating, drinking, and talking. A man in a turquoise cap was looking my way, his dark eyes taking in everything about me. Right away I knew he was my father. When I saw who was with him, I realized I didn't have to worry about proving it. My mother rose and hurried toward me, her eyes brimming with tears.

PART III: WENDY

Chapter Eighteen

THE OLD TIMES

"I can't believe people fall for this crap," Maris said when she returned to our dorm from her latest rally. "Here we are, trying to get a degree and take on the world, and these people come along with their Family Values crap and screw everything up royally."

With Maris as my roommate, I couldn't help being aware that large groups of people were demanding that our nation return to some mythical former time when everyone was happy because women stayed home and minorities knew their place. Busy with classwork, I hadn't spent much time thinking about it. We had government for, by, and of the people, so our checks and balances would keep the crazies from gathering too much power.

"What's he done today?"

"Miller insists that women, along with people of darker skin, of course, have caused universities to dumb down their curricula." She lowered her tone to do a parody of the man she called the Recently-elected Whack-a-doodle. "'A college degree doesn't mean what it did back when I received very high, I could say extremely high marks from all of my professors.' He wants to 'raise the standards' by having classes filled first by 'traditional' students, meaning white males. They'll let the rest of us in if there's room."

"Let 'em try arguing that pathetic idea in court." I grabbed the materials needed for my organic chemistry class. "If everyone's rights don't matter, then nobody's rights matter."

But the people in the new administration didn't listen to the courts. They ignored civil rights. They insisted that whole groups of the population were incompetent, undeserving, and dedicated to undermining the nation. When a student on campus was shot in a heated exchange with police, I finally began paying attention, and I got angry.

I was shocked when I went home over the summer and learned that my parents agreed with such ideas. "It might seem unfair on the surface," they insisted, "but something has to be done to set the country back on the right path." Mom believed Gerald Miller had been sent by God to save the nation, and she wasn't the only one. Though his methods were extreme, she claimed it was because the forces of good had to act forcefully to stop the encroaching evils of terrorists, deviants, and "elite ignoramuses." Dad admitted he wished Miller were a little more civil, but in general he supported his contention that our "Christian ideals" were being eroded.

Back at school, Maris grew more and more furious with Miller and his ilk. "It's horrible that we have to put up with these people!" she'd gripe, stomping across our tiny shared space. "We'll vote them out next election, but still!"

Except that began to seem unlikely to happen. The arrests began, and our very freedom was at stake.

We spoke out, Maris and I and others of like mind. We protested at least once a week. We made signs. We chanted slogans. We supported politicians who worked to halt the nation's turn away from freedom, but more and more of them disappeared over time. Some lost elections they'd been projected to win. Others quietly resigned and left public life. A few died, one from a freak house fire, another from falling off his own balcony. Maris and I went on, but in the end we recognized that nothing we did changed what was happening to our nation.

At the beginning of Miller's second year, protesting was declared illegal. Police were given permission to use force to stop it, even deadly force when dealing with "losers and scum." Maris was apparently in the latter category. To my everlasting regret, I was not there when she was shot and killed while objecting to the replacement of all females in governmental jobs. I might have warned her to be quiet. I might have pulled her back from facing down the officer who pulled out his weapon, shot her in the chest, and said, it was reported, "One less noisy, nosy bitch."

The official ruling said the officer's action was justified because my friend, an unarmed twenty-year old who weighed a hundred pounds soaking wet, had made him fear for his life. It was clear Maris was a threat, the report concluded, because she'd been there. If she hadn't been a troublemaker, she'd have been attending her morning class.

Jolted from assumptions that my country would always be my country, I looked for new ways to oppose the regime. In my search, I met a charismatic man named Sri Afzal, who spoke eloquently of true fairness. To combat government power, he recruited computer-savvy types who could delve into records and find proof of the misdeeds Miller and his henchmen performed daily. While I was no tech genius, I had a talent for explaining. Sri's people gave me the information they gleaned from statistics and algorithms, and I translated the material into words any fair-minded person could grasp.

The problem was that by then the nation was so flooded with lies that we had become only one of many voices crying in the wilderness. Confusion led people to shut down and stop listening to either side.

As our world got weirder, our work got darker. Our group continued to dig for secrets inside Miller's machine, where we found one heart-breaking blow to democracy after another. We learned that Miller planned to cheat in the mid-term elections, and no one seemed able, or willing, to stop him. It was almost too easy to find evidence of how his people used their offices to enrich themselves, and we did our best to get word of that out to the public. The lack of response was frustrating. Many were afraid to speak out. Some insisted that both sides were to blame. And far too many accepted anything Miller said, no matter how outrageous it was.

When logical arguments and appeals to Constitutional law didn't work, we turned to disruption. Sri formed what he called a Resistance Force, which looked for ways to sabotage Miller's government. T-group (for Tech), worked remotely, sending bots deep into government computers to create havoc in their files. A-group (for Action) broke into government offices and destroyed paper records, particularly files listing citizens who wouldn't keep quiet about Miller's abuse of the democratic system. Sri and I were active in A-group, and we trained vigorously to make ourselves both effective and elusive. As time went on and things got worse, we began hiding small bombs in government office to disrupt operations. We always planned the explosions for off-hours and phoned in last-minute warnings to assure that no one got hurt.

As we did all that together, Sri and I fell in love.

I didn't tell my parents. I could imagine the look on my mother's face if I brought home a man who looked "foreign," whose family worshipped what she'd consider the wrong God. And though Dad would have claimed to be fine with us being a couple, he'd have offered solemn, well-meant reasons why Sri wasn't a good permanent mate. I knew what they would be: Our vastly different backgrounds would eventually cause friction between us. I'd spend my life defending my marriage from bigots. My future children would suffer due to the mix of cultures and religions. Not that he was prejudiced, Dad would assure me. He was simply proud of his heritage and hoped that someday my children, his grandchildren, would share it.

Both my parents also began commenting on the unhappy state of dating in our culture. Mom claimed it was simply bed-hopping, and marriage had become an afterthought. True childrearing was impossible, she insisted, when parents either juggled work schedules haphazardly or hired caregivers who didn't share the family's religion, culture, and values. Dad argued that couples would be better off if parents had a say in the match. "Look at all the young women who marry a man who looks good or talks a good game," he'd say. "They have a kid or two, and then they realize they picked a loser." Shaking a finger, he'd add, "And what happens then? Her parents step in and help out, for the good of their grandchildren. That could all be avoided if Grandma and Grandpa had a say in the first place."

Dad often called me when Mom wasn't around, voicing his hope that I was "staying out of the craziness." He wasn't against protesting if it was done correctly, he often assured me, but the pictures he saw on the news, students harassing police officers who were simply doing their jobs… That was sickening.

So I didn't tell my parents I was in love with a man whose name had started showing up on government watchlists. I certainly didn't tell them about my own anti-establishment activities. Conditions grew worse in my little college town. Students refused to stop gathering, and as the protests grew larger, the response became more violent. Police officers and sheriff's deputies quit, unwilling to fire on students, angry women, and people who'd lost their jobs for criticizing Miller. We took it as a good sign. People were starting to stand against the Troglodytes.

Then came the Miller Men.

Unbeknownst to most of the nation, Miller had from Day One begun training bands of what he called "strategic interventionists." Chosen from the most extreme nationalist groups, they arrived at protests ready to disperse crowds, intimidate protesters, and arrest activists, meaning anyone they didn't want around. They were armed to the teeth and allowed, possibly encouraged, to "use extreme force." They wore masks, supposedly as protection from projectiles and chemicals, but the added advantage was anonymity. Violence without fear of reprisal attracts a certain type, and their ranks were full of such men.

Along with them came journalists chosen and cultivated by Miller and his cronies. The newly-formed Office of Media hired reporters who were willing to slant every story the government's way. Protesters were depicted on the evening news as violent, drug-crazed, and out of control. Only tear-gas, take-downs, and arrests stopped them from burning homes, looting businesses, and hurting innocent pedestrians. Those who were killed at protests deserved to die, Miller claimed. They should have been at home, where innocent people belong.

"He's dead, Wendy!" Sri burst through the door to our apartment, waving his phone. "He dropped dead mid-rant!"

I didn't need to ask who. Jumping up from my chair, I danced around the room with him. "I can't believe it's over."

Sri frowned. "Well, it isn't over. All the people Miller put into power are still there."

"But everyone knows they're crooks. Without his—what? Charm? Persona? Bullshit? Anyway, we'll get them out—"

"And hopefully into prison."

"For sure." It was my turn to frown. "I wonder who'll be willing to try to fix the mess Miller's made of the country."

"I don't know," Sri said. "Too many still believe the crap he spouted, even after two years of chaos."

"They do seem to be everywhere, but at least—" Sri joined me, and we crowed together, "He's gone!"

I really hoped things would smooth out after that, but they did not. Miller's successor, Timothy Ryan Dupree (of course we called him TuRD) was tougher than expected. He claimed the administration needed more time to complete "the great work of the greatest man." He said protests had to stop so that Miller's work could be completed.

Sri had appeared on the government watch lists almost from the first. Charismatic, well-spoken, and fearless, he represented exactly the type of influencer Miller, and now Dupree, needed gone. The watch list turned to a wanted list. Sri's picture was posted everywhere, with a reward offered for his capture. We hid in the basement in the home of a sympathetic friend, and between news reports telling what a dangerous man Sri was, how he'd destroyed property and even killed innocent people with his wild-eyed, misshapen views, we got married. A few days later, Azalea was born.

Having a child changed Sri's outlook. While I'd been his equal partner to that point, he suddenly turned protective. As we sat together on the sagging, musty couch, staring at the miracle that was our child, he said, "Wen, you should leave the country for a while. I have a friend who has a plane, and he'll take you to Canada."

I hated that idea. "We're in this together, Sri."

"But you have a new job now." He touched Azalea's face reverently. "Your first responsibility is protecting our child."

"So the male fights while the female runs and hides?"

"You're her mother, her best chance to grow up strong."

"That's bullshit," I contended. "If I'd died in labor, you'd have raised her by yourself, and she'd be fine." With all the stubbornness I could summon, I finished, "We stay with you. Azalea will learn to be a fighter against injustice."

I won, but my victory was short-lived. Days later, our hiding place was invaded. Sri was tased and carried out, still twitching. I was cuffed and arrested. My baby was bundled into blankets and taken away.

For a day and a half I was visited in my bare, comfortless jail cell by person after person with "a few questions." They came in pairs, one standing by the door as if on guard to stop me from escaping. The other would sit on the bunk opposite mine and ask things like, "What can you tell us about your husband's plans to destroy the capitol?" My only response was, "Lawyer." Eventually each questioner gave up, leaving me alone again. The harsh overhead lights in the cell never went out, so I had no idea of the time, but I tried to rest between visits. My demand for a lawyer was ignored, and I guessed the interviews would become less polite over time.

The next day, or maybe the day after, I heard a voice outside my cell. "Take a break, son. I can handle one skinny girl."

The door ground noisily on its track, and a man I'd never seen before stepped in. Though only about my height, he brought to mind a commanding officer in a combat movie, upright posture, brisk step, and a dead-pan, don't-let-them-know-what-you're-thinking expression. Mid-fifties, physically fit, he brought with him an air of…not arrogance, really, but certainty of his worth.

“Mrs. Afzal, my name is Allen Vox.” I learned later that he was an army general, but he didn’t mention it then. “I’m sorry about…” He gestured at our surroundings. “This.”

“Did you have anything to do with it?”

“No, ma’am, I did not.”

I shrugged off his sympathy. “You can sit on the other bunk.”

Metal scraped on metal as Vox sat. His back remained straight. His head remained erect. He lined up his feet as if someone would be checking later with a ruler. “I’m here to talk with you about your husband.”

I’d meant to be reserved, but I couldn’t be. “Have you seen Sri?”

“He’s in a Special Detention Center. No visitors allowed.” His eyes met mine with the faintest glint of humor. “Apparently, you are considered less dangerous. From what I’m hearing, Afzal duped you with charm and visions of his heroic deeds.”

“That’s not true.”

He shrugged. “If playing the misled wife gets you out of prison, it might be worth keeping your convictions to yourself.”

My first impression was beginning to sour. “What do you want, Mr. Vox?”

Folding his hands at his waist, he thought for a while, either about what he’d tell me or how he’d phrase it. “There are people in this country who want to see an end to the hatred and the fighting.”

I raised my chin. “If you think we’re to blame for—”

Vox raised a hand. “I’m not blaming anyone, but Dupree’s people are doing a great job of making people like your husband look like demonic terrorists.” Leaning toward me he said earnestly, “I’m saying it's time to end it, and I'm wondering if your husband would be interested in partnering with others to achieve that."

I took a second to study his face, looking for a hint as to his motive for asking. "Explain what you mean by that."

His explanation began with a question. "If he could go free and have a significant role in forming a new government, is he the type of man who can accept certain limits in order to build a strong society?"

I felt my hands tightening into fists. "I suppose it would depend on what those limits were."

Vox turned away for a moment, looking at the blank wall to his left. When he returned his gaze to me, he said, "The nation we thought we had is gone, Mrs. Afzal. Miller has wrecked it, and we can't just snap our fingers and get it back." He licked his lips. "Though it's unfortunate, in some ways it's a good thing."

"I doubt that!" The words erupted from me without conscious decision. Setting my fingers against my mouth, I looked at Vox encouragingly. I needed to hear what he had in mind for Sri.

"The institutions we had, many of which were a mess even before Miller came along, are now useless. They've been defunded or filled with Miller loyalists or beaten into submission by constant harassment. The rest of the world, allies and enemies alike, look on with amazement at what Miller was able to do. Our democracy, or as some insist when splitting hairs, our republic, is dead. We will need something new going forward, a middle road, if you will." He put a hand out, palm raised. "Your side wants every person to be treated with respect."

"That's not my 'side,' I responded. "It's a principle that any strong society is founded on. But yes, that's what we want."

He put the other hand out. A balance. "Others want to feel safe in their homes and secure in their values."

"But—"

Vox shook his head. "Again, Mrs. Afzal, I'm not here to argue who's right and who's wrong. I came to ask if you believe that your husband would support ending the problems our nation faces."

It sounded good, but I hadn't been born in that cell. Raising my chin, I replied, "If fairness is at the heart of it, he might."

"I, along with a few others, intend to propose a government that will give each side some of what it wants. With strong leadership, we believe the nation can heal and move forward."

Tiny alarm bells rang in my head. *Some* of what it wants? "Will you reverse the changes the Miller administration made?"

A tensing around his eyes hinted I'd asked a question he didn't want to answer, but he did. "We would of course stop Dupree's war on the people of this country. But you must admit that some of what's been done was good in that it stream-lined a slow, inefficient government."

"By 'streamlined,' do you mean ignoring the Constitution and the courts?" I couldn't hide the sneer in my voice.

"There's a pretty wide belief that the Constitution was stronger before we started amending this and changing that."

"You mean before we said women and black people could vote? Before we guaranteed rights to everyone? Before we made sure the government can't establish a national religion?"

A tightening along his jawline told me Vox had imagined this would be easier. "Anyone who's paying attention knows we need serious reforms, but first we need new leadership. At this point I'm simply investigating whether your husband would support a middle-of-the-road approach to solving the nation's issues."

Looking into Vox's eyes, I saw no light behind them. Though his words were carefully planned, he felt no passionate desire to save our nation. That meant, I decided, that his passion was for something else. "If you intend to ignore human decency or stifle anyone's rights, Mr. Vox, Sri will never go along."

"I see." Vox rose. "Then I won't take up any more of your time."

And that is how I assured my husband's death. At least that's what I believed for eighteen years.

More time passed in the cell: concrete walls interrupted only by the metal sliding door, which looked out onto yet another concrete wall. Mostly I saw nothing. My days were interrupted only by the serving of unappealing food, shoved through a slot in the door morning and night. I kept track of time by the meals, so I knew it was three days after Vox's visit when I heard my father's voice in the hall. The door opened, and there he stood. His mouth tried to smile, but his eyes were sad.

I shrank back on my bunk, imagining what Dad saw. I was still wearing the clothes I'd been arrested in, a pair of Sri's jeans and his t-shirt. My pants were stained with post-partum blood, since I hadn't been allowed to clean up. I'd received a black eye resisting arrest, and while I could see out of it now, the skin around it was still tender to the touch. Since I could no longer feed my baby, my breasts were swollen and sore.

That wasn't all. Dad knew by now that I'd lied, claiming I was busy at school and couldn't find the time to come home for a visit. I'd made up chirpy stories about difficult classes and impossible professors. I hadn't told my parents about my marriage, my anti-government activities, my pregnancy, or my infant child.

Stepping into the cell, Dad turned to the guard. "Thank you." The man closed the door and left us together.

"Wendy." In that word was a world of sadness and a ton of disappointment. I knew I should apologize, but I couldn't.

Realizing I wasn't going to start the conversation, Dad said, "I've arranged for you to come home with me. Your name has been kept out of the media, so the public won't know you were involved in this—" He couldn't come up with a term for what I'd done, so he started a new sentence. "Be glad I have friends in high places. Otherwise, you'd be on your way to a place much worse than this."

"And Sri?"

Dad shook his head. "I can't help him."

"You won't."

He shrugged. "There's nothing I can do, even if I wanted to. He's a well-known ring leader for these...renegades."

Miller had come up with the term, and now Dupree used it a lot. Unlike the decent citizens of our nation, renegades deserved no consideration from the courts, no due process, no "comfy prisons with weight rooms and libraries." Renegades should be locked up in places suited to their bestial nature. Better yet, they should be dead.

I shook my head. "If Sri's going to prison, so am I."

Dad's face darkened, and I saw determination beneath his calm demeanor. "No, you're not, Wendy. You're going home with me, even if I have to have you sedated."

I could see that he meant it, and I guessed he could make good on his threat. My father meant to erase my crimes and provide me with a new chance at life. That wasn't something I wanted if Sri and I couldn't be together.

But Sri's words came back to me like an echo in my head. *Your first responsibility is protecting our child.*

Sitting up straight on the narrow, lumpy mattress, I said, "I'll come home. I'll do whatever you want me to, on one condition. Find my daughter so I can bring her with me."

Dad had the contacts—and the money—to get it done. What did it cost him to amble into that prison and take a charged felon home with him? Probably more than he'd intended, but he hired a man to track my baby through the maze of records of children whose parents had been arrested or deported. Once Azalea was found, he paid for identity papers that listed me, under my maiden name, as her mother. The space for the father's name was left blank.

When I held Zalea for the first time in eight days, I told myself she had to be my focus. I could do nothing for Sri. No one even knew where they were holding him. My life, at least the life I'd chosen, was over. My only consolation was that maybe people would learn from the disasters of Miller's horrible government. Maybe next time, they'd choose leaders who weren't out for themselves. Holding my baby close, I climbed into Dad's car to begin the long ride home.

Chapter Nineteen

PRESENT

Loss is a shock. Grief is a burden. When I heard that the Woods Tribe's leader, my father, was dead, I wasn't sure how to feel. My first thought, I will admit, was relief.

But the next morning, we discovered that my girls were missing. That whole day I was frantic, wandering the burg, looking for them in places I'd already looked, and considering possibilities for their absence that I knew were ridiculous.

Zalea had run away, dragging Milla with her. Where had she imagined the two of them might go?

After a day of fruitless searching, they were declared missing. Rolf made the announcement to the tribe, his face a mask but his tone smug. He didn't glance at me as he spoke, and I kept my face turned down. Because of the promise I'd made to Father in that prison long ago, my brother expected me to bow to tribal law. For years I'd hidden every rebellious look and gone about my assigned tasks with willful obedience. I'd buried my emotions where even I couldn't find them. Though I'd never been able to pretend to be happy, I'd forced myself to fit in. I'd done all that to keep my girls safe.

Father's death changed everything. While I'd disagreed with most of what he stood for, I'd at least known he'd loved us. Now that his protection was gone, life would be different. As Zalea had no doubt understood, different meant worse.

In the days following those horrible events, I hid the re-awakening I experienced. I acted the way people expected me to. I helped with planning Father's funeral. I listened to the changes Rolf proposed to tribal procedures. I answered my mother's questions and comments with suitable deference. But over and over it repeated in my head: *I will leave Tribe Woods. I will find my girls. I will become a real mother to them.* After years of sleepwalking, I was making a plan and building the courage to follow it.

Mother was devastated by Father's death. After four decades of marriage, losing her spouse was like having an arm ripped from her body. Grief for the loss of their leader flowed from the tribe. People stood outside our home, some crying softly. They brought more food than we could ever eat, and I smuggled most of it to SQ to keep from offending their generosity. In the burg square, men hung strips of black cloth over the meeting house doors, an old-fashioned, heart-warming signal of mourning. Father's people knew that he'd cared about them.

Opposing the sadness of the community was Rolf's poorly-hidden glee at finally being in charge. He had to wait forty days—the period Christ was tested in the Bible—before he could be officially installed as the new leader, during which time other men could offer themselves for the role. Since Father had named Rolf as his heir after Benny died, there was little likelihood he'd be challenged, but still, the waiting period was required. Rolf could barely contain his impatience. His funeral speech, which he'd made me read to correct any grammatical errors, had a lot about his vision for the glorious future of the tribe and not much about Father.

Within days Rolf informed me I'd be getting married for a third time, since without children to care for, I was now a Non-Contributing Member. I could choose a man, he said as if offering me a gift, but if I had no one in mind, he'd choose for me. I guessed that would be some elderly man wealthy enough to slip Rolf an appropriate bribe.

Rolf wasn't just pleased to be moving into Father's place. He seemed almost gleeful about it. There'd been no sighting of the second stranger, the one who'd supposedly killed Father. Was it possible that was because he'd never existed?

No. My brother could not be so depraved as to murder his own father. Grief and worry were making me delusional.

Father's funeral was held four days after his death. As I stood beside his grave, emotions I hadn't felt for years surfaced. The promise I'd made to him was now void, and I could allow my anger to burn again. That fire destroyed my fears and minimized the difficulties I faced. I had to find my girls. Once we were together again, I'd protect them with my life.

As hundreds of people left the cemetery and the plain grave that held my father's earthly remains, I lingered behind, thinking, *Where are my daughters?* While I was desperate to find them, I couldn't simply walk away from the tribe. I had no money, no transportation, no idea which direction to take. I had to make a plan.

Absorbed in the business of becoming leader, Rolf didn't notice when I began asking questions about the days before the girls disappeared. Zalea had no confidants, so there was no one I could question about what she'd been thinking, but Milla had Mary Ann, who couldn't keep a secret if it were handed to her in a locked box. Going to her house when I knew her parents were out, I slipped inside, went upstairs, and found her in her room. Dresses were laid out all over the bed, the dresser, and the chairs. "I'm trying to decide what to wear to the fair," she said in her breathy, little-girl voice. "I know it's bad to be thinking about it so soon after Grandfather's death, but I'm sure you understand, Aunt. I need to get my marriage settled before Uncle Rolf starts changing the rules."

Even ditzy Mary Ann knew that life would soon be more complicated.

"If you know where Milla went, you need to tell me."

She brushed a lock of hair away from her face. "No, Aunt Wendy, I don't. I was as surprised as anyone when they r-- left."

"When did you talk to her last?"

She avoided my gaze. "I—I'm not sure."

"Be honest with me, girl, or I'll tell your father you've been up to no good and you'll miss the fair entirely."

Her eyes widened. I could almost see the wheels turning in her head as she arranged the story into the least damning version she could manage. "That night when we delivered food to AQ, we heard noises, so we went to see what was happening." She put her fingers over her mouth as she finished, "We saw that man get hung."

Part of that, I guessed, was true. "Milla saw it?"

"She hid her eyes at the end."

Tempted to slap her for taking my innocent child to such an event, I said instead, "What do you know about the man?"

"Well, he was a trespasser." Something clicked in her feather-lined brain. "Jeremy saw him talking to Zalea that day."

"The stranger spoke to Azalea. You're sure?"

"He heard them planning to meet up later. Jeremy told Rolf, and Rolf got some men together. They found him and—well, you know what happened." She put a hand on my arm. "That's all I know, Aunt Wendy. Please don't tell Father, because I have to go to the fair. Who knows what poor excuse for a man he'll pick if I'm not there to help him decide?"

The gibbet sat about twenty yards off the main road into Woodsburg. Though we seldom had a Final Punishment in the Woods Tribe, any man hanged was left there as a warning to others. Making sure there was no one around to take note, I approached the gibbet, gagging as the smell of the days-old corpse hit me. Holding my breath, I kept going. When I got close, I forced myself to look up at the bloated face. It was a relief to find that I didn't recognize him. I went through his pockets. Nothing. Next I felt his belt, looking for a bulge that would signal a secret compartment. None. There was one more hiding place we'd used in the old days. Tugging off his boot, I pulled out the liner. Nothing there. The other one was the payoff. Under the insole was a folded piece of paper. Excited by my find, I retreated into the woods, sat on a stump, and unfolded the paper. In handwriting I hadn't seen for years was a message.

> Azalea,
>
> I don't know if your mother has told you about me. I am called Sri Afzal, and I am your father. Wendy believes I am dead, and until a few months ago, I thought both you and she were. Her parents arranged that so we would never try to find each other.
>
> If you are happy where you are now, burn this letter and forget me. But if you want a different life for yourself, the man who carries the message will bring you to where I now live, in the country of Dorado.
>
> If you doubt the authenticity of this letter, ask your mother how you got your name. I had meant to call you Shaina, which in my language means "Beautiful," but she had recently read a short story by O. Henry with a character called Azalea.

> Because I loved her so much, I agreed to her choice.
>
> Your father, Sri

I knew the handwriting, and I also recognized the logo at the top of the sheet, *ΣΩ.* As a gift for Sri's twenty-fifth birthday, I'd had a ring made for him with a stylized *S* for Sri and *W* for Wendy. Apparently he'd adopted that as an identifier and was still using it all these years later.

Sri was alive. A part of me that had been as good as dead stirred, like a bud responding to sunlight. I felt joy but also regret. Doesn't common wisdom hold that if love is true, a person feels the presence of her soul mate in the world? But no. I'd accepted what I was told and kept accepting it for years. In that all-important thing, my mother was right. I was wrong-headed and always had been.

THE OLD TIMES

Miller's death and Dupree's struggles to maintain power plunged the nation into civil war. Fighting broke out, mostly in cities, where the rebels tended to be. Using guerilla tactics, rebels battled troops in riot gear. Soon tanks rattled down main avenues in major cities. While there was no fighting near us, people in our farming community felt the repercussions. Services we'd taken for granted flickered, fizzled, and died. Electricity stopped buzzing through the wires. Information stopped flowing through cyberspace. Phone calls no longer connected. We learned to do what we could with what we had, but for months it was still a surprise when I turned a switch and got nothing. I picked up my phone a dozen times a day, forgetting I'd only find a blank, black screen.

“When are we going to get our power back?” people asked, expecting a return to normal life any day. It didn’t happen. Miller had filled every job in his government with an eye to loyalty, not competence, and his unqualified yes men, now working for Dupree, had no idea how to cope with rebellion and disruption. Government agencies became slower and slower and finally stopped operating entirely. Contracts went unpaid, as did anyone whose income depended on government funds: retirees, dependent children, disabled workers, and the employees themselves. No one admitted the problem was serious. “We’re working day and night for you,” Dupree claimed. “Once we’ve dealt with the rebels, services will return.” But it didn’t happen. Things only got worse.

Then a man stepped onto the national stage, an army general with a distinguished record. Well-spoken and convincing, he offered a way to end the chaos: “We must hold a national referendum on leadership,” he said with calm certainty. “The people should decide how they want to go forward.” He proposed a vote that would tell us if our citizens wanted the current administration to keep running things, the opposing party to take over, or something else entirely.” For himself, the general said, he’d like to see a Middle-of-the-Road candidate offered to voters, someone with no baggage and no obligation to either party.

The man’s name was Allen Vox.

Of course he was investigated seven ways from sundown. What the nation learned was that General Vox was known for intelligence and courage. He’d led an amazingly blameless life. He was happily married with three adult children. He was a regular attender of his local Methodist church. No one could find a single incident where he’d used his rank for questionable purposes. There was on his record only one stain: a traffic ticket for doing seventy in a fifty mph zone. When a reporter asked about it, Vox replied with a rueful smile, "I was listening to an audio book, and I'd come to a good part. I think I was subconsciously trying to help Jack Reacher escape the bad guys, so I pressed on the gas pedal in real life."

People chuckled at his honesty and self-deprecation. They said it would be good to have a leader of integrity, with a clean past and a sense of humor. When asked if he might consider the job of guiding the nation out of chaos, Vox said, "Let's talk first about what needs to be done. Then we can talk about who we want to do it."

Though I remembered Vox visiting my cell months earlier, I pretty much ignored what was happening outside our community. I slept in my old bedroom in my parents' home. I took care of Azalea and helped out where I could. The spotty availability of electrical power had brought renewed interest in canning, but local women could no longer consult the internet to learn how. They were pleased when I offered to pass on what I knew from a college course I'd once taken on food preservation. Sugar became expensive and hard to get, but we had sugar beets, so we learned to make our own. I thought about Maris sometimes and how she'd have laughed to see me back on the farm, sterilizing Mason jars and wearing a for-real, god-awful gingham apron to protect my shirt from stains.

"I like General Vox's idea of a referendum," Dad said one night at dinner. "We'd find out what people want in a leader."

"I think we should wait until the next election," Mom said. "Give Dupree a chance to finish Miller's work."

Looking at my plate, I remained silent. The country was sliding into full-scale revolution with Dupree in control. It was a breach of Constitutional order to hold a referendum, as Vox proposed, but what else could make things right?

"The military is backing the idea." Dad took another potato. "So are some pretty influential organizations."

"I suppose the army wants Vox to take over, since he's one of theirs," Mom said. "But Miller warned us it would take a while for things to get better. I'm sure they will if people just learn to behave themselves."

Spooning squash into Zalea's open mouth, I asked, "How would a referendum be done?"

"Vox says each county will hold a vote at a central location. People will have three days to go there and cast their ballots."

"Who gets to vote?"

"Registered voters, as long as they can prove they're who they say they are." Dad spoke as if I'd asked a silly question, but I thought of all the people whose lives had been disrupted, the government buildings where services were no longer offered, the technology that could no longer provide replacement for lost documents or verify identities.

I wasn't sure how the referendum went from one man's idea to reality, but it did. Dupree fought the idea, of course, but powerful politicians and businessmen spoke in favor of it. Dupree's jack-boot style of government had not been kind to anyone, and it had seemed like there was no way to get rid of him until Vox made his proposal.

Pressure was applied, and in the end Dupree accepted the referendum. He was the candidate for his party. The other side chose their best-known guy, a man who was well-liked, though perhaps a little naive about what the job would entail. He spoke of "taking up our lives again" as if that were possible with ruined cities, massive numbers of dead, wrecked infrastructure, and a destroyed power grid. Vox ran as a Fair Center candidate. His platform was "Peace and Fairness."

Of course Dupree tried to rig the vote, but when he announced that Miller Men would stand guard at polling places, Vox put forth a different idea. "Let's have the United States Marines secure the voting," he suggested. "As far as cheating goes, the Marines don't believe in it, and they sure won't help some old army guy get promoted over their heads."

Marines it was. Polling places were open to all registered voters, and no one who attempted to vote was harassed in any way. There were quibbles about voters having to show up in person, but the overall mood seemed to be that we'd let the question be decided by those who cared enough to get themselves to their proper polling place.

Mom was still unsure about Vox, but Dad said, "He might be exactly what this country needs, Linda. He wants us to feel safe in our homes but still allow for the differences between us."

Vox had nothing bad to say about either side. He despised the violence, he claimed, but he understood the factors that had brought us to war. He looked forward to a time when we could talk again without name-calling, nasty memes, and AI-generated fakes.

If he won the referendum, Vox said, he would ask the high court to examine the process and decide if it had been fair. That pleased many who felt that legality had fallen by the wayside under Miller and Dupree. Vox also assured us that lawbreakers on both sides would be punished. Corrupt members of the current government would pay back what they'd stolen from the nation's coffers. He would also try any rebels who had destroyed property and endangered lives.

"Peace and fairness," Dad said the day before the vote. "It's exactly what we need." That time, Mom nodded agreement.

Seventy-one percent of the votes cast went to Vox. Some said it was unnecessary to ask the high court to approve such a stunning result, but Vox did it anyway. The finding was that the election had been a "legislatively referred process" and therefore legal.

It was a huge change from the two-party system, but most agreed that was irretrievably broken anyway. For too long, both sides had stood behind their lines of division, sniping at each other, and getting nothing done. People were tired of "what about-ism" and dirty politics, so they'd chosen a new type of leader. In that spirit, Vox announced that he preferred to be called simply the Chief. "It's short and to the point," he quipped, "like me."

The first problem Vox had to deal with was areas on both coasts that had announced they were seceding from the nation. The west had quickly reformed itself into the nation of Dorado and made alliances with several powerful nations. Vox made no attempt to lure them back and cut off all further contact. The east coast rebels were less organized. After some negotiation, they rescinded their announcement of secession and rejoined the nation under its new name, Fairica.

Once our boundaries were decided, Vox outlined his central idea for rebuilding. "The country is in chaos, financially, socially, industrially, and every other way," he said in a national speech that we watched at the home of a neighbor who'd kept his ancient TV antenna in place. "We have nowhere to go but home, so the people of Fairica will form tribes made up of like individuals. They will mix to do business, but they'll live apart, each on its own land, each choosing its own lifestyle. While we'll be respectful of each other's differences, we'll live among those who know us best."

If I'd heard any of that at eighteen, I'd have laughed out loud. People would never agree to move hundreds, even thousands of miles, to be part of some tribe-slash-kibbutz. But I was wrong. Pastors preached the virtues of close-knit communities in church. Educators liked the promise of local control. Wealthy men pledged financial support to new tribal businesses. Families received encouraging, welcoming letters from their new tribal leaders.

I saw it from the inside. Combining a hefty financial investment with an agreement to abide by the new National Standards, Dad asked for and received the lands around our long-time home. His plan was for a farming tribe, but his vision was a return to his conception of what the old days of farming had been like. Success by the sweat of a man's brow. A woman in the home, raising his children and easing his path. Church on Wednesdays and Sundays. No tech. No lascivious movies. No odd religions or lifestyles. People who wanted that could apply to join some other tribe.

People clamored to become members of the Woods Tribe. I saw them arrive daily, vacant-eyed, beaten-down, often physically wounded. They wanted out of cities that had been toppled by bombing raids. They didn't want to have to decide between helping the rebels or cooperating with government troops. Father offered them homes, work, and emotional support. All over the nation, people chose a tribe that felt right for them. Felt safe.

I was not surprised when it became clear that Vox had intended all along to become a despot. His glorious vision for the nation was personal, drawn from his views of citizenship, family, and happiness. Once he had the reins of government firmly in his hands, Vox used the damage Miller and Dupree had done to democracy to have his own way everywhere. Miller Men stuck around, renamed Mobil Officers for National Compliance and known to most as Monkey Men. The Office of Media remained too, churning out continuous success stories of tribal life and blissful happiness.

In theory, tribes were autonomous, but in reality, what was now called the "Govt" limited their actions by controlling their finances. To get money for health services, a tribe had to ban sexual deviance. Public works grants were unavailable to tribes that allowed women to vote. School funding required that leaders had strong policies to deal with members who criticized the Govt. While some expressed doubts, most insisted that Vox had taken a firm stand to right the ship of state. Changes to the rules could be addressed in a year or two, when we'd all recovered our footing.

Vox followed through on his promise to punish wrongdoers. Dupree (who resisted giving up his office until armed men showed up in his bedroom and offered to help him pack) was allowed to move to South America, but he and other members of Miller's government were stripped of the wealth they'd accumulated through grift. That was a "boatload" of money, Vox told the nation, and it would fund the Govt's activities until the tribes were up and running.

As for the rebels, Vox claimed he wanted to be fair. While they'd broken the nation's laws, most had acted from altruistic motives. To deal with the problem, Vox called for a public hearing where rebel leaders would explain the grievances they'd fought against. Once their motivations were clear to everyone, the Govt would decide how to respond.

The hearings were scheduled at the nation's capital, now relocated at the geographical center of the country. The new Chief sent his own plane to collect a half-dozen rebel leaders who'd been imprisoned by Miller and Dupree. Members of the press went along to assure the integrity of the process, and Vox's younger son served as host and guarantor of the Chief's good intentions.

When the last of the rebel leaders had been picked up, the plane started its return to the capital. Twenty minutes before landing, it crashed, killing everyone aboard. The tragedy was blamed on a flock of geese that flew into the engines. A full investigation was promised, but aside from a few updates that said little, the matter disappeared from the news. On the passenger list was Sri Afzal, who'd been released from prison to make his case for leniency for all rebels, including himself.

Chapter Twenty

OLD TIMES

It took my father over two years to implement his plans for the Woods Tribe under the TRA. As Zalea grew from infant to toddler, Dad welcomed men from all over the nation, some named Woods, others willing to become Woods in order to be part of his successful farming operation. He arranged homes and jobs for them and figured out what the rules would be among us. Having begun as a small farmer who worked his way to a large agribusiness, Dad simply widened his scope even farther. The land granted to the Woods Tribe was about the size of what had been his county of residence. Not all of the men now under his leadership were farmers, of course, but those willing to learn became hands for experienced farmers while others set up other businesses our people would need. Each of our four burgs had a meeting hall where tribal business was conducted. Any member could share thoughts and ideas in meetings—if that member was male. Our tribe required weekly church attendance, and the men Father chose as pastors could be counted on to remind the congregations that the New Times was good for everyone, being aligned with the lives God intended us to have.

Dad stuck to what he knew well, growing wheat, corn, oats, potatoes, and soybeans. A cousin who'd been an agricultural engineer before the war helped farmers decide what to grow each year. A Woods who'd worked in media out west designed handbooks, charts, and checklists for the tribe's use. Another who'd been with Human Resources at a big company worked to fit each Contributing Member to a job. My oldest brother Benny, who'd once been CFO at a large corporation, resisted coming home for as long as possible but finally returned and soon became indispensable to the tribe.

Having no husband, I lived with Mom and Dad (now Mother and Father, terms we were told were more respectful) and received a small stipend as Zalea's mother. It wasn't always comfortable. Mother treated me as if I were part of her past she'd rather have forgotten. Father seemed to forget all my sins, reverting to the doting relationship he'd had with his "Li'l Girl" when I was five. Neither of them took much interest in what went on outside the circle of the tribe unless it affected grain prices or delivery methods. I learned not to care either, since there was nothing that I could do to change it.

When he first came home, Benny and I talked a lot. He knew the truth about my past, and I had long known the truth about him. We bonded over our disgust at Vox's changes to our society, though we had to be careful not to show it publicly. Benny did his best to avoid our parents' attempts to marry him off. While they spoke obliquely of Benny's "problem," they held the determined belief that he'd "get better" with time and family support. My brother always smiled when we spoke of that, as if our parents still believed in the tooth fairy.

While our discussions of life "before" were cathartic at first, they became depressing. Talking with Benny made me long for things that were no longer available, like tolerance for different ideas and cultures. Benny wished he could change my situation. "You're a person, Wendy," he'd say. "You shouldn't have to sit down, shut up, and be a good girl."

As my life changed, to wife again and then mother to two girls, I saw Benny less and less. When we met, he seemed okay, but I did notice that while he always smiled and spoke politely, he never engaged emotionally with anyone.

While Benny worked and asked for nothing, my second brother wanted more and more. Rolf had always been nasty, though Mother insisted he was simply more competitive than other boys.

Dad also ignored Rolf's darker side, citing instead his cleverness and dogged pursuit of goals. As tribal attorney, Rolf took to the Govt's intricacies like a trout to a grasshopper. People who hold power seldom expect to abide by the rules laid down for the rest of us, and Rolf excelled at getting favors like lucrative contracts from energy companies or permission from the Govt to use banned fertilizers. A disgusted Benny shared with me that Rolf bribed Govt inspectors to close their eyes to certain irregularities in the way we conducted business. Tribe Woods was soon a powerhouse in the Green Section. While Benny did his best to rein Rolf in, he admitted that Father took Rolf's side, winking as he opined that doing business "requires a little wiggle room."

While we'd never gotten along as kids, now Rolf despised me. When Father wasn't around, he referred to me as "the Prodigal Daughter" and pointed out that Zalea should be living with her father's tribe, not ours. He often commented on Benny's reluctance to take a wife, bragging that he and Sally had been providing the leader with grandchildren for years.

I didn't realize how much Rolf resented me until one day when Father paused in the kitchen doorway after dinner. As I cleared the table, he said, "Wendy, you know I love having you here, but it's time you remarried. Your girl needs a father, and my daughter should be an example to the tribe."

I knew it was Rolf's idea, and he'd gone so far as to present Father with a candidate. Fifth cousin Eric Woods was "a Godly man" whose wife had died at the age of thirty. He had three half-grown boys at home who needed a mother.

The memory of the promise I'd made Dad choked back my negative reply. He'd saved me from going to prison. He'd found Azalea. In return, I'd vowed to do as he asked. Still, I'd never expected to be given in marriage to a man I'd never met. Dad tried to soften the deal by making it a request. "Meet the guy," he urged.

"If you don't like him, we'll look for someone else." The underlying message was that I would marry. It was only a question of how much fuss I put up about the husband chosen for me.

Eric and I had three dates. We met first at the burg's only restaurant, where he bought me a steak and clearly thought it was a big deal. He wasn't bad-looking, and he was clean and polite. I told myself it could be worse. The second time we went for a boat ride on a local lake, during which he entertained me with stories of what a great fisherman he was. Finally, we attended church together. Sitting in the same pew had become a way to announce to the tribe that a couple was in a serious relationship. We entered the sanctuary with his boys behind us like stair steps. Eric carried Zalea, a sign to all that he would accept her as his. Older women's faces revealed pleasure. Younger ones looked faintly irritated. There were only so many eligible men available, and Eric was considered a catch.

We married six weeks after we met. I saw no reason to delay, since it was unlikely I'd find a new love at that point in my life. The loss of Sri was a wound that would never heal, but I ordered myself to give Eric a chance. While I might never love him, we might achieve mutual fondness through shared goals and experiences.

That hope lasted until the first time he hit me. Though I made every effort to be a good wife, my new husband railed constantly on what he saw as my faults. He harped on the deficiencies of the female brain. He maintained I should be more grateful than I appeared to be, since he'd taken on a wife with a past full of bad choices. There were rituals for every aspect of our lives, and I struggled to learn and observe them. Meals should be served at the same time every day. The family came to the table and sat, except for me. I dished out food from a bowl or a platter, setting an appropriate amount on each plate. Eric was served first, being head of the household, but if I didn't move quickly enough, he'd snap, "My food is getting cold, Wendy." Serving myself last, I'd slip into my place and try to eat a little before it was time to get up and serve the next course.

I was expected to keep every closet in the house in order, which to Eric was more than simply neat. The clothing in each child's area was arranged by use: everyday things on the right and special occasion on the left, and then by color, dark to light. I couldn't see why it mattered, but Eric checked periodically and often disagreed with my placement. "That shirt is more gray than blue, Wendy," he'd say, moving a hanger two garments to the right. "I don't know how you could have made a mistake like that."

The sexual part wasn't too bad, since he heated up fast and finished quickly. I learned to watch for signs that he was thinking about having sex. When I saw it, I applied a little oil, forced myself to smile, and waited for it to be over.

I thought I'd adapted well. I thought I hid my frustration. And then one day I was hanging clothing on the line to dry. Zalea stood beside me, handing up one clothespin after another. When we were done, I handed her the basket to carry inside. She put it over her head then turned to mug at me. Laughing, I told her she looked cute.

Zalea went into the house. As I followed, I noticed Eric standing in the shed doorway, watching. The look on his face was a warning, and while I didn't know exactly what would happen, I sensed it would be bad. "Run down to Grandmother's house," I told my daughter, "ask for a jar of pickled green beans for our supper."

She trotted off. I waited. Eric came into the house, slamming the door behind him so hard the place shook. "I can't stand the way you coddle that girl of yours."

"Zalea is fine." She was more than fine. She was great, amazing, wonderful. She was my joy, my only reminder that my life had meaning.

The open-handed slap sent me reeling. "Did you just contradict me, Wendy?"

For a moment I felt like my old self. "She's my daughter," I said, wiping blood from my lip. "You can't—"

I don't recall much after that. I woke up on the floor, my ribs aching from what I assumed were kicks he'd administered after I was down. By the time Zalea returned, I'd dragged myself upright, cleaned my face, and started preparing dinner.

For a while I let myself consider the possibility that this would release me from Eric. I'd tell Father what he'd done. I'd—what? *Divorce* had become a dirty word. A man could set his wife aside for immorality or barrenness, but I belonged to Eric by law. I was already an embarrassment, a woman who, it was whispered, had engaged in criminal behavior. If my father had to step in to save me a second time, he'd be accused of acting with self-interest, to the detriment of the tribe. A man like Eric might even report him to the Govt for investigation.

Beating one's wife or children was fairly common. Father had made it clear he didn't approve of it, but in the end men were responsible for the behavior of their family members. It wasn't spoken of openly, and women explained their black eyes and even broken bones with stories of clumsiness on the way to the bathroom in the dark.

Over time I learned to avoid Eric's anger—most of the time—by anticipating and diffusing it. When I became pregnant, he was thrilled. Suddenly I was the Cradle of Life, the holy vessel that would turn my husband's seed into his child. He would stroke my hair, left to grow long now because he liked it that way. He'd tell me how happy we'd be once we had a child who truly joined us. I would of course agree, but my real reaction was dread. Which parts of my husband would I copy and paste into the world? A boy who'd grow up to beat his woman? A girl who'd accept that she must have deserved it? I hated him, and I couldn't imagine loving what he'd inserted into my womb.

Until I held Camilla in my arms. She was perfect. She was wonderful. When I showed her to Azalea, she touched her soft cheek with a finger. "You won't let Father hurt her like he hurts you, will you, Mother?" I don't know how she knew, but I assured my serious, beautiful Zalea that I would never let anyone hurt either of my daughters.

Camilla's presence intensified Eric's dislike of Azalea. I watched over her like a mother kildeer, going to great lengths to lead Eric and his sudden, angry fists away from her. If I even sensed that he was becoming irritated at Zalea, I'd send her outside with a harsh command meant to convince him I wasn't "coddling" my older child. When she was gone I faced him alone, often taking blows meant for her on myself. Though I saw confusion in her expression, I had no way to explain my behavior without admitting that her stepfather was a monster.

Having been taught that women were useful only for providing food and clean underwear, Eric's boys never warmed to me. They seemed unaware of me as a person and unable, maybe unwilling, to notice when I limped around the house or carried one shoulder hunched due to pain.

Though Zalea said nothing, I saw awareness in those dark, beautiful eyes, so much like Sri's. Little as she was, she knew how I was treated. Helpless as she was, she felt the injustice of it. Strong as she was, her dislike of Eric showed in ways she didn't recognize. When Milla was almost one, he said to me one evening,

"I bet your parents would take Azalea in. They have lots of room in that big house, and she'd be company for your mother."

It was becoming customary to send "extra" girls to live with other families, where they earned their keep doing household chores. It was seldom done with a child as young as six, and while Zalea might be safer with my parents, I was unwilling to give her up. I loved her. I'd changed myself completely in order to be able to keep her with me. In addition, I'd seen that my mother couldn't hide her dislike of my daughter. While she'd never mistreat a child, disapproval rang in Mother's voice any time she spoke to her.

Knowing Eric wouldn't like people gossiping that he was cheap, I framed a careful reply. "That's a good idea for when she's older, but for now, we don't want people thinking you can't afford to support your children."

Though he didn't send Zalea away, Eric's proposal made me even more careful not to show her signs of favor. I seldom touched her, lest my husband or one of his sons see and resent it. I often spoke harshly to her in their presence. Zalea learned not to come to me for comfort, so she turned to my father, who let her tag along behind him and ask question after question about what he did and why he did it. Later she would bond with Benny, who was also willing to teach her. She became confident in her own intelligence. She grew strong in her beliefs. But she wasn't feminine and malleable like other girls. The only real softness Zalea ever showed was for her little sister, Milla.

One summer day when the girls were ten and five, a man came to tell me, in a gibbering rush of words, that there'd been an accident in the field. While auguring corn into a grain box, Eric had stepped too close to the tractor's power take-off. The tail of his flannel shirt caught in the shaft, which spun at 540 RPMs. Before anyone could shut the machinery down, he'd been pulled into it and killed.

Days later, I heard that the messenger reported I'd been too shocked to respond to the news. The truth was that I'd struggled to conceal the relief I felt at being freed from that monster.

Eric's house was taken over by a man with a family, as tribe rules required. His boys went to live with their uncle, who welcomed the increased stipend three strong sons would provide. My daughters and I returned to my father's house, where I made a case for being allowed to remain single. Mother disapproved of the idea, but whispered rumors about my past, the fact that I'd borne two girls and no sons, and the growing realization that Milla was mute and therefore "damaged," meant that even though I was only thirty, no men came beating on the door with requests for my hand.

Life with my parents was certainly less violent than it had been with Eric, but it wasn't idyllic. Father had fully adopted the New Times beliefs. Women should subject themselves to men. People of other races, while useful at times, could not be trusted. The tribes' children were raised on such ideas, with no first-hand knowledge beyond our homogeneous group. There were no Black kids at school, no Hispanics in the burg, no Muslims at work in the fields. Our schools taught that other religions and cultures were eccentric and wrong. Given the chance, members of some tribes would eat your dog. Others would steal your children and sell them into slavery. And, it was said, a few were composed almost completely of unpredictable, violent drug addicts. While our wise Chief Vox charged their leaders with keeping them in check, it paid to stick with your own kind whenever possible.

Essays my daughters were assigned at school made me sick: *Describe your coming role as a mother and a wife. What parts do you feel will most fit your talents?* While Milla willingly wrote about her devotion to children and the recipe book she was compiling with her grandmother's help, Zalea objected to the inequalities she saw. Why, she would ask at dinner, did girls wear dresses when pants were much more practical? Why shouldn't she ask the Sunday School teacher how it was possible that Jonah had lived for days in the belly of a whale without being digested? The story made no sense.

I was sometimes called to the school to smooth some young teacher's ruffled feathers. Azalea didn't speak respectfully. Her questions were impertinent, her tone sarcastic. "I'll talk to her," I'd promise, but on the way home I'd wonder where her rebellion came from. Why did she long for rights she'd never have, times she'd never known? How did Zalea sense what she and other women had lost, what it was like before?

PRESENT

Finding the letter from Sri made my path clear. If my daughters were on their way to where he lived, that would be my goal too. Though it hurt to know Zalea had thought me so useless that she hadn't even hinted at her plans, I admitted she was right. I'd buried any sign of my real self in women's work to please my father, to placate my husband, to still my mother's disdain, and to be like the women I saw every day. Now I was determined to break free, to awaken the old Wendy and find my girls. I didn't let myself think about seeing Sri again. That was simply too much to contemplate.

Though I'd often dreamed of escape, of moving to some faraway country where there was no winter, my dreams had come to nothing. A lone woman with a child, later two children, would have been easy to catch and return to her tribe. In addition, I'd been emotionally incapable of planning anything. The effort it took each day to fit in, to play my role, to hide my unhappiness, was exhausting. Rolf carped constantly about the "privileges" I was afforded and my abnormal desire to remain single. "Marriage is ordained by God, Wendy. What's wrong with you?"

Soon the power to "fix" me would belong to Rolf. I had to go.

My biggest problem was finding transport to Dorado. I'd never be allowed to take a vehicle, and if I tried to steal one, I'd be stopped at the checkpoint. An idea I'd entertained on and off over the last year returned to mind, a possibility but not an easy one. The tribe owned a single-engine airplane. While neither of our two licensed pilots would agree to take me anywhere in it, I had discovered a third pilot living in our midst. That presented an opportunity, though the devil was, as always, in the details.

The plane, though seldom used, was regularly maintained. Aviation fuel was incredibly expensive, but the tribe kept a store of it for emergencies. With a little coaching, I thought I could get the plane ready to fly. That left me with only the question of how I'd spring my pilot from Special Quarters.

Sixty-two-year-old Betsy Woods had been a commercial pilot in the Old Times. She was a vocal and vociferous critic of the New Times, but because she had MS, and because her husband Cecil was hard-working and well-liked, people mostly ignored her complaints about the tribal system. When Cecil died suddenly of a massive stroke the year before, Betsy, who had no children, had been forced to move to Special Quarters.

That's where I'd come to know her. I often helped out at SQ, partly to demonstrate that I was useful despite being single and partly because I didn't like the way the place was run under Rolf's oversight. Though he sneered at my "playing Lady Bountiful with the loons," the work was meaningful to me.

Despite Father's well-meaning efforts, residents with problems ranging from congenital birth defects to difficulty with social interaction to full-blown schizophrenia were jammed into tiny, cell-like rooms. Those who lacked self-control spent most of their time locked in, alone and ignored. Treatment was minimal, since medicine was expensive and hard to come by. Though doctors were required to take turns visiting AQ and SQ facilities once a week, most focused on private clients, who were able to pay for the care they received. Workers at SQ understood that their job was to clamp a lid on the place, to keep unappealing and unwholesome members of the tribe away from those who combed their hair and didn't drool. To me, the worst thing about SQ was the finality of the place. Very few who entered those doors ever returned to society.

Betsy's multiple sclerosis grew worse each month. One hand moved constantly. Her speech was hard to understand. And her vision was going. "I see like a fly does," she told me. "A slice of what's in front of me repeated dozens of times."

This was the person I hoped would fly me away from Tribe Woods.

Though I'd decided to leave, I delayed for a week, then two weeks, and then three. For one thing, I was scared. For another, I had trouble putting my request to Betsy into words. How does one ask a person to risk her life for a cause that's probably hopeless from the outset? Several times when I visited SQ, I thought, *Today's the day I tell Betsy my idea.* Then I'd chicken out, excusing my cowardice with the lack of privacy or an imagined conviction that she looked tired. Then one day I looked at the calendar and asked myself, *Why are you dragging your feet? In three days Rolf will be Woodsleader.*

Taking a cake I'd made that morning, I left the house without saying where I was going. Mother spent most days in her room alone, and I often heard her mumbling prayers. I was mentioned, as was Rolf, and sometimes she cried. Though we had little to say to each other, I recognized that she was devastated at losing Dad. I suppose she also missed Milla, who'd been like a puppy at her heels for years.

SQ was a red brick, one-story building with three wings flanking a round entry area. It was surrounded by a high fence with a large gate at the front and a smaller pedestrian gate off to one side. Residents who were mobile and could behave might sit in the yard on nice days and watch the squirrels. I'd seen them out there, walking and talking to each other, or to themselves if that was their choice. I rang the bell and was admitted by a young staffer I hadn't met before. That was no surprise. Turnover at SQ was constant.

The guy eyed the cake with something like delight, and I told him, "I'm going to take a slice to my friend in B Wing. I'll leave it to you to dole out the rest."

With a plate, a spoon, and a square of carrot cake, I made my way to Betsy's room. Her wing was outfitted for people with physical disabilities, with low sinks and toilets to accommodate wheelchair users and easy to grip door and drawer handles. A Wing held the developmentally disabled, and C Wing was sometimes called, unkindly, the Mad Wing. There almost everything, including the residents, was stored in locked spaces.

I passed the front desk, where two caregivers examined a chart, one sitting with pen in hand, the other reading over his shoulder. As I made my way through the common area, I spoke to residents I knew and nodded to others. A few greeted me. Others seemed unaware of my presence. Tim, who had Parkinson's, reached out a shaky hand, hoping I'd stop and talk. On another day I would have, but at that moment, I hardened my heart, gave him only a smile, and went on before I lost my nerve yet again.

"Wendy," Betsy said when I knocked and entered. "It's g-good to s-see you."

"I'm sorry I haven't been around much. Since Father died, things have been crazy."

Shadows moved behind her eyes. "Rumors are f-flying about—upcoming ch-changes here at SQ."

"What changes?"

Her mouth twisted. "It a-appears we'll be r-required to work for our k-keep."

"Work?" I glanced out the doorway. "What work can the people here do?"

Looking at her wandering arm, she quipped, "I'm sure I'll be great at knitting potholders."

Her sarcasm calmed the last of my qualms, and I made my pitch. "Betsy, I need to get away from here. If I could get you to the plane, do you think you could fly it?"

The look on her face might have been funny if I hadn't been so anxious. "Wendy. L-look at me."

"But if I set your hand on the stick or whatever they call it, you could grasp it, right?"

"Y-yes, but I d-don't guarantee I'd have f-full control."

"I'd help. You'd tell me what you need and I'd do it."

She frowned. "B-but I don't s-see well anymore."

"I'll be your eyes too." Aware of how desperate I sounded, I knelt beside her and soldiered on. "I'll do whatever you tell me to, Betsy. We'll leave here tonight, fly as far as we can on a tank of gas, and then we'll figure out what to do from there." It sounded crazier and crazier, but I finished, "I'll support us both somehow.

I'll—" I stopped, unable to believe my own words, but then I pressed on. "—do whatever I have to."

Betsy sat very still, except for the arm that never stopped moving. It swooped out as if rejecting my words, but then it dipped, paused, and returned to her side. Did it represent her thinking, or was it only obeying the fractured impulses of a damaged brain? Finally she said, "It's l-likely to end b-badly."

Rising, I took a step back. "I'm sorry. I'm a little crazy right now. I didn't mean to—"

"Wendy." Betsy's expression, which had been doubtful a few seconds ago, turned almost mischievous. "Are you s-saying you're w-willing to risk dying in a p-plane crash to g-get away from this p-place?"

"I guess I am."

Reaching out with her good hand, she took hold of my wrist. "M-me too."

"Really?" Her pronouncement of willingness brought an immediate wave of overwhelming doubt. "You know there's only about a twenty percent chance we'll actually get away with it."

"Sweetie, m-my life has been a m-mess for s-some time. Now that Rolf's the leader, it w-will get a l-lot worse." Her smile was sad. "Y-you're the one t-taking a risk. I'm s-simply t-taking ch-charge of my own d-destiny."

"I'm willing if you are."

Betsy glanced out the reinforced window. "H-how would w-we m-manage it?"

I sighed. "First, I'll have to fuel the plane. I need you to tell me how to do that."

It took a while, but Betsy explained how to attach a grounding line so a spark wouldn't ignite the fuel vapor. I'd need two stepladders, one for the storage tank and one for the plane. I'd fill gas cans, haul them to the plane, and pour the fuel in by hand. "F-fifteen t-trips with a two-gallon c-can in each hand. That sh-should be enough."

I sighed deeply before speaking. "I can do that, but to be honest, I have no clue how we'll get to where I want to go."

"I know a p-place we c-can hide for a wh-while," she replied after a moment. "If we can g-get there, w-we'll be s-safe and t-taken care of."

I was surprised at how calmly she accepted the idea of escape, because the thought of it had made me fizz with tension for days. There was wisdom in her approach though. Worrying about all of it at once was at best counterproductive and at worst obstructive. I needed to focus on escaping the tribe. The rest, finding a destination, locating my girls, deciding how I'd make a living, and avoiding pursuit—The tribe would want their plane back—could be sorted out later.

"Okay," I said. "If I don't get caught filling the tank, I'll come for you at midnight. I'll find some excuse to get in and—"

"N-no." Again her expression turned mischievous, as if we were planning a surprise party. "Come to the l-little gate."

"You can get outside?"

"Helen can." Betsy's friend Helen was a dour sort who seldom spoke and never smiled. "Her n-niece s-smuggles cigarettes in t-to her, and sh-she g-goes out at night t-to s-smoke them. Sh-she knows all the staff's l-little s-secrets."

There was still the gate itself, which Betsy would never be able to climb. Sensing my question, she said, "Helen can h-help with the g-gate too, b-but it will t-take some effort on your p-part."

I had to trust her, so I went on to the next problem. "Do you think you can ride on the back of Zalea's bike?"

Betsy sniffed. "I don't c-care if you have t-to wrap me in a t-tarp and t-tie me on. J-just get m-me out of here."

Leaving SQ, I started for the airstrip, which lay a half mile outside the burg. I went through the woods rather than along the road to avoid meeting people who might wonder what I was up to. The silence under the maples and elms reminded me of the days when I'd first come here with Zalea. Seeking ways to accept my lot, I'd walked with her for hours, lamenting the loss of my freedom, my country, and my husband.

News of Sri's death made me a mess, though the people around me seemed mostly relieved. Chief Vox had been willing to work with the rebels. Fate had intervened. Now, with the most extreme fighters on both sides out of the way, the country could settle down and rebuild.

Every day back then, more people had arrived to join our tribe. Benjamin Woods, now called "Leader Woods" welcomed them personally and saw that they were settled in. Every man got a job that would allow him to support his family and a house for their use. Unlike the Old Times, when laws had been twisted by those with abnormal ideas and desires, Father's rules were clear. While a person might not agree with all of them, we all agreed to abide by them.

Vox talked a lot about returning to simpler times, and people wanted that. Tired of trying to figure out what was fair, they were willing to let a strong leader make those decisions. The world of cyber-this and AI-that had made life complicated, and a surprising number of people were willing to give all that up in the name of simplicity. There were gripes for a while about inconvenience: no more credit cards, no social media, and no on-line banking, but most eventually convinced themselves that doing without them led to better, less complicated lives. Those who didn't were silenced. Shame and ridicule came first. In extreme cases, a tribe could banish a non-cooperating member. That was serious, since other tribes were unwilling to take in renegades who got no stipend and were therefore a drain on resources.

My mother's shift from computer-savvy educator to what the Bible called her husband's *helpmeet* surprised me. She wasn't allowed to attend meetings, vote, or offer opinions in public. I waited for her to run out of patience with the New Times, but she continued to smile benignly and say nothing as we gave up technology, professional entertainment, and most of all, women's rights. Once I asked her outright. "You used to run a school. How can you let them tell us what we can read and how we can dress?" The look she gave me made me wish I'd kept quiet. "We needed this, Wendy, and you're an excellent example of why. Look at the mess you made of your life, hiding what you were doing, rejecting your family's values, and taking up with some..." I waited for the ethnic slur, but she caught herself, "—stranger. Your father forgave your foolishness, but now he's stuck supporting you and your—" again I sensed her curbing her tongue, "—alien child."

I could have argued that Zalea was as much a citizen as she was. That I hadn't asked to be dragged back to the farm. That Sri wasn't a stranger to me. But none of that would have convinced Mother that she was wrong. She wanted this life, rules she was comfortable with and the people who looked and thought as she did. That was why she supported Rolf, despite the fact that she knew how greedy, corrupt, and unkind he was. While she loved her "baby boy," I'd heard her say more than once that Byron was too weak to lead the tribe. Having her least worthy son in charge was a sad goal for a woman who could have run the tribe herself if the fact that she was female didn't preclude it.

Reaching the airstrip I paused, momentarily uncertain. Mother would say I'd taken the wrong road again. Standing there, still and unsteady, I watched a lone bird fly over, heading southwest. Taking courage from its solitary flight, I vowed again that I would leave tonight. My girls needed me, no matter what they thought. I couldn't let them down again.

The minimally maintained airport runway had once been a cornfield. It ended at a building just large enough to hold a small airplane and its necessary accoutrements. Taking out the keys I'd stolen, I fumbled through them until I found the one that unlocked the hangar door.

Now that I was actually putting my plan into action, I set my doubts aside. That wasn't easy, since facts nosed at my heels like a snarling terrier. My pilot was half-blind and mostly disabled. The Cessna was decades old. The airstrip was narrow and edged by weeds. At its end stood a grove of sturdy pines and tall maples. I imagined all sorts of tragedies, from being caught getting into the plane, to tearing the wheels off if we failed to clear the treetops, to veering off the runway and crashing before we ever got off the ground.

Those thoughts served no purpose. Setting my shoulders, I checked the hangar to assure that I was alone. Then I did a decidedly amateur check of the plane. It appeared to be airworthy, but what did I know?

Toting two fuel cans out to a tank set on a raised platform out back, I filled them, carried them inside, hauled them up the stepladder, and poured the fuel into the plane's tank. The next hour was a repeat of filling, carrying, climbing, and pouring. Though I was careful, I spilled fuel on my jacket sleeve on one trip. I would have to ditch it before I got home.

When the fifteenth trip was complete, I replaced the gas cap, returned the cans to where I'd found them, and relocked the fuel tank and the hangar. Aside from a slight, lingering smell of fuel, no one who happened by would notice anything different. I peered through the window for one more look at the plane that would become my means of leaving the tribe. Tonight I would escape the place where I'd been a prisoner for years. I was done being complicit in my own captivity.

Rolf was at the house when I returned. His sharp gaze made me glad I'd not only jettisoned the jacket in the woods but left my shoes on the back porch as well.

"Where have you been?" he demanded.

"Walking in the woods. It calms me down."

Rolf let out a huff of disgust. "Well, while you were wandering and grieving—" he gave the words a whine, as if I'd been indulging myself, "—we finalized the arrangements." He explained the agenda for the installation ceremony as if I were clueless. Mother came in as he talked, carrying the stole of office she would place around his neck to signal the transfer of authority. My only role would be to stand at the back of the stage, next to Byron and his wife, and look approving.

I'd had years of practice hiding my feelings, so when he finished I said, "Sounds like you've got everything figured out."

"No thanks to you."

“Son,” Mother said in a coaxing tone, “We need to work as a family now. Wendy and I—”

“I don’t need help from either of you.” Rolf seemed to feel the time was right to show his hand. “While you’ll be honored as Father’s widow,” he told Mother, “you need to understand that Sally is First Woman now. You’ll be moving in with Byron and Ariel, and I’ll thank you to keep your opinions to yourself as we go forward.”

Turning to me, he shook a finger under my nose. “And you will not be living like a princess in a tower anymore. You’ll marry, as will Azalea if she ever comes dragging her ass back here.” He sniffed. “Milla can go to SQ. She’s a good little worker, so they’ll be happy to have her out there.”

I didn’t argue. In fact, I did my best to appear cowed by what Rolf thought was his authoritative manner. I was surprised, however, when I glanced at Mother. Her jaw worked, her lips went tight, and a glint came into her eyes that went beyond anger. If I’d had to choose a word for it, I’d have said what she was feeling toward her son was *rage*.

Chapter Twenty-One

Our escape that night was bold, risky, and possibly comical. The night favored us with clouds that blocked the moonlight. Using a flashlight when necessary, I pedaled Zalea's bike right up to the fence surrounding the SQ building before I saw Betsy's pale face peering through the wrought-iron gate. Behind her stood her friend Helen, who had cerebral palsy, with a smoldering cigarette pinched between her fingers. While I wondered briefly how safe a smoking habit was for a person without much physical control, my next thought was more personal. Could Helen be trusted with our secret?

Betsy sensed my concern. "H-Helen is r-really good at p-playing dumb." Pointing my flashlight at my face, I smiled a thank-you at Helen. She did not smile back, probably unhappy at the prospect of losing her friend. Betsy leaned heavily on a cane held in her left hand. Her right waved wildly in the darkness, like a tethered bird trying to take flight.

"Follow me along the fence," Helen said in a low, wavery voice. I walked with her along the cyclone fence, slowing my pace to accommodate her halting gait. "There." She pointed, and I turned to see a lamp post behind me. "There's a magnetic box stuck on that, up near the top. The night men keep it there so they can sneak in late to work."

I went around the post, nervous at standing in the spill of its light. "I don't see a box."

"You're not supposed to." Helen's tone held a hint of irritation. "Climb up onto the base and feel around the collar." I did as she said, clinging to the post with one hand while the other skimmed the smooth metal that attached the lamp to its post. My fingers found what my eyes hadn't seen, and I stepped down, waving the box. Sliding it open, I took out the key and went back to the gate. When I opened it, Betsy shuffled through. As she said goodbye to her friend, I relocked the gate and replaced the box in its hiding place. Let the staff scratch their heads, wondering how Betsy had escaped.

My duffel bag was fastened to the handlebars with stretchy cords. I'd brought only essentials except for one thing. At the last minute, I'd remembered the Barbie doll Zalea had given Milla. Going to her room, I rummaged in the closet until I found the doll. It wouldn't take up that much space, and Milla would know I'd been thinking of her when I left the tribe.

Stuffing Betsy's smaller bag in next to mine, I stabbed her cane between the two. The bike had a platform on the back for carrying boxes, which made a tolerable seat. Mounting sidesaddle, Betsy wrapped her wandering hand in the folds of her skirt and then tucked the fabric under her knees, trapping it there. Taking a firm grip on the metal post that supported my seat with her good hand, she said softly, "R-ready when y-you are." We took off, following secondary, unlit streets until we came to the dark road leading out of Woodsburg.

I hadn't ridden a bike in decades, so I was rusty, and Betsy's weight pulled me to one side, making it hard to pedal. I adjusted, leaning the opposite way, and, weaving and bumping, we headed down the dark road toward our flying chariot. When we were some distance away from the building, I stopped pedaling and turned on the motor, my quads already shaky from unaccustomed exertion.

Even with mechanical assistance, it took us a while to reach our destination. Twice we had to pull into the shadows when a vehicle appeared ahead of us. Once Betsy slid off the bike and tumbled into the ditch. "I'm okay," she assured when I circled back to her.

"I'll d-do better this t-time." I dusted her off and, resuming our positions, we putted forward again.

The night was turning frigid. The handlebars felt like ice, and the cold air whipped past my ears, making me wish I'd smuggled a hat out of the house. Betsy shivered behind me, and I berated myself for making the poor old woman suffer. Then I reminded myself she'd already been suffering for months. A little cold could not, would not, stop us.

The hangar had a single yard light mounted over its door. As I approached, I watched carefully for signs the place was occupied, but the interior was dark and there was no movement in the spill of light out front. Reaching the building, I dismounted, helped Betsy steady herself, and then unlocked and opened the overhead door. We both winced at the rattle the rollers made, but once it was up, there was silence. I kicked the chocks away from the rubber wheels and pulled the plane outside, maneuvering it to a spot Betsy indicated.

There'd been a dusting of snow the day before, but the wind had swept most of it away. The nose of the plane now pointed at a dark wall of trees at the far end of the runway. I'd have sworn they were too close to miss, but Betsy seemed unworried. Leaning on me, she walked around the plane, inspecting as I aimed the flashlight where she directed. When it was done, she admitted grudgingly, "They've k-kept the old girl in good s-shape."

"Have you flown this plane before?"

She snuffled a laugh. "Once upon a t-time it belonged to m-me—well, to Cecil and me."

"I didn't know that."

"Help me up." I held Betsy's waist as she climbed the steps and ducked into the cockpit. Betsy took the pilot's seat. I strapped her in and took the one next to her. "The l-last time I flew was the d-day we arrived h-here," she said as she surveyed the instrument panel. "The p-plane b-became tribal property, and I w-was informed m-my pilot's license was n-null and void." Old anger sounded in her voice. "They c-claimed female p-pilots, like f-female doctors and executives, only m-made it into the w-workforce because the s-standards that men had been h-held to were relaxed."

"I remember that. I couldn't believe so many people nodded their heads and agreed that it was so."

"I d-didn't! I s-spoke out, but they s-said I w-was b-bitter." Betsy chuckled. "B-bitchy too."

I got a quick lesson on the plane's instrument panel, what would happen in the next few minutes, and what I was expected to do. I asked a few questions, and Betsy answered them, her speech halting but her mind clear and focused. "Are w-we ready?" she asked, and I knew it was a last chance to change my mind. Giving her a thumbs up, I fastened myself in.

Then came the noisy part. The moment we started the engine, our danger increased and our time to act decreased. Betsy placed her good hand on the yoke as I reached overhead to flip the switches she named for me. She asked for readings from several gauges, and I reported how they changed as we made adjustments to the fuel/air mixture and performed other operations she ordered.

As the engine purred to life, Betsy gave commands in a calm voice. I obeyed, terrified I'd cause the plane to blow up or to dive nose first into the ground. As we began to move down the runway, my heart thudded in my chest. It looked short—too short! Betsy had me turn what she called the flap handle, and we picked up speed. When it seemed we were doomed to crash into that dark line of trees, we rose like a bubble instead, taking to the air.

Suddenly the ride was smoother, quieter, and darker. Watching the dots of light below fade, I said goodbye to my home, feeling no hint of remorse.

"They'll report us," Betsy said calmly, "but in twenty minutes or so we'll be over the b-big lake, where it's likely the r-radar will l-lose us." She explained that flying over water made something called *clutter*, which confused radio detection. Earth Lake was huge, so it was unlikely stations on the ground would be able to tell where we were until we landed on the other side. Even then, Betsy said, if we set down in a remote place, our trail would be difficult to pick up.

"And you said you know a place."

"I d-do," she replied. "We're t-taking H-Hamlet's advice: 'G-get thee to a n-nunnery.'"

"Did you say a nunnery?"

She smiled. "I d-don't intend to continue w-west with you, dear. I p-plan to end my l-life as a nun."

Betsy's sister, she explained, was part of the Convent of the Beloved Ruth, a group of nuns living on the west shore of Earth Lake. Near the end of the Miller Administration, a wealthy woman had bought an old resort and turned it into a home for aging nuns. In return for a large annual donation and the promise they'd keep to themselves, the Vox Govt had agreed to leave the group alone. "Th-They receive no f-financial support from the G-Govt," Betsy said. "N-nobody cares what h-happens to them."

"If they figured out a way to get around the Govt's paternalistic crap," I responded, "I like them already."

"They c-can only t-take two n-new members a y-year. Diane j-joined t-ten years ago, and sh-she offered t-to get m-me in when C-Cecil died. Rolf s-said no."

I frowned. "Why would he do that?"

"I h-hear he's s-started counting some SQs as C-Contributing Members. H-he k-keeps the s-stipends for himself."

"That snake. If he were caught doing that, the whole tribe's future would be in jeopardy."

"T-True." Betsy shifted in her seat. "E-even if we c-crash and burn, W-Wendy, I'm g-glad I won't die in that sad p-place."

The drone of the plane was hypnotic, and after a while we settled into silence. Betsy estimated a three-hour flight, which would put us near our destination right around daybreak. Her prediction was correct. By the time creeping sunlight allowed a dim view of the ground, we were approaching the lakeshore near the point she sought. "The convent is a l-long, low b-building with a huge c-cross at one end," Betsy said. "It should be to your left."

After a few minutes I said, "There. I see it."

"Good. Now l-look for a l-landing spot, a flat f-field or a straight s-stretch of road."

"Um… The road that runs along the shore is pretty straight."

"I w-won't be able to s-see where we a-are until w-we're q-quite low, so y-you need to h-help me line the plane up. Tell me w-what you see, where we are, and give me the altimeter reading every few seconds. D-don't worry if we d-don't make it the first t-time. We can t-try again."

I failed twice. As the road rose to meet us, I panicked and shouted, "Go back up! Go back up! We haven't got room."

Betsy was patient. "That's okay," she said each time. "We'll go around again."

The arrow on the fuel gauge looked alarmingly low. How many screw-ups did I get before the engine choked and died?

In that instance, the old saying "The third time is the charm" made sense. The first time, what I saw was unfamiliar, and decisions came at me too fast. The second time was still scary, but I began to see how the landing had to go. The third time we came around, I'd begun to trust that we had enough room to set down safely. As we dropped from the sky, I gave Betsy a running account, telling her things she probably didn't need to know along with things that were vital. When the wheels hit, I gave a little yip but managed to stay focused. "Right," I called out. "Now left." Betsy pressed first one rudder petal then the other, keeping us on the road as she slowed our speed. When we coasted to a stop, there was still plenty of straight road ahead. The cockpit went silent except for my ragged breathing.

"W-walk d-down the road," Betsy ordered. "F-find a h-hole in the w-woods where we c-can hide the p-plane."

"You—"

"I'll g-get out b-by myself. Go."

Hoping she didn't fall and break a bone, I started down the road, peering right and left. After about a quarter mile, I spotted a two-track that led to a cabin set deep in the trees. Hunting property, I guessed. It appeared that no one had used it for years.

I returned to the plane to find Betsy leaning against a tree, recovering from the effort of getting herself to the ground. She held a coil of rope in one hand. "P-put this through the sh-sheave in front and then m-make yourself a h-harness," she ordered. "I'll p-push from behind to g-get you st-started."

A sheave turned out to be what I'd have called an eyelet. Passing the rope through it, I made loops at either end. By slipping one onto each shoulder, I was able to pull the plane like an ox drawing a plow. With a nudge from Betsy to get me going, I started up the road. The trek was easy on the asphalt, but it got a lot harder when I turned onto the dirt road that led to the cabin. The sandy track made it hard to keep my footing. The ground was uneven, so I got pulled backwards each time the wheels hit a dip.

Sweating, grunting, and saying words my mother would have disapproved of, I fought my way forward. Behind the cabin was a fairly steep downslope, the perfect place to ditch the plane. I dragged my burden toward it, so focused on the task that I made a potentially fatal mistake. When the wheels finally tipped over the edge of the depression, the loosened tension on the rope made me realize I was directly in the way of the plane's tumble. Slipping out of my home-made harness, I dove to one side, rolling away from the wheels and ducking under the wing as the plane bumped past me, continued down the incline, and jiggled to a stop. Getting up, I dusted myself off and regarded it with satisfaction for a moment before starting back to where I'd left Betsy.

The terrain and the plant life around me was similar to what we'd left the day before. The November air was cold, the sky above me gray. Now that I wasn't laboring physically, I felt a chilly wind invading any uncovered spot, my calves, my wrists, my neck. I needed my jacket, which made me realize I'd left our bags in the plane. I turned back, slid down the incline, and retrieved them from the cockpit. Leaving for the second time, I noticed the marks the plane's wheels had made. I went into the woods, found a pine branch, and used it to sweep the tracks away.

"Good," Betsy said when I reported what I'd done. "N-now we n-need to figure out where the c-convent is from here."

Through the trees on the opposite side of the road, I saw sunlight sparkling on water. "Let's walk down the lake shore."

It was the easiest way to locate the place, but not, I soon realized, the easiest way for Betsy. She was a trooper, but walking in sand was nearly impossible for her. Her balance was terrible, even with the cane. Her face was blue with cold, and her MS had sapped what little strength she had left. After falling onto one knee for the third time, she said, "You g-go find my s-sister, W-Wendy. I'll wait here."

Leaving her felt wrong. We'd formed a bond with our crazy escape, and I imagined some local busybody coming along and ordering her to explain her presence. Since we didn't have other options, I agreed. I found her a seat on a hummock and promised to return ASAP. Hurrying down the beach, I passed dozens of lake cottages, all shuttered and locked. The chill in the air and the gray color of the water confirmed that it was too late in the year for lakeside vacationing.

Beyond the cottages, I came to a sign that said *Private Property - No Admittance*. Ignoring it, I continued along the beach. When I came around a spit into a small cove, there it was. The main building looked like an old motel, two stories with doors along each level. Though it was early, women moved busily about, all wearing gray dresses, all with white caps covering their hair. Shuffling through the sand, I approached one of them. "Good morning. I'm looking for Sister Diane."

The woman was suspicious. "Who are you?"

I kept my tone and my expression polite. "I'm looking for Sister Diane."

A second woman approached. "Who is she, Ginger?"

"She says she's looking for Diane."

They regarded me as if I'd asked them to donate a kidney. "What does she want Diane for?"

Still trying to be nice, I kept my tone pleasant. "I'll explain when I see her." They frowned, unable to make a decision. "I'm not here to upset anybody," I told them. "Please tell Diane I have a message for her."

They looked at each other. One of them shrugged. "I'll go," the other woman said, and she hurried off.

Five minutes later, the messenger and a woman of probably seventy-five approached. Her features resembled Betsy's, but I saw no sign of my friend's easy smile. "What do you want here?"

"Are you Diane?"

"Yes. Are you connected to the airplane that landed near here this morning?"

Uh-oh. "I hope it didn't cause you any trouble."

"It hasn't yet, but someone's bound to report it." Diane's lips were tight, and the words came out like bullets. "We're sure to have toppers, maybe even Monkey Men, stopping by to ask questions about it."

That didn't sound good. "Can we speak alone?"

Diane gestured for the other two to move away. They went, though clearly disappointed. "What is it?"

"Betsy's with me. She wants to stay here with you." Briefly I filled her in on Betsy's unhappy status at SQ, my decision to leave, and her willingness to help me get as far as the convent.

"She flew her old Cessna here?"

"We kind of worked together. She told me what to do, and I did it."

"And where is she now?"

"Down the beach a bit. She's worn out."

Turning to the nuns, Diane said, "Grace, will you get the dune buggy? We're going to have guests."

Within an hour, Betsy was resting in one of the empty dormitory rooms. The reunion between them had been heart-warming, though Diane was clearly upset by her sister's physical decline. "If only I'd known," she said.

Betsy shook her head. "As l-long as I had C-Cecil, I was ok-kay, but now..." She made a rueful grimace.

The nun's lips set firmly. "Well, you'll have the best life we can provide from now on."

Leaving Betsy to nap, Diane led me to her office, passing a doorway left open to reveal a large open area filled with crates. Inside, the women of Beloved Ruth worked busily, boxing wheels of cheese. Except for their sober dress, they didn't seem much like the nuns I'd seen as a kid. The convent, I deduced, was a way for them to avoid the tribal system, much as women in the Middle Ages had "taken the veil" to escape unwanted marriages and dictatorial men.

I was assigned a room and provided the schedule for meals. Then I was sent to a small cubicle where a woman named Ellie ordered me to sit down and present my arm. When I did, she painted some sort of glue over my tattoo and then applied a thin patch that identified me as Georgina Fry and listed a birthdate that put my age at forty. "That won't fool the fancier scanners," she said as she tested to make sure the edges were stuck in place. "Our local toppers have older models, so you're okay for now."

For the rest of the day I wandered the place, peering into rooms and exploring the grounds. Everywhere I went, women smiled at me but didn't engage. They were busy. I was temporary. That night I slept peacefully, pleased with my progress.

The next morning I met with Diane, who asked pointed questions about my plans for the future. When I explained that I wanted to leave Fairica for Dorado, she said in the direct manner that was typical of her, "Your arrival has no doubt been noted. That means it's in our best interest to send you on your way as soon as possible."

Raising a brow, I asked, "Do you have a magic wand that will whisk me off to a different country?"

Putting her index finger over her mouth, Diane rested her chin in her hand. "Not a magic wand, no, but we might be able to help." Smiling at my look of surprise, she explained, "This area is known for its cheese. We make our own version of sharp here, and it's very popular." Pride rang in her voice as she finished, "Aging is everything, and we here at Beloved Ruth are very patient about that."

I wasn't getting the connection, though I figured there had to be one. "Dorado has become a wealthy country," she went on. "The people there love our cheese, which pairs nicely with their excellent wines."

"I didn't think Fairica traded with Dorado."

She smiled at my naivete. "Officially, no, but commanders do as they like. Dunn sells our cheese to wealthy customers in Dorado and makes a hefty profit." She raised her brows. "In exchange for our product, we get Dunn's protection."

I was stunned. "The commander of the Green Section illegally transports your cheese to Dorado to make himself a buck."

"His personal pilot makes the deliveries." Glancing out the window, where a few dead, curled leaves swirled in the wind and skidded across the grass, Diane tied the story to my need. "He's coming for a shipment soon."

Still stunned, I said, "I can't believe our commander is a crook."

"Jesus said the poor will always be with us. I'm afraid the rich will as well, and of the two groups, the rich are greedier by far." Another sigh ended her philosophizing. "Anyway, it's possible you could travel to Dorado on Dunn's plane."

"How would I do that? Hide in a cheese box? Crawl into a corner and hope to go undetected?"

"We'd have to offer the pilot a bribe."

I shook my head. "I don't have much money."

"The sisters who deal with him might know what would tempt him to help us."

A little glow started when she used the word *us,* but a sharp rap on the door interrupted. A woman put her head in without waiting for permission and said, "The toppers are here."

"Thank you, Caroline." Diane gestured to me. "This way." Down a hallway, she opened a door and led me into a small laundry. Gray dresses hung on racks along two walls, and she ordered, "Put one of those on, quickly." While I selected one that seemed likely to fit, she opened a drawer and took out a white cap. I buttoned the dress. She covered my hair. "Our local topper, Drew Baker, is a twenty-four carat ass," she said as she worked. "As I said, Commander Dunn keeps him from harassing us most of the time, but your plane has given him an excuse."

"Will he find it, do you think?"

"It's been seen to. A few of the younger women dragged it down to the lakeshore last night, towed it into deep water, and sank it. They swept the road and raked the sand, erasing all signs of the Cessna's final trip."

"You people are amazing."

She frowned. "You're pretty young to be one of us. Let's hope he doesn't notice."

Leading the way to the packing room, Diane ordered me to stand between two women who were boxing wheels of cheese. While they showed me what to do, Diane left briefly. Soon she returned, accompanied by five men with hard, stupid eyes and expressions that were meant to appear tough. They were almost comically mismatched. Some had pistols. Others carried deer rifles, and one had a sawed-off shotgun. Except for the head topper himself, they wore regular clothes, with only TOP ball caps to identify them as officers of the law.

Head Topper Baker wore a uniform so outrageously contrived that I had to bite my lip to keep from smiling. Tan camouflage pants were topped with a black t-shirt that was almost invisible under a tactical vest that bristled with weapons, up to and including a hand grenade. He carried a scary-looking gun with a banana clip. On his belt were more weapons: a pistol on one hip, a stunner on the other, and at the back, two sets of handcuffs and a can of what I guessed was pepper spray. His hat, an Aussie Breezer, had crocodile teeth strung along the band. I guessed we were supposed to think he'd hunted and killed the croc himself. That was unlikely for a guy who lived on a freshwater lake in a deciduous forest.

"Head Topper Baker is here with questions, Sisters." Though Diane was perfectly composed, I noted a twinkle in her eye as she finished, "Please be as helpful as the dignity of his office requires."

Baker stared at us for a while as if his steely glare might prompt a confession without him demanding one. Stepping toward a woman down the line, he asked, "How long have you been here?"

"Nineteen years, sir."

The topper's gaze moved on to me. "How about you?"

I made the reply I'd been coached to give. "Six weeks, sir. My husband died recently, and I was sick with grief. Commander Dunn gave me permission to stay with the sisters until I feel ready to return to my tribe."

"Scan her." A deputy stepped forward with a device that looked like a TV remote. At his command, I put out my hand, working to keep it from shaking.

The man waved the scanner over my arm. "No alerts," he reported.

"I'm gonna check back in a week or so," Baker said, coming so close we were almost nose to nose. "Woman young as you should be having babies and supporting her tribe, not hiding out with a bunch of queers."

I almost replied, but a look from Diane suggested I should keep quiet. Baker wanted to make me afraid. I wanted to punch his flat nose even flatter. I could not give in to either of those wishes.

Stepping back, Baker addressed the room. "An airplane landed near here yesterday. I know you heard it." Glaring at a woman whose red face and blinking eyes betrayed nervousness, he demanded, "What do you know about that, Sister?"

"I heard a big noise early yesterday morning," she responded in a shaky voice. "I thought it was a truck going by."

Baker's eyes swept the room, looking for signs of weakness. "I'm not fond of this place," he said, his tone turning oratorical. "There's unnatural things going on out here, things it makes me sick to think about." He raised a finger to the sky. "If one of you perverts came anywhere near my kids, I gotta tell you, I'd go nuts. I know you're the commander's pets, and he's the boss, but if I had my way, you'd all be lined up against a wall and shot."

A couple of the toppers grunted assent. One called out, "Amen!" Not one woman said anything.

"We'd like to have a look around," Baker said in a falsely pleasant tone. "You won't mind that, will you, Sister Diane."

She gave him her best smile. "We are happy to make your work easier, Topper Baker."

Baker and his men searched the buildings and grounds for hours, making no attempt to be respectful. Finding nothing incriminating, they climbed into their trucks, still muttering, and left. With a collective sigh of relief, the women of Beloved Ruth began putting their belongings to rights.

Kay and Alice were the two nuns in charge of delivering the cheese to a nearby airstrip. Since a woman driving a vehicle was a rarity, they were the only ones at Beloved Ruth who had licenses. They knew Dunn's pilot fairly well, they said, but at first they could think of nothing that might convince him to take me to Dorado with him. Certain we'd find something, Diane asked question after question. Finally she hit on the right one: "Does he talk about his children?"

That brought a gasp and a memory. "He has three daughters," Kay said. "The youngest loves dolls, so he often buys her special ones when he travels. He mentioned a rag doll he found for her once, and a—"

"I have a very special doll," I interrupted excitedly. "A Barbie that's still in the original box." It was Milla's doll, not mine to give away, but if that was what it took to get me to Dorado, I'd gladly hand it over.

That Friday, when the plane was due to touch down, we left for the airstrip, Kay and Alice in the truck and me hidden in the back, under a tarp, among the cheese boxes. I'd said goodbye to Betsy, who seemed happy in her new home. "G-good luck, Wendy," she said. "I hope you f-find your girls very s-soon."

Now, as we bumped along a narrow road, I imagined what could go wrong in the next hour. Already suspicious of the nuns' activities, Topper Baker might show up at the airstrip. The pilot, a man named Kurt, might refuse our request that he transport an illegal passenger. Even if he agreed, I might be found by inspectors or members of the ground crew. If any of that happened, it wasn't only my life that was ruined. Betsy would be found and returned to Rolf. Topper Baker would make sure the nuns' punishment was harsh and long-lasting. And Diane would be held responsible for everything. It felt like the ride took forever.

Sister Kay, the bolder of the two nuns, was charged with making the offer. I heard it from my place of concealment, and I had to admire her cool approach.

"Good afternoon, Kurt. Did you have a good flight?"

"Fine," the man replied. "Ten cases, right?"

"Right. How is your littlest daughter, Daisy, was it?"

"She's good."

"You mentioned once that she's quite taken with dolls. Would she like a vintage Barbie, do you think?"

"A real Barbie doll?"

"Yes. In excellent shape."

"Is it for sale?"

She hesitated. "It might be available for trade."

His tone turned suspicious. "What kind of trade?"

"Suppose a person needing to get to Dorado was willing to trade the doll for a ride. Would that be a deal you'd consider?"

Kurt thought about it. "Can I see the doll?"

I heard Kay open the door, rummage briefly, and close it again. A few seconds later the man said, "This is nice."

"I bet she'll love it."

He thought about it for what seemed like a long time. "Before I agree, I need to talk to this mysterious passenger."

In for a penny, in for a pound. Rising from my place in the pickup bed, I asked, "What do you need to know?"

Examining me from under dark brows, the man asked, "What's your deal?"

"I'm looking for my two daughters. I think they're in Dorado."

"Why'd they run away?"

"Our leader died suddenly. The new one will trade my girls like they're bags of oats."

Kurt's mouth tightened. "It's hard raising daughters these days." Shifting his feet, he turned to Kay. "I'm going to walk into town and have dinner. Please get the cheese loaded and have the inspector sign off on it. I plan to take off in, say, an hour." With a meaningful glance at me he added, "I won't need to look in the back, because you ladies are honest."

An hour later I sat squished between boxes of cheese in the plane's cargo area. I heard Kurt approach, whistling as he came. He spoke to someone and the man answered. I had a moment of terror, thinking he'd brought Baker back with him, but only one set of footsteps came toward me. There was shifting of weight, and things squeaked and clicked as he went through pre-flight checks. Finally I heard him announce by radio that he was ready for takeoff. More flipping of switches. The radio squawked as he was given permission to take off. We began to move. I felt the moment when the plane left the ground and took to the sky. I was on my way.

"You might as well come up here and enjoy the view," Kurt called when the many sounds faded to one monotonous whir.

Clambering out from the back, I took the co-pilot's seat. "Thanks." It wasn't enough, but I didn't know what else to say.

His tone turned warning. "When we get there, I'll turn the plane so the door faces away from the hangar. If you get caught, I'll claim I had no idea you were aboard."

"I wouldn't expect anything else."

With that settled, we moved on to casual conversation. Kurt opened a small soft cooler and gave me the choice between two sodas. I took a Mountain Dew, having not had one for almost twenty years. It was sweeter than I remembered, but the cold and the fizz were pleasant. From my backpack I took a dozen muffins the nuns had sent. He ate two of them. I talked about the good things in my life, the farm, the sense of safety it offered, and my girls. When I explained why I distrusted my brother's intentions for them, Kurt confessed, "My wife and I have started keeping our oldest girl at home."

"Why is that?"

I thought he wasn't going to answer. Finally he said, "Commander Dunn is…fond of very young, very pretty girls."

How awful to fear that your child will be pawed by some old pervert! "That's horrible. How can men like that—? Ugh."

His shoulders twitched in an angry movement. "Could be power. Maybe a need to feel young again." He sniffed. "I know people who consider it an honor for their daughters to be noticed. They claim he's generous with them…afterwards… but Letty and I don't want—" His voice choked. "We won't let him put his hands on her." He took a long breath. "It's getting harder though. Twice now he's mentioned it's been a while since he's seen her."

How long could the anxious parents protect their child? I had no doubt there were evil men—and evil women—who pandered to the commander's sick desires. Some flunky would say to Dunn at some point, *Your pilot's kid has grown into a beauty, sir. Would you like me to arrange for her to visit your home?*

"I'm sorry," I told Kurt. "This isn't the way things should be."

"My wife wants to…you know…do something. Have a few teeth removed, maybe." He was silent for a moment before adding, "I guess we could get her dentures when she's…older."

Did people really maim their daughters to deter powerful men from raping them? A bigger question arose in my mind. Was it inevitable that rich men got their way, no matter what it was they wanted?

Chapter Twenty-Two

We made two stops to refuel. Each time, Kurt pointed out the nearest bathroom and then distracted the ground crews while I hurried off to visit it. When we crossed the border into Dorado, he announced it as if he sensed I'd feel better knowing, though we had some distance yet to go. Finally, he landed at his destination and turned the plane, as he'd indicated. "Good luck, Wendy," he said as he opened the door. "I hope you find your girls."

"Thanks. And I hope Commander Dunn's dick shrivels and drops off."

Kurt got out, carrying the remaining muffins the nuns had given me as a distraction for the ground crew. I followed him out of the cockpit in a crouch, but instead of going down the steps, I climbed onto the wing and hunkered there like a frog on a lily pad. While I was now out of Fairica, I had no right to be in Dorado. Peeping over the roof, I saw Kurt begin handing out muffins. Hurrying down the steps, I headed for a stand of scraggly pines. When I looked back, the men were happily munching their treats. "Thanks," I whispered to Kurt. I'd left the doll on my seat, where he'd see it first thing.

I'd seen plenty of photos of the west coast, but being there felt open and wide in a way home never had. The airstrip was at one side of a huge flat space, but mountains lined the horizon. They appeared to be only a mile or so away, but I'd heard that distances are deceiving where mountains are concerned. The city was called Landon, and Kurt had described it as mid-sized and prosperous. Most of it lay east of the airport. Outside the cyclone fence surrounding the airstrip was a well-maintained highway with lots of traffic. I'd forgotten how much noise dozens of vehicles moving at speed make, and it took a while for my brain to be able to block out the commotion so I could think. I needed to get a sense of the area, but the airstrip where we'd landed was commercial. That meant no terminal, no tourist-friendly amenities, no cab stands.

A whistle sounding in the distance helped me decide on a plan. Train stations were sure to be full of strangers, so I'd blend in. People wait there, sometimes for hours, so I wouldn't stand out if I stayed for a while. There'd be food, rest rooms, benches, and a wall map that I could use to orient myself. That would be my next goal.

I did my best to stick with Betsy's one-step-at-a-time philosophy. I'd got myself out of Fairica, which was good, but now I faced the reality that Dorado was a big place. I had no way of knowing if my girls had made it this far. My first move had to be finding Sri in hopes he'd heard from them. If he hadn't, perhaps we could look for them together. I took a deep breath, filling my lungs with Dorado air. I had a long way to go, but I was no longer a prisoner of my tribe or my nation.

Waiting in my hiding spot, I watched as night fell and the area quieted. Trucks and planes stopped arriving. Most of the workers left, zooming out the gate in pickups and sedans. I watched a lone security man walk the boundary fence, checking the storage units as he passed to make sure they were locked. When he was a good distance away, I shouldered my pack and crept through the shadows to the ten-foot fence. The strands of barbed wire at the top discouraged me briefly, but I reminded myself how often Sri and I had gone over fences like it. We'd done it to spray paint *FREEDOM!* on government buildings. We'd done it to enter offices and destroy lists of "disruptive" citizens. We'd done it to wreck computer centers with sledgehammers and homemade bombs. We'd been fearless back then.

Two decades ago I'd been younger and lighter, but my determination to find my girls made the fence into simply another barrier I had to conquer. Taking off my denim jacket, I held it in my teeth as I gripped the metal and climbed. When I reached the top, I tossed the coat over the barbs, rolled myself over, and half-climbed, half-dropped to the ground.

It wasn't a graceful dismount. I fell the last few feet, pinching my fingers painfully in the wire before I managed to let go. Still, I remained upright, stumbling only a little. Running across the highway, I dived into the darkest spot I could find, a culvert that smelled of oil and something dead.

I waited in my stinky space until I was sure no one had seen me. Then, skulking through the shadows, I followed the road into town. Dirty, dusty, and a little bloody, I bore no resemblance to an upright citizen. I had no food left, and I was emotionally exhausted. Turning down one street after another, unsure what I was looking for, I spotted a child's treehouse in the yard of a modest-looking home. Lights shone inside, but the yard itself was dark. The treehouse, which had once been cute, now appeared abandoned, its nailed-on slab steps cockeyed and its window overgrown with branches. Climbing up, I sprawled on the plank floor and promptly fell asleep.

The next morning I woke early, shivering in the morning damp. The sun's first rays showed over the mountaintops, so I guessed it was between six and seven a.m. Since the owners of the property were apparently still fast asleep, I took further advantage of them. I washed my face and hands in their pool, cringing as the cut on my hand stung from the chemicals in the water. Next I used their shed as a changing room and put on my spare set of clothes. Finally I stole three oranges from a tree in the yard. They were seedy but delicious, and I ate all three as I walked, following the sound of whistles to the train depot.

Despite the fact that I now looked pretty much like any other woman on the street, I felt constant prickles down my neck. Years of submission to authority were hard to forget, and I kept imagining a man demanding to see my identity tat or my travel permit. At a traffic light, I stopped next to two uniformed police officers. The dark-haired woman was teasing her blond partner about his love of gummy bears. He laughed good-naturedly. While they seemed watchful, scanning the street for possible trouble, neither gave me a second glance. I walked on, moving fast to warm myself. I'd left my jacket tangled in the wire atop the airport fence.

The train depot sat beside a maze of tracks, with benches at one end and a row of machines along the other. It felt like I'd stepped back in time, or maybe forward. I saw dozens of devices people at home no longer had, cell phones, tablet computers, and earbuds. I watched passengers approach the row of machines and purchase what I guessed were train tickets. *If I knew where Sri lives, I could get a ticket—* No, I couldn't. I had no cash, no credit card, no ID.

Sitting down on a bench, I observed the people around me for a while, studying how to blend in. They were well-dressed and relaxed, giving the lie to Fairica's contention that everyone here was miserable and afraid. If Dorado had suffered in the war to free itself from Fairica, it had apparently recovered completely.

Noticing a bulletin board with bits of paper tacked to it, I went over and read ads for services like pet-sitting and computer repair. At the top right corner was one that stopped me: *Help for Travelers.* It had a phone number, but what caught my attention was the logo. It was the Σ/Ω I'd designed for Sri almost two decades earlier.

Excited by the discovery, I asked a woman sitting nearby if I could borrow her phone. She clearly wasn't thrilled with the idea, but I begged, "Please. I only need it for a minute, and I'll sit right here so you can hear what I say."

Grudgingly, she handed the phone over. Once I had it, I had to ask for help making the call. I'd memorized the number, so I said it as she punched it in. "It's ringing." She handed me the phone.

"Hello?" A woman's voice, not young. Suddenly I had no idea what to say, and she repeated, "Hello?"

"Um—I saw your number on the wall at the train station."

"What do you need?"

"I don't know. I'm—new here, and—" Should I mention that I recognized the logo? I decided not to until I knew more. "I wondered what kind of services you offer."

"Do you have a place to stay? Money? A phone?"

"No."

"Where are you?"

I'd forgotten the name of the city, but I looked around until I found it posted. "Landon."

"All right." There was a pause, and then she said, "In twenty minutes, a man wearing a red baseball jacket with white trim will come into the station. Tell him you're looking for Clara."

"Clara."

"Yes. He'll buy you a ticket and put you on the right train." The voice stopped, and when I looked, the phone had gone black. Giving it back to the owner with my thanks, I took a seat that faced the entry door and waited. It happened as the woman had said. A man came in, stopped and scanned the crowd. I rose and made eye contact, and he gave a little nod that invited me outside. When we got there, he asked, "Do you have an ID I can scan?"

"Why?"

"It helps us determine if you're legitimate."

Though it scared me to do it, I pulled up my sleeve, peeled off the plastic overlay the nun had made, and showed my real tattoo. He scanned it with his phone. "You've come a long way." Pocketing the phone he said, "Let's get you a ticket."

It was so simple from there that I almost couldn't believe it. Red Jacket bought me a ticket to Lugar, printing it out, since I had no phone. With it in hand, I followed him to the correct train. He wished me luck and turned away, but then he called, "Wait." Reaching into a pocket, he took out a bottled water and a candy bar. "She said you'd be hungry."

Thanking him, I climbed onto the train, which again brought on the feeling I was in a time-warp. There were no suspicious guards with guns. I saw women wearing pants, halter tops, and lip rings. Men had long hair, short hair, or no hair, as they pleased. Tense with anticipation, I took a seat. Soon there was a hiss as the air brakes disengaged, and the train began to move.

The trip took three hours. Most of the time I looked out the windows, reminding myself that I was in a place where no one would choose a mate for me or demand that I find one. I was nervous about getting off at the right stop, but a friendly fellow passenger, seeing me craning my neck as stations approached, asked the name of my destination and then assured me he'd see that I knew it was coming in plenty of time.

I went back to thinking about my great good fortune. I was out of Fairica. I'd met people who wanted to help. It was exhilarating to think that in a few days, or even tomorrow, I'd find Milla and Zalea. And the husband I'd lost so long ago.

The train reached my stop just after six p.m. Red Jacket had said I'd be met at the station and driven to Clara's house, so I stepped into the warm evening, alert for contact. A man waved me over and then turned to lead me to a baby-blue sedan. When I asked where we were going, he simply said, "It's perfectly safe," and opened the passenger door. People lie to people every day, I knew that. He might have said it to trick me into cooperating, but it didn't feel that way. I sat back in the man's comfortable car, letting him choose both the route and the radio station.

After about a half hour, we pulled up outside a modest two-story home among dozens like it. People walked along neat sidewalks and sat on porches, talking and laughing. Almost all of the homes were brightly lit, and through large front windows, I saw the flicker of TV screens. It appeared everyone in Dorado had one.

Leading me to the front door, the driver knocked twice. "Clara will take care of you," he said. Then he turned and left.

When she opened the door Clara, who had grayish hair, greenish eyes, and skinny little glasses that sat halfway down her nose, was already smiling. "Hello, hello!" she said, pulling off the glasses. "Please, come in."

Suddenly shy, I hesitated, but she waved me in like a first-grade teacher welcoming the new kid. Gathering my courage, I stepped over the threshold and into a combination dining/living room with a large table and six chairs on one side and a couch and two upholstered chairs before a fireplace on the other. At the back of the room was a doorway to the kitchen, and past that, a hallway disappeared into darkness. A lovely stairway curved upward on my left, its banister shiny with use. Doors lined the second-floor hallway, bedrooms, I guessed. Logs burned in the fireplace, adding warmth to the chill that had settled at evening. It felt like more than that, like trust was transmitted through the fire's crackle and hum.

"Your driver probably told you we're in southeastern Dorado, near the border with Fairica."

"He didn't tell me anything. Not even his name."

She shrugged. "Just as well, I suppose. If one isn't a chatterbox in our line of work, that's not a bad thing."

"Before this goes too far," I warned, "I should tell you that I haven't got any money."

That brought a dismissive shrug. "Very few of our clients do, hon. Later there might be ways you can assist us, but there's no requirement to do so." She raised both hands. "We do what we do with no strings attached."

"You help escapees from Fairica just because you're nice people?"

"There." Again she seemed like a proud teacher. "You've got us all figured out." Her glance swept my rumpled clothes. "You'd probably like a bite to eat, a shower, and a good rest. We can talk tomorrow about what comes next."

The wooden floor of the playhouse had been neither flat nor comfortable, and I hadn't realized how tired I was until she said it. "That sounds great."

Clara had prepared a whole pizza. "They have take-and-bake where I shop, and since almost everyone likes pizza, it seldom goes to waste."

I hadn't had pizza since my college days, and I ate three pieces. "In the tribe," I said when I finally pushed my plate away, "we always had meat-and-potatoes meals because that's what my father wanted."

Hearing myself say it aloud made me realize how long it had been since I'd questioned adhering completely to a man's tastes. Dad had disapproved of "foreign" food, so we never served it. No sweet and sour chicken. No lasagna. No tacos.

"Bring your stuff." Clara showed me to a cozy bedroom across the hall from hers. "Get up whenever you feel like it; we don't keep much of a schedule."

I slept well, and when I emerged from the bedroom, Clara was sitting at a computer, leaned toward the screen, head tilted back to get her bifocals in the right spot as she read. "Good morning," she said without turning. "There's cereal on the counter and milk in the fridge."

I ate Cheerios while Clara finished up whatever she was doing online. I surprised myself with how easily familiar terms returned to me after years of disuse. *Surfing. Google. Apps.* How long since I'd even thought about them?

Clara joined me at the island, refilling her coffee cup on the way. "Are you ready to talk about why you left Fairica?"

"My two daughters ran away because our leader is…not a good person. I think they meant to come here."

"Describe them, and I'll see if anyone has reported two girls traveling on their own." Clara went back to her computer, and her fingers flew over the keyboard. "To the general public, we're a hostel for foreign students, but our real purpose is helping people get out of Fairica. We have people on both sides of the border, so someone might have seen your girls."

As the morning went on, Clara's contacts responded, one by one. No one had seen Milla and Zalea.

I did some mental calculating. They'd been gone from the tribe for almost six weeks, but they were on foot. They'd had a lot of ground to cover, so they might still be on their way. *Please, please let that be true.*

Because I had begun to trust Clara, I offered a bit more information. "I think the girls will try to reach the older one's father, who lives somewhere in this area. His name is Sri Afzal, if that helps with—"

I stopped, because Clara's gray brows had risen almost to her hairline. "You have a child with Sri?"

"He's my husband. I thought he was dead, but he recently sent a letter to Azalea, inviting her to come and live with him."

"Mail in Fairica is monitored, so how would he send such a letter?" A note in Clara's voice hinted she already knew.

"A man brought it." Though I felt ashamed, I finished, "She never got it, because the man was caught and hanged."

"We guessed it was something like that." Clara swiped at her eyes with her fingers. "He was a good man."

"I'm sorry." My sympathy changed nothing, so I went on. "I found the letter after he…afterward, and I recognized Sri's symbol." I licked my lips. "I'm the one who designed it, a long time ago."

Clara seemed amazed. "You and Sri were married."

"Yes."

Taking a sip of coffee, she stared past me for a moment. "Well then," she finally said. "Let's let him know you're here."

"You're in contact with Sri?"

"My dear," Clara said, "He is the driving force behind this whole operation."

I should have known. Sri was not the kind of man who could simply ignore the injustices Fairica had imposed on the people he'd left behind.

I spent an anxious hour trying to decide how it would be to see Sri again. I'd loved him madly once, but I'd gone through the grieving process, believing he was dead. Did I still love the man, or did I love an old memory?

In the room I'd been assigned, I looked at myself in the mirror atop the dresser. What would Sri think when he saw me? *She looks like she hasn't smiled in years.* That was true. I hadn't felt like smiling for a long time. I did what I could, hand-pressing my clothes, combing my hair, and trying out words of greeting.

Then I heard him in the great room. His voice was unchanged, and the years fell away like autumn leaves from the maples back home. Hurrying out of the bedroom with a smile on my face, I stopped, keeping the expression in place only with effort. Sri was older but still handsome. Beside him, a woman with dark eyes held his arm with both hands. The message: *He is mine.*

There was only one way this could go. "Sri," I said, keeping my tone even. "It's good to see you again."

Seeing how I was going to play it, he relaxed a little. "Good to see you too, Wendy." His tone was as casual as mine, but I knew Sri's face, his body, and his mind. I saw the effort he made to keep his expression blank. I saw the twitch of his hand. I heard the tiny tremor of emotion in his voice. Sri wanted to take me in his arms, to comfort me and wipe away the grief of our years of separation. He could not do that, so instead he said, "This is my wife, Nina."

Working against every urge in my being, I stepped forward and put out a hand. "It's nice to meet you, Nina."

She was clearly unconvinced of my sincerity, which suggested she was nobody's fool. Still, Nina shook my hand and gave me a tight smile. "Nice to meet you too."

"I've prepared some goodies," Clara said in her bustling manner. "Nina, will you help with the serving?" To me she said, "We'll have a bite to eat while the four of us see what we can do about finding your girls."

"Girl," Nina corrected.

Clara's gaze flicked to Sri, but she touched Nina's arm, urging her to follow. Nina went, clearly unhappy to leave Sri and me alone together. Aware of her gaze, I kept my face blank as I said in a low voice, "I thought you died in a plane crash."

"Your mother wrote to me in prison to say that rebels blew up a bus you and Azalea were on," Sri said, his tone immeasurably sad. "She said she blamed me."

That was all the time we had. Nina returned with a tray of sweets, followed by Clara with a carafe of coffee in one hand and a pitcher of iced tea in the other. She herded us to the table, where Nina pulled out a chair for herself and the one next to it for Sri. I sat down opposite them. Clara chattered brightly, ignoring the tension in the room, and passed me the tray of pastries. I didn't want food, but I took a doughnut and bit into it. I needed the tea to wash it down, since my mouth had gone dry. I didn't want to sit there looking at Sri. I wanted to touch his face, to bury my own face in his shoulder while I wept for all we'd missed. Raising our child together. Living in the country we'd once known and loved. Growing old as husband and wife. Never having been branded a disgrace to our nation and our families.

I took another bite of my doughnut with sprinkles, swallowing my emotions along with it. I'd focus on finding my girls.

I told again what had happened when the man, whose name was Chad, was captured on my father's land. Sri took the news stoically. Nina made a *tsk* sound as if to say, *What can one expect from savages?* Clara studied her sticky bun as if the secret to life lay inside its folds.

Next I described the events that had led to my leaving the tribe: my father's death, the girls' disappearance, my conviction that Rolf would do his best to make our lives miserable. Sri smiled as I told the story of my plane ride with Betsy, but when his wife shifted in her chair, he resumed a bland expression. I could read his thought, and it pleased me that he appreciated the boldness our escape had required. No matter what I'd been in the years we were apart, Sri saw that I still had some of my old fire, and he approved.

"You lived with your tribe all this time?" Nina's emphasis on *tribe* indicated what she thought of the system. "You did nothing to get away from them?"

Realizing I could relieve her mind a little, I said, "I got married and had Milla. I wanted to give my girls happy lives."

"Under the thumbs of men," Nina said disdainfully. "I wonder how they found the courage to run away."

"We shouldn't judge the pressures others operate under, my love." Sri said it gently, but it was a reprimand, nevertheless. Nina's lips tightened, and she said no more.

Once I'd finished my story, Sri gave a brief version of his. "When we were...when they arrested us, I was sent to a prison worse than anything I could have imagined. We lived like animals, desperate for food, for safety, for one second without noise and bright lights shining down on us and abuse from the guards." His tone turned bitter. "I think the only reason I was given the letter from your mother was that it added to my pain. Our jailers always approved of that."

I saw hints of what he'd suffered. A pale, raised scar disappeared into his hairline. The fingers on his left hand were knobbed and crooked, as if they'd been broken and allowed to heal untended. Seeing me looking at them, Sri put his hand under the table.

"One day I was taken to the prison warden's office, where I was told I could be a free man again. The new man in charge, Allen Vox, proposed what he called 'a pathway to peace.' Rebels who'd stood against the Miller regime could help the nation heal by publicly supporting Vox and his reforms. If we did that, our crimes would be forgiven."

"Did you believe them?"

Sri's wry smile was so familiar that it hurt my heart. "Let's just say that my promise to support Chief Vox was given in the same spirit as his promise to set me free. Vox's man talked a good game. He told me that other rebel leaders had already agreed to attend." Sri shrugged, which I read as disgust for their naïve acceptance of the offer. "I guess they weren't the only ones in the country who wanted to believe Vox was the answer to all our problems."

"But you knew better."

Sri waved a hand. "I didn't *know* anything, but it felt wrong."

I had to bite my lip to keep from saying, *That's exactly how Vox affected me!* The fresh reminder of how closely Sri and I had shared everything, even intuition, made it hard to keep silent, but I let him continue. "What Vox's offer did provide was a chance to escape. I told them I'd be happy to air my concerns to the new Chief."

"And then you started plotting." I couldn't bury the visions in my head, Sri and I huddled before a computer, discussing how we'd accomplish a goal despite dangerous possibilities.

Sri grinned, and I guessed he was revisiting those same memories. "I did."

Nina shifted impatiently in her chair, and Sri buried the grin. "You will recall that Vox made a big deal out of his peace summit. He sent his own plane to circle the country, picking up rebel leaders at several locations and bringing them to the meeting. Though I was leery of his promises, I wanted to get on that plane."

I'd been thinking ahead, and I said, "Get on it but not stay on it."

Again Sri's eyes met mine. *You always could read my mind!* He didn't say it aloud. "I figured since Vox was playing the whole peace conference thing for the media, we'd be allowed to board the plane without physical restraints. I managed to get word to a friend, who came up with a plan. As I went up the air stairs, my friend popped off a few small charges near the nose of the plane. It was just smoke and noise, but some of the guards went to investigate. The ones who stayed with us peered out the windows, trying to see what was happening. I grabbed a bunch of blankets from the steward's shelf, made them into a vaguely human shape in my seat, and then covered it with another blanket. My friend Yaris was still setting off his little pop bombs, so the guards were distracted. I walked to the back of the plane like I was headed for the lavatory, went down the interior stairs, located the cargo bay, and exited the plane through the loading hatch. Yaris was waiting in an empty baggage cart, which became our getaway vehicle."

"The plane took off."

His tone turned hard. "And eventually crashed."

"I never believed it was an accident."

"No. Vox downed his own plane to get rid of a bunch of problems."

"But one of the dead was his own son."

"Who had a drug problem and a tendency to screw up everything he touched," Nina put in.

"Vox wanted to kill you and the other rebel leaders," I said. "Once he did that, he could show his true colors."

Nina frowned. "I never understood why the people of Fairica didn't rise up and kick him out."

"People choose their leaders," Sri said, "whether they do it by actively supporting them or by simply ignoring their duty as citizens. Keeping them in tribes where they don't know much about each other helps him to control them. Every tribe is afraid those 'other' tribes are out to get them."

I turned back to Sri's story. "What did you do once everyone thought you were dead?"

He sighed. "This part of the country had seceded and become Dorado. Neither government had established firm border policies yet, so I simply rented a car and drove home to my family. Once here, I applied for and was granted citizenship."

"Everyone who could get out of Fairica was doing so," Nina said. "I worked in a large pharmaceutical lab, but I reached a point where I could not endorse the lies those idiots wanted me to agree to."

"We weren't the only ones," Sri said. "What Fairica has today is men who exchanged their rights as human beings for what they believed was security."

Men like my father. “How do you make a living and fund this…rescue service?”

“We smuggle goods into Fairica, items the Govt can’t or won’t provide. With the profits, we help those who have escaped Vox’s clutches and assist others who want to.” Sri leaned back in his chair. “It’s very satisfying.”

His phone signaled a text message, and Sri leaned over the tabletop to read it. “Hector says he’s got Azalea.”

Feeling relieved and scared at once, I asked, “What about Milla?”

“He doesn’t say.” Sri rose. “We’ll get you to Azalea ASAP. Maybe she’ll be able to tell us where her sister is.”

PART IV

Chapter Twenty-Three

MILLA

Living with the Vails was okay, though a lot of the food they ate was kind of spicy and being Isa's friend was a bit like walking on eggshells. Aside from rock collecting, which she considered her area of expertise, I was expected to be interested in whatever Isa was at a given moment. When she lost her temper, I was likely to get punched or pinched. When that happened I also got glances of disappointment from Madame Vail, hinting that I'd failed in my duty. I did my best to anticipate Isa's frustrations and either prevent or soften them, as I'd once done with Aunt Sally's rambunctious twins. Life with the Vails wasn't exactly happy, but they'd rescued me when I had nothing and no one. I had to be grateful for that.

They were generous too. I got new clothes without asking. Each new outfit exactly matched Isa's, but I smiled brightly and signed *Thanks* every time.

I woke up each morning long before Isa or Madame did. The commander was gone a lot, but when he was there he rose early, shut himself in his office, and had breakfast delivered on a tray. I spent the early hours with the servants, helping out where I could. I cut up vegetables, scrubbed pot bottoms until they shone, and applied lemon oil to the furniture. Though Mar said we mustn't let Madame Vail know, she seemed to enjoy my company.

I also stayed behind at the stable after our rides whenever possible. It was the one time Isa didn't want me beside her, because she spent at least an hour arranging the rocks she'd collected that day on the balcony railing. That meant I could help Grae or the grooms feed Dolly and brush her down.

One day Madame Vail passed on her way to the lake and saw me mucking out a stall. "Misa, you're getting your nice new shoes dirty," she said in the tone I recognized as irritated but trying not to show it. She'd started calling me by a new name because it rhymed with Isa. "Isa and Misa," she'd say. "My two pretty girls."

Though most of the people who worked on the estate were nice, I liked Grae best. He was what I imagined a big brother would be like, and his calm presence eased the grief I felt at losing Zalea. We were careful to be formal when Isa was around, since her crush on Grae made her fiercely jealous. She often embarrassed him, asking things like, "Grae think Isa new boots sexy?" She held onto him longer than necessary when he helped her into and out of the saddle, batting her eyes. Though he was always polite, Grae was careful not to encourage her.

Once she decided she and I were friends, Isa was open about her admiration for Grae. "I choose husband for me, I pick him," she said in a wistful tone unlike her usual blare. "Grae very nice-looking."

Madame Vail had noticed her daughter's infatuation, and for once she took a stand. "Isabel Joanna! What would your father think if he saw you mooning over the help? Show a little dignity." As usual, her mother's words didn't stop Isa. She went on flirting with Grae. He went on pretending he didn't notice.

While Isa wasn't clever, she could be crafty. One night as we got ready for bed she told me, "Grae will fight. Make lots of money for Father. Then he and me get married." It took me a second to process that. Isa believed Grae's success in the fight ring would make her father see him as an acceptable husband for her.

I was sure she was mistaken. In fact, I'd figured out that my presence in their home was an attempt to get Isa ready for a candidate her father already had in mind. The commander needed Isa to behave herself long enough for him to marry her off. After that, her husband could deal with her mental difficulties and her tantrums.

My presence had made Isa less volatile, but it was mostly because she liked having a person who was completely hers. For all her breathless concern for Isa, Madame Vail was self-absorbed, and the commander could seldom be bothered to notice his daughter. I was Isa's example, her teacher, and her plaything.

One afternoon a few weeks after my arrival, Madame Vail said, "I'm concerned about your vision, Misa, so I made an appointment for you with our optometrist." I doubted he'd find anything wrong with my eyes, but it was kind of Madame Vail to care, so I signed *Thanks*.

The nearest eye doctor was two hours away. On the day of my appointment, Madame Vail, Isa, and I got into the car with Grae and set off for a place called Theisburg, where there was a whole building full of doctors. The one for eyes found nothing wrong with my vision, but Madame Vail had a suggestion anyway. "I want her to have brown contact lenses." While he frowned, she turned to me. "Wouldn't it be cute if you and Isa had the same color eyes?"

Though he looked uncomfortable, the doctor said he could arrange it. I shook my head no, but Madame Vail didn't notice. Lenses that changed my blue eyes to brown were provided, with instructions on how to care for them. I didn't like the way they felt when I blinked, but when I appeared the next morning without them, Madame Vail said in the overly-sweet tone I'd come to associate with her demands, "You forgot to put your contacts in, Misa. Run back upstairs and take care of that, and then come back for your breakfast."

Next it was my hair, which was a few shades lighter than Isa's. In the tone that had begun making my stomach twist, Madame Vail said, "The girl who does my hair is a whiz with color. I'm going to ask her what she can do to make your shade the same as Isa's."

The stylist turned my light blonde hair to a honey color that was nice but no longer felt like mine. With the contacts in and the color change, Isa and I did look more alike, which made Madame Vail clap her hands. "It's not a perfect likeness," she exclaimed as we stood side by side, "but you make a beautiful pair."

While I didn't enjoy my new look, I reminded myself that the lady had been really good to me after Zalea died. I'd be ungrateful to resent a few changes that pleased my benefactor so much.

Isa and I had lessons together every day. "Miss Vail" wasn't what anyone would call a cooperative student, and most of the time spent with Tutor Matthew was dedicated to him coaxing her to do some small task that could loosely be called educational. On days when she chose to cooperate, Isa could write her numbers and stick the correct number of shiny gold stars into boxes below each one. While she could print her name, she was uninterested in writing anything else, so she filled every piece of paper she was given with *Isa, Isa, Isa.*

Unaware that I was close enough to hear, Tutor Matthew told Mar, "It's hard to tell how much she's capable of, because she knows I can't make her do anything. Now that Milla's here, she makes her do any work I assign."

Madame Vail referred to Isa as "special" and insisted that she required "extra patience" from everyone who dealt with her. I'd known mothers in the tribe who didn't admit their children's faults, but never one as determined as she. In her mind, Isa was always on the cusp of turning into the perfect child. Whatever she did wrong didn't matter. In fact, all Isa's wrongs were necessary steps toward growth. "We learn from our mistakes," Madame would claim, though it was clear Isa didn't. One day she chucked a rock at me because Grae helped me into the saddle first. Her mother viewed the cut on my cheek as evidence of her daughter's awakening femininity. "Isa didn't intend to hit you, Misa. She was just letting off steam."

The growing sense that the Vails saw me as Isa's permanent companion bothered me. Would I always be expected to serve as a buffer between her and the world? Would I always have to defuse Isa's tantrums, do tasks she didn't want to do, and bear the brunt of her anger? I got pinched. I was called vile names. I had to clean up Isa's messes while she stood back and laughed about it. Five minutes later Isa had forgotten, but the injuries I suffered became harder and harder to forget.

The commander avoided his only child whenever possible, but one day the door between my room and Isa's had been left open a few inches. When I came out of the bathroom, I saw him in the gap, standing with his back to me. He held Isa's arm with one hand while his other squeezed her cheeks so hard that her face was distorted. As his fingers dug into her skin, turning it white, he delivered a message in a tone of naked threat. "The Meyers are coming for dinner tonight. You will be downstairs exactly at six, dressed in the clothes Mar lays out for you. No boots. No rocks stuck in your bra. No cowboy hat. When you are introduced, you will smile at their son and say, 'Good evening, Adam.' We will sit down to dinner. You will eat what you're given, watching your mother and doing exactly as she does. You will answer if you're spoken to directly. Otherwise, you'll remain quiet and keep your expression pleasant. When the meal is over, I will dismiss you.

Turn immediately and leave, walking softly enough that your steps are silent. I'll have no pouting, no tantrums, no throwing dishes. Do you understand?"

Isa nodded. When he was sure he'd made his point, the commander let her go with an abrupt motion that sent her staggering back a step. As she rubbed her jaw resentfully, he turned and left. As soon as the door closed, Isa said in a low, angry tone, "Bastard!"

The incident told me I'd been right. Plans were under way for Isa's marriage. Would I be expected to move to a new tribe, dressed as her twin and dedicated to Isa's needs for the rest of her life? It seemed likely. In me, the Vails believed they'd found their solution to their daughter's fractious nature. As for Isa, she only saw what she wanted.

We go where the Lord puts us, and we do what we're given to do. I almost heard Grandmother's voice telling me what she'd have said if she'd been there. I knew she was right, so I vowed that whatever my role was in Isa's future, I'd accept it cheerfully. Even if it wasn't what I'd imagined, service could make life worthwhile.

A second unintentional eavesdrop destroyed my cheerful intention. While we were at lessons the day after the Meyers' visit, Isa smelled cookies baking in the kitchen. Shoving at my arm, she ordered, "Want cookies." She put her fingers close to my face, adding, "Three."

Madame Vail disapproved of eating between meals, but I knew better than to argue. With an apologetic smile at the tutor, I slipped silently down the hall and into the kitchen. It was empty, but the cookies had been left on the counter to cool. I was making a little stack of the still-warm treats when voices sounded in the hall, coming my way. With no way out, I backed into the pantry, out of sight.

"—actually a good thing the girl doesn't speak," Madame was saying. "For one thing, she can't gossip to anyone about Isa's behavior."

The commander's reply was, "Mmm."

"Isn't it amazing that they look so much alike, Darling?"

Another "Mmm." I heard the rustle of waxed paper as the commander helped himself to a cookie.

"Except for their noses. Do you notice that Misa's nose is longer than our Isa's?"

"Mmm." The refrigerator opened. Something landed on the counter with a gentle thud. A cupboard door opened and closed.

"So I was thinking, we could have Misa's nose done."

That got his attention. "What?"

"It's really no big deal, Darling. They'll put her to sleep, do a little reshaping, and when she wakes up, she'll be perfect. Misa would really look like Isa if we fix her nose."

"Isn't that a bit much, Giselle? Why do they need to look alike?"

"Sweetheart." I heard the brush of fabric on fabric. "It would make me so happy if our little girl had a perfect twin."

There were more sounds, and the commander made an odd groan. After a while he said, "Do what you want, Giselle. I like it when you're happy."

When I was sure they were gone, I emerged from the pantry. The jug of milk sat on the counter, and two more cookies were missing. So much for not eating between meals. I put the milk away, my mind heavy with what I'd heard.

"Took you long enough," Isa complained when I returned. I gave her four cookies, my own desire for a treat gone.

For days I kept touching my nose, wondering how long I'd get to keep it as it was. I felt sick and scared. And, I realized, angry. No matter what the Vails had done *for* me, what they intended to do *to* me was wrong. I wasn't Isa. I didn't want to be Isa's lookalike. But what could I do? Spying on Madame Vail, I tried to discover if an appointment had been made. Every morning I looked at her calendar, and finally it was there: *Appt. M, Wednesday 10:00 a.m.* Next week.

My mind whirled with images: a doctor, a scalpel, anesthetic, an awakening. No longer Milla but Misa, Isabel Vail's unwilling twin.

How could I stop this? No idea I conjured was practical. I couldn't report the Vails to the authorities, because they *were* the authorities. I couldn't leave, because the guards wouldn't let me through the gates. I longed to call home and beg Grandmother to send someone to get me. I wouldn't care what punishment the tribe doled out if they'd take me back. I'd live in Special Quarters. I'd scrub floors and spoon-feed residents and never give anyone a minute's trouble. If I could just talk to her!

But the phones in the commander's home were useless to me. I'd never used one, didn't know how they worked, didn't know a number that would reach my tribe. And even if I figured all that out, I had no voice to speak my concerns across the miles.

Chapter Twenty-Four

ZALEA

I was shy with Sri at first. We sat in the diner, with the clink of silverware in the background, while he and Mother told their stories. It might have made me feel like a normal teenager to be sitting there with both parents, but Mother's presence was a huge surprise, and I hadn't yet decided how I should view Sri Afzal, smuggler and newly-acquired father.

Sri seemed to understand. "Order something, and then we'll talk."

The menu offered foods I'd never heard of before. "Try the nachos," Mother advised.

When the woman went off with my order, Sri said, "You've been told I'm a criminal." His sideways smile revealed where mine had come from. "It's true, but only in Fairica. I oppose those who control the nation that was once my home."

"They say your people blow things up."

Sri's mouth turned down. "Those claims come from the Govt. They excuse their own incompetence and keep the citizens angry and afraid of outsiders."

The server appeared and set a plate of food before me, crisp triangles piled high with meat, vegetables, and melted cheese. Tentatively I took a triangle loaded with toppings and tasted it. That was good, so I tried another. "Just be careful with those." Mother pointed out a green circle about as big as my thumb. "Jalapenos are hot."

I tried a bite and immediately went for my glass of water. "Good," I said after a moment. "But hot."

Mother chuckled into her fist then stole a chip from my plate and ate it. She seemed like a different person, and yet one I had dim memories of. Once she and I had played games together. We'd sung songs. We'd laughed. When had that ended? The shadow of my stepfather fell over my good memories. Eric had been the end of my mother's joy.

Sri was smiling too, but they weren't making fun of me. It was more like they were enjoying my new experience. Mother and Father helping their child explore new possibilities in the world.

While she was careful not to be the least bit affectionate toward Sri, I noticed that Mother's eyes lingered on his face when he wasn't looking her way. I'd never seen her emotions so plainly displayed, but what I saw was a mix of love and regret.

Once we'd eaten, we prepared for the drive to the house where Mother was staying. She suggested we visit the ladies room before leaving the restaurant, and, taking the opportunity, I asked, "What's going on with you and my father?"

She stared at her reflection in the spotty mirror as she answered. "Sri has a wife and kids here in Dorado, Zalea."

Seeing the glint of tears in her eyes, I obeyed an impulse I hadn't felt in years. Sliding my arms around her, I pulled her close. "I'm so sorry, Mother."

She responded by holding me tightly, stroking my hair and sniffing back her tears. In my ear she said, "Please don't ever call me *Mother* again. From now on, I want to be your mom."

Sri had a nice car, and it purred smoothly down the well-kept highways of Dorado. He pointed out landmarks and told little stories to entertain us, but my thoughts were jumbled. I'd learned so much in the last hour. Perhaps most important was that there had not been a happy reunion between them and there never would be. Was that hard for Sri? If they'd known about the lies, would my mother and he have searched until they found each other again? That certainly would have changed my life completely. I wondered what Sri would do right now if his feelings were all that mattered.

Whatever the answer to that might be, he was polite and carefully unemotional with Mom. She seemed to understand, expressing gratitude to him in equally polite, equally unemotional terms. "Now that you and I are together," she told me as we turned into the driveway of the home of a woman called Clara, "Sri and his people are willing to help us find Milla."

"I know where she is."

They both turned to me in surprise, but Sri said, "Let's go inside, so Clara can hear what you have to say."

Clara was nice, welcoming me to her home and setting out some cookies she'd made and cold cans of Coke and Sprite. Sri's wife Nina was there, and I met my half-siblings Chad, Cher, and Cari. The kids seemed excited to have an older sister. Sri's wife was polite but not warm. I tried to imagine what it would be like to find that your husband's first wife and daughter suddenly dropped out of the sky and into your family. She had to be a mess inside.

"Tell us about your journey," Sri said. "Start at the beginning."

I told the story of our trek across Fairica, leaving out the parts that would have shocked them. When I got to the train wreck, Clara slid her laptop over and began typing. "I found the Govt's cover story on that," she reported when I stopped for a sip of Coke. "Saboteurs wrecked the train to, and I quote, '…sow discord among the citizens of Fairica.' That's their story, but independent journalists say track maintenance has been neglected for years. The commander of the Rose Section, one Peter Vail, has made no investment in infrastructure for years, so there are bound to be problems."

"But that's who has Milla," I said. "Commander Vail, from the Rose Section." I finished my story, telling how I'd seen Milla with the Vails on TV then gone to their estate to see her.

"You didn't talk to her?" There was a hint of the old Mother in the tone of the question.

"You should have seen that place," I said. "Milla's got everything she could ask for."

"Except her family," Mom responded. "Milla loves you, Zalea."

"And she thinks I'm dead. I didn't want to force her to choose between another long, hungry road trip with me and all the nice stuff she has living there."

Mom didn't seem convinced, but Sri took a practical approach. "Things are different now. We can offer Milla a safe place outside Fairica. We need to ask her if that's what she wants."

That night I had trouble sleeping. So much had happened, so much was going to happen, that it was hard to shut my brain down. Clara had a fenced back yard, and the night was warm, so I put on the sweat pants and shirt Clara had provided and slipped out the back door. Moonlight lit the yard, and I stepped off the patio onto the grass, feeling it with my bare feet as a way of grounding myself. I didn't see Nina Afzal sitting in an Adirondack chair on the far end of the patio until it was too late to pretend I hadn't.

"Azalea."

"Mrs. Afzal."

“Are you comfortable here?”

“It’s very nice. Clara seems to sense what people running away from their homeland need to feel safe.”

“She’s very good at what she does,” she agreed. “And we have been at this for a long time.”

“I think it’s good, what you do,” I said. “I never thought about leaving the tribe, never thought I had anywhere else to go. But then I heard about my—about Sri’s letter, and suddenly getting away was all I could think about.”

“You never saw the letter?”

“Not until today. Mother—Mom—showed it to me.”

After a moment, Mrs. Afzal said, “That was my doing, though I didn’t realize it at the time.”

I took a step closer to her. “What do you mean?”

Pointing to a nearby chair, she invited, “Would you like to sit?” I did, eager to hear what she had to say. When I was settled in, she began, “Several months back I was visiting Clara, and I’d brought Cari with me. There was a refugee staying here at the time, a girl named Ursula. She’d been sent away by her family because she got pregnant. Like you, Ursula had more courage than most. She ran from her chaperone and somehow made it to Dorado. She was eight months along and desperate by the time one of our people found her and brought her to Clara.”

“I’m glad for her,” I said. “I liked Ursula. The boy who practically raped her got some other boys to say she was a slut, so her parents sent her away.”

Mrs. Afzal’s lips curled. “Not nice, but not very original either. She and her little guy are doing well. That day, Ursula told my

Cari that she looked almost exactly like a classmate of hers. This girl was something of a local legend, because she actually ran the financial operations of her tribe. I didn't pay much attention until she said the name of the tribe was Woods. Ursula couldn't get over the likeness. 'Your daughter even smiles like Azalea,' she told me." Nina shifted in her chair. "Azalea. Not a common name."

"No."

"I asked questions about this classmate. Her age, her family, her background. Everything fit." Her feet shifted on the cement patio surface. "I fretted over it for a full day. I tried to tell myself it couldn't be Sri's Azalea, but I knew it was. Old Ben Woods' wife had lied to Sri. Eighteen years later, I knew I had to tell him the truth."

I didn't know what response was equal to the sacrifice she'd made, so I kept it simple. "Thank you, Mrs. Afzal. Thank you very much."

Mother wasn't happy when I insisted on going along on the mission to rescue Milla. "She's too young, Sri," she said as if expecting him to forbid me to go.

But Sri was not a Fairica-type male, prepared to tell me what I could and couldn't do. "Zalea knows the layout of the place," he responded, "and she's agreed to follow my orders. The plan works better if we have two people Milla will recognize. We can split up if we have to, Zalea and I going in one way and you and Yaris another."

I noted the team choices. Mrs. Afzal would stay in Dorado, taking care of their kids and overseeing their operations. Four of us would go after Milla: Sri, Mother, me, and Yaris, a fireplug of a man who didn't say much but seemed like someone you'd want on your side on a clandestine mission.

We'd studied the Vails, collecting bits and pieces of information about the wife, who was pretty but seemed shallow; the daughter, who had something wrong with her that nobody talked about, and the commander, who ruled his section like a king, collected ancient art, and loved primal sports like boxing and cock-fighting.

Sri's plan for finding Milla was practical, so Mom made no more objections at that moment. But over the next day and a half, as the plan took shape, she made comments clearly designed to scare me into staying in Dorado. "I worry," she said at one point. "You've never had any training in the kinds of actions we'll have to take out there."

I thought about reminding her that she'd been out of the "action" loop for two decades, but I said, "I'll do what Sri tells me to." I couldn't call him Father yet, much less Dad, as his kids with the current Mrs. Afzal did.

The main reason Mother's ploys didn't work was because I felt so guilty about leaving Milla behind. No matter how happy she'd looked, I should have at least asked her what she wanted. If I'd been thinking straight, we wouldn't have to take on the risks a trip to Eden posed. I figured it was only right that I went along and did my part.

As I packed for the trip, Mother stopped in the doorway to my room. I'd dumped my stuff onto the bed so I could re-pack with clothes Clara had provided, sturdy shoes, quick-dry cargo pants, and shirts I could layer, depending on the weather. Seeing the spangly dress, Mother stepped in and picked it up. "Where did you get this?"

"At Uncle Benny's house. I think it belonged to a woman he knew, Bonnie. Do you remember her?"

Mother sat down on the bed, the dress on her lap. She held one hand over her mouth for a few seconds, apparently trying to come to a decision. Finally she said, "This was Benny's, Zalea. He sent me a picture once from his phone of him and Kent at some event. Benny was wearing this dress."

As understanding hit, I stopped folding and met her gaze. "Benny was Bonnie."

"Yes."

"Then the letters signed 'Mother' that were tucked inside Bonnie's journal, they were from…"

"Your Grandmother." Mother's smile was sad. "She knew about Kent. I don't think she knew that Benny had arranged to transition." I frowned, and she explained, "To become a woman."

I ran a hand through my hair. "I knew Benny pretty well. He was…male."

Mother shook her head. "I don't think you and I can understand what life feels like for people like Benny." Looking out the window behind me, she said, "When we were kids, he'd say that his name was really Bonnie. Dad would insist he go outside and hang with the neighborhood boys, but he never wanted to. Once Mother caught him trying on clothes from her closet. That was the first time I ever saw her cry."

"So Benny felt like a girl—a woman—on the inside."

"Yes. When I was about twelve, which means Benny was seventeen, it got to the point where my parents couldn't ignore what they called his "unnatural behavior" anymore. They started spending an hour every night, kneeling on either side of him and praying for healing."

"It didn't work?"

She smiled sadly. "I don't think it ever does, Hon."

"So Benny left the farm as soon as he could."

"Yes. His life in the city made him happy. Not many at home knew what he was up to, but Mother had her ways of finding out. Benny was happy with Kent, and Kent was okay with the transition plan. Then came the unrest and the war and all the 'return to values' rhetoric. Kent was murdered by a gang of fundamentalist thugs, and Benny was a mess. We talked on the phone, but then things got really bad, and nobody could talk to anybody.

"When Vox took over and required everyone to return to their so-called roots, Benny was forced to come home. Dad promised to find him an understanding wife. To explain why he'd never married, they made up a story about a girlfriend who'd died tragically young." Mom took a deep breath. "By Dad's own rules, Benny would have a *D* for *Deviant* tattooed on his forehead if the tribe ever saw the real Benjamin Woods, Jr." Mom bit her bottom lip. "I told Benny over and over that he was fine the way he was, but he always felt he'd let our parents down."

"But he was smart, and he did so much for the tribe." I shook my head. "And for me."

"Agreed." As she'd talked about the past, Mother's face had taken on the sad expression I remembered well. "The first year or so, I'd put you in the baby carrier and Benny and I would wander the woods, talking. We agreed that what was happening to our country was horrible, but we didn't know how to change it. But then I married Eric and Benny got busy with the tribe's business. We sort of drifted apart." She pushed her hair away from her face. "The last time I talked with him alone was about six weeks before he died. Knowing Dad's mind was failing, Mom was pushing even harder for Benny to get married. He needed to step up, she said, to take on his God-given role and become the next leader." Her voice quivered. "She pushed until Benny-who-was-really-Bonnie took a gun into the woods and…ended them both."

Taking the sparkly dress from her, I folded it neatly and set it on the dresser. "I wish I'd known. I might have helped."

"Benny was so proud of you." Mother gave me a wobbly smile. "My sister knew quality when she saw it."

Using information I provided, Sri and Yaris made a plan for contacting Milla. We would leave on the weekend, enter through the tunnel, and go on in a camper registered in Fairica with Rose Section license plates. We'd drive the eighteen hours it would take to get to Eden in two nine-hour segments. I heard Yaris on the phone, instructing his contact on the other side to pack a small tent and two roll-up mattresses for the men to use. Mom and I would sleep in the vehicle.

The fact that I'd been told Milla was dead meant we couldn't simply knock at the Vails' gate and ask if she wanted to leave. We planned to go in the way I had, along the lake. Sri and Yaris spent hours discussing possible snags. They had a Plan A, a Plan B, and even a Plan C. That one sounded scary, since it laid out what they'd do if one of us got caught and the mission turned into a double rescue.

It felt weird going back to Fairica, but as we motored through the tunnel on ATVs, with its funny echo-y sounds coming at me from all directions, I comforted myself with the knowledge that Sri and Yaris did this all the time. With their plans, the equipment, and our clandestine entry, I felt like an extra in one of Grandfather's John Wayne movies.

The van Yaris had arranged contained false papers for each of us. Sri and Yaris posed as engineers, sent to do an annual checkup on the safety of oil and gas wells across the southwest. When asked, they explained they'd made it into a camping trip as a treat for the "little ladies."

Both men wore caps with an oil company logo on the front and black-framed eyeglasses. Mom and I sat in the back, wearing special blouses Sri had provided. "The fabric is called 'adversarial patch,'' he told us. "The print is designed to fool facial recognition cameras." They were hideous, and Mom and I giggled when we looked at each other. I couldn't remember the last time we'd shared a laugh, so it felt good. As we drove along under sunny skies, Sri gave us packs of chewing gum. "When we approach a check point, slip the gum into your cheeks to change the shape of your jaws."

"Do you think they're looking for us?" Mom asked.

"Doubtful, but in this business, we think ahead to prevent problems, so we aren't stuck solving them last minute."

Mom looked at me and rolled her eyes. I made an answering grimace to show I was nervous too. All in all, it was a little thrilling and a lot scary.

Chapter Twenty-Five

MILLA

As the day of my first appointment with the surgeon approached, it seemed time passed faster than before. I went around in a daze, trying to appear normal but unable to sleep for any length of time or eat without feeling sick. My misery was interrupted on Monday, when the commander called for the staff and the family to meet on the patio for an announcement. After we'd waited there for about twenty minutes, he appeared and delivered bad news. Thieves had broken into the family's house in the capital. When Cara came home and caught them, they'd killed her.

Shock traveled through the little crowd, expressed both vocally and physically. Madame Vail wiped tears from her eyes with a lace-edged handkerchief. Mar's face went pale. Lucia's eyes scanned the little group, noting reactions. Angry words, growled in low tones, cursed the faceless killers who'd murdered a woman they all knew. I heard soft prayers for Cara's soul. A man with an eyepatch rubbed his own throat, as if stopping himself from speaking. Beside me, Isa muttered words I didn't catch, but I could have sworn she sounded pleased. I looked for Grae's tall form at the back of the group, but he wasn't there. As soon as I was able to get away, I went to the stable to find him, but Grae wasn't there either.

Early the next morning, I returned and found him among the horses, his face pinched with grief as he scattered fresh hay in the stalls. Approaching, I put a hand on his arm. To my surprise, Grae turned and pulled me close. The embrace was brief; the message that followed was shocking. "Milla, I'm leaving soon. I won't be back, but I want to—" His tone wavered. "Thank you for being my friend."

Had the commander ordered Grae to move to the capital? Looking into his eyes, I saw that wasn't it. Grae met my gaze only briefly and then looked over my shoulder, at the hills behind the house. He planned to leave Eden and the Vails.

I made a decision I needed to communicate with him, but at first I didn't know how. Then, going to a nearby bin, I took a scoopful of grain, sprinkled it on the stable floor, and wrote my message. *I go too.*

Grae looked surprised—no, shocked—which made me realize how much I was asking of him. Why would he burden himself with a girl who didn't know the area, was noticeable due to her defect, and would have trouble keeping up with his long strides? The answer came to me: I could offer him a place to go.

It wasn't a perfect idea, since Grae didn't fit Rolf's idea of tribal purity. But I'd been thinking a lot about going home, and I'd come up with a way to secure my uncle's cooperation. I'd write down the awful things Rolf had done to Zalea and give it to someone I trusted, like Uncle Byron or Teacher Foster. Then I'd tell Rolf he had to let Grae stay or everyone would find out what a bad person he was. Grandmother would take my side. If necessary, I'd marry Grae to secure his future as a Woods member. We weren't in love, but that hardly mattered. Grae was kind. He'd be a good husband. It would work.

First I needed to convince Grae. Erasing my first message, I wrote, *Live with my tribe.* After a moment I added, *Free.*

Grae said the word aloud as I brushed the message away. "I didn't know where I'd go," he admitted. "I planned to find some renegades, but—Are there horses where you come from?" When I nodded, he smiled. "I'd like that." He allowed himself a moment of optimism, but I saw reality return when his brows met over his nose. "You know this is going to be dangerous, right? Even if we manage to get out of Eden, we'll have a long, hard trip to get you home."

I knew more about how long the trip would be than he did, but I tried for a humorous touch, bending my arms and tightening my fists in the classic pose of strength.

He didn't smile. "Think about what will happen if they catch us." I shook my head angrily, indicating I wouldn't entertain that possibility.

Sitting down on a bale of hay, Grae chewed at his lip for a moment. "You might be able to solve a problem I've been worrying over. Do you think you could sneak into the Vail's office and steal two travel passes?" When I nodded, he looked slightly ashamed. "You'll have to fill them out. I can read okay, but I never got good at writing." I nodded again to let him know I could handle that. "Good. Make up fake names for the passes. Put your tribe as the destination. There's a guy living not too far out of our way who'll alter our tattoos if we pay him."

I rubbed my fingers together to ask about money. "Aunt Mar gets Fairbucks from the commander every week for buying groceries and stuff. She gave me what she had saved up." He shifted his weight on the bale. "Are you sure you want to do this, Milla?"

I wished I could explain about Madame Vail's plan for me and how desperately I wanted to escape it. Unable to do that, I simply gave him a steady look and a firm nod.

"All right. Get the passes. Tomorrow night, fill a bag with food from the kitchen, stuff we can carry easily. I'll bring water, Mar's money, and the tools we'll need." Looking out a window, he said, "Come as soon as Isa goes to sleep. We'll need to get a good distance away before anyone knows we're gone."

Hearing the idea of escape formed into the steps of a plan, I felt a shiver of doubt. We were young and inexperienced. We were both easily identifiable. We would be pursued by powerful people. Commander Vail would see Grae's departure as an insult. Madame Vail would be furious at what she'd interpret as my ingratitude. Though our leaving together was comforting, it doubled our danger. Bending down, I wrote in the dirt, *You don't have to take me.*

Grae gave me a long look. "I'm guessing you have a good reason for not wanting to be here."

I wrote a new message. *They can kill us.*

"That's exactly why I can't stay here, Milla. The commander had Cara killed, and it was because of me." I felt my eyes widen, but Grae didn't explain further. "I'll wait here until midnight tomorrow. If you don't show, I'll go alone."

Tuesday was torture. I crept downstairs very early, before the commander woke, and sneaked into his office to steal two blank passes from a stack of them in a drawer. Sitting in his comfortable leather chair, I filled in the required information, using a sample of Vail's writing and practicing for a few minutes until I was satisfied with my approximation of his scrawl. Rummaging in the desk, I found his official seal and applied it over the signatures. Sliding the passes into the waistband of my skirt, I returned to my room and hid them under my mattress. As I often did, I made the bed so Lucia wouldn't have to. Long before Isa began stretching and groaning next door, I'd accomplished Part I of my mission.

At lessons that morning, Tutor Matthew commented that I wasn't at my best. In the afternoon when we went riding, a different boy accompanied us, saying Grae was sick. Though I guessed he was using the time to prepare for our departure, I had to tamp down feelings of panic. What if they'd caught him sneaking into the tool shed? What if he'd changed his mind and left without me? I looked behind so often that Isa swatted me, ordering, "Watch where you go, Dummy!"

The Meyers had been invited to dinner that night. Isa was required to attend, but I was not. I used the time to make a pack for myself, which I slid under my bed with a pair of sturdy boots. I put the clothes I'd wear, a long skirt, a short-sleeved blouse and a warm jacket, under my pillow.

When dinner was over and the Vails and their guests went to sit by the pool, I went downstairs and waited until Mar and the others went outside to serve them. Darting in, I took two sleeves of crackers, a jar of peanut butter, a bag of dried fruit, and a packet of almonds. Back upstairs, I put the food in my pack just as Mar came in. Dusting my hands, I pretended I'd been looking for a shoe.

"I brought you a piece of cake," Mar said.

The thought of eating made my stomach flip, so I signed *No, thanks*. Meeting her gaze, I added, *You extra kind.*

"All right, then," Mar said. "Be well, Milla." It sounded like a benediction. Or maybe a goodbye.

I couldn't tell if Isa was particularly irritating that evening or whether it was my nerves, but I had to fight to keep from punching that nose that was shorter than mine. I tried to fake sleep when she came upstairs, but that didn't matter to Isa. Plopping down on my bed, she related every detail of the dinner with her prospective mate.

"Meyer kid is dork," she proclaimed. "He fat." She puffed out her cheeks. "He talk funny." She made her voice high and squeaky. "He got no horses. Not one!" She went on for what seemed like hours, telling in detail everything the boy had said and done that she found irritating.

When Isa finally went to bed, leaving the door between our rooms ajar, I waited until her breathing turned deep and regular. Sliding from between the covers, I got dressed. Dragging the pack out from under the bed, I slid my arms into the straps and listened again. Isa stirred once but didn't wake. After a full minute standing frozen in place, I went to the doorway to Isa's room and looked in. Again she stirred. "Uh?" she muttered. "Uh?" I remained perfectly still, and she relaxed again. When I heard a soft snore, I pushed the connecting door closed and crept away.

I knew where the security cameras were and had figured out how to avoid them. While there were none in the bedrooms, one covered the corridor and another showed the stairs. That was not the way I chose to go. On the terrace, a camera panned back and forth. I slipped my pack onto my back and, waiting until the camera pointed away from me, darted across to the railing, grasped it like it was a tree branch back home, and twisted my body over to the other side. Letting myself drop so that I hung on the outside of the balustrade, I waited while the camera made its arc. When it turned away again, I slid my hands along the railing until my foot touched an upright post. The scrollwork that made it beautiful also provided places to grip. Once I found a foothold, I transferred one hand, then the other, and then my other foot to the post. From there I was able to climb to the ground with little difficulty.

When my feet touched the patio floor, I breathed a sigh of relief. Ducking behind the pillar, I waited until the ground-floor camera was fully turned away from me before darting into the orchard. From there I was safe from view until I reached the stable. It was cool in the shadows, and I considered stopping to put on the jacket I'd brought along, but I decided against it. I was too scared, convinced that any moment I'd hear, "Hey! Someone's moving around the house!"

As Grae had instructed, I approached the stable's long side wall, where Dutch doors opened from each of six horse stalls. The doors were usually bolted on the inside, but he'd left the center one open for our use. Ducking under the closed top half of the door, I entered the stable. I had a moment of panic when I thought someone had grabbed me, but it was merely my pack catching on the door. Crouching a little lower, I got through.

Grae was waiting, pacing, in fact. "Milla! Are we good?" When I nodded, he took his pack from behind the bales and shrugged it on. "Let's go."

He knew the rhythms of Eden well, which guards would be paying attention and which ones napped on duty. He knew how often they patrolled. And, he told me, he knew of a narrow space just behind the north guard shack that wasn't covered by cameras. I followed as he headed for that spot.

When we reached the back exit gate, Grae and I crouched behind a clump of bushes. After about ten minutes, one of the two men in the guard shack left to make his patrol. The other sat bent over in a chair, whittling. His focus was on the piece of wood in his hands as he cut away tiny bits and blew them away. A nice hobby. A fine distraction.

As soon as the first man disappeared from sight, Grae led the way to the wall. The guard inside the shack was only a few feet away from us, so quiet was essential. Boosting me onto his shoulders, Grae handed up a pair of wire cutters. After a nervous glance at the guard shack, I went to work. Cutting the concertina wire that spiraled along the top of the wall, I pushed it out of the way and pulled myself up onto the bricks. Once I was off his shoulders, Grae backed up a little, made a running jump, and pulled himself up beside me with the softest of grunts. I looked down at the guard shack, where I could see only the woodcarver's hands. He never stopped what he was doing. Grae turned quickly on his rear and then dropped to the ground on the opposite side. Hands up, he signaled me to follow, and he caught me, softening my landing and keeping it silent. Our first step was complete. We were off the estate grounds.

From our daily rides, I knew that Vail's property stretched before us for miles in all directions. The route Grae had chosen led up over the ridge, harder terrain, he said, but it would provide more cover. The moon glowed bright white over our heads as we began along a trail that led upward. It looked different, harder, on foot than it had from the back of a horse. On the other side of the ridge, I remembered, the trees gave way to low-growing vegetation that had to push its way up through rocky ground. We wouldn't have much in the way of cover there, so we'd travel as far as we could while night served as a cloak.

By the time the sun peeped over the horizon, I was exhausted. The pack weighed heavy on my back. The adrenaline that had fueled me at the outset faded. I concentrated on two things: putting one foot in front of the other, and not running into Grae's back when he paused to get his bearings.

I was relieved when he said, "By now they know we're gone. We'll hole up and wait for dark again."

The place Grae found was a cave-like indentation in a wall of rock that stretched for some distance. An outcrop above it gave us shade and concealment from all but a direct line of sight. Settling onto the gravelly surface, we pulled our feet in, hiding ourselves as much as possible.

By mid-morning the sun beat down. What probably felt like a mild day elsewhere got hot as the rocks around us absorbed heat and radiated it back onto us. Grae passed me the canteen, cautioning me to take sips of water rather than long drinks. When I gave it back, he poured a little water onto a bandana and handed it to me. "Wipe places where you have a pulse," he instructed. "That cools your blood as it circulates." He was right. While I wasn't exactly comfortable, I felt a little less like a pancake on a griddle.

Leaning our backs against the irregular surface, we passed the time in silence. Somewhere a bird screeched one long note over and over. A faraway piece of metal clanged like a lonely gong. Grae slept, snoring gently, but the hard ground, fear, and the heat made it hard for me to do the same. My ears seemed to shift like a cat's as I listened for any hint of pursuers approaching. My thoughts wavered between *We can do this!* and *What were we thinking?*

Grae's solid presence was a comfort. I wasn't alone in this strange place, and the fact that he could sleep seemed to indicate optimism about our future.

When the sun began to sink in the west, Grae stirred, wiped his mouth, and looked around. "Another hour, maybe, and it'll be dark enough to move. It will be cooler then too. We'll reach Cougar Canyon tonight, and we'll follow the ridge until we reach a spot where we can cross the river that flows through it. On the other side is the outer boundary fence. Once we climb that, we'll be off Vail's land." After dredging crackers in peanut butter, we had dried apricots for dessert. As we ate, I tried to imagine the moment when we'd leave Commander Vail's land. Would I feel free then? Safe? Probably not.

That reminded me of Grae's statement that Cara had been murdered. Smoothing a spot in the dirt I wrote, *Why Cara die?*

The reply came in a toneless voice, hinting that Grae was suppressing his emotions. "Aunt Cara told the commander if he made me fight for him, she'd tell Madame about stuff she'd seen." He shifted his body on the hard ground. "Stuff he doesn't want her to know about."

I saw where the story was going but sensed Grae needed to tell it. "Last week, Donnie left the estate for a couple of days without telling anybody where he was going. Next thing we know, Cara's dead." Grae's voice turned hard. "Donnie came and told me about it personally, and you should have seen the look on his face. He was all 'I'm so sorry, Grae,' but he had that slimy half-grin he gets, like he thought he'd got back at me somehow." Picking up a pebble, he flung it away. "A few minutes after he left, Isa came into the stable. I was still trying to take in what happened, and she said, 'Cara gone now. You fight for Father. Good for you and me.'"

The bird screeched overhead, louder than before. Grae's voice was thick as he finished. "I got my aunt killed, but I'm not really the one responsible. I'll never go back there, no matter what—"

He was interrupted by a distant mechanical buzz. Rising onto his haunches, Grae peeped out at the quickly darkening sky. "Damn," he muttered. "A drone."

I didn't know what that was, but looking up, I saw a metal object above us, lit like a seagull in the rays of the setting sun. "It picks up body heat," Grae said. Pulling two odd-looking objects from his pack, he handed one of them to me and ordered, "Cover yourself with this and stay still."

Though I didn't understand, I obeyed. Unfolding the metallic blanket, I draped it over my head and then made myself as small as possible beneath it. Above us the drone came closer, its soft hum odd to my ears. As we sat motionless under our silvery coverings, I imagined the machine sniffing the area like a hound on a scent. After what seemed like hours, the sound faded to nothing. "You can take it off now." As Grae gathered our things, he said, "When I broke into the supply shed, I noticed these Mylar blankets and grabbed a couple, thinking they'd protect us from cold and heat. That was lucky, because they just saved us from something a lot worse."

Chapter Twenty-Six

ZALEA

It took forever to reach the Vail estate, at least that's how it felt to me. The country we passed through, while exotic and beautiful, seemed to go on and on. The weather was monotonous too. While at home winter would be setting in, here the days were moderate and the air was dry. Only the nights were cool, and I was glad for my cozy sleeping bag.

Yaris drove carefully, abiding by speed limits and observing all signs. As we traveled east, we passed through several checkpoints. Some were a breeze. A guard would ask a few questions, take a look at us, and then wave us onward. Other guards were more thorough, but Sri and Yaris knew the ropes. They appeared both respectful and relaxed, joking when it seemed appropriate and remaining serious when it didn't. Mom and I stayed quiet unless asked a question. At her suggestion, we undid the top few buttons on our crazy-loud blouses. "Most men don't look at faces when there are boobs to gape at," she said, and I tried not to blink at the unlike-Mother comment. I began to understand that Wendy Woods, tribe member, had adapted to survive in a society she'd hated. I was seeing the rebirth of the old Wendy.

Late Tuesday afternoon we reached the turnoff to the estate. As we passed Dick's diner, I got a glimpse of Renee at the front of the building, watering her flowers. I wanted to let her know I'd succeeded in finding my father, but that would have to wait. We had agreed not to endanger them a second time unless it became necessary. Instead we pulled off the highway about a half mile south in a secluded spot well into the trees. Setting up a simple camp, we readied ourselves for dark and the long trek. While Mom and I cooked dinner, Sri and Yaris found the outer fence and cut a hole big enough for us to crawl through. Sri figured it would take four or five hours to reach the inner wall. We'd enter via the lake, which meant crossing the water barrier I'd described to them. Yaris said he had that part under control, and I believed him.

By the time we reached the estate grounds, day would be dawning. Our plan was to find a place to hide near the stable and wait for afternoon and a chance to talk to Milla. Depending on what happened then, we had several different exit strategies. None of them would be easy, due to the cameras, the wall, the fence, and all those armed guards. Again, Yaris said it was under control, and the guy had a way of making me believe him.

As we waited, Mom got nervous. "What if we can't find her?"

"We know she rides most days," Sri said for the third time. "We'll wait near the stable. Zalea will signal her to come into the woods. She'll be gone before they realize she's missing."

"If she wants to come with us," Yaris cautioned. "And if they go riding tomorrow."

"What if they don't?" She was in negative mode, more Mother than Mom.

"If we have to enter the house to find her, we'll do it."

"There's four of us. It'll be harder to hide from the cameras," I said, though I knew they knew that.

Yaris tucked strands of his long blond hair behind his ears. "Like I said, we avoid them if we can, blind them if we can't. Now come and help me with the equipment."

I followed him into the camper, where he removed a false partition, revealing a backpack for each of us. The heaviest one Yaris took for himself. "What's in here?" I asked as I shouldered the one he handed me.

"Food. Water. Flashlights. Other stuff we might find useful." We took the other two to Sri and Mom, who stood close, talking earnestly to each other. They stopped as we approached, and because they avoided looking at me, I guessed I'd been the topic of conversation.

Yaris took a bandana out of his pocket and tied it over his blond hair, hiding its brightness. "Let's go."

He led the way, using a shuttered flashlight. We followed in silence, first me, then Mom, and Sri bringing up the rear. It was a weird experience, being out in the dark *with* my mother instead of hiding what I was up to *from* her. I'd wondered how she'd fare on this trip, but she kept up, exhibiting stoic cheerfulness. She even joked with Sri when he tripped on a root and went stumbling into a tree. "Klutz."

"And here I was trying to impress you with my physical grace," he replied with a grin.

That was all that was said, but for a second I sensed the easy relationship they'd had before. This was tough for them. With a big job ahead, they also had a lot to get past. Years of separation. The fact that Sri had a new family. The need to work closely without getting too close. I was proud of how Mom was handling it. Sri had a life, but right now, she didn't have much except hope.

I did my best to recall the details of my earlier visit, but a tree is a tree and night is dark. For a long time, nothing looked familiar. That was okay, because Yaris had a phone with something called GPS, a ray of some sort that kept us on track. Somewhere between two and three Wednesday morning, I saw the lake on the right, moonlit and calm. "The wall is about a quarter mile from here."

"Good," Sri said softly. "We'll have time to get past the water barrier before daylight."

We moved down the lake shore. Not only was it shadowed by trees, but the way was weedy and mucky. At some points the only way to get past driftwood or marshy spots was to wade out into the water. "I can't believe you made this trip all alone," Mother muttered as she bent to retrieve a shoe sucked off her foot by deep mud.

Sri chuckled softly. "Our girl did all right, didn't she?"

It was the first time he'd acknowledged the fact that the two of them had created me together. I felt a little twinge of satisfaction, but nobody commented further. Instead we concentrated on keeping our footing in the slime.

As we neared the inner wall, I heard an engine start up, then another, and then a third. "Boats," Sri said. Fearing we'd been spotted, we retreated inland, but when the boats took off, they turned away from us and headed north. Once the noise faded, we moved forward again.

Then the estate wall stood before us, with its metal mesh disappearing into the water. I'd passed over it disguised as a clump of weeds, but it was unlikely four people could get away with that.

Yaris helped Mother remove her pack, and we watched as he unloaded the contents, two headlamps and four snorkeling masks. Handing each of us one, Yaris showed us how to access the valves that fed oxygen into the faceplate. "We'll have about eight minutes of air," he told us. "I'll go first. If we can get under it, great. If not, I'll have to cut a hole, which will take a while. When I signal, swim out to me, pass through the barrier, and follow it back to shore. We need to come out of the water close to the wall, behind the camera's range."

They all looked at me, and I realized I was the only one who'd never done any scuba diving. Swallowing hard, I gave them a thumbs up. Yaris turned immediately and waded into the water, the slosh of his steps fading as the water deepened around him. A few minutes later we heard a call that sounded like a bird but probably wasn't. Sri said, "There's room to go under. Stay close and follow my light." Mother had already put on her mask and was wading into the water.

The diving mask scared me at first, but all I had to do was breathe normally and let it do its work. The passage was eerie too, going from dark night into darker water. Once we were far enough from shore that silt didn't interfere with my vision, all I had to do was follow Sri's bobbing light. Mom stayed behind me, and I swam hard, not wanting to be the weak link in our little chain.

Sri easily located Yaris, who wore the other headlamp, and by its light we could see there was a foot or so of space between the bottom and where the mesh ended. They motioned me through, then Mom. With only a slight brush against the metal, I scooted under and headed for shore, pulling myself along the mesh until my hands found the lake bed. I raised my head cautiously. There was no sound, no movement on the shore. Still, as I crawled from the water I imagined being surrounded by men with guns and bad attitudes. I might have sobbed out loud. Feeling a hand on my shoulder, I turned to see Sri beside me. His touch was a question. *Okay?* I wasn't sure, but I set a hand on his arm and squeezed. *Okay.* We were in. So far, so good.

Now I led the way, circling through the orchard so we approached the main stable doors from the cover of a stand of grapefruit trees. Stopping out of range, I pointed out the camera positioned at the peak of the roof.

During a planning session, I'd drawn a very amateur sketch and labeled the camera with an *X*. "I think it's the only one around the stable," I'd told them. Indicating the long wall where the corral was, I went on, "On this side there are Dutch doors that open from each horse's stall. I didn't see any cameras over there."

"Stall doors won't open from the outside," Yaris said, eyeing the sketch. "We'll need to blind that door camera to get inside."

"Disabling a camera will bring the guards to see what's wrong," Mom objected.

When an idea hit, I'd put a hand on Yaris' arm. "If you can blind the camera for just a few seconds, I'll run into the stable. Once I'm inside I can open a Dutch door in one of the empty stalls, and the rest of you can get in that way."

Mom had fussed about it for a while, but I'd argued it had to be me. I'd been there before, I was the smallest of us, and I was younger and, I insisted, faster than any of them. Though she'd rolled her eyes, she hadn't said any more.

Now Yaris eyed the building, making his plan. Pulling a branch off a nearby tree, he stuck it in his back pocket, approached the stable from the side, and shinnied his way up the wall at one corner. Once he reached the roof, he moved hand over hand along the edge, his short legs dangling as his powerful arms held his weight.

Watching, I set my feet firmly, ready for a mad dash. Reaching the camera, Yaris hung briefly from one arm as he draped the branch over the lens. He grunted, "Go!" and I ran to the door, flung myself through, and closed it behind me. Yaris would wriggle the branch a few times and then drop it, leading anyone watching to assume it had landed on the camera by accident, fluttered for a moment, and then fallen off.

The stable was empty, which was a relief. Making my way down the stalls on my right, I located one that didn't contain a horse and opened the bottom half of the divided door. Seconds later Mom ducked inside, then Sri, and finally, a grinning Yaris. "Smart," he said softly, and I felt my face warm. I was more accustomed to being called smart in the sense of "smart aleck" than "smart thinking."

Mom, Sri, and I climbed to the loft, where we planned to wait until Milla arrived. Yaris left us for a while, and Sri explained, "When he gets back, we'll know all we need to about this place."

As the sun lit the sky outside, Yaris returned, carrying a hand-drawn map with *X*'s where there were cameras and circles where there were guards. "Weird stuff going on," he told us. "There's only one guard at each gate, and I didn't see a single one on the grounds. The boats we heard going north earlier are still somewhere out on the lake. The shed where they keep ATVs has space for a dozen, but there's only one there." He raised his brows. "If I had to guess, I'd say the guards are all out looking for someone."

A scrape alerted us to the door opening below. Looking down, we saw a boy of about ten enter, take up a broom that looked too heavy for his skinny arms, and begin sweeping the floor. Moving silently to the ladder, Yaris waited until the kid was turned away and then descended, quickly and quietly. Stepping up behind him, Yaris put one hand over his mouth and the other around his body. The boy struggled, but Yaris said softly, "Calm down, kid. I'm not here to hurt you."

The boy stopped fighting, though his posture remained tense. "There's a girl staying here," Yaris said. "I need to talk to her. If I take my hand away, will you tell me where Milla is right now?"

The boy nodded. Yaris removed his hand far enough to let him talk. "Milla ran away in the night," he said. "Grae too." He waved his arm in a wide arc. "Donnie's got all his guys out looking for them." That explained what Yaris had seen.

Letting go of the boy, Yaris turned him around so they faced each other. “Can you keep quiet about me being here if I give you something good?”

The boy’s brown eyes narrowed. “Like what?”

“This.” Yaris took a candy bar from his pocket. “And this.” From another pocket he took a silver dollar. It was a clever offer, one item the kid could have for himself and another that would benefit his family. “Act normal, but keep quiet about seeing me. And if they find Milla, come back here and let me know. Deal?”

After a moment, the boy took the items, one with each hand, “Deal.” Pocketing his rewards, he took up the broom and began sweeping so vigorously that Yaris coughed at the cloud of dust raised. “Why don’t you come back later to do that?” he suggested. “No one’s likely to notice with all that’s going on, so you could have an hour to yourself.” From where I lay in the loft, I saw the glint of pleasure in the kid’s eyes at the idea of free time.

When he was gone, Yaris joined us. “What now?”

No one answered for a long time, but finally Mom said, “I don’t see how we’d find Milla before Vail’s people do. There are a lot more of them, and they know the area.”

“Wendy’s right,” Sri said. “We’re four against forty and strangers against locals.”

I didn’t want to think that way. “What if they find her and kill her?”

Yaris frowned. “You said they were treating her well.”

Mom shook her head. “Milla isn’t the type who’d run away unless she was in trouble.”

"We need to find her." I looked to Mom for support. In her eyes, I saw that she'd made a decision.

"Sri, this isn't your problem. You and Yaris take Zalea and go."

He put out a hand as if reaching for her, but he stopped himself. "What about you?"

She looked around the dim loft as if seeking inspiration. "I'll distract them, give Milla time to get away." After a moment she added, "Take Zalea—"

"I'm not leaving!" I almost shouted.

"Keep your voice down," Yaris cautioned. "Nobody's leaving, at least until it gets dark again. Let's try to figure out what comes next."

Sri had already been figuring. "Let them look for Milla. If she gets away, we make a new plan. If they find her, we go in and get her."

He made it sound simple, but I knew it wouldn't be. We were still four against forty, in unfamiliar territory. The only advantage we had was that they didn't know we were there. I doubted it would be enough.

Once it was established that we'd stick together, Sri, Yaris, and Mother turned to fine-tuning the plan. I watched in awe, seeing the full scope of their expertise and their bold approach to the problem. I gasped when Yaris opened his waterproof backpack and started removing brick-sized packages wrapped in tape. Each had a small timer attached to it with wires.

"Do you remember how to use these, Wendy?" Sri asked.

My mother gave him a smile unlike any I'd seen from her until that moment. "Nothing to it."

"Good. When it gets dark again, that will be your part. Yaris and I will see to your girls."

Chapter Twenty-Seven

MILLA

When full night came, Grae and I left our hiding place and started off again, the Mylar sheets draped over us like cloaks in case the drones returned. After an hour or so, we came to the canyon he'd mentioned and turned to walk along its edge. "It's not all that high, more of a ravine than a canyon," Grae explained as we went, "but somebody a long time ago called it Cougar Canyon and the name stuck." In the moonlight I could see that the drop to the water was about twenty feet. I didn't like walking so close to the edge, which seemed to pull me toward it like a magnet, but the river's babble was a soothing accompaniment to the occasional scrape of our feet on the rock ledge. The trail was narrow, and the moon sometimes disappeared behind clouds. When that happened I moved closer to Grae, fearing I'd lose him in the dark. He would extend a hand behind him, letting me grip it until the light returned and I felt safe on my own again.

Grae could no doubt have traveled faster alone, and that bothered me. Maybe I should have stayed behind and accepted whatever Madame Vail had in mind for me. Questioning my decisions was new to me because *making* decisions was new. I didn't like it at all. Grandmother had been right when she said the world was a hard place. Without rules, without guidance, a girl didn't know what was right and what was wrong.

After a half hour of silent, determined trudging, Grae flashed his light ahead briefly to let me see that we were about to begin our descent. "Once we cross the river, we'll be good."

"But you won't be crossing." Donnie's voice came from somewhere up ahead. "You're in trouble, my friends."

"Run, Milla!" I turned to do as Grae said, but there was a man behind me. I plowed directly into him. Though he tilted a little at impact, he grabbed my arms and held on.

With sweeping blows of both arms, Grae knocked aside two men who tried to grab him. As they stumbled backward, he turned on the man who held me, giving him a sideways blow that sent him staggering to the ground. My captor dragged me down with him, so I didn't see what happened next. I heard a shot ring out, heard Grae grunt in pain. A bright light came on, and Grae was illuminated against the blackness beyond the canyon ledge. His shirtfront was stained with blood.

"Run!" he repeated. Rolling to my feet, I started away, but in only seconds I was tackled from behind. I fell forward, my face making painful contact with the ground and my mouth filling with dirt. As I fought to get away, the sounds behind me made no sense. Later I was able to put it together. A second shot. A strangled sound from Grae. The scrabble of his feet on the loose gravel. When my captor turned me back toward the cliff edge, Grae was gone.

One of the commander's men shone his light over the edge. "I see him. He's floating downriver."

"Is he dead?" Donnie asked.

"As good as, I'd say. Two bullets in his chest and a twenty-foot fall shoulda done it."

I stopped fighting, sagging in the arms of my captor and blaming myself for what had happened. Without me, Grae would have been off Vail's land by now. Like Zalea, Grae had tried to get me out of trouble. Like Zalea, Grae was now dead.

"No sense wandering around down there in the dark," Donnie said. "Let's get this one back to the house." Raising his voice he called, "Over here, Mel," and an ATV engine started and roared toward us. The driver spun it in a circle beside Donnie and got off, leaving it running.

Donnie aimed the flashlight beam directly at my face, making me squint. "You can ride back to the house on this, or I can drag you behind it. Your choice." When I nodded to indicate I'd go quietly, he ordered, "Get on." I obeyed, dimly aware that I was making soft hiccups of sorrow.

The ride was fast and bumpy. Unwilling to hold on to Donnie, I grasp the metal frame instead. I even considered letting go and rolling off the back of the speeding ATV. If I survived the fall, I might run into the darkness and find a hiding place. It was more likely I'd be hit and killed by one of the other ATVs that followed us, but I wasn't sure that mattered anymore.

Commander Vail waited in the spill of light on the wide patio surrounding the ranch house. Using my hair as a handhold, Donnie escorted me to him, giving me a shove so that I stumbled the last few steps. Vail looked to Donnie first. "Grae?"

"Dead. It's dark out there, but I'll send some men out to find the body in the morning."

"What a waste," the commander said without a touch of emotion. "The boy could have done great things." He turned to me. "And you, Little Miss. I invite you into my home. I treat you like a daughter. You repay me by turning Grae against me and sneaking away in the night." He made a *tsk* of disgust. "Whatever became of grat—?"

A scuffle behind me caught the commander's attention, and he looked over my shoulder. "What's this?"

"We found him on the grounds, sir."

I turned to see a man in his forties being forced toward us by two guards. His face was bloody, and he seemed cowed by his captors.

"Who are you?" Vail demanded.

"My name is Mark Woods." The man shot me a look I couldn't interpret, but I thought I was being asked to go along. "I'm this girl's father, and I came to take her home."

Confusion bubbled in my head. This man certainly wasn't my father, though there was something familiar about him. His eyes were dark. His skin was coppery. When he smiled to indicate that he was harmless, his mouth went a tiny bit crooked. It came to me like an electrical shock. The man looked like Zalea.

Zalea's father had once sent a man to find her. Had he now come looking for her himself? If he had, he was too late.

The commander's tone turned amused. "How did you manage to misplace a daughter, Mr. Woods?"

"She ran away," the captive said. "She and her sister imagined having some kind of grand adventure outside the tribe."

"Ah, yes. She was traveling with another girl when we first met."

Again the man met my eyes briefly. "I already found her. She's back with her mother."

A bubble of joy welled inside my chest. Zalea was alive! My next thought was less joyful. The Vails had lied to me.

The commander made no attempt to explain. "Either your tribe doesn't educate its children well, Mr. Woods, or your girls are less obedient than they should be."

"We did our best with them," the dark man said, "but they are young and foolish, as girls tend to be."

Commander Vail nodded. “I assume you have proof the girl is yours.”

“Our identity papers are in my knapsack, which I left outside your boathouse.” The man cleared his throat. “I’m aware that you have supported my daughter for several weeks.”

“That’s true. She came to us with nothing.”

“I am obliged to repay you, and I believe I have something that will serve.”

“What can you offer me?” There was condescension in his tone.

The man looked at him sideways, as if he knew he had the right answer. “I’m told you collect Olmec art.”

The commander’s expression changed. “I do.”

“I have with me an Olmec head in jade with gold trim, dated around 600 BCE.” Mr. Woods gave a little shrug. “I can’t provide provenance for the piece, but I doubt that matters to a private collector.”

The commander made an effort to appear calm, but I could see he was excited. “If it’s genuine, I would be interested.”

“An exchange, then. The treasure I have for the treasure you hold.”

“I’ll take a look, but I warn you, I am not easily fooled in such matters.”

“I think you will be pleasantly surprised.”

Commander Vail’s tone took on a falsely hearty note. “How did you learn the girl was here?”

“I happened to see a news report. She was with you at the capital.”

“And you came all this way alone?”

The man's head dipped a little. "I prefer that my daughters'…mistakes remain private in order to preserve their reputations. When they went missing, we said they were visiting an aunt in another tribe."

"Does your family know where you are right now?"

"We have no private phone in our home, so to avoid gossip..." The man shook his head.

To his men the commander said, "Go with him. Let him get his bag and then bring him to my office with the art piece."

Was it possible that the man couldn't see what Vail had in mind? I tried to send a message with my eyes: *Run!*

He missed it. "Thank you, Commander Vail. I'm grateful for your understanding, and I will count on your discretion."

When they were gone the commander turned to me. His eyes were hard as he ordered, "Inside."

Madame Vail hurried toward us with tears in her eyes. "Misa, Misa," she said sadly. "We did so much for you, and this is the thanks we get. Your disloyalty upsets me."

I had never in my life regretted my muteness more. *Help me?* I wanted to shout. *You entertained yourself with plans to change me, as if I were a toy you'd bought for your spoiled, horrible daughter.*

"Where is Isa?" the commander asked.

"I sent Mar up to check on her."

As Madame spoke, Mar entered the room, her face pale. "Isa is not in her room. I don't think she's in the house."

With shouted orders and wild threats, the commander ordered a search. When a boy came to say that Princess was missing, Madame Vail sank into a chair, weeping. Her husband grabbed my arm. "Don't worry, Giselle. I'll secure this little bitch. Then I'll see that Isa is found."

Dragging me into the hallway, he opened a closet under the stairs that was so small I had to crouch to fit. "It's uncomfortable," he said before closing the door, "but you won't be alive much longer anyway."

The closet was completely dark and smelled of cleaning oils. Awaiting my doom, I comforted myself with the knowledge that my sister was alive. The stranger who looked like Zalea had to be her father. Somehow she'd found him and convinced him to come to Fairica for me. That was brave of him, but now he would die, as Grae had, because of me. I would rob my sister of the father she'd missed all these years.

As I waited in the stuffy closet, the door hinge poking my hip, I wondered why Zalea's father, supposedly a long-time criminal, was so trusting. It had been dumb to admit he had a valuable piece of art with him. He'd come without telling anyone where he would be. How could he be that naïve?

Then I heard the first explosion. It was some distance away, but the reaction in the house was immediate. Shouting. Excited questions. Hurried footsteps going this way and that.

A minute or so later, there was a second explosion, this one closer to the house.

"What *is* that?" Madame Vail asked in a squeaky voice.

"We're being attacked," her husband answered. "Go and lock yourself in the safe room. I'll be along soon."

“But Isa’s out there. How can I—”

“Go!” he ordered.

There was more, but it became a muddle of orders and exclamations. I heard Madame Vail call Isa’s name several times. Shouting and running continued, and her voice faded in the general confusion.

Then I heard a crash at the latch of the closet door. A second later it opened, and a man grasped my arm. “Come with me.”

I exited the cramped space, relieved to stand upright again. We were in Madame Vail’s sitting room, which was dark. I couldn’t see the man clearly, but he was shorter than the one who’d claimed to be my father. I hesitated, unsure what to do. Shouts continued outside. The whine of passing ATV engines hinted at reckless speed. There was another explosion. The chaos offered a chance for escape, but did this man intend to help me or harm me? Jerking my arm free from his grip, I turned and ran out of the room. In the hallway, a figure grabbed me, stopping me in my tracks.

Chapter Twenty-Eight

ZALEA

My sister clawed at my arms, making panicked noises. "Milla!" I said, holding on. "Milla, it's me."

Her face came up. Her eyes widened. Finally, a smile lit her face, and she hugged me tightly. I felt her tears warm my shirt as she made little sounds of joy.

"We have to go." I pointed. "Follow Yaris."

She obeyed, and we trailed him through the house and out a side door onto a patio lit by sconces. Despite the crazy situation, my heart felt light. Milla and I were together again.

Yaris stopped, putting a hand up to signal danger ahead. Dragging Milla with me, I followed him into the shadows, stepping behind a supporting pillar where we all bent to a crouch. Only a few feet from us, five men came onto the patio and stopped to confer. One of them was the man I'd seen on television, Commander Vail. Signaling for us to stay where we were, Yaris left the patio and disappeared into the darkness.

"What's going on out there?" the commander asked the men around him.

"Someone set charges," one replied. "They're small, but they seem to be all over the estate."

"What's the damage?"

"Not much damage, but we don't know what's going to explode next."

Pointing at two of the men, Vail said, "Form teams. Find the charges and disarm them."

"How do we—?" one started to ask, but Vail made an angry gesture, stopping the question.

"Find them. Bury them in the sand. Toss them in the lake. Just stop that damned noise!" The men went off, their expressions doubtful. I didn't blame them. Who wanted to go poking around for a device that might explode in his face?

Taking hold of Milla's hand, I spelled out *Mother* on her palm and then pantomimed an explosion. She frowned, but I spelled it again. *Mother* with a *Boom!* gesture afterward. Her eyes widened, and I nodded to affirm it. Worrywart Wendy was planting bombs to cover our escape.

The commander turned to the men who remained. "This has to be that guy who wants his daughter back. Find him!"

The men hurried off, leaving Vail alone on the wide veranda. When an explosion sounded some distance away, he swore a vivid oath. After a moment he turned and went into the house, passing within a few feet of where Milla and I hunched, holding our breath.

When the door closed behind him, I whispered, "The stable is our rendezvous point." The patio seemed quiet, so I stood and peeped cautiously out. A second later I was pulled into the open by a man who pinched my arm painfully between his fingers and thumb. "Who the hell are you?" he demanded.

I tried to pull away, but he held on. I reached for his eyes, but he swatted my hand away. I kicked at his man parts, but he caught my foot and pulled, landing me on my back. As I lay stunned, he leaned over and said, "Little thing like you ain't going to beat old Donnie."

That's when Milla landed on his back like an oversized wasp. Digging her feet into the man's middle, she covered his eyes with her hands. When he released my foot to deal with her, I kicked him in the crotch. Though it felt good to hear his howl of pain, the kick was off a little and didn't stop him. He fought to peel Milla's hand away from one eye, but as soon as he let go to work on the other, she covered the first eye again. Realizing my legs were my strongest weapons, I stayed on the ground and kicked at his knees, ankles, and groin. We did okay for a while, but the guy was strong. He freed one eye, got a bead on me, and kicked me hard in the ribs. I curled into a ball, fighting to get my breath back. Able to concentrate on Milla, the man backed into the pillar hard, pinning her between it and him. The blow stunned her, and she released her grip on him and fell to the ground. Reaching down, the man picked Milla up with one hand, shook her like a dust rag, and then dropped her beside me on the marble surface. We both struggled to get back on our feet, but neither of us succeeded. I didn't know what was keeping Milla down, but my limbs felt like they'd forgotten how to work.

"I've got this, Zalea." My vision was a little wavery, but I saw that Yaris had returned.

With the realization that he faced a more dangerous enemy, Donnie's expression changed. "Who are you?"

Yaris tilted his head toward us. "Friend of theirs."

"Well, they ain't going anywhere," Donnie said.

"We'll see."

The men regarded each other, shifting their weight as each mentally calculated what the other was capable of. Donnie was a head taller; Yaris seemed unworried about that. Donnie's reach would far surpass Yaris', but he didn't seem concerned about that either. Instead Yaris stood patiently, waiting for his opponent to make the first move. Opting for the quick win, Donnie reached for the pistol at his belt. Yaris lunged forward, chopping Donnie's wrist with the side of his hand. It was an almost playful gesture, but Donnie's face contorted with pain and the gun went spinning to the ground. Pulling his arm close to his body, Donnie rubbed it to ease the sting.

"No guns," Yaris said in a pleasant tone, "and no more beating up on kids."

Donnie flexed his shoulders and swiped a knuckle under his nose. "All right then. A contest between gentlemen."

I wanted to yell that Donnie was no gentleman, but the grim nod Yaris returned hinted he already knew that.

The fight began in earnest, though it was one-sided from the start. Yaris went about his task in a businesslike manner, hitting Donnie where it hurt and dancing out of the way of return blows. The big man grew angry, which only contributed further to his downfall. He made more and more flailing, desperate attempts to connect his fist to any part of Yaris, but he failed every time. When the big man hesitated for a second, red-faced and panting, Yaris took a long step forward and delivered a vicious blow to his jaw. Donnie went down and stayed there, eyelids fluttering.

"We need to go," Yaris said.

Commander Vail stepped out of the shadows, holding the pistol Donnie had dropped. "You're not going anywhere."

Movement behind him was so sudden that my mind didn't comprehend it at first. Something swept toward Vail, and I saw him stumble, stagger a few steps to the side, and then fall forward, making no attempt to catch himself. Skull hit stone, and he didn't move.

Mom stepped into the light, hefting an oar in both hands. "Did I kill him?"

Yaris touched the commander's neck. "No, but I think he's down for a while."

"That works." She turned to us. "Come on, girls. Sri's waiting."

Running single file through the orchard, we made our way to the stable. My side hurt like crazy, but I kept going. We had to stop a few times as pairs of guards went this way and that. "We're almost out of bombs," Mother said in a whisper as we stopped in the shadows to make sure there were no guards near the stable. "I set twenty, two minutes apart. That last one had to be number fifteen, maybe sixteen."

"As soon as we find Sri, we'll be on our way out of here," Yaris replied.

The sound of clopping hooves quieted us. Into the spill of light over the stable door came the commander's daughter, Isabel, leading her horse. Slumped in the saddle was the oversized groom I'd seen on my first visit. He seemed only half-conscious, holding the horn with his left hand. His clothing was wet, mostly with water, but on one side, also with blood.

"We fix you, Grae," Isabel told him. "You and me getting married."

Poking me, Milla signed, *Help him.*

While I didn't understand the request, I got the urgency. A whispered conference with Yaris began with him shaking his head, but when I insisted, he raised his hands in surrender. "Wendy, go find Sri and bring him here." She left without a word, circling widely through the orchard. To Milla and me, he said, "You two immobilize the girl. I'll see to the giant."

Snatching the bandana off Yaris's head, I handed it to Milla. "I'll grab her. You make sure she can't holler for help."

With Milla at my elbow, I sneaked up behind Isabel, who'd led the horse inside and was trying to line it up with a bale of hay to help with the groom's dismount. I grasped her arms from behind. Though she immediately began struggling, the surprise put her at a disadvantage. Milla—my timid little sister—slipped the bandana over Isabel's mouth and tied it tightly at the back of her head. Her initial shout turned to a strangled grunt of protest. I pulled, Milla pushed, until we backed her against a support post. She kicked and squirmed, but I held her there while Milla found some twine and tied her to it with a half-dozen granny knots. The girl growled in outrage the whole time. While I might have imagined it, it seemed to me that my gentle sister was enjoying herself.

By the time we had Isabel secured, Yaris stood atop the hay bale, cutting away the wounded man's shirt with his jackknife. He examined the man's wounds, one in the upper chest and one near the waist. Flashing his light around, Yaris ordered, "Bring me that roll, will you, Milla?" Going to the post he indicated, she took down a roll of veterinarian wrapping tape that hung on a nail. Yaris used the tape to wrap the big man's wounds, going around and around until the tape was gone. "Hopefully that will stop the bleeding," Yaris said, jumping down from the hay bale. "We'll leave him on the horse as long as we can, because there's no way we can carry him very far." To Milla he said, "You couldn't have chosen a regular-sized guy for your knight in shining armor?"

She looked to me, confused by his grumpy tone. "Don't worry," I told her. "Yaris is one of the good guys."

Sri and Mom ducked into the stable through the open Dutch door. With a yelp of joy, Mom pulled Milla into her arms, fighting back tears as she pulled her close. Though Milla seemed dazed by our presence, she was happy too. Raising an arm, she signaled that I should join her and Mom in a group hug.

After giving us a few seconds, Sri said, "Most of Vail's men are dealing with Wendy's bombs, but they've got boats patrolling the lakeshore. We'll have to leave through the gate." Another explosion sounded, and he added, "With all that's going on, we should be able to overcome whatever guards are left on duty."

"Milla," I asked, "Can you get us to the front gate without going into the open?" She nodded.

Yaris helped Milla get onto the horse in front of the wounded man and then pulled his hands around her waist, giving him something to hold onto. Turning the horse in a half-circle, Milla left the stable and started through the trees. Mom followed, then Yaris, then me and Sri. Though there was commotion elsewhere, the only one of us that made noise was the horse, clopping along and huffing every once in a while as if confused about the reason for her late-night journey.

When we reached the wall, Sri helped Milla dismount. Together, with the three females standing ready to lend assistance if necessary, he and Yaris got the wounded man to the ground. He'd rallied a little, and he seemed to recognize Milla when she turned the flashlight toward her face and touched his arm. We let the horse go, and it trotted back toward the stable. Another explosion sounded, this one far away. We heard shouts and then voices moving away as the guards ran toward it.

"What now?" Mom asked.

"They've probably alerted the Monkey Men." Sri's voice was calm, though the news wasn't exactly welcome. "They'll be setting up roadblocks."

"How can we get past them?"

"You've given us a way, I think." Quickly he outlined his new plan, which was creative if not brilliant. Neither of those terms necessarily translated to workable, but we were low on options. Sri and Yaris left us with the young man whose name Milla spelled into my hand: G-R-A-E. When I heard the wail of an ambulance in the distance, I felt a spark of hope. Sri had predicted there'd be one, and it was critical to our escape. Perhaps fifty yards from where we waited, the vehicle stopped at the gate, waiting to be allowed through. As its mournful note faded to nothing, the world went silent.

"Zalea," Mother said after maybe thirty seconds. "Sneak up to the house and see what's happening."

Holding my bruised ribs, I hurried toward the bright lights that winked between trees and stopped at the edge of the orchard to survey the scene. At the far side of the house, the commander lay on the ground, where Mom's blow had left him. A dark-haired woman knelt beside him, possibly checking his pulse. Several yards away, Donnie sat with his back against a pillar, rubbing his jaw and muttering. I recognized Mrs. Vail, who strode back and forth on the patio, demanding that someone do something. Help her husband. Find her daughter. Catch the intruders. Three guards in the vicinity hesitated, unsure what to do, until her voice rose to a scream. "Go! Do your jobs!" They left, no doubt eager to get out of her sight.

The siren wailed again. In only a minute, the ambulance pulled up in front of the house and stopped. Two men got out, their movements purposeful, their expressions sober. Sri, wearing glasses, a cap pulled low over his face, and a vest with a medical emblem on it, went immediately to Donnie. Taking a syringe from a case he carried, he spoke encouragingly as he gave him an injection. In seconds Donnie's head nodded, and he dropped into unconsciousness.

Yaris spoke to Mrs. Vail, and I heard him tell her the commander and his head of security would be transported to the nearest hospital. Going to the ambulance, Yaris pulled out two stretchers. He ordered one of the guards standing nearby to help him lift Commander Vail onto one while Sri and another guard lifted Donnie onto the other.

All the while, Mrs. Vail paced and babbled. I heard "my daughter" and "missing."

"Ma'am," I heard Sri say, "your husband needs medical care now. Will you come with us or follow in your own vehicle?"

She hesitated, torn between concern for her husband and her child. Finally, she said, "I'll have one of the men bring me along as soon as we find Isa."

"All right," Sri said. "If your daughter is hurt, just call us, and we'll send help." He climbed into the back with the two patients. Yaris closed the doors and then got in the driver's seat. The siren sounded again, and they drove off.

Hurrying back to our hiding place I said, "Let's go."

With some difficulty, Mom, Milla, and I helped Grae stand. We formed a clump, Mom on one side of him and me on the other. Milla walked behind, holding Grae's belt to keep him from falling on his face or keeling over backward. He did what he could, and together we made slow but steady progress. When we reached the gate, Sri and Yaris hurried forward to help. They'd already removed Donnie from his stretcher and laid him out next to three bound and gagged men, the gate guard and the two EMTs who'd arrived in the ambulance. Lowering Grae onto the empty stretcher, we used our combined strength to pick it up and slide it into the vehicle.

"We have a golden pass now." Sri indicated the unconscious commander. "One look at him and we'll get through all the nearby checkpoints."

"What about the rest of us?" I asked.

"Wendy will pose as the commander's personal nurse," Sri said. "She'll ride in the back with him. Yaris and I are the EMTs, so we're good." He sighed. "I'm afraid there's only one place for the two of you to ride."

That's how Milla and I rode for ten miles tied to the top of an ambulance. Mom wrapped us in blankets, and Sri and Yaris secured us with gurney straps. "I'll leave my window down," Yaris told me. "If it gets to be too much, just yell."

It wasn't fun. It was cold up there, we couldn't change position, and we were battered by the wind, like birds in a storm. It might have been too much if either of us had been alone, but Milla and I were together. Every so often I'd call out, "Better or worse than a grain truck?" and she'd giggle.

Once we'd passed the outer fence, we came to a roadblock set up by a team of Monkey Men. We listened intently as they barked questions at Sri. We heard him leave the driver's seat and open the rear doors so they could look inside. Everyone in the Rose Section knew Commander Vail's face, and even Monkey Men trembled at the idea of delaying the medical care he obviously needed. The tone of their voices changed, and soon we drove on.

When we came to the place where we'd left the van, Sri and Yaris climbed up and released us. Milla and I tested our shaky legs, shivering but almost giddy from the experience. While Yaris and Sri figured out the next step, Mom took hold of our hands and fretted about how cold they were. I assured her we were fine. We hugged a lot, there in the open, in the night, all together and reasonably safe.

It was decided that Yaris, Milla, and Mom would travel in the ambulance, with Yaris playing the part of EMT, Mom the commander's caregiver, and Milla Isabel Vail. Sri and I would follow in the van, using the forged travel passes. It was good to ride with Sri and get to know him better, but at each stop I worried that someone would remember there'd been two couples in the camper a few days ago. Perhaps because the gravely wounded commander of the Rose Section had passed through minutes before, no one did.

"What if he wakes up?" I asked when we stopped along the way.

Yaris' teeth gleamed in the headlights. "I'm making sure he doesn't."

Since we had to cross the Gold Section to reach Dorado, our ruse of taking the commander to a hospital couldn't hold. We drove through both mountains and deserts on primitive roads that jounced my bones and scared me, long stretches of nothing. Terrifying narrow roads that edged steep rock walls and overlooked drops that made my gut clench. To make matters worse, a November rain storm pounded the vehicles all one night. Lightning bigger than I'd ever seen cracked across the sky as the accompanying thunder rolled behind us. At times the wipers couldn't keep up with the rain, and we had to pull over and wait for a lull before we could continue. Sri and Yaris remained cheerful, but I saw anxiety in my mother's expression and sheer terror in poor Milla's. The next day the sun lit the sky as if no such thing had happened, and we went on. Only once did we have to retreat, when a river glutted with rainwater blocked the way ahead. Yaris plotted a new route, and once again we continued west.

It was a scary time. We constantly scanned the roads and the air for the approach of Monkey Men. Once it was likely our ruse had been discovered, we no longer dared to stop at service stations for gasoline. Yaris "borrowed" it, first stealing a can to hold the gas and then filling the tank from road construction worksites after hours. While I recalled feeling it had seemed to take forever to get to Eden, it felt even longer going back. After three days of travel, with stops and detours to avoid danger, we finally arrived at the old mine entrance that disguised the tunnel to Dorado.

Milla's eyes went wide when Yaris removed the cover and revealed the tunnel. With the commander's stretcher strapped onto the back of Sri's machine and Grae doggedly holding onto Mom as she piloted hers, Milla and I rode behind Yaris as we wended the maze of passages. The headlights bounced off the walls as we turned and bumped along, and I felt Milla's grip on my waist tighten. At the far end, Sri opened the door and we entered the garage, so bright after the dark of the passageway that we all blinked and squinted. Only Commander Vail didn't react to our safe return. He was still in what Yaris called "La-la Land."

Mom couldn't seem to get enough of hugging us. "You're safe now," she kept saying. "Both of my girls are safe."

"Milla," I said, "You're in Dorado now." She looked back the way we'd come, her expression one I couldn't interpret. "Are you happy?"

Her reply was strange. *I happy you happy.*

Chapter Twenty-Nine

MILLA

When we got to Dorado, Zalea's father, Mr. Sri, took Commander Vail to a hospital for treatment. I wondered what kind of story he'd tell about how the commander got so far away from home. Zalea had suggested we dump him in the desert and leave him to die. I was glad Mr. Sri didn't agree to that.

"We'll let the authorities know where he is," Mr. Sri told them. "I would expect that our government will use the opportunity to get some things they want from Fairica."

"Will Vox negotiate to get Vail back?" Mother asked.

Mr. Sri nodded. "Vail is one of Vox's strongest supporters, so he *needs* him back. With people in Fairica starting to reconnect to the internet, their lies don't hold up. The Govt is failing, and I believe there'll be big changes in a year or so."

I didn't think Fairica was weak, but I didn't let that show on my face. Zalea's father was nice. He'd come with Mother to find me, and now Mother, Zalea, and I were safe in Miss Clara's big house.

Grae went to a different hospital, one Mr. Sri knew about where they'd take good care of a guy with bullet holes and not ask a lot of questions. He was weak from everything he'd gone through, but he responded well to treatment. In fact, the first chance he got, Grae told Mr. Sri he wanted to join his group and help harass the Govt of Fairica. The commander had created an enemy in Grae, one who'd never give up trying to defeat him. While he certainly had cause, I believed revenge was wrong. Yes, the commander was a bad man, but not everyone in Fairica was evil. As Grandmother said, "A bad apple can show up in any basket."

Two days after our escape, we got word from Eden through a surprising source. Mar showed up at Miss Clara's house with fourteen other former workers from the estate. "When the security team figured out that Commander Vail wasn't with the real ambulance crew, Donnie ran around like a madman," she told us. "His face was all bloody, and his shoulder was dislocated, but he kept screaming at everyone, 'Find that girl! Find the commander! Find those trespassers!'" She turned to me. "You can imagine the tantrum Isa threw when she was located and set free. Madame Vail had to be sedated. But I was happy to hear that you and Grae got away."

Taking advantage of the chaos on the estate, Mar had announced that anyone who wanted to be free of the Vails should leave. While the guards combed the woods, one of Grae's cousins drove them out the main gate in one of the commander's vans. Another cousin knew of a two-track that allowed them to circle around the Monkey Men. They'd gone to a couple Zalea knew named Renee and Dick, who'd called another friend of hers, Ernesto. He'd picked them up early the next morning and took them across the desert and through the tunnel.

I was sad to part with Mar and the others again, but Clara's house couldn't hold all of us, so they went off to a hostel in another town. Starting new lives would be a challenge, but they seemed happy. Before they left I signed to Mar, *I glad you choose future.*

"You as well," Mar responded, giving me a hug. "You can choose your future now too."

That was a topic of discussion for several days. Mrs. Nina and Mr. Sri stayed with us at Mrs. Clara's. Mrs. Nina fretted that her kids were missing too much school, but I suspected she wasn't about to leave her husband to deal with his first wife's future without her there to remind him of his obligations.

Though Mr. Sri was nice, he wasn't like the men I'd known all my life. He was the boss over lots of people, but he seldom gave orders. Around the house he wore shorts and sandals, nothing else, and it took me a while to get used to his mostly-naked body. Still, he tried to be good to me. One day when I came down to breakfast, I saw a rectangular box at my place at the table. Opening it, I found a flute, almost like the one I'd lost. I looked up to see Mr. Sri smiling broadly. "Your mother says you're an excellent musician."

Pleased with both the gift and Mother's praise, I signed *Thank you* several times.

I noticed that Mother and Mr. Sri's friend, Mr. Yaris, had begun talking to each other a lot. Watching them through the window one warm evening, I noticed Mother gesturing with her hands, showing emotions on her face, and chuckling at things Mr. Yaris said. It was like seeing a different person.

Mother was more affectionate with us too, always reaching out to touch my arm or Zalea's cheek. She said my short hair was pretty, though I still missed the feel of long tresses down my back. She taught Zalea how to drive a car, and once she was comfortable in traffic, Clara let the two of us go to the hospital to visit Grae. After a week, I figured out that Zalea wasn't driving me to the hospital to be nice. She and Grae talked a lot, and it was weird. I'd never seen my sister act like a girl before.

Mr. Sri was looking for a house for us. "As soon as we find you a place, we'll get you enrolled in school," he told me. I must have looked worried, because he added, "Your mother plans to open a business. If you don't want to go to school, I suppose you could help her with that."

That idea was even scarier. What could I do in some shop? I hated math. I couldn't answer the phone. And how would customers react to a clerk who didn't speak?

I didn't fit in. I'd seen lots of places over the last few months, but not one of them had felt like home to me. Dorado was too…Grandmother would have called it *worldly*. People, even women, swore right out loud in the street. I turned my eyes away from girls who went around with their bellies showing. I'd even seen a pregnant woman at the hospital, walking along with the waistband of her skirt tucked under her bump and a cropped shirt above it. I was embarrassed that Sri's son had started calling me *Sis,* and I was irritated when he punched my arm to show affection. Life in Dorado wouldn't be horrible, but it didn't feel like the way things were supposed to be either.

Chapter Thirty

WENDY

After a while, I started feeling guilty that my mother didn't know if we were dead or alive. While she and I didn't agree on much, she deserved to know that the girls were safe. Sri made the call, phoning the Woods Tribe's business office posing as a buyer looking for barley. He acted surprised when they told him Ben Woods was dead. Winking at me, he asked, "Is it possible I could speak to his wife? I'd like to offer my condolences."

The man said he'd have to wait while he went and got her, and Sri assured him he'd be happy to. Then he handed the phone to me. As I waited, I tried to read the looks of the people who sat nearby, who'd be listening to my end of the conversation. Milla's serious little face almost glowed at the thought of hearing her beloved Grandmother's voice again. Zalea looked slightly resentful, perhaps angry at any attempt to revisit our former lives. Sri merely waited. Yaris watched me, and though his expression was bland, I sensed he was worried about the effect the call might have on me.

Clara was in the kitchen. Nina had taken her kids to a movie. She and Sri would return home tomorrow and pick up the thread of their life together. I would be simply another refugee to be settled and encouraged and, I was sure Nina hoped, never seen again.

"Hello, this is Linda Woods."

"Mother?"

After a pause, I heard her say, "You can go back to what you were doing, George." A moment later she whispered, "Are you all right, Wendy?"

"I am. I found the girls, and we're safe. Friends here are going to help us start a new life."

"But you can come home now. Byron is the leader, or he soon will be."

"How did that happen?"

"Rolf is…he's dead."

"What happened?"

"He…fell from a hayloft."

"He fell? What was he doing?"

"He just *fell.*"

Her tone was a warning, but I had trouble accepting the words. "Did he have a dizzy spell or trip or what?"

"It doesn't *matter.*" That sounded more like an order than a statement. When I hesitated, still confused, she said in a rush, "Wendy, Rolf killed your father. He—" She didn't finish. Clearing her throat, she went on in a calmer tone. "Come home now. Bring the girls and take your place in the tribe again."

"I'm not sure I want to do that."

"You need family around you. Milla needs people who understand her problem. And after what Rolf did to Azalea, she—"

"Wait. What did Rolf do to Zalea?"

In the pause that followed, I realized two things. My brother had abused my daughter. My mother assumed I'd known and ignored it, like I'd ignored everything else that was wrong in that place.

"She'll tell you about it when she's ready," Mother said. "When she does, please let her know that I put a stop to it as soon as I realized it was happening."

I pressed my stomach, afraid I'd vomit all over Clara's computer desk. My brother had been a pedophile. My mother had known about it and decided that ordering him to leave Zalea alone was enough. No justice for my child. No punishment for Rolf. "If he weren't dead, I'd come home and kill him myself."

"It's been taken care of."

The way she said it brought a weird scenario to mind. Mother had been aware of what Rolf had done to Zalea. Somehow she'd found out he killed Dad. Had she lured him to the barn on some premise? Had she smiled at her son as she maneuvered him toward the open hayloft window? Had she pushed—

No. Mother couldn't have murdered her own son. A quarrel between them might have come to blows. Maybe she'd pushed him in an emotional response to harsh words. "Mom, if you…hurt Rolf, I know you had good reason."

There was a long pause before she said, "I hurt you, Wen. I knew Eric mistreated you. I knew how depressed you were, and I ignored it."

I tried to keep my voice level as I asked, "Why, Mom? If you knew what I was suffering, why did you let it go on?"

"I was angry at you. You married that…man. You fought against our government. You planted *bombs,* Wendy."

"To try to save our country."

"What you did was wrong." She said it harshly, but a second later her tone changed again. "I suppose I was wrong too." Her voice choked with sorrow. "Now Byron is all I have left."

I swallowed an angry response. Even now, only her sons counted.

"He's a good man, Wendy. He's organized. He's fair. He'll be a good leader."

"I wish him all the success in the world but—"

"Come home." Her tone was pleading.

Sri had promised to help me set up a business. Zalea was trying to decide between studying for a career in finance and attempting to make it as a singer. While I'd rolled my eyes at the range of those opposites, Sri said, "Let her try both. She'll know when she finds what feels right."

Women had careers in Dorado. They made their own decisions. They chose their own partners, or chose to have no partner at all. It was pretty exciting stuff.

Mother was still talking, and I tuned back in. "—suppose Azalea will stay with her father's tribe, but Milton Woods' son Jack is quite taken with Milla. Everyone knows Zalea made Milla run away, so when she comes home, Milton and I will match the two of them. Milla can stay right here in Woodsburg, so you won't lose both your daughters."

"Milla's too young—"

"I know that," Mother snapped, "but she won't get many offers, so I'm thinking ahead. Jack's a hard worker, so she won't want for anything. And being mute won't affect her ability to give him children."

"I see."

Actually, I didn't. My mother had grown up free to do pretty much anything she chose. She'd obtained an advanced college degree and worked in education for years. How did a woman like that want nothing more for her beloved granddaughter than marriage and babies? For years I'd resented her and deferred to her. Would it do any good at all to tell her how wrong she was? I doubted it. People who have already decided how they feel about something seldom want to be forced to think it through again.

Unaware of my thoughts, my mother said, "Let me know when you're ready to come home. I'll make the arrangements."

I gave her the only encouragement I could. "We'll talk it over and let you know."

Zalea was the interpreter between Milla and the rest of us, and it thrilled me to watch them communicate. The phone was on speaker, so they'd all heard what Mother said. Milla signed something to her sister, and Zalea's response was disbelief. "Home? You want to go back to the tribe?"

Milla's hands flew as Zalea translated aloud. "She says she'll be okay now that Rolf's gone." Zalea shook her head in frustration. "Milla, if you go back you'll be just another female serving the men of the tribe." Milla signed again, and the reply made Zalea's tone rise. "But what if you're sorry someday? What if after you have three kids you wish your life was different?"

The answer to those questions was that women have faced that prospect since the beginning of time. Hoping Zalea could convince Milla to stay, I chose to keep that thought to myself.

"You know I can't go back with you," Zalea said, her tone wavering between anger and grief. "If you go back, we might never see each other again."

Milla's chin quivered as she signed her reply. Zalea translated. "She says she loves me and she loves you, but she doesn't like the heat and too many people and everyone asking her what she wants to do. She wants to be back home, where she knows how things are supposed to go."

Before I could speak my next words, I had to steady my voice and my heart. "I'll go back with her. I'll—"

"No," Zalea interrupted. "You're not going back."

"But Milla needs someone who'll stand up for her."

Zalea turned to Milla again. "Are you sure this is what you want to do?" When Milla nodded, Zalea abandoned her earlier arguments and took Milla's side. "Grandmother will take care of her. She loves Milla, and Uncle Byron listens to her. She'll make sure Milla has a good future." Looking into her sister's eyes, she finished, "Milla needs people she knows and places that are familiar. The rules you and I disapprove of so much make her feel safe."

Zalea knew Milla better than I ever had, possibly better than I ever could. I looked at my younger daughter, who nodded vigorously in support of what her sister had said. She signed one more message, her enthusiasm obvious, and Zalea translated. "She says to tell you that Jack is really nice and she likes him a lot."

Milla's easy dismissal of my presence from her life was hard to accept, but I acknowledged that my mother had been her guide, her mentor, and her pillar of strength. It should come as no surprise that Milla preferred life with her. My future as a parent, it seemed, would be with Zalea alone. While her independent spirit made it unlikely she'd seek my counsel or heed my advice, I could be there in moments when she might need a listening ear. Maybe we'd come to a point where she could talk with me about what Rolf had done. As a survivor of abuse myself, I could relate. Together, we might be able to heal and move forward with new lives, new goals, new understanding.

About the Author

Peg Herring lives in northern Lower Michigan, where she reads, writes, and loves mysteries and women's fiction. She and her husband enjoy travel and gardening, two great pastimes that don't coexist well. Peg also writes cozy mysteries as Maggie Pill.

Books by Peg Herring (listed in series order)

The Simon & Elizabeth Mysteries (Tudor Era Historical)

Her Highness' First Murder/Poison, Your Grace/The Lady Flirts with Death/ Her Majesty's Mischief

***

The Loser Mysteries (Contemporary)

Killing Silence/Killing Memories/Killing Despair

***

Clan Macbeth Historical Romance (medieval Scotland)

Macbeth's Niece/Double Toil & Trouble

Thrillers

Shakespeare's Blood/Charlie Dickens' Documents

***

Standalone Mysteries

Somebody Doesn't Like Sarah Leigh (cozy mystery)

Not Dead Yet... ('60s-era mystery/suspense)

Her Ex-GI P.I. ('60s-era mystery)

Yesterday's Murder (contemporary mystery)

***

The Dead Detective Mysteries (paranormal but not scary)

The Dead Detective Agency/Dead for the Money/Dead for the Show/ Dead to Get Ready—and Go

***

Caper Novels: Suspense with Humor

Kidnap.org/Pharma Con/The Trouble with Dad

***

Women's Fiction

Deceiving Elvera

Sister Saint, Sister Sinner

Aunt Marge

FAKE

Peg's website: http://www.pegherring.

www.ingramcontent.com/pod-product-compliance
Lightning Source LLC
LaVergne TN
LVHW050915080826
845145LV00001B/91

* 9 7 8 1 9 4 4 5 0 2 5 6 0 *